Nathan knocked. "Let me in, Adrienne."

Eventually, his new wife opened the door a few inches. "Go away. I do not intend to consummate our marriage tonight."

"Indeed?" He came into the room, following her. "Are you going to make me guess what I've done wrong?"

"Leave me alone." Adrienne renewed her battle against the intoxicating power of her attraction to him.

"A lot of women marry men much worse than me, you know." Courting danger, he added, "Perhaps you have forgotten that you belong to me now."

"I curse your bloody men's laws!" She whirled on him. "I belong only to myself. Get out!"

Nathan stared back at her, eyes flashing. "I trust that you remember where to find me, my dear."

"Snow will fall on Barbados before I come to your bed!"

"An empty threat." A hint of a smile played at the corners of his mouth, and Adrienne blushed. "Good night, for now ... Mrs. Raveneau."

By Cynthia Wright
Published by Ballantine Books:

BARBADOS

Cynthia Wright

Library of Congress Catalog Card Number: 89-91456

ISBN 0-345-38172-9

Manufactured in the United States of America

First Edition: November

BALLANTINE BOOKS • NEW YORK

Copyright © 1995 by Cynthia Wright Hunt

All rights reserved under International Pan-American Copyright Conventions. Published in the United States by Ballantine Books, a division of Random House, Inc., New York, and simultaneously in Canada by Random House of Canada Limited, Toronto.

Library of Congress Catalog Card Number: 95-94038

ISBN 0-345-38172-6

Manufactured in the United States of America

First Edition: August 1995

10 9 8 7 6 5 4 3 2 1

Dedication

For the extraordinary Catherine Coulter,
who took me under her wing during my divorce,
let me hug her husband when I was lonely,
played the piano at my second wedding,
and just matched me up with my new agent.
This is a friend beyond price!

Acknowledgments

Special thanks to John Chandler and his staff at the historic, eccentric Ocean View Hotel on Barbados. John's enthusiasm for his island's history helped me discover the world created in *Barbados*.

PART ONE

Yet, Freedom! yet, thy banner, torn, but
    flying,
Streams like the thunderstorm *against* the
    wind.

—George Gordon, lord byron

Chapter One

March 1818
London, England

HOLDING A CANDLESTICK IN ONE HAND, ADRIENNE Beauvisage eased open the door to the Frakes-Hogg nursery. Little Ellie and Beth were sleeping peacefully in their beds as their governess tiptoed over for a closer look. Angelic pink cheeks, long lashes, and dark curls made them appear unscathed by their mother's recent death.

Sensing Adrienne's presence, Beth opened her eyes and whispered, "I wish you could be our mummy now."

How could she say that she despised their father and had stayed this long only because of the girls? "I couldn't love you more if I were your mummy."

"Good." Smiling, Beth went back to sleep.

Adrienne's heart ached as she tucked her in again, then returned to the corridor. Not a day passed that didn't find her struggling anew with the problem of the insidious attentions paid to her by Ellie and Beth's father, Walter Frakes-Hogg.

Two years earlier, when Adrienne had completed her education at age eighteen, her parents had begged her to come home to the family château in France, but she'd insisted upon seeking employment and fulfilling her ambition to teach. Above all, Adrienne craved independence. Though bright and beautiful, she had no desire to pursue a place in London society, which she considered superficial.

After Walter Frakes-Hogg persuaded her to become the live-in governess to his tiny daughters, Adrienne had fallen in love with the girls instantly. Because their mother, Jane,

3

was bedridden, they needed more than knowledge from Adrienne, and she had tried to bring some warmth and cheer into the gloomy house. Adrienne was encouraged to feel like a member of the family, and to call Mr. and Mrs. Frakes-Hogg by their Christian names.

Now, making her way down the arched corridor lit only by her single candle, she was grateful that Walter was away tonight, paying a condolence call on his newly widowed sister-in-law. When had she first begun to have doubts about her employer? Surely there had been unsettling moments before Jane's death, but in those days he'd been home so seldom and Adrienne had been so busy that she hadn't allowed herself to ponder Walter's odd behavior. At times, she'd had the sensation that he was staring at her from across the room, but then he'd smile at her calmly and Adrienne would shake off the feeling.

Since Jane's death, however, Walter had begun to make remarks that gave her chills, all the while staring into her eyes and smiling. He hinted that she could be well taken care of if she considered his needs as well as those of the little girls, but his threats were always so subtly veiled that Adrienne doubted her own instincts.

Once, when she had been climbing a tree with Ellie and Beth, Walter had offered to help them down from the lowest branch. He caught the girls, then insisted that Adrienne fall into his arms—and when she did, he slid his hand under her skirts while pressing her breasts to his ribs. His scent, a mixture of sandalwood and strong spirits, caused Adrienne's stomach to lurch.

Finally, there had been the night she awoke from a deep sleep to the sound of her doorknob rattling. If she hadn't taken the precaution of bolting her door, who knew what might have happened? Yet, in the daylight, Adrienne wondered if it had been a nightmare.

Many an hour she daydreamed about surrendering to convention and either going home to the safety of Château du Soleil and the love of her family, or joining London society with her friends from Mrs. Harrington's Seminary for the Daughters of Gentlemen. Anything would be preferable to this gloomy place. Adrienne might be unconventional, but she wasn't a recluse. If only there was a solution for Ellie and Beth . . .

Her bedchamber, though spacious, was dark, cold, and lonely. Adrienne used her candle to light oil lamps on the bureau, then turned toward the bed and nearly screamed aloud.

"Good evening, my dear." Walter Frakes-Hogg was sitting in a hard chair next to her bed, his coat lying near her pillow. The lamplight played eerily over his long face and tall, spare frame. Though only middle aged, he had prematurely white hair, and drink had reddened the ends of his ears and nose.

Her heart was hammering, but she strove for composure. It wouldn't do to let him sense her terror. "I must ask you not to enter my rooms uninvited, sir. If you like, I will speak to you in the sitting room. . . ."

"No. I like it here, and I make the rules. Had you forgotten?" He drank from a glass on the nightstand and loosened his cravat.

She hated the way he could smile and be evil at the same time. "Why have you come home from Mrs. Halper's, sir?"

"My sister-in-law means to move into the house with us, to take care of the girls."

"But that's wonderful news! I think highly of Mrs. Halper, and she will be able to give them so much that was lost when their mother died."

"I don't want her here. I'd rather have just you." His dark eyes glittered. "But she hasn't any money, no place else to go. I came home early to think of a way to foil her plan."

Adrienne felt dizzy with fear as she noticed that Walter's speech was impaired by drink. Should she run from the room? "Sir, you really must consider the needs of the children. You're away a great deal, and they need the love of their aunt."

"We'd rather have *your* love." He got to his feet and advanced toward her. "I'm certain we can discuss arrangements . . . hmm?" Bleary-eyed, Walter looked her up and down, nearly salivating over her lush curves and delicious-looking mouth. He began to unfasten his shirt, muttering "Wouldn't you like that?"

Before she could run for the door, he had captured her wrist and was drawing her into his arms. Adrienne realized that there was only one way to ensure her escape. She returned his feral smile. "You are so commanding, sir."

"Ah, charming, charming." He began to fondle her breast. "We must get rid of these missish gowns you favor, find something more revealing. You certainly have the shape for it."

Bile rose in Adrienne's throat. "No man has ever made me feel attractive until now."

"I can teach you things you never imagined."

"Oh, sir, I—I feel faint." She backed away from his looming mouth. "Can we sit down on the bed?"

"By all means, my dear girl! That's passion, going to your head. Come to think of it, I feel a bit lightheaded myself. Perhaps we ought to rest together. . . ."

Adrienne watched him lie back. When his shirt fell open, she saw a strawberry birthmark in the middle of his bony white chest. There was a bulge in his trousers, and he was breathing hard. "Sir?"

"Yes, my beauty?"

She sat down beside him. "I feel so shy. Will you close your eyes and let me practice kissing you the first time?"

Overcome by lust, Walter squeezed his groin with one hand and put the other back on her breast. "Christ, you're so young and firm. I can't stand it—"

"Close your eyes, sir," she whispered coquettishly. When he obeyed, Adrienne reached under her pillow for the dagger that she had placed there after the night he'd tried to come into her room. Now, trembling inside, she pushed it against his flabby throat. "I despise you! You have tried to use power to have your way with me, and I hate you for it. Now get up."

Disbelief and rage clashed in his eyes. "Little strumpet! Give me that thing before I turn it back on you."

"If you try, I'll kill you. I would have no regrets."

"Don't be stupid. If you do this, I'll make you pay!"

"There are ways I could make *you* pay if you threaten

me. Couldn't I ruin your reputation if I chose? Now get up. Put your hands in the air. Higher!" Adrienne moved the knifepoint to the middle of his back and poked it in far enough to draw blood. "You know, I wish I could kill you. Your daughters would be happier without you."

Something in her tone gave Walter Frakes-Hogg pause. She meant it. He let her force him into the tiny dressing room, then listened as she locked the door.

"You are going to be exceedingly sorry!" he yelled.

"Save your breath. You'll never see me again!" As she spoke, Adrienne dragged a satchel out from under her bed. It had been packed and ready, just in case, since the day she'd hidden the dagger under her pillow. Thank God for her darkest suspicions! Now she stepped out of the room, locked the door, and fled down the shadowy corridor. She would take the girls with her in a hackney, drop them at Mrs. Halper's, and trust her to look after them.

For her own part, Adrienne knew that she must conceal her whereabouts from Walter Frakes-Hogg. He was capable of all manner of revenge, for she had humiliated him in the worst way a woman could humiliate a man.

As she got little Ellie and Beth out of their beds and prayed that Walter wouldn't break free and kill them all, Adrienne realized that she'd give anything to have her papa come to her rescue.

"Won't you have a whiskey, Papa?" Adrienne paused hopefully beside the celleret in the corner of her father's sitting room. Nicholai Beauvisage was occupying an elegant suite in the St. James Royal Hotel, but after a fortnight away from his French château and Lisette, his beautiful wife of twenty-five years, he was unappreciative of his surroundings. He wanted to leave London—and take his daughter with him.

"I don't want a whiskey. I'll tell you what I *do* want—"

"You are frightfully edgy!" she interrupted quickly. "Perhaps a drink would settle your nerves."

"I don't need whiskey to settle my nerves," Nicholai replied with a dark stare. "What I need is obedience and respect from my wayward offspring!"

She blinked. "I detest the word 'obedience.' While I was at school, Mrs. Harrington insisted that I must have been *born* with a rebellious streak, since I could not respond to her efforts to subdue my spirit."

"I suppose you mean to turn your behavior back on *me* somehow!" He watched his daughter laugh and tried not to betray the softening of his heart. Gad, but Adrienne was magical—an effervescent mixture of beauty, keen wits, blind courage, and sheer charm. Who could resist the sight of her, with her chestnut curls caught up in a soft Grecian knot, her thick-lashed green eyes sparkling with mischief, and her dimples setting off a flawless, creamy complexion? If she could cultivate manners to match her appearance, eligible men would clamor for her hand in marriage, and then someone else could worry about her safety.

"I recognize that wistful expression, Papa," Adrienne said more gently. Joining him on the Sheraton settee, she patted his hand. "I know that you still hope to convince me to return to France with you—"

"My dear child, when you wrote to us last month, you didn't seem to need convincing. If you're in danger here in London, why have you changed your mind?"

"It was just a passing mood, Papa. I'm feeling much braver now, and I know that a quiet existence at Château du Soleil wouldn't make me happy. Nor am I suited to marriage, so you may as well cease gazing off into space and dreaming that I will be transformed into a proper member of London society." Adrienne leaned her head on his shoulder, as she had as a little girl. "We've had this same conversation every day since you came to London to take me home. Just because I am finished with school does not mean that I must either marry or live with you and Maman in France!"

"You are aging me decades each day," Nicholai lamented.

"Why can't you trust me to manage my own life?"

"Perhaps because you have gotten into one scrape after another ever since you were old enough to walk!"

"If you are referring again to that silly adventure I had when I ran away from Miss Harrington's school, please do not." Adrienne's cheeks were pink as the past returned, unbidden. It was embarrassing to think that she and her friend Venetia Hedgecoe could have foolishly fallen in with a woman like Mrs. Sykes, who took them in and promised to introduce them to London society. However, the lavish parties she'd taken them to had been filled with conniving, debauched men who had plotted to steal the girls' innocence. Mrs. Sykes had been searching for "suitors" for Adrienne who would pay for her lascivious brand of matchmaking.

"By the look on your face, my dear, I surmise that I still do not know the true extent of your imbroglio." Even four years later, Nicholai's torment was fresh.

"I escaped unscathed, and I've grown up tremendously since then, Papa. I would never do anything so foolish now, but I did learn some important lessons, especially about men. They can be charming, attentive, and cultured, but in the end they try to use their male dominance to achieve their selfish ends. I would rather take care of myself than trust a man."

Frustrated, Nicholai nearly poured himself a whiskey. "I would not judge all men against the standard of Frakes-Hogg or those you met through Mrs. Sykes! When I hear you talk this way, I only worry more."

"I am nearly twenty-one, Papa: a grown woman." Stubbornly Adrienne continued, "I have supported myself since school as a governess, and although that situation ended badly I do not intend to surrender and retreat from a life of self-sufficiency. You insisted that I receive a proper education, and I am grateful. I can make my own way in the world."

Nicholai's face grew stormy as he thought of the villainous Walter Frakes-Hogg. Adrienne's letter had only hinted that he had made unwanted advances toward her and that she had made him angry when she fled, taking his daughters to the home of his sister-in-law. What *hadn't* she told him?

"But what of Frakes-Hogg?" Nicholai said in low tones. "Has he not threatened you?"

She shrugged, eyes flashing. "I was a *little* afraid when I wrote to you, but I have since realized that Walter is a coward. I am not afraid of him, but he is afraid of *me*—and the damage I could do his reputation!"

"For God's sake, Adrienne!"

Her pretty chin set in a hard line. "Never mind. I have decided to accept another post. I will be able to leave London and Frakes-Hogg will have no idea where I've gone. There's no need to worry from this moment forward."

"What's this all about?"

"I have been offered a wonderful position as a companion to Lady Thomasina Harms, the ancient widowed mother of that exceedingly handsome dandy, Huntsford Harms." She gave Nicholai a grin. "Perhaps he will fall madly in love with me at first sight, propose, and take me off your hands, Papa!" Noting that he was not amused by this sally, Adrienne hastened to add "I'm only teasing. Lady Harms has informed me that, should I accept her offer of employment, we will depart immediately for her grand estate in Hampshire, where we shall languish for weeks—"

"I thought you'd be dead bored by such a routine," he put in.

"This is different. I will be *paid* for my boredom, thus maintaining my independence. And Harms Castle has one of the most extensive libraries in all of England! I shall immerse myself in the role of scholar."

It all sounded utterly mad to Nicholai. "What about this fellow Huntsford Harms? If he is there, and his mother is a decrepit widow, you'll find yourself in a compromising position again, my dear."

"I was only teasing, Papa. Huntsford Harms will doubtless be ensconced for the entire Season in her ladyship's house in Cavendish Square, thrilled to death to have his mother out of the way so that he can indulge himself in peace. You know how self-absorbed the nobility are." Adrienne waved a hand airily.

"In any event, I can take care of myself. Haven't I proven that yet?" She jumped up and stood before the pier glass, smoothing her blue spencer and white muslin skirts. "Now I must go, Papa. I have an appointment with Lady Harms to deliver my decision to become her companion after all. She'll be delighted!"

He put a large sum of money into her reticule. "Indulge me, won't you? Buy yourself some new gowns."

"If it will make you feel better, Papa. Thank you!"

Adrienne was tying the ribbons of her chipstraw bonnet when a knock sounded at the door. In the hallway, a footman delivered an envelope with her name on it, and Nicholai watched as his daughter broke the seal.

"Rather odd, isn't it?" he said. "Who would know that you are here?"

Her eyes moved rapidly over the paper, then she laughed with false gaiety and tore it into pieces. "Oh, Papa, it's nothing. People in London are very odd. They love to send mysterious messages to amuse themselves, but it's just a game." With that, Adrienne tossed the bits of paper into the bottom of her father's fireplace, then sought to distract him with an embrace. "Do stop worrying about me and begin packing for your journey home to Mother. She needs you far more than I do!"

Nicholai stood at the window, watching until she had emerged from the hotel onto St. James and climbed gracefully into a hack. When it started off into the crush of vehicles, Nicholai crouched in front of the sitting room fireplace and picked up the pieces of his daughter's note. Several minutes later he had fit the tiny squares together and read:

Lock your doors, strumpet!
I mean to make you pay, and you know how!

Oxford Street was jammed with the vehicles of well-to-do patrons who, attended by servants, were fluttering among the shops.

From her open hack, Adrienne found herself staring at window displays of linen-drapers, haberdashers, silversmiths, and silk mercers. She cared little about fashion but adored objects of real beauty, and at that moment, she was desperate for a distraction. Adrienne felt as if her problems—the vengeful Walter Frakes-Hogg, her father's displeasure, and the impending interview with Lady Thomasina Harms—were coiling about her like a python.

She shivered at the thought. "A python!" she murmured. "How hideous!"

Deliverance intervened. Her eye was drawn to a tasteful display in the window of E. Ralna, Fanmaker, where Adrienne beheld a true work of art. The fan was an exquisite concoction of ivory, embroidered silk, and lace. One glimpse in passing was not enough.

"Coachman!" she called, leaning out the window in a most indelicate fashion. "I must go into the fanmaker's— there!—this *instant*!"

The fellow assumed that a crisis was in the offing and yelled to the phaeton that was approaching on the left, between his hack and the raised flagstone walkway. When Adrienne's coachman attempted to cut off the phaeton, its raven-haired driver would not give way, and the confused horses reared back, whinnying in confusion.

"Are you trying to cause an accident?" the dark-haired man shouted angrily. "Get out of my way!"

"My mistress desires to reach that shop!"

"Why should that piece of news interest me?"

Adrienne, perceiving the problem, interceded. "You there, coachman!" she addressed the phaeton driver. For emphasis, she leaned farther out, so he would be sure to see her, and pointed her delicate parasol at him. "Do be a good fellow and let us over, won't you?"

One of his eyebrows flew up, then he gave a harsh laugh. "You have a very high opinion of yourself, miss, which I do not happen to share. You do not possess the road."

Outraged by his rudeness, Adrienne shocked her own driver by jumping out of the hack and pushing her way through the crush to reach the side of the phaeton. Still pointing the parasol, she stared up at the scoundrel, her cheeks hot with color.

"You, sir, are horrid! Has no one ever taught you to show respect for ladies?" She didn't like the sound of her own voice, or the things she was saying, but he'd pushed her past reason.

"Is there a lady present?" He caught her parasol and pulled it from her hand. "Stop aiming that weapon at me."

In spite of her mounting temper, Adrienne noticed the driver's compelling sea-blue eyes and the crisp, expertly tied cravat that set off a deeply tanned visage. It was even more maddening to perceive the laughter that lurked just behind his reprimand. Was he really a common coachman?"

"I do not wish to waste another moment of my time with the likes of you, sir." Adrienne tried to salvage the scraps of her dignity. Head high, she turned and walked coolly to the fanmaker's window.

Eugene Ralna himself came scurrying out to greet her. Spectacles bobbed on his long, thin nose. "Ah, it's young Lady Adrienne, is it not? I still remember the day last autumn when you accompanied your mother to my humble establishment. How may I serve you? Have you come to choose a fan on her behalf?"

Hoping that the odious man in the phaeton was watching, Adrienne let the fanmaker fawn over her. "I have business of my own, Mr. Ralna. In passing, I could not help admiring this exquisite creation in your window."

"Ah! You have flawless taste, just like your mother!" He smiled broadly. "That fan is made with the rarest ivory, fifteenth-century embroidered silk, and priceless Arles lace. Rumor has it that Marie Antoinette herself commissioned it after receiving the silk as a gift." Ralna paused, allowing his words to sink in, then murmured, "Shall we step inside for a closer look?"

"Why, the fan is part of *history*!" Wide-eyed, Adrienne had turned to follow the elderly man, when she was distracted by a tap on her shoulder. A backward glance revealed the phaeton driver's face, and she found that the sight of him made her furious. "Leave me alone," she hissed.

"Don't tell me that you made all that fuss, disrupted traffic, and endangered my horses over a bloody *fan*?" came his acid reply.

Adrienne refused to look back. "A brute like you would not understand. Do not speak to me again."

She had progressed several steps and was about to precede Eugene Ralna into the shop when the voice she despised called out, "Did you intend to make a *gift* to me of your parasol?"

Whirling, Adrienne met his mocking eyes and watched as he held out her parasol. The frilly thing looked ridiculous in his male hand. Did he mean for her to walk over and retrieve it? An instant later the parasol came sailing through the air toward her, and somehow she reached out and caught it. Her tormentor laughed, then bowed low.

"Don't let me keep you from your urgently important *fan* inspection," he taunted, and returned to his high-perch phaeton.

Adrienne hurried past Eugene Ralna, into the safety of his shop. Meanwhile, outside on sunlit Oxford Street, two young women were tittering as they stood, with a lady's maid, in front of the haberdasher's shop and discussed the impertinent rake who had caused Adrienne Beauvisage to blush to the roots of her chestnut hair.

"Isn't that Nathan Raveneau?" the first girl whispered.

"Definitely," her friend agreed. "I have heard the most outrageous stories about him from my sister and her friends. Since he returned from the West Indies, he's been setting London society on its ear!"

Not to be outdone, the first girl pronounced, "My cousin told me that everyone has taken to calling him 'The Scapegrace'!"

Just then Nathan Raveneau seemed to sense their scrutiny and turned his head to stare at the two gossiping girls. They went pale, then pink, and scampered away like frightened bunnies.

Chapter Two

"I DON'T KNOW WHY I BOTHER TO COME HERE ANY more," Nicholai Beauvisage muttered under his breath as he looked around White's Club. "Nothing's the same as it was, and even if it were, I'm too old for this nonsense."

Raggett, the proprietor of the legendary gentlemen's establishment, brought him a brandy. "I was not aware that the club had changed since your last sojourn in London."

"Don't play the dunce with me; you know perfectly well what I mean. Brummell and Byron have exiled themselves in Europe, and even the Regent is perpetually under a cloud of gloom since the death of his daughter, Princess Charlotte, in childbirth. For years the bucks of St. James have been allowed to behave like a lot of spoiled children, but the pleasure's gone out of it now, don't you think?"

"Not for everyone, sir," Raggett replied, inclining his head toward the green baize tables where an assortment of fops, young and old, continued their endless party. As the host, it was his task to help each guest relax and join in the fun. Noting the approach of Nathan Raveneau, Raggett seized the opportunity. "Don't sink into the doldrums yet, sir! Here's our young sea captain, Raveneau, back from the West Indies, and perfectly unspoiled as far as I can see."

Nicholai perked up. "Raveneau?"

"Indeed, sir. He's a man after your own heart." Raggett decided not to mention that all the dandies at White's were fascinated by the mysterious Raveneau, who partook of society's sophisticated pleasures only on occasion and fol-

15

lowed none of its rules. People were calling him The Scapegrace.

Staring as if he'd seen a ghost, Nicholai exclaimed, "My God, you are the image of your father! Do you remember me, m'sieur? I am an old friend of both your parents."

"Of course I remember!" Nathan's face lit up with genuine enthusiasm. "When I was a boy, eight perhaps, your wife sailed on my family's brigantine from America to England . . . searching for you, as I recall. The fair Lisette was my first love, and I hoped that she would come to her senses and decide not to marry you."

Nicholai's smile widened. "Infatuation with Lisette would be a noble beginning for any lad! Good God, that was twenty-five years ago! Come, sit, and tell me about your parents. I know that they keep a house in London, but I have been so embroiled in the affairs of my wayward daughter during my fortnight here that I've had no chance to call on old friends."

Explaining that his parents, André and Devon Raveneau, were at home in Essex, Connecticut, Nathan elaborated, "I am not even staying at our London home myself. I don't want to trouble the staff to fuss over only one person, and I spend more and more of my year in the West Indies. Since I don't even know how long I'll be in London, it's easier for me to put up at a hotel—"

"If I remember my own tendencies at your age, I might venture to guess that you also like your privacy and prefer not to have your parents' servants hovering at all hours?"

They laughed, finished their brandies, and decided to sup together. In the dining room they ordered champagne and turbot, which was served with turtle soup, boiled potatoes, pickles, smelts, and peas.

"I'll never get used to English food," Nathan remarked.

"Do you know Captain Gronow?" Nicholai's green eyes danced with mischief. "He advises putting a bit of everything onto your fork at once. Claims that technique enhances the tastes."

Nathan stared in consternation before giving way to more laughter. "I can't tell you how much my spirits have improved since meeting you, sir. I was out of sorts when I arrived tonight, thanks to a hot-tempered little hoyden in Oxford Street who nearly challenged me to a duel!"

"I needed a bit of cheering myself," Nicholai admitted. "London's not what it used to be, and I was feeling quite bored listening to the fops criticizing everyone. I'm relieved to know there are still other men like me at White's."

"Don't forget," Nathan cautioned, "I'm really American by birth, just like you, my friend!"

"London should be grateful to have us, then." Nicholai poured more champagne and sighed. "I suppose that my dark mood might actually stem from concern for my daughter. Your mention of a hoyden reminded me of my own irrepressible Adrienne. You see, she is the reason I am here from France—to try to persuade her to come home, where she would be safe and cared for. Instead, Adrienne prefers to seek *employment*, like a common servant!"

"Is that so terrible?"

"Perhaps not, but she is headstrong, and I believe that she's in danger." He told the story of Walter Frakes-Hogg in a rush, his eyes turning stormy as he recounted the scoundrel's attempts to take advantage of Adrienne, and the threats he had made in recent weeks. Nicholai finished with today's episode of the unsigned note as the table was cleared and dessert appeared. "Why won't she listen to me and come back to France?"

"Hasn't she given you an explanation?"

"Well, yes, but I don't like it. Adrienne insists that she wants to support herself and to continue her education. She has always been incorrigible. A few years ago she ran away from school and fell in with a woman who was being paid by noblemen to find them young . . . ladybirds. Thank God she was rescued in time." He shook his head. "Adrienne's grown up since then, but she still fights convention, and she's seen enough of unscrupulous men to want to look after herself. I'm sleepless with worry."

"It must be difficult to stand back and trust her when you fear for her safety. I've had Walter Frakes-Hogg pointed out to me as a person to avoid, so I understand your concern."

"If only she'd listen to me!"

Nathan sought another topic. "My own parents have had their share of sleepless nights over me as well. I learned too well from my father and became a sea captain myself, and now I spend most of the year in Barbados."

"Barbados! Odd you should say that; the island is my favorite of all I've visited."

Pleased to have found a distraction, Nathan smiled and leaned forward. His dessert, a particularly heavy trifle, went unsampled. "I share your sentiments, sir. When I began sailing my own ships to the West Indies, I had no intention of lingering. I meant to load up sugar and rum and be on my way, but I found that Barbados worked on me in the subtlest ways—"

"Yes!" the older man exclaimed. "Everything seems exotic there, from the sun on one's back to the turquoise sea to the scent of the frangipani and the sight of the bearded fig trees—"

"And the food and drink!" Nathan broke in. "I could live forever on Bajan rum, papaya, flying fish, limes, pigeon peas and rice, breadfruit—"

"And yet one can still get a proper cup of tea, thanks to the British influence. I'm so fond of Barbados that I purchased fifty acres of land along the eastern coast and am loath to sell it ... just in case Lisette agrees one day to leave France."

Nathan cocked an eyebrow. "The east coast, you say? That can be a treacherous location, and not only because the wild Atlantic Ocean batters that side of Barbados. Perhaps more treacherous is a *person* who lives in the eastern parish of St. Philip."

He sipped his brandy, then slowly explained, "Xavier Crowe is my nemesis. You see, I have bought my own home, on a sugarcane plantation farther north, but Crowe is the sort of sea captain who gives the rest of us a bad name and does everything in his power to spoil the pleasure I take in living on Barbados."

Beauvisage's expression was concerned. "What can one man possibly be doing to cause you such aggravation?"

"Crowe is just twenty-five: spoiled, dishonorable, crafty, and far too rich. His mansion, called Crowe's Nest, overlooks the ocean, and he has plenty of henchmen to carry out his plots. More than once, when a ship has drawn near in bad weather, Crowe's men have strung lanterns along the beach's palm trees. The incoming ships have been fooled into thinking that they've reached the safe haven of Bridgetown, and they sailed toward the lights."

"Let me guess," Nicholai interjected grimly. "The ships were dashed on the reef."

"That's right," Raveneau confirmed, "and Crowe's men looted the wrecks before they sank. Since Xavier was always careful to be conspicuously absent from Crowe's Nest during the actual crime, he's never been caught. Most Barbadians are afraid of him and his power, while I simply despise the man—and the feeling is mutual." He paused to light a cheroot, calming himself with a visible effort. "I'll admit, I've had personal conflicts with him that've deepened the bad feelings between us, but it is his character and his deeds that I detest most. You ought to think twice before becoming Crowe's neighbor."

Nicholai scratched his head. A plan was brewing in his mind. "From your description of Crowe's Nest, it sounds as if our estates might adjoin." He watched the spark of interest kindle in Raveneau's eyes. "You'd love to get your hands on my fifty acres, wouldn't you?"

"To watch over Crowe—and likely catch him in his crimes—yes, I would. Intensely." A decanter of port, with two glasses, appeared, but Nathan didn't notice. His knuckles were white on the arms of the chair, and the sparks in his eyes had caught fire. "I wish that I could ask you to name your price for your land, but unfortunately my funds are nearly all tied up in the estate I have purchased in St. Andrew's Parish. The house and plantation buildings date back to 1660, and they've gotten rather shabby. When I bought that land on Barbados and began planning the restoration of my new estate, I thought that nothing could mar my happiness, but Crowe has managed to strike me on every front."

Nicholai Beauvisage met the younger man's eyes with a penetrating stare. "I perceive, my friend, that we may be able to assist one another. If you will come to my aid, I am prepared to *give* you the fifty acres you covet."

"I accept!"

"You are young and full of fire." Nicholai chuckled. "Perhaps you should hear your side of the bargain before you agree."

Nathan was already imagining what would happen when the land adjoining Crowe's Nest belonged to him. What a fantastic stroke of luck it had been for him to meet Beauvisage here tonight! "Tell me then," he said. "I'll do anything."

"I want you to guard my daughter from danger until her twenty-first birthday, four months hence." He poured ruby-hued port into his own glass. "Adrienne has accepted a position as companion to Lady Thomasina Harms and shortly will travel with her ladyship to Harms Castle, there to pass the summer in musty boredom."

"Sounds like Harms Castle will be protection in itself." Nathan suggested hopefully.

"Lady Harms has a randy son called Huntsford, and then there's Frakes-Hogg, who doubtless won't give up so easily. Perhaps I'm making a tempest in a teapot, but I will feel a good deal better about returning to France if I know that someone I trust is keeping an eye on Adrienne."

"Are you suggesting that I protect your daughter from danger and . . . romantic seduction?"

"Why not?" Nicholai shifted in his chair. "Is it asking too much that she remain pure until she is twenty-one years of age? Adrienne is certainly capable of managing her own life, but I cannot help worrying because she is hotblooded and impetuous. If I am going to allow her to go off to a strange estate in Hampshire, can I not be assured, as her father, that some scoundrel won't be able to take advantage of her at a weak moment?"

"Well, then . . ." Nathan looked ahead to autumn, when he'd be back in Barbados, standing on his new fifty acres on the eastern coast. Xavier Crowe would be utterly crazed to find Nathan close enough to monitor the goings-on at Crowe's Nest! The thought made him grin suddenly. "I can stand anything for four months, even—" He caught himself.

"Even being exiled to the wilds of Hampshire for the summer!" His laughter was edged with relief, for he'd very nearly slipped and made an insulting reference to Nicholai's bluestocking daughter. No doubt Nicholai was a doting father, but surely Adrienne would be married by now if she were as attractive as all that.

It was an odd arrangement indeed, and it seemed to indicate that Beauvisage was an overprotective father, but who was Nathan to judge? The outcome for him would be fantastic. During his four-month exile in a drafty castle, he could read all the books he'd postponed, meanwhile keeping one eye on Adrienne Beauvisage, who was doubtless a temperamental spinster. Although it sounded dull, 'twould be a small enough price to pay for Beauvisage's strategically located land. Soon those acres would belong to Nathan, and he'd finally have means to thwart Xavier Crowe!

"You can perceive, my dear Miss Beau, that I have a method, can you not?" Lady Thomasina Harms waved Adrienne into her dressing room, which was arrayed with clothing and books being packed for the journey to Hampshire.

It was late, Adrienne was exhausted, and she had long ago given up saying her name properly for her new employer. Lady Thomasina had fixed upon "Miss Beau," and so it would be. It was the least of the old woman's eccentricities. From her lace turban and plump face, painted with too much crimson lip salve and rouge, to her pudgy body swathed in an elaborate embroidered gown and excessive jewelry, Lady Thomasina was a startling sight. Adrienne's interview had stretched into an endless supper, after which her employer had insisted on this visit to her dressing room.

"No doubt a bright girl like you can make sense of my method, hmm?"

Adrienne stared at the veritable stew of aging gowns, misshapen slippers, petticoats, chemises, bizarre hats and turbans, pieces of jewelry, fans, reticules, muffs, gloves, and such. She pursed her lips and made an attempt: "I do seem to notice a pattern of *colors*. . . ."

"Bravo!" Lady Thomasina cheered, clapping her hands.

"You'll learn in no time. At all times, even in transit, my possessions are arranged according to color *and* size, and I am very sensitive to even one item out of place!" She brought her thickly powdered face close to Adrienne's. "I am relying on you, Miss Beau, to watch over my things with a vigilant eye."

It was quite late by the time Adrienne returned to her own furnished rooms, and she was too tired to do anything more than prepare for bed. Lady Thomasina had announced that they would depart morning after next, so Adrienne decided to spend the following day packing. She would be taking everything that wasn't in France, since her home would henceforth be with Lady Thomasina.

The prospect of rusticating with an eccentric old woman in the Hampshire hinterlands couldn't help but give Adrienne pause, but she lectured herself while snuggling into bed. "Don't be gooseish. It will be an adventure," she insisted. "Much better than going home with Papa, where everything is familiar!"

The threatening note from Walter Frakes-Hogg leaped into her mind then, as she lay quietly in the dark. To keep her fears at bay, Adrienne conjured fanciful images of her future at Harms Castle, lingering on the prospect of visits from that legendary dandy, Huntsford Harms, until sleep carried her away . . .

In the morning, Adrienne sent word to her father that she would meet him at noon to make her farewells. She chose a pretty walking dress of lilac muslin, with satin ribbons that trailed down loose from the middle of her back, and concealed most of her curls under a jaunty tartarian turban with a lilac-striped band. Her scent, a light essence of lilac mixed for her in Paris, completed the effect.

Then, after organizing most of her possessions and luggage, Adrienne left the actual packing until after her appointment. In the doorway, she remembered her priceless new fan and took it with her. Her landlady was waiting downstairs in the vestibule, wearing a long face.

"How I shall miss you, dear Adrienne." Miss Hedgecoe, the aunt of Venetia Hedgecoe, a close friend from school and Adrienne's partner in numerous adventures, had welcomed her when she had fled Walter Frakes-Hogg's house.

"And I you." She embraced the older woman.

"Still, I don't want you to end up a lonely spinster like me. I'm glad you're venturing back out into the world." Miss Hedgecoe held out a letter. "This just arrived by messenger."

Adrienne paled at the sight of Walter's handwriting, but didn't want to worry her friend. "Thank you, dear. I must dash to meet Papa, so I'll read it on the way."

Once inside a hack, she gave the name of the hotel to the driver, then sat back, staring at the missive as if it were a poisonous snake. "I ought to simply tear the thing up and toss it away!" Adrienne thought. "That bully cannot hurt me!" But curiosity won out again. She broke the plain seal and read:

I will find you!

Nicholai had a light luncheon served in his private sitting room. Servants from the hotel's dining room had just finished laying out the dishes on a table set with fine white linen when Nathan Raveneau peeked out of his host's bedchamber.

"How long do you want me to hide in here?"

"You won't be *hiding* exactly," Nicholai amended. "Waiting is a better word. You're just waiting in here until I have Adrienne prepared for our plan."

"And then I should go out into the hotel corridor through this other door—" Nathan pointed to the narrow exit in the corner of the bedchamber. "—and knock, as if I'm just arriving?" He was looking amused yet dashing in his top boots, fawn breeches, and a blue coat he'd meant to throw away last year because of some frayed spots. It was a costume ordered by his new employer, to add to Nathan's new image of middle-class hired protector.

"That's right—you go out and knock at the other door when you hear me say 'Mr. Essex will be here at any moment.' "

"Who? Oh, right, that's me! And I thought I'd been so

clever, choosing to be called after my family's town in Connecticut. It wouldn't do for me to forget my name in front of your daughter!" Then Nathan pressed, "What if that note you forged and I delivered this morning doesn't work? What if she isn't afraid?" And he thought, How did I get myself into this absurd coil? Could I have drunk so much more last night than I remember? It was insane, and yet the prospect of bringing down Xavier Crowe in the near future was irresistible . . .

"Don't worry," Nicholai was saying. "I know how to handle my daughter."

Raveneau couldn't suppress a sardonic laugh. "Yes. Clearly you have young Miss Beauvisage completely in your power!"

"Very amusing." A sudden thought brought him up short. "I nearly forgot to give you your spectacles!"

"Spectacles?" Nathan put the gold-framed lenses on and stared at himself in the mirror.

"They're clear, but seemed a good addition to your new costume. Nothing like Nathan *Raveneau*, hmm?"

At that, there was a knock. Startled, Nicholai pushed the younger man into the bedchamber, closed the door, and went to greet his daughter.

Adrienne's embrace was warm. "Oh, Papa, you are so good and patient and I am hopeless. Are you going to forgive me before we part and you return to France?"

"Perhaps." In the face of her affection, he felt a pang of guilt. Adrienne might be full of mischief, but she'd never lied to him. "Of course I forgive you. Come and eat while the food is warm."

"Look at my beautiful new fan!" She opened it and waved it delicately to and fro. "It belonged to Marie Antoinette!"

"Stunning, my darling." Nicholai privately suspected that the shopkeeper had concocted that bit of whimsy.

"Thank you, Papa." She kissed his cheek. "I bought it with the money you put in my reticule!"

Adrienne discovered that she was famished after the morning of preparations for her journey. Her father looked on admiringly as she devoured salmon mousse and chattered about the upcoming journey, with Lady Thomasina Harms, to the legendary Harms Castle in Hampshire.

"Listen to me!" Adrienne exclaimed suddenly, between bites of lemon bread. "I've prattled on hopelessly. You must tell me all your news. What have you been doing in London since last we met?"

He reached across the table to clasp her hand. "Only hoping that you'll change your mind and travel home with me. How pleased your mother would be—"

"You're very unfair, invoking Maman like that!" she scolded. "Besides, she was an independent woman, and I know that she would be the first to understand that I'm too old to cling to her apron strings."

"I'm not just behaving like a stuffy father now." Nicholai paused, staring into her lively eyes. "I have real cause to fear for your safety, and I can't just walk away under these circumstances. You see ... I pieced together the note you tossed away in my fireplace yesterday. I know that Walter Frakes-Hogg is far from the harmless bully you have made him out to be."

Adrienne looked crushed. Lowering her eyes, she set down her fork, and her shoulders drooped. "Will you force me to go with you?" When he didn't reply immediately, she straightened again hopefully and went to kneel beside her father's chair. "Oh, Papa, my feelings are all bittersweet. It's certainly nothing against you, or Maman, or our wonderful home! And I am fully aware that life at Harms Castle will doubtless be dull ... but something deep within me yearns for fresh experiences."

Filled with pride, he cradled her fine-boned face in his hands and kissed her tousled dark-auburn curls. "I understand better than I care to admit. Did you imagine that you acquired your character out of thin air?" Nicholai stood, lifting her to her feet. "I will let you remain in England on one condition."

"Anything!" She was flushed with excitement.

It occurred to Nicholai that his daughter was as incautious as Nathan Raveneau had been when they'd exchanged these same words. "I want you to allow someone to look after you until your twenty-first birthday. That's just four months from now, but my hope is that Walter Frakes-Hogg will lose interest by then if he realizes that you are being guarded."

Clearly taken aback, Adrienne searched his face. "A—protector? How very odd, Papa! What sort of person would want to hover over me in Harms Castle?"

"As it happens," he boomed, "I've discovered a grand fellow! His name's Nathan—uh—Essex, and he's had experience at this sort of thing—"

"Do you mean he's some sort of *thug*? Really, Papa, it just won't do—"

"Mr. Essex will be arriving at any moment to meet you," he insisted. "I am afraid that you have no choice, my girl."

No sooner had she opened her mouth to utter another protest then a sharp knock came at the door to her father's suite. Adrienne's heart was beating fast; she felt rather like a doe, cornered by hunters in the forest. Reaching for her new fan, she opened it and created a calming breeze.

"Welcome, Mr. Essex," Nicholai was drawing the younger man into the sitting room. When Adrienne beheld them together, her first traitorous thought was that the Essex fellow was nearly as handsome as her father. Gleaming black hair, fashionably wind-blown, set off a face that could have been a buccaneer's but for a simple pair of gold spectacles. He gave her a faintly sardonic grin that heightened her first impression. Essex was tall, with a lithe yet powerful physique, and he moved with graceful self-assurance, suggesting a person of quality.

But then Adrienne remembered that he had been hired by her father to look after her, and she noticed his worn top boots and coat. Nathan Essex was a working man.

He seemed to know his place, for when he approached her, he bowed his head and didn't extend his hand. "It's an honor to meet you, Miss Beauvisage."

Even as she began to reply, Adrienne knew a delayed shock of recognition that was sharpened by the sound of his voice. "You—you're the *coachman*, aren't you!"

His eyes came up, blue with a glimmer of sea-green in them, and settled on the open fan. "Oh—*no* . . ."

"What's this all about?" Nicholai demanded, stepping between them.

She stamped her foot. "Where did you find this rude, hideous—*person*, Papa?"

Nathan heard himself bark, "Before you call others rude, miss, you might examine your own behavior! Besides rude, you're spoiled—"

"Arrogant!" Adrienne pointed back at him.

"Pretentious!" he parried.

"Oooh! Insolent!"

Horrified, Nicholai held up a hand. "You both will be silent this instant!" He could feel the sparks flashing through the air between his daughter and his young friend. "I will hear Adrienne first, then Nathan."

"Papa, I hope you have proper references for this brute, because I don't believe that he can be qualified to protect me from a mosquito, let alone a dangerous man!"

"Gammon," Nathan muttered.

"I want only to hear—*briefly*—how and where the two of you met previously," her father said. "Leave out your opinions of Mr. Essex's character."

"Oh, all right. I was proceeding along Oxford Street after my appointment with you yesterday, Papa, when I chanced to see a simply exquisite fan in Mr. Ralna's shop. It happens to be an historical *relic*." She fluttered her new possession for emphasis. "My own hack driver was making an effort to move out of the flow of traffic, but this odious beast refused to give way. He's a common coachman, Papa, nothing more! I asked him myself, very politely, and he laughed at me! We quarreled, and he pursued me and mocked me, nearly following me into the fanmaker's shop!"

Nicholai turned concerned eyes on Nathan Raveneau. Certainly he was not a coachman, but—could he have misjudged the man?

"Your daughter has a curious way of twisting the truth to suit her needs," Nathan said coolly. "As I saw it, her overpowering need to acquire this frivolous fan nearly caused an accident among the rest of us on Oxford Street! Her hack tried to cut me off, frightening my horses, and they reared back and nearly collided with another vehicle. When I dared question her driver, Miss Beauvisage proceeded to address me as if I were a chimneysweep who could barely manage the King's English! A moment later she jumped out into the traffic and bore down on my phaeton, yelling and pointing her parasol at me as if she might stab me!" He paused to give her a quelling glance. "To defend myself, I removed it from her grasp. She insulted me further, and I followed her to the shop to return her *weapon*."

"I am speechless," Nicholai pronounced. "I can only wonder if either of you realize how inconsequential your altercation sounds? Why not forget about it, laugh, and start fresh?" The couple met this suggestion with dark stares.

"Well, I don't really care whether you get along or not, because this arrangement is fixed. Adrienne, I trust that Mr. Essex will guard you with the same zeal he has devoted to your quarrel, and I can assure you that he comes highly recommended. For my part, I am ready to wash my hands of it all. I leave at dawn for home and the arms of my wife— and will leave the pair of you to your sulks and insults."

Nathan Raveneau stole a glance at his headstrong young charge. She might make his blood boil, but at least she wasn't the odd bluestocking he'd expected. Harms Castle might not be a crashing bore after all. . . .

Nearly four miles of masted ships lined the Thames, mimicking a narrow forest from London Bridge to Deptford. Extensive docks had been built on the Isle of Dogs for the convenience of vessels trading in the West Indies, and there rested the splendid *Golden Eagle*, her sails furled in the late-afternoon sunlight.

Captain Nathan Raveneau stood on the quarterdeck. His eyes took in every detail of the packet he'd acquired only two years before. The clean-lined ship boasted an exceptionally fine, well-trained crew, and it pained him to consider the prospect of being away for four long months.

Had he been drunk to agree to such madness?

Zachary Minter, whose Uncle Halsey had been André Raveneau's trusted right hand on board the *Black Eagle* during the Revolutionary War, approached his old friend.

Zachary and Nathan had shared childhoods, amusing themselves on board ship during pleasure voyages to England and France, and their friendship was more powerful than the boundary of a captain's authority over his first mate.

"I still can't believe you're going to do this thing." Minter drew himself up to his full five-and-a-half feet of skinny strength and shook his head, his red hair agleam. "Can't you just explain that you were in your cups, and—"

"I've already considered doing that, or worse, but the devil of it is that I want Beauvisage's land in Barbados. It'll all be worth it if we can have access to Crowe's Nest." His face wore a familiar expression of impenetrable determination. "I can trust you to see to the ship, can't I, Zach?"

"I never thought I'd live to see the day that you would put any other consideration before the *Golden Eagle*."

"You tread on thin ice, old friend," Nathan murmured. "I ask you to do my bidding for a mere four months. We'll sail to Barbados when August arrives."

"Your crew wants to sail now."

"And they must wait."

Minter's hair seemed to smolder in the setting sun. "While their heroic captain plays nursemaid to a spoiled chit in the middle of—"

"Be silent," Nathan warned, and pushed a folded note into the other man's freckled hand. "Here is a map Beauvisage obtained for me of the route to Harms Castle, where I must remain until the first day of August. Do not seek me out unless the situation is dire; I will discharge you if you attempt to lure me back with tricks. However, I *ask* that you come to me if I do not return on time." A smile touched his hard mouth. "I have no idea what to expect. With a spinster and a dowager for company, I feel certain it will be deadly dull, but one never knows."

Zachary Minter shook his head. "I hope that you don't die of boredom, Captain Raveneau. What an ignoble end that would be for The Scapegrace!"

Dawn had pinkened the mist on the Thames when Adrienne climbed into Lady Harms's ancient berlin. Her trunks were to travel separately, with her employer's belongings, but the berlin gained little speed from its lightened load. The coach was a load all by itself.

"I've never seen anything quite so extraordinary," Adrienne ventured as she surveyed her surroundings.

In its day, perhaps a half century ago, the berlin had doubtless been magnificent. Huge and ponderous, with the Harms coat of arms emblazoned on the door, it was meant to be a vehicle of luxury. The interior was roomy, with tattered decorations that were beaded, braided, and fringed.

"My late husband maintained that this was the only fit means of transportation for persons of quality," Lady Harms asserted. They were passing Green Park, where the cows were mooing to be milked. "Look under your seat, Miss Beau."

When Adrienne leaned forward, she discovered that she was sitting on a padded trunk. She lifted the lid momentarily and glimpsed lanterns, a small cooking stove, and a chamber pot inside.

"How very remarkable!" she exclaimed after regaining her seat. Her lace-turbaned companion nodded with satisfaction, but Adrienne held the private view that the berlin was so equipped because it could move only at a snail's pace. Passengers would be forced to live inside the coach for days—perhaps weeks!—and thus the stored items would become necessities rather than luxuries.

At least that hideous person is not traveling with us, she consoled herself. Luckily, the lesser servants, including abigails and footmen, were bundled into a third coach; only Lady Thomasina's companion accompanied her in the regal berlin.

"This is a near-perfect replica of the coach used by Marie Antoinette and the king during their attempted flight from France!" her ladyship announced.

Adrienne stifled a yawn. "Very ... interesting."

"See here, my girl, you are not making any effort in the least to be good company!"

"I do apologize, my lady, but it's shockingly early! I'm something of a night owl. . . ."

"I believe it is customary for hired companions to suppress such expressions of discomfort." Lady Thomasina gave her a decidedly sharp look, then sniffed. "It appears to be prodigious good fortune that we are to acquire another passenger at the Black Swan Inn! I have every confidence that he will make a better effort to entertain me."

Before Adrienne could take in the older woman's announcement, the berlin rumbled into the yard of a coaching inn, preceded by their outriders. Puzzled, she drew back the curtain and beheld Nathan Essex, striding toward them.

"*That*, Miss Beau, is a fine figure of a man! Don't you agree?" As spellbound as a young girl, she added, "Furthermore, I perceive that Mr. Essex is in his element at this early hour."

Adrienne gaped inelegantly. How on earth had that knave managed to acquaint himself with Lady Thomasina and squirm into her good graces? "I—how—"

"Mr. Essex paid me a call and explained a bit of your situation, persuading me to allow him to protect *both* of us." The old woman beamed and raised her jewel-encrusted quizzing glass. "I'd be a fool to refuse such a delicious offer, particularly given the dearth of entertainment one usually suffers at Harms Castle. You, my girl, must surrender to the inevitable and be grateful that your father thinks enough of you to enlist Mr. Essex's services."

Adrienne's head was spinning, and Nathan was about to open the coach door. "But why must he ride with us?"

"Because it amuses me."

A wild sort of energy came into their midst when Nathan climbed aboard. His wide shoulders seemed to fill Adrienne's vision, and his clean male scent filled the air. As he settled into the space beside her, he turned bespectacled eyes on her that snapped with all manner of wit.

"I knew I would enjoy this!" Lady Thomasina proclaimed, beaming. "If I were smaller, I would ask you to sit by *me*."

"I would that that were possible, my lady," he replied, then gave Adrienne a dark look, murmuring, "We meet again, my charge."

She was incensed by the way he bent his head in mock deference. "Pray do not forget your station, Mr. Essex."

"If you will not forget yours, Miss Beau" came his retort, and it pricked her. "We are both paid employees of those more fortunate than we, are we not?"

Fuming, Adrienne pressed her lips together, turned her body away from him, and stared out the window as the berlin rolled back onto the road.

"Once again I must express my appreciation, my lady," Nathan said to Adrienne's mistress. "Perhaps your companion neglected to tell you that she has received threatening messages from her former employer, who made advances toward her when she was governess to his children. Although it would seem that she will be safe in your household, her father is concerned and wants to be certain also that no danger comes to *you*, my lady. As I have mentioned, it would be my honor to look after both of you."

The old woman appeared to swoon momentarily. "How *gallant* you are, sir."

"Not at all. Now then, how would you prefer to pass our journey, my lady? We could have a game of cards, or—" Nathan reached into his pocket and brought out a worn, travel-sized volume of *Ivanhoe*. "—I could read aloud, if you like."

Lady Thomasina's rouged cheeks reddened further, and she sighed, ecstatic. "I wonder if you do not misrepresent yourself, Mr. Essex! Perhaps you are a scholar in disguise."

"I fear not." He dipped his head, but his eyes twinkled. "I am merely conscious of the courtesy you do me by allowing me close access to my ... charge." Nathan slipped his hand around Adrienne's wrist and gently held her until she squirmed free, blushing. "I would make myself useful in return."

"Delightful." Her ladyship beamed. "Simply irresistible. Don't you agree, Miss Beau? Yes, of course you do. And we shall have *Ivanhoe*. Do begin, Mr. Essex. Your audience is rapt."

He opened the book and obeyed in tones laced with amusement. " 'In that pleasant district of merry England which is watered by the river Don ...' "

Adrienne heard his voice through a mist of confused embarrassment. Her wrist burned where Nathan's fingers had encircled it, and she felt the persistent, steely line of his thigh, even through her gown and pelisse. Did he *mean* to press against her? Cheeks flaming hotter at the thought, Adrienne clenched her teeth. She reminded herself that he was only a servant, a hired guard, and ought to be respectful to her. After all, her father was paying him to take care of her! There had to be a way to force him to treat her with the same sort of respect he paid Lady Thomasina Harms.

It galled her that he made her think such things. Adrienne despised aristocrats who put on airs and pretended they were somehow above untitled folk, and yet here she was, trying to put Nathan Essex in his place. Why was he so infuriating?

As the procession of vehicles wound deeper into the verdant Hampshire hills, her ladyship interrupted Nathan from time to time in order to scold her young companion. "Are you listening, Miss Beau? Sit up straight, child, and show some breeding!"

Was Adrienne mad, or did she feel the pressure of his thigh intensify at such moments?

Chapter Three

When dawn broke at Harms Castle for the fourth morning since Adrienne's arrival, she lay in her narrow bed and realized that she profoundly regretted every decision she had made leading up to that moment. How many times did she have to entangle herself in wretched coils before she would learn to listen to voices of reason?

Her body ached with fatigue. She might be paralyzed—but couldn't be that fortunate. Adrienne knew that she was perfectly healthy, and so must crawl out of bed, bathe with cold water, dress, and begin one more endless day of servitude.

Lady Thomasina Harms's own schedule was considerably less taxing. She favored an array of bizarre pastimes, which Adrienne had glimpsed that first night in London, when her ladyship hinted about her color-and-size Systems. They were currently being practiced in the sprawling library at Harms Castle. Lady Thomasina spent most of each evening there, making precarious stacks of bottle-green or bloodred books, aided by her reluctant companion.

"My husband insisted on grouping the books alphabetically," her ladyship would complain as yet another pile of old books got too tall and toppled over. "Can you imagine? We had horrible rows about it, and I could scarcely wait to organize them all with a *real* system. Of course, he's just been dead a few months, and it may take years."

Then, long past midnight, she would waddle off to bed, leaving trails of powder from her wig. Lady Thomasina liked to sleep late and have a leisurely breakfast in bed. Adrienne, meanwhile, quickly discovered that she was expected to rise with the rest of the household staff and "get down to business" making more precarious piles of colored books.

On this fourth morning, as she finally managed to fasten her own gown, a sharp knock came at her door. Lady Thomasina's tallow-faced abigail, Hortie, seemed to delight in rousting the newest servant out of bed. Each day Adrienne rose earlier, and each day Hortie arrived earlier. Adrienne wished she didn't have to answer. The rapping only grew more insistent, however, forcing her to yank open the door to the corridor.

"I'm coming!" she cried. "Why can't you—" Her voice broke off at the surprisingly welcome sight of Nathan Essex.

"Yes?" A slow smile crept up to his eyes.

"I thought you were Hortie."

"I'm not. I begged to come in her stead."

"Hortie hates me because Lady Thomasina's given me her old chamber, and now she's forced to sleep in the dismal servants' quarters." Adrienne walked back into the narrow room, which adjoined her ladyship's grand suite, in search of hairpins and a ribbon. "I despise this place! I should have listened to my father."

Boldly Nathan closed the door and followed her. "You only say that because he cannot hear you recant."

"Well, I would like to know, where have *you* been? What are you being paid to do, frequent the taverns in Winchester?" She brushed her hair furiously.

"Have you missed me?"

"Only in the way that misery misses company, sir! Eternity in Hell could not be worse than twenty hours of each day spent taking books from shelves and sorting them by color and size, while listening to Lady Thomasina's tirades!" She spoke in a ragged whisper, aware that only a heavy door separated them from her ladyship's bedchamber. "At least you might *help* me!"

"The night we arrived, supped, and were shown our

rooms, you made it quite clear that you preferred to be spared another moment of my company—"

"I had just spent an entire day in your lap, while you read *Ivanhoe*!" she protested.

"You were not in my lap, Miss Beau. I would remember it clearly if you had been." He removed his spectacles and began to polish them.

She felt his eyes roam over her in a way that made her breathless and warm. Nathan was clad in a loose white shirt, a worn cravat, and the familiar buff breeches paired with top boots that needed shining. Yet his appeal was shockingly potent.

His hair gleamed. Glossy and black, it was recklessly long, curling over his collar. Adrienne, who had been overwhelmed by exhausted boredom, knew a spark of interest. She hated him but welcomed the diversion.

Feigning contrition, Adrienne sighed. "I *know* I was not in your lap, but I felt awfully closed in during our journey. Perhaps my manners suffered."

Manners? Nathan thought, wildly amused. Is she in jest? "Have you grown new manners since arriving at Harms Castle?"

"Must you be so relentlessly infuriating?"

He laughed and watched as she lifted her slim arms and fashioned a soft knot of chestnut curls atop her head. Feathery baby tendrils trailed along the nape of her neck. He was sorely tempted. "I was right all along. You *don't* like me."

"Not in the least," she agreed. "However, if I must perform acts of slavery in my role as servant, you might as well join me. My shoulders ache beyond reason, so if nothing else, you can lift the books."

"A thrilling plan."

Harms Castle was only a few decades old, built by Lady Thomasina's father-in-law with a fortune acquired through an advantageous marriage. Located a half-dozen miles from the ancient town of Winchester, the Nash-designed country house was nestled into a lush fold of hills and bordered by the trout-filled River Itchen.

Adrienne found the maze of rooms confusing, since they all seemed to look alike and the arrangement was much different from that of her family's château, where she had grown up.

Harms Castle featured a great entry hall, a saloon, a drawing room, a long gallery, a dining room, and, of course, the infamous library. The west wing consisted of apartments, most of which were vacant, since Lady Thomasina was the only noble in residence.

She was catered to by a score of servants, ranging from the house steward, butler, and cook, to housemaids, liveried footmen, and scullery maids. Yet either the staff was too small for the castle's size, or they were lazy, or they were not instructed to clean properly, for the place was as rundown and musty as the berlin Lady Thomasina preferred for travel.

Adrienne regarded her new state of servitude as odd indeed. Although well born, she had always been too spirited to enjoy lolling about, so she had not expected to be put off by physical work. However, Lady Thomasina's tasks were tiresome, because they were queer, pointless, and demanding.

Walking with Nathan to the servants' dining room, Adrienne was brightening already, though she would never admit that to him. They breakfasted on grayish porridge with Hortie, some housemaids, and Jarrow, the fat butler who looked like a man overly fond of spirits. It was Hortie who reminded Adrienne that her ladyship expected work to begin in the library by six o'clock. Nathan casually rose and followed her.

Climbing a dark staircase from the servants' wing, she glanced back at him. "What are you up to now?"

"I'm going to help you, just as you asked. You don't really object to my company—do you?"

He knew just how to get under her skin and turn it pink. "I have discovered that even *your* company is welcome in this godforsaken place. Besides, Papa is paying you, isn't he?"

"Handsomely."

"It seems that neither of us has a choice."

Adrienne watched as he paused in the arched corridor to examine a painting by Fragonard. What a puzzle Nathan Essex was! He seemed misplaced somehow in his decidedly middle-class clothing and occupation, and Adrienne had to remind herself continually that he was probably someone her father had met at a cockfight or in a pub on the docks.

"Well, then, if Papa is paying you to watch me, where were you these past three days? I have realized that you didn't give me a proper answer when I asked earlier."

He glanced back at her, one dark brow arching slightly. "I had business in town. Perhaps you might consider the possibility that protecting you involves more than standing in your shadow."

"I see." How dare he be secretive? After all, in one way, he was working for *her*, wasn't he? Whirling, Adrienne walked down the corridor and entered the library, wishing she could lock Nathan out. It was especially galling that he could come and go as he pleased in view of her punishing descent into the serving class.

"Tell me how I can help you."

How could she resist? All morning long, Adrienne sent him up the ladders in search of more bottle-green books, and it did her heart good to watch as he tried to carry stacks down while maintaining his balance. Once, when it appeared that a particularly large armload would break free and crash to the floor, Adrienne intervened to hold the volumes in place long enough for Nathan to reach the threadbare carpet safely.

"This is a magnificent house, but it certainly needs more upkeep," he remarked.

"You should see Lady Thomasina's home in Cavendish Square. I wonder if she does not *prefer* cobwebs and tarnished brass. . . ."

Nathan fingered the draperies and bit his lip. "And motheaten fabrics?"

"I've awakened each night to the sound of mice in my walls," Adrienne confessed in a whisper.

"I'll suggest to the house steward that a rat catcher be called. I am surprised that one isn't on staff." He glanced up in time to see Lady Thomasina herself trundling into the library. She was clad in an old-fashioned gown made of fraying striped silk and distinguished by a creaking set of paniers. A Welsh terrier followed in her wake, a chicken wing clutched between his bared teeth.

"At last you have deigned to join us, Mr. Essex!" her ladyship exclaimed.

Adrienne rejoined: "It seems that my *protector* has been at his leisure these past days, since his own employer, my father, is in France now and knows not whether I am being guarded."

"Sweeten your tongue, Miss Beau, or you shall drive him away again, and then you'll have only a mad old woman for company!"

Adrienne reddened, but Nathan laughed, as if it were all a jest. He stepped forward, sketched a bow, and lifted Lady Thomasina's hand for a brief kiss. "I can only say, in my own defense, that there is more to keeping Miss Beauvisage from danger than standing beside her. A related matter took me to Winchester."

"So gallant!" her ladyship pronounced, while Adrienne privately suspected that he had been passing his time with a local strumpet.

"And now that I am with you both again, I must inquire after your comfort. Are you feeling safe and secure, Lady Thomasina?"

"Infinitely more so now that you have returned, sir." She allowed him to help her into an old velvet tub-shaped chair, then called to the terrier. "Angus, darling, come to Mummy with your sweet little bone." When the dog had obeyed, Lady Thomasina returned her attention to Nathan. "Angus was one of his lordship's six Christian names, and when I gave it to my pet, it quite annoyed him. Every time he heard me call out to dear Angus, his face would turn blood-red. Apoplectic fits, I'd venture. The poor fellow was completely lacking in humor. . . ."

Adrienne didn't know what to do, so she sidled over to the worktable, leaned over the newest stacks of books, and made a show of counting them. Nathan Essex had apparently lost interest in helping her, for he seemed perfectly content to sit close to Lady Thomasina and make amusing conversation. Soon even Angus had traded his smelly chicken bone for a nap on Nathan's booted foot.

Watching the cozy scene from afar, Adrienne knew just how Lord Harms had felt when he'd had those blood-boiling spells.

Minutes passed, and a maid wearing a soiled apron appeared with a tray of tea and miniature cakes. Lady Thomasina called for another serving for Mr. Essex, but seemed to forget that Adrienne was present. Instead, the pair shared cake bits with Angus.

An hour passed. Nathan read another chapter of *Ivanhoe*. Adrienne developed a raging headache from the mold spores that contaminated nearly every volume in the Harms library. She discovered a copy of Christopher Marlowe's *Passionate Pilgrim* and was reading happily, perched on her ladder, when, suddenly, she was noticed.

"Gadzooks, there you are, Miss Beau!" the old woman cried out as she craned her neck. "Hard at work? Good, good. Aren't we grateful to have this handsome creature here to make our labors more enjoyable?"

She couldn't manage more than a stiff smile for her employer but gave Nathan a stare that was meant to cut deep. Adrienne had been used to speaking her mind, often to excess, all her life, and no aspect of her new position was more frustrating than holding her tongue.

"On the subject of Miss Beau's labors," Nathan remarked conversationally, "I hope that you will allow me to make an observation. You do trust my judgment, don't you, my lady?"

"Of course!" She raised her quizzing glass. "What is it? Something about the Systems?"

"I would never presume to interfere with your Systems," he said gravely. "However, I do wonder if Miss Beau's true talents are being properly used these days."

"True . . . talents?"

"Perhaps she is too modest to tell you herself, but I have been informed that your companion possesses a keen intellect. It is *she*, not I, who is the scholar. Miss Beau is not only blessed with a vivacious temperament, she is an expert on literature, a lively reader, and an accomplished pianist as well. When her father agreed to her wish to travel here rather than return to the family's vast estate in France, it was with the understanding that his daughter would be given an opportunity to enrich her life with new experiences—and to help your ladyship to better enjoy your own life."

Lady Thomasina squinted, scratched her head, and ignored the clump of powder that dropped into her lap. "That was quite a speech, sir. Did you make it because Beauvisage is paying you?"

"I made it because I believe that Adrienne has a great deal to offer you—as a true companion, not as a filer of books. That job could be relegated to a few of your strong young footmen."

Her heart pounding with elation, Adrienne came toward them, wiping her hands on her apron. "Oh, my lady, if you would agree to Mr. Essex's ... suggestion, I would be more than happy to *oversee* the work on the library. It would probably be a much more efficient plan, after all."

Lady Thomasina pursed her lips. "The pair of you haven't been conspiring against me, have you?"

Nathan's response was masterful. He leaned toward her, his deep-blue eyes holding hers, and murmured, "You don't believe that, do you? No, of course not. I am a fair man. I have only told you what I know to be true." A smile tugged at his mouth. "As for Miss Beau being in league with me on any matter, I fear that we have yet to exchange pleasantries about the weather without plunging into an argument."

"Well then, perhaps there is some merit in the case you've made. I'll consider altering Miss Beau's duties."

"We all may benefit from her increased good spirits." His tone was wry. "I suspect that this young lady hasn't been used to much physical labor, and it's taken a toll on her mood."

"Hmm." The old woman regarded Adrienne, who had inched forward to stand near them and was beaming. "If that smile is any indication, you're right!"

Adrienne blushed then, unable to look at Nathan. "My

lady, while you ponder this matter, I shall return to the books."

"I'll bring more down from the upper shelves," Nathan announced.

Watching as the couple began to work together, Lady Thomasina realized that there was no one left to entertain her. "This won't do at all," she whispered to Angus. The terrier was looking bereft himself, without Nathan's boot to doze upon. "We shall have to devise a better system. A system for the Systems."

All afternoon Adrienne could see that Lady Thomasina was preoccupied—and frustrated. How could she fault Nathan for working beside Adrienne after she had complimented his gallantry so often? So, as the day unfurled, Lady Thomasina was forced to amuse herself, pretending to read volumes of Boswell and Pepys when in fact she was watching the young pair over the tops of pages.

Suddenly Adrienne found her labors more enjoyable. Perhaps her good cheer was due to the sense that a victory over her irascible employer was at hand. Yet there was another kind of charge in the air. It seemed to have to do with the sight of Nathan Essex, coatless. The white expanse of his shirt heightened his rakishly sun-darkened visage, and the sight of his wide back and shoulders when he walked away from Adrienne carrying an armload of books made her feel oddly breathless. . . .

"I cannot recall a duller afternoon!" Lady Thomasina cried suddenly.

Nathan stopped midway up the ladder and looked back at her. "My point exactly, my lady. If this work were more efficiently delegated, your companion and I would be free to devote ourselves to *your* needs."

"My head aches." She scowled. "I will take supper in my chambers."

"Let me help you." After jumping lightly to the floor, Nathan scooped up his coat, shrugged into it, and was at her side in an instant.

"I'm not a cripple," Lady Thomasina complained.

Angus peered up at Nathan and emitted a low growl.

"What sort of mood is this? Are you angry with me for telling the truth?" He gave the terrier a quelling glance, then slipped one arm around the stout old woman as he drew her out of the tub chair. For a moment, it seemed that she was stuck. "Lean forward a bit, my lady. There we are."

She visibly melted. "I like my own way. Always have."

"So I see. And you shall have it, if you don't mind sacrificing companionship for the organization of your library."

"You're stubborn."

He gave her a dazzling grin, their faces inches apart. "We understand each other."

Adrienne watched as they went out of the room together, arm in arm, Angus leading the way. Just before they disappeared through the doorway, she called, "Good day, my lady! I hope you feel better after a little rest. If there is anything I can do, please call upon me."

"Yes, yes."

Sighing, she returned to her awful labors. The sun began to slip toward the curve of the hill beyond the garden, and still Nathan did not come back to help again. So much for chivalry, Adrienne thought, despising him anew. Everything the man did was a performance, a means to an end. There wasn't a sincere bone in his body.

Her hair was coming loose, curls falling down her back as she clambered up the ladder one more time. The library was growing dark, yet no one had appeared to light candles. It was the worst place in the world. A volume of Fielding's *Tom Jones* caught Adrienne's eye and, biting her lip, she peeked inside. Her hip settled between ladder rungs as she strained in the dusky light to read a scene between Tom and a lusty tavern wench. How could such graphic behavior be in print for all the world to read?

Warm blood crept into her cheeks, and she forgot about the smell of mildew that clung to her skin and the aching of her shoulders. A strange, rather naughty feeling stole over her.

"I have good news."

The sound of Nathan's voice, shockingly close, gave her a terrible start. Instinctively trying to hide the book,

Adrienne lost her balance and tumbled off the ladder. Nathan deftly caught her and managed to grab the forbidden volume of *Tom Jones* as it sailed past.

"Don't worry," he assured her. "I have you."

In agony, and all too aware of her disheveled state, she cried, "I'm fine! Let go!"

"Are you spending more time reading than sorting these days?" Nathan examined the book with lazy amusement. "Tsk, tsk. This is hardly fit for the eyes of an unmarried young lady. Were you enjoying it?"

"You are beastly!" Did he notice her sweaty old-book smell? He must think that she had degenerated into a scullery maid, in need of a bath *and* decorum! "Only a horrid *man* would enjoy a book like this! It's shocking!"

Nathan was shocked too by the force of his response to Adrienne in his arms. Her curves were even more alluring than he had imagined, and she had a salty-sweet scent that was enhanced by the sight of her curls tumbling from their pins. Her mouth reminded him of crushed cherries, inviting beyond belief. "You needn't be alarmed. I'm not going to hurt you, Adrienne."

"Just put me down!" Everything about him excited her: his hard male body, his appealing scent, the gleam of his hair and his eyes, and even those incongruous spectacles.

"Hold still a moment. Perhaps you've twisted your ankle?"

"No such thing!" Panic began to set in. Her breasts were crushed against his chest in a way that made her want to reach up for his shoulders, his mouth. . . . "I mean it, you—you scoundrel! Put me down before I scream for help!"

His eyes were thoughtful, and then he set her lightly on her feet and stepped back. "No need for hysterics."

"I was not hysterical!" Her voice broke, and that made her angrier. Why did she have to sound like a harridan at such a moment? "Stop smiling at me like that! I hardly think that Papa would approve of your behavior!"

"Your papa wouldn't ask the wolf to guard the chicken coop, would he? He trusts me implicitly." Shadows played over his face. "Perhaps you ought to as well."

She thrust out her chin and made no reply, while a chill spread over her body. As if reading her mind, Nathan hunkered down before the marble-faced fireplace and set about laying and lighting a fire. "God only knows when this chimney was last cleaned. Look at the soot! I've never been in a worse-run house," he declared. "It's a bad piece of luck for both of us."

The flames licked upward, and Adrienne felt better as she held out her hands toward the comforting rays of warmth and light. Nathan had dusted himself off and was circling the library with a taper, lighting candles. When he returned to her side, they were both quiet as they soaked up the fireglow.

Finally Adrienne spoke tentatively. "Earlier, when your voice frightened me out of my wits, did you say something about good news?"

"I did. Lady Thomasina is going to assign a pair of footmen to the physical labor of carrying books. You will help her oversee the project, but in the main, your duties will revert to those you were originally engaged to perform: providing companionship, reading, playing the piano, and so on."

Euphoric gratitude made her feel buoyant. "Oh, Nathan, thank you!" Beaming, she nearly hugged him. How attractive he looked in the firelight!

"Not at all. As you are so fond of pointing out, your father hired me to take care of you. Perhaps now you will believe in me a bit more."

Instantly Adrienne was suspicious. "Was that the only reason you took my part with Lady Thomasina? To lull me into allowing you to take control of my life?"

Nathan nearly laughed. She had a rare, effervescent beauty, her tousled hair agleam with chestnut lights, her thick-lashed green eyes snapping. "Why can't you like me?"

"Because. Because I simply cannot. And I can't explain." The prospect of surrendering to him, to his aura of competence and desirability, was frightening to Adrienne. Too many strong men had tried to control her. "I am ravenous. I'm going down to see what the cook has made for supper."

"Tomorrow evening you shall dine with Lady Thomasina."

"Perhaps *that* fare will be edible." Adrienne turned away and started toward the doorway, only to realize that Nathan was following her. "Can you not give me a moment's peace?"

"I thought you had been lonely without me."

"You flatter yourself."

"Perhaps." He gave her a smile that prickled the back of her neck, for it said that he knew her secrets. When she strode away again, Nathan caught her arm. "You are too headstrong for your own good, my dear. I understand more and more why your father felt need of me."

"Again I must ask you to loose me!"

"I'm afraid you cannot be rid of me." His chiseled face loomed above her, shadowed by the play of a nearby candle. "I have told you as reasonably as I can that you must endure me, and I continue to suggest that you trust me." Nathan tightened his grip on her arm. "In fact, you will have to trust me and obey me, Adrienne." He paused. "You see, Walter Frakes-Hogg has been seen near Winchester, and I do not intend to allow you to put your life in jeopardy."

She gasped. "You—you're lying!"

"Cease your tirades against my character." Nathan caught her other arm and held her fast.

"You are nothing more than a—hired thug! You have no right to give me orders!"

His eyes went hot and dark, but he spoke softly. "I may be a working man, but I will not be lorded over by anyone, especially a spoiled, harum-scarum baggage like you." Not for the first time, Nathan Raveneau wished Nicholai had never invented this new identity for him. It didn't fit him any better than the frayed costume he was forced to wear. "I will not fight you at every turn." He pulled her closer until their bodies touched full length. "Furthermore, I suggest that you not underestimate me."

Adrienne nearly spat in his face. "I hate you!"

He gambled. "Do you want me to leave permanently?

Would you prefer to protect yourself from Walter Frakes-Hogg?"

Her catlike eyes shot daggers at him, but Adrienne's intellect prevailed in the end. "All right. You can stay. If there is one person I despise more in all the world than you, Nathan Essex, it is the odious Walter Frakes-Hogg!"

Chapter Four

"SOMETHING BY HAYDN, PERHAPS?" LADY THOM-asina inquired sweetly.

After untold hours of playing the piano, Adrienne's fingers were stiff and sore. Across the drawing room, the old woman was tucked into her favorite chair, munching contentedly on sweetmeats while Angus dozed in a pool of sunlight.

"Perhaps I should step into the library for a moment and see how Tavis and Sam are coming with the Systems. They do grow confused from time to time."

"Well . . ." Lady Thomasina's painted mouth turned down in a pout. "If you must, run along then. But be quick about it! If I'm left alone very long, I shall grow bored and ill-tempered!"

Fleeing, Adrienne nearly collided with Hortie, who was carrying a tarnished silver tray with a letter on it. "This just arrived by post, my lady," she intoned, pretending that her rival was not in the room at all. "I believe it is a letter from his young lordship."

"From my Hunty?" Lady Thomasina leaned forward anxiously. "Oh, dear, will someone read it to me? I've forgotten my spectacles."

Adrienne knew that she ought to volunteer, but the opportunity to slip away was too promising. From the doorway she called, "No doubt Hortie will be glad to oblige, your ladyship. And you must be missing her companionship since I've joined the household." She gave the skeletal abigail a hopeful smile.

"I am forever at your disposal, ma'am."

"I'm used to Miss Beau's reading voice, or that of Mr. Essex, but I suppose you'll do, Hortie. . . ."

It did Adrienne's heart good to see the other girl drawing a stool up beside Lady Thomasina. She was more than glad to share her own position, the burdens of which had shifted from physical labor to emotional suffocation. Like a child, Lady Thomasina demanded relentless entertainment and attention, and Adrienne was growing increasingly resentful.

Out in the cavernous corridor, it came to her that there really wasn't any escape. There could be no change of scenery except other parts of dreary Harms Castle. She wasn't allowed to go to town, for even if Lady Thomasina would loosen her grip, Nathan Essex had forbidden her to wander away alone.

Through an arched leaded-glass window on the landing, Adrienne gazed out over the garden. It was in need of grooming, but daffodils were blooming in clusters, and a boxwood maze caught her eye. How wonderful it would be to breathe fresh air after the assortment of stale smells inside Harms Castle!

Lifting her gray skirts, Adrienne looked right and left, then hurried down the stairs to the heavy doors leading out the rear of the house to a mossy terrace rimmed by shallow stone steps. Nearby, a man who apparently was the estate gardener was poking at a plot of earth with a hoe. He tipped his hat to her as she passed, then shuffled away as if he'd forgotten why he'd been hoeing in the first place.

For a quarter of an hour, Adrienne wandered in the maze. She listened to the songs of birds that were gathering material for nests, ventured to the edge of the meadow to pick cowslips and budding red clover, and watched the activity of some beetles. It felt rather exciting to do something forbidden like going outside without permission, but what fun was it if no one knew?

Just then a stormy-faced Nathan Essex came around the hedge toward her and took hold of her by both arms. "Are you mad? I have given you clear orders not to go anywhere without telling me!"

As her heart began to pump, Adrienne realized that she wasn't bored any more. "Take your hands off me, sir! Must you manhandle me at every turn?"

"Only when you insist on behaving like an incorrigible child who deserves a shaking!" His eyes blazed into hers. "Would you rather be in the hands of Walter Frakes-Hogg?"

"Aren't you a bit of an alarmist? Really, it's broad daylight, and I am within sight of the house. Have you no sympathy for my plight? You come and go as you please, but I am trapped with that woman for hours on end, forced to perform as if I were some sort of trained pet!"

Nathan stubbornly shook his head. "I think it's more than that. I think that you enjoy breaking the rules and misbehaving."

"To what end?"

"That is a question only you can answer, chit."

She found herself being tugged back up the stone steps by his unyielding hand. "Don't call me that," she complained. No sooner were the words out than Adrienne regretted them, for a wicked gleam shone momentarily in his eyes that told her he would probably make "chit" a pet name for her in the future.

Inside the garden doors, Nathan pressed her into a corner and said in low tones, "If you must have a walk, ask me and I will take you. Understood?"

Hating him, she nodded. When he released her and she raced away, up the stairs to the drawing room, Adrienne was already plotting ways to rebel against her jailer.

"My dear Hunty will be joining us to celebrate my birthday!" Lady Thomasina rhapsodized. Her good cheer was such that she had scarcely scolded Adrienne for her lengthy absence. "Wait until you meet him, Miss Beau. My son is everything that a man might aspire to."

They were just finishing a small supper, served in front of the fire in Lady Thomasina's sitting room. Nathan, apparently having taken pity on Adrienne, had agreed to join the women, and he toyed with his strong boiled mutton as they talked.

"Perhaps young Lord Harms can provide male companionship for Mr. Essex," Adrienne ventured.

"I don't believe that Hunty fraternizes with commoners, as a rule," the old woman said with puckered brow. "Perhaps he will make an exception in Nathan's case. However, I don't know whether they would get on well together. Hunty is a different breed of male."

Adrienne saw Nathan's brow arch at that, and indeed she wondered herself exactly which breed Huntsford Harms might be. Aloud, however, she murmured, "No doubt his lordship is refined in his manners and tastes; a *gentleman* in behavior and appearance."

"Exactly so, Miss Beau. Those are the qualities that distinguish nobility, don't you think? There is a certain refinement in the blood."

One of the kitchen maids appeared then with the dessert tray. Nathan took one look at the goblets of trifle and folded his napkin.

"I find that I am tired this evening. Will you excuse me?"

When he had gone, Lady Thomasina turned to her young companion. "You see? He is very attractive in a . . . potent way, but completely unrepentent in his manners. No true gentleman would leave the table before I had." Frowning, she shook her head so that powder from her wig showered the dishes. "I have a feeling, though, that he knows better and does as he pleases. A reckless type, don't you think? One might even describe Mr. Essex as a rogue."

"Without a doubt. And I think that his disregard for good manners goes far beyond the dinner table, my lady."

The rest of the evening was taken up with a reading of one more chapter of *Ivanhoe* and Adrienne's efforts to play Mozart's Sonata in C well enough to please Lady Thomasina.

As the hours passed, she felt increasingly trapped. It made no sense to blame her father, who was far away and had meant well. Instead, Adrienne's resentment built toward

Nathan Essex. He knew full well the extent of her ordeal, and yet he not only left her to it, he refused even to help her—escaping instead, always, at the earliest opportunity!

Lady Thomasina began to nod off around midnight. Hortie came in with her toddy and took her off to bed, and Adrienne was alone at last, and wide awake, fuming. She went into her bedchamber and threw open the window casement to admit the cool evening air. Below, the garden stretched haphazardly, starlight flickering over the pathways. Adrienne inhaled the spicy scent of boxwood.

What harm could there be in a little midnight stroll? If she didn't release some of her pent-up energy, after all, her temper would only be worse on the morrow.

Smiling to herself and feeling fiendishly naughty, Adrienne pulled the pins from her hair, letting it spill down her back. She dabbed lilac cologne on her throat and breasts, decided to leave her shawl behind, and carried her slippers to ensure a silent escape. Then she padded into the darkened corridor in search of moonlight and at least the spirit of adventure.

Nathan also had been looking out a window over the garden. For hours he'd been walking from one end to the other of the long gallery, which afforded views of the garden or the drive leading to Harms Castle's main entrance. His task was numbingly dull, requiring him to remain in darkness so that he could not be seen from outside.

He hoped that his feeling about Walter Frakes-Hogg was right. If he could catch him trespassing on private property tonight, the authorities would step in, Adrienne's safety would be assured, and perhaps the spoiled girl's father would release Nathan from this prison and—most important—give him his reward in Barbados.

Through hooded eyes, he gazed out over the ill-tended gardens and tried not to think about Adrienne Beauvisage. She stirred up a hornet's nest of conflicting feelings inside him, all the more vexing because of the masquerade he had to enact. He wasn't sure how he'd handle her differently as Nathan Raveneau, but he did know that she was dangerous—and so was he when they were together. Nathan opened another button on his plain shirt. The thread broke and it fell off in his hand. Damn, but he missed his own clothing, each piece of which had been created to fit him to perfection. The sooner this charade was ended and he got away, the safer—and happier!—he'd be.

A faint rustling in the garden reached his ears, and he straightened. Was it an animal? The badgers were venturing out of their tunneled setts lately. Nathan listened until he was able to distinguish the sound of human footsteps crunching softly on a pebbled pathway. Adrenaline coursed through his veins. He had warned even the servants to stay indoors tonight (not that any of them were energetic enough to venture forth). Only one person could be sneaking around the garden at midnight: Walter Frakes-Hogg! The long hours spent sitting in darkness, watching, had paid off.

For an instant, Nathan envisioned the lush beauty of Barbados. He could almost taste a bright papaya and feel the heat of the sugary sand between his toes. Soon he'd be sailing home, reunited with Minter and his crew, and when he arrived, he would claim the precious acres that adjoined Xavier Crowe's estate on the island's eastern shore.

Best of all, Nathan thought grimly, he would be Raveneau again, not Essex, a guard for hire.

First things first. He shrugged into a blue coat to blend in more easily with the darkness. Nathan decided to slip not only a pistol into the waistband of his breeches but a sheathed dagger as well, then he left the house through the other door, so that he might creep quietly round the side and into the garden.

Outside, the air was damp and cool, unwilling to shift into summer just yet. Nightingales were singing in a distant hedgerow, and a tawny owl called *kee-vit* as he hunted for mice in the meadows. All of Nathan's keenly sharpened instincts told him that his own prey was human.

Slowly he circled the high boxwood maze, entering from the north.

His nostrils flared at the scent of lilac. Odd. There were no lilac bushes blooming yet in this garden, as far as he could remember . . . but Nathan remembered then that lilac was Adrienne's scent. He'd even seen the hand-labeled crystal bottle on her bureau the morning he visited her in her chamber.

Walter Frakes-Hogg was an exceptionally tall man, but there was no sight of him.

And the footsteps, still audible, were awfully light. Nathan had a sinking feeling that gave way to yet another surge of fury. If he'd gone to all this trouble just to catch Adrienne Beauvisage in another act of defiance, then she must pay a price.

Every muscle in his body was taut as he soundlessly tracked the lilac fragrance and the intermittent sounds of Adrienne's midnight ramble. When he saw her at last, his jaw clenched. She stood in one of the maze's circles, holding a bouquet of daffodils to her cheek. Moonlight spilled over her mane of curls, her exquisite profile, and her creamy throat and bosom. Oblivious to the chilly air, or the hour, or the danger she had placed herself in, Adrienne beamed heavenward.

Unseen, Nathan glowered at her. The chit would drive him to an early grave before he could complete his four-month sentence in this godforsaken dungeon—or she'd die herself as a result of mad, rebellious escapades such as this one.

Humming like a mischievous child, Adrienne turned down another boxwood-edged lane. Nathan decided quickly, and angrily, on a plan. He crept after her, watching round the corner of the hedge, and when she paused, then bent to pick another furled bloom, he sprang. In an instant he was upon her. Adrienne cried out, but it was too late. One of Nathan's arms went round her waist like an iron bar, while the other imprisoned her shoulders. His elbow pushed into her open bodice, then he let her feel the cold prick of his dagger at her throat.

"Don't try to scream," he growled hoarsely, "or I'll kill you."

"Who are you?" She strove to sound brave, but there was a throb in her voice. "What do you want?"

"Did you think I wouldn't find you here? That I'd let you go so easily?"

"W-Walter?"

"Of course! You ruined my life, and now you'll pay."

"But—it doesn't sound like you—" Wildly she wondered why he would disguise his voice, then realized it didn't matter. Oh, God, why hadn't she listened to Nathan? Why was she such a fool? And why was this villain determined to hurt her? It was maddening to know that he could feel the thudding of her heart against his arm. "Please, leave me alone!"

"Did you really believe I would let you go?"

Adrienne was terrified by the knife yet furious with this man for abusing her freedom. Why were so many men sexual predators who believed that the seduction of innocent females was nothing more than a sport, like fox hunting? "You have to let me go. I had a perfect right to decline your advances." Tears crept into her voice. "I loved your little girls. It broke my heart to leave them, and it was wrong for you to put me in that position. Do you care more for your own gratification than the welfare of your daughters?"

Nathan couldn't believe that she was going to launch into moral lecture while being held at knifepoint. In guttural tones, he challenged, "Will you give up your life to be right, always?"

"Perhaps."

Enraged beyond reason, he threw down the dagger and spun her around, his fingers digging into her soft upper arms. "Damn you, chit, it's me! You won't even let me teach you a lesson, when your life depends upon it, without going off on a headstrong tangent!"

Her mouth dropped open, and her eyes flashed in the shadows. "Nathan Essex! How could you do something so cruel?" She struggled in his grasp, but he only held her more tightly. "Let me go this instant! Horrid bully!"

"Do you think you can have your own way, no matter what, even when your life is at risk? Do you imagine that your will is so strong that it can overpower anyone who opposes you? Hold still and listen to me, because this is a les-

son you cannot afford to dismiss." His voice was low and
hot with more than anger. "I was not pretending to be Walter Frakes-Hogg in order to torture you and amuse myself
at your expense. I did it to show you that you could have
been killed tonight as a result of your determination to rebel
against me. I spent hours watching for that man to try to
sneak into the castle and reach you, and he may well have
shown up and been warned off by the noise you and I have
made!"

"You're obsessed with threats of danger," she said defiantly. "You create them out of thin air."

Nathan wanted badly to shake her. "Why can't you allow
me to do what I've been hired for by your father? If we
trap this villain, who is, I assure you, lurking no farther
away than the next town, then you can run wild if you
choose and I may be able to escape altogether!"

In spite of herself, Adrienne was stirred by this masculine creature. He loomed above her, wide-shouldered,
raven-haired, exuding a wild strength that was magnified by
the moonlight playing over his carved features. How dare
he proclaim that he wanted to escape from her forever?

"You are a—a *beast*! Just like nearly every other man
I've met since coming to England. None of you have
hearts, or *souls*—you just live according to your male pride
and your need for conquest! Men thrive on truly base passions, so is it any wonder that women are revolted by
them? If most women didn't need men in order to have
children, and to provide financial support, they'd do just as
I am, seeking independence and—"

"Will you never shut up?" His eyes drilled into hers.

"I hate you," she muttered.

"A stinging retort, Miss Beau." Nathan knew he should
release her and walk away, but it seemed that her infuriating speech had put a demon in him, and he was now pos-
sessed. "So, you have no use for men or our passions? You
find men physically revolting?"

Adrienne stiffened, pressed her lips together, and felt her
heart begin to hammer. His grip relaxed on her arms, but
she couldn't move. When Nathan slowly drew her closer,
until her bodice touched his hard chest, she started trem-

bling, awash with a terrifying yearning. All at once, the place between her legs was hot, then wet.

Nathan's breath was warm on her cheek. "I don't think you're revolted now."

Feebly she tried to defend herself. "Men—men like Walter—are so base—"

"But we aren't all like Walter."

"You frightened me."

"You frightened me first. I was afraid for your safety."

When his strong arms enfolded her in the cool night air, Adrienne knew a sense of bliss that surpassed anything she had ever felt. A sob rose in her throat. Helplessly she turned her face up for his kiss, and his mouth was a wonder: firm and sure, working her lips, then parting them to make magic with his warm tongue. Adrienne's knees went weak as long-buried needs burst forth in waves.

"You see?" he whispered gently. "Men can be useful."

She stared at his face, entranced. He wasn't wearing his spectacles. Her hands crept upward, feeling the planes of his chest, then the unyielding strength of his shoulders, until her fingers clasped around his neck. Their bodies were pressed together full length in a way she found thrilling.

Kissing her again, Nathan dimly realized that he didn't need to keep teaching her this lesson. She understood, and now he was also beginning to understand more than he cared to. Dangerous! he warned himself, but Adrienne's incautious streak seemed to be contagious. Besides, whom was he fooling? He'd known his share of those brutish male passions she described, ever since the day he and Adrienne had first made clashing contact on Oxford Street.

Her mouth was sweet, her skin enticingly soft, and she was beautifully made, just like the other women he'd made love to, but Nathan couldn't remember experiencing this added element of complex excitement with any other woman. It was something personal between them. Baffling . . .

Both of them were alarmed yet unable to turn back. Adrienne ached for him to cup her breasts with his bare hands, and she nearly pulled down her own gown for him. Her eyes stung with tears of need. Hungrily they kissed, then she threw her head back, beckoning him to explore lower. His lips were burningly stimulating as they touched all her pulse points. She sank her fingers into his hair, panting. Her nipples were so hard they ached, and Nathan was hard and hurting as well.

"Dear God." He gasped, amazed at what was happening.

"Yes," she urged.

They knelt on the damp, mossy path. She wanted to rip open his shirt, to press her face to his chest to smell him and taste him, but now her sleeve was falling, and his lips grazed the first swell of her breast. "Oh!" Adrienne cried. If he were actually to touch her bare nipple with his warm, wet mouth, she might die, or come apart—

"Essex?" A gruff voice was calling from the castle's stone terrace. "Are you out there? It's me, Fred."

"Christ." Nathan rose halfway, squinting, until he spied the ancient gardener, swaying in the light of the lantern he held with two hands. "What is it?" he yelled.

"I seen an intruder, hidin' in the bushes near me tool shed! He threatened me and ran off to his horse, but afraid I am—lookin' fer you everywhere—and Mr. Jarrow said you'd be the one to help me—"

Through the thick haze covering his brain, Nathan realized that the intruder must have been Walter Frakes-Hogg. "Adrienne, it was—"

"I know. Go to him. I'll get myself together and slip back inside shortly." In response to his sharp look of worry, she gave him an unflinching gaze. "I'm fine. I'll hurry, and I'll behave myself."

Nathan was already on his feet then, calling to the old man, running, while silently cursing himself for this perilous lapse in his own vigilance.

Meanwhile, Adrienne's heart beat fast with scrambling emotions. She waited just until Nathan and Fred had disappeared inside the castle before she hurried out of the boxwood maze and around to one of the side entrances. Just before the heavy door closed behind her, a movement in a distant grove of elm trees caught her eye. Quickly Adrienne pushed the latch that locked her safely inside.

Outside, on the other side of the trees, Walter Frakes-

Hogg mounted his spotted gelding and started off in the direction of Winchester.

There was no point in waiting around so that the black-haired fellow who'd been manhandling Adrienne might have an opportunity to catch him. Frakes-Hogg had every intention of finishing his business with Adrienne Beauvisage without ever coming face to face with that hired thug.

Chapter Five

NOTHING NEEDED TO BE SAID THE NEXT MORNING when Adrienne and Nathan met in the servants' kitchen. Both of them realized full well what a frightening mistake had been made and how fortunate they were to have been interrupted by Fred.

"Your friend won't escape the next time," Nathan said to her in businesslike tones as they sat together eating bowls of overcooked oatmeal.

She knew that he avoided using Frakes-Hogg's name because Hortie was watching and listening, but couldn't he have chosen a less annoying word? "I'll remind you that he is hardly a friend of mine."

"A figure of speech, Miss Beau." He stirred milk into his tea and tried not to look at Adrienne. In spite of the dark circles under her eyes, she flushed whenever she spoke to him, and her curls were pinned up in a haphazard way he found particularly fetching.

"Don't you two have work to do?" Hortie scolded as she rose. "Lord Harms arrives tomorrow evening, you know, and her ladyship will have a list of preparations."

When Lady Thomasina's abigail was out of earshot, Nathan murmured, "You don't suppose the old peahen will want to do a complete spring housecleaning by tomorrow? The staff would probably revolt."

"It would take a year, not a day, to clean this place."

"My point exactly."

Adrienne pushed her bowl away. It made her nervous to

be so close to him. "I should check on Lady Thomasina. She may be too excited to stay in bed until her usual late hour."

He followed her partway up the servants' staircase, waiting until they were out of earshot of the kitchen. "I must speak to you."

A hot tide rose in her face. He had grasped the back of her skirt, and their fingers tangled when she tried to free herself. "I don't want to talk to you," she hissed.

"It's not about our interlude in the garden, if that's what's worrying you," Nathan said bluntly, then softened his tone. "More important, at this moment, is tracking down Walter Frakes-Hogg before he tracks *you* down. I want you to be on guard during the times I am not within your sight, but I'll try to join you just as soon as I've had a good look around outside and another talk with Fred, now that he's sobered up."

"It's all like a terrible dream," Adrienne protested.

"Well, it was not a dream." He caught her gaze in the dawn shadows for one meaningful instant. "Every moment was quite real."

She started away, up the curving steps. "I'll see you later then. I hear Lady Thomasina's bell."

"Do you know, my Hunty has the most beguiling brown eyes!" her ladyship rhapsodized from her tub chair in the library. "Lady Caroline Lamb once said that Hunty's eyes were more beautiful than Lord Byron's!"

Adrienne looked up from her sketches of the still-in-progress Systems and managed a wan smile. "How nice."

"Are you listening, Miss Beau?"

"Of course, my lady. However, Tavis and Sam are about to embark on the next phase of the Systems, and I want to be certain that the instructions are quite clear—"

"The maroon bindings are next?"

"Just as you have written, my lady."

"Good!" She bent to pet Angus and fretted, "I do hope the staff has begun preparing in earnest for my son's arrival. There is so much to do! When do you suppose the floors were last scrubbed?"

"Which room were you thinking of?" Adrienne wondered cautiously.

"Why, all of them, of course! Jarrow and that new housekeeper, Mabel, have been organizing the rest of the servants, haven't they? Where is the house steward?"

"Visiting his mother in Cornwall, I believe, my lady."

"Oh!" She fell back dramatically, and her brocade turban came loose. "Does no one understand the value of a hard day's work any more? Is this the way these people repay me for all my kindnesses?"

"I'm sure that your son's true concern is for you, my lady. He doubtless won't even notice the condition of Harms Castle—"

A while later Lady Thomasina heard the hall clock announce the noon hour and put a pudgy hand to her brow. "I am faint with hunger. Where is that girl with my tray?"

"Let me go and see." Seizing the opportunity, Adrienne hurried out of the room and nearly collided with Nathan. "Oh, thank goodness it's you! I've never been so glad to see anyone in my life!"

"A gratifying change of heart," he replied with decided irony. Reaching in his coat pocket, he found his spectacles and put them on. "Particularly since I must speak to you."

Adrienne checked to be certain that Lady Thomasina's meal was on its way, suggesting that Hortie sit with her mistress while she ate, and then Nathan led her off into the conservatory.

"Sit down. Don't worry; her ladyship will be occupied for quite some time. The rat catcher is roaming the house, and I assured him that Lady Harms would be eager to discuss his findings, so he'll visit her in the library within the hour. When I left him, he'd already killed five beasts of gigantic proportions."

Adrienne shuddered. "Hideous! Never mind." She took a gilt chair bathed in sunlight and looked around. Clearly, although the glass conservatory had great potential, Fred the gardener had no vision. There was one row of orange and lemon trees, barely blooming and in need of water, and a few half-dead flowers. "What a shame!" Adrienne remarked. "My mother would weep to see such waste."

"I'm afraid time does not allow a discussion of the plants at this moment." Nathan, whose boots were scuffed, drew his own chair close to her and lowered his voice. "I found fresh footprints in the dirt where the gardener saw the stranger. They looked as if they were made by boots to me—"

"Walter always wears Hessians!"

"I thought as much. Has he particularly long, narrow feet?"

"Yes!" Looking stricken, Adrienne jumped up and began pacing to and fro.

"Nothing to be gained from hysterics, unless you become more cautious as a result—and obey my orders!" He gave her a stern glance, then continued, "I followed the footprints to the place where Frakes-Hogg had tied his horse. That was when Fred lost sight of him."

"Oh!" She paced faster, remembering what she and Nathan had been doing at that same time. "If only—"

"If only you had stayed inside, as I instructed? I doubtless would have captured Frakes-Hogg rather than you, my provoking midnight prowler."

"Scolding me now won't help a bit."

Nathan sighed. "I wish I knew what *would* help." He was vaguely gratified to see her go suddenly pink. "At any rate, while our gardener went racketing about the castle in his cups, looking for me and consulting with Jarrow, who was doubtless foxed as well, Walter Frakes-Hogg walked his horse through the trees until he reached a spot where he could view the gardens."

"You—you don't mean—" She gasped for breath, one fair hand splayed over her bodice. "How could you draw such a horrifying conclusion?"

"Quite easily. I followed the prints left by his boots and his horse's shod hooves. They both stopped in that crescent-shaped grove of elms that protects the garden—"

"—and continues to the castle's west entrance?"

"Yes." Nathan watched her pace for a few moments, considering how to phrase his next speech to best effect. At length, he leaned forward and caught her skirt as she passed by. "Will you sit down? This situation isn't one we can run from."

She obeyed but could not meet his penetrating gaze. "I have been so very foolish."

"Have you? Well, it is time for both of us to deal with reality. It seems probable that Frakes-Hogg saw all or part of what transpired between us in the garden last night."

Wringing her hands, Adrienne moaned. "I fear it's true— that he did see us—because just as I was letting myself back into the castle, I saw a movement in the elm trees. I confess that I had a sense of foreboding, even then."

"Why didn't you tell me?" Her anguished blush was answer enough. "See here, there is one thing we must clear up before any other. No matter how many regrets either of us has about last night, we must own up to what happened and handle the consequences. No more pretending that you can merely erase those . . . stolen moments." A faint, wicked smile tugged at his mouth.

"You are horrid."

"Yes, yes. Now then, on to capturing Walter Frakes-Hogg. You'll have to help me, since you know him and I don't. Agreed?"

Adrienne nodded miserably. "Agreed."

It was Nathan's turn to pace. "Right then. First, tell me about his physical appearance. I've seen him from a distance, once or twice in London—and just recently the Winchester butcher pointed him out to me on the street. I know that he's very tall and thin, with prematurely white hair and dark eyes. What are the details that come to your mind?"

"He has very ruddy cheeks, because he's always at the brandy," she replied immediately. "And he has an odor— brandy mixed with a sandalwood scent he uses to try to hide the smell of spirits. His face is long, and his nose is long, but it has a reddish knob on the end of it. And the edges of his ears are always red."

"That's quite an attractive picture you paint. Anything else?"

She fussed with the folds of her skirt. "There is a strawberry birthmark in the middle of his chest."

"Don't worry," Nathan said lightly, dropping back into his chair. "I won't ask how you know about that. I'm sure your knowledge couldn't have been gained through pleasant means."

"Quite true." She met his gaze squarely, her eyes like fiery emeralds. "I despise Walter Frakes-Hogg. He is a bully and is all the more lethal because he pretends to be so very amiable. All his advances toward me were made with a smile on his face, and he would continue to smile later, when he'd counter my rejections with veiled threats." She shuddered. "He's a monster! If only there were a way to help his daughters. I stayed far too long because I loved Beth and Ellie and couldn't bear to think of them not being properly cared for."

"What would happen to the girls if their father should die?"

His casual tone sent a chill down her spine. "Their mother's sister, Mrs. Halper, would raise them. She was recently widowed and has never been able to have children of her own, so she adores Beth and Ellie. However, the problem is that she is now penniless. Before I left the girls with her, she was considering moving into Walter's house. . . ."

"Might she have taken the girls back home for that reason?"

"It's doubtful, unless they are all living there in his absence. I warned her about him. And Walter told me that he didn't want her in his house, interfering with his . . . pleasures." Adrienne shuddered at the memory. "His decision had nothing to do with Mrs. Halper's problems. I suspect he enjoys denying other people's wishes—but he's sly about it. Unfailingly polite."

"It sounds as if he's one of those fellows who uses whatever power he has to toy with other people."

"Exactly!" Adrienne cried. "It took me the longest time to realize that Walter Frakes-Hogg really is a terrible person. I hoped that he would change, or that deep inside he was good. . . ."

"And now you know better?"

"Sadly, yes. I am much older."

A grin lit his tanned face. "Verging on spinsterhood?"

"I wish I could be, so that people would stop expecting

me to marry! My notion of hell on earth is lifelong dependence on a member of the male species."

Before Nathan could reply to that strong statement, Mabel, the stocky Irish housekeeper, stopped outside the conservatory door and rapped on the glass. He rose, motioning for her to enter.

"Been lookin' everywhere for the pair of you! Her ladyship's fit to be tied!" Mabel shook her finger at them. "An outrider's just come in advance of Lord Harms's party. Seems that he an' his friends are due to arrive within the hour!"

Wielding a long driving whip, Huntsford Harms tooled his own high-perch phaeton and team of chestnuts up the weed-dotted drive to Harms Castle. The young Corinthian was attended by an assortment of footmen, outriders, his valet and other personal servants, and another traveling coach filled with friends.

A coachman sat next to Huntsford, looking panic-stricken as his employer narrowly missed turning over at the last curve. By the time the phaeton came to a halt several yards beyond the castle's grand entrance, a crowd had assembled to greet the party.

Jarrow had put on a fresh tailcoat and cravat for the occasion, and he stood at the forefront of the ragtag band of castle staff. Nathan and Adrienne had agreed to go down together on behalf of Lady Thomasina. The old woman's ankles were, she claimed, too swollen for her to climb stairs. Her son might attend her in the library, where she was waiting with Hortie and Angus the terrier.

"He certainly makes a striking picture," Adrienne whispered.

"That's one choice of words," Nathan replied sardonically. "Very kind of you."

She was fascinated in spite of herself. Resplendent in a curly brimmed beaver hat and a driving coat with innumerable capes, Huntsford Harms allowed a great fuss to be made as he came down from the phaeton. The servants behaved as if he were royalty, and he did nothing to discourage their obeisance.

"Ah, Jarrow, there you are. Good to be home, as it were." Huntsford waited for the old man to do a sufficient amount of bowing before he continued, "I trust that the necessary preparations have been made for my house party?"

"We are honored to have you among us again, sir. Indeed." His red face brightened further. The situation was all the stickier because no one was quite sure what to call young Huntsford since his father's death. As the son of a baron, he'd never been a lord before, and Jarrow didn't consider barons to be real nobles, anyway. Still, the boy did have power, at least in this house. "Not to put too fine a point on it, I suppose it is my duty to say . . . ahem! That is, we, the staff, did not have sufficient time to prepare as we might have wished. Her ladyship's requirements, for the normal run of events, are rather . . . less stringent."

"I'm sorry to hear that," Huntsford replied coldly. "And where is my slothful mother?" Upon hearing the story of her swollen ankles, he flared his nostrils and rolled his eyes at the same time. "Perhaps it's just as well. She doesn't make a very favorable impression, does she, and my guests might've been frightened off if they'd met Mummy straightaway."

Jarrow kept one eye trained on the good looking and extremely fashionable persons of quality approaching from the other coach. The two young men looked just alike, from their exaggerated shirtpoints to their tasseled Hessians, and the females were clad in nearly identical redingotes and elegant hats. One of the ladies was carrying a small, fluffy dog that began to yip as they approached the group of strangers.

"Little Peter must need to straighten out his affairs!" his mistress exclaimed. She put the dog down, and he promptly relieved himself on the steps.

Huntsford Harms gave the young lady a withering stare. "Confound it, Lucy, I told you repeatedly to leave that smelly little beast in London. If he spreads fertilizer all through Harms Castle, you'll never be asked again!"

One of the male guests cleared his throat. "Appalling manners, Harms. Do show us your breeding instead."

At the back of the crowd, Adrienne lifted her eyes to meet Nathan's and they shared a look of amused consternation. "I wish we could escape," she whispered.

He nearly took her arm and whisked her away, but more than duty made him stay. Huntsford Harms was so repellent a character that Nathan sensed that he bore watching. The young buck now appeared ready to advance toward the doorway, but turned back to Jarrow on an afterthought.

"This news about Mummy's ankles gives me pause, old chap. A pang of filial concern, and all that. Is she in failing health? I mean . . . shall I brace myself to be shocked when I see her?"

Adrienne could bear no more. Impulsively she walked forward to stand in front of Huntsford Harms. "Sir, I could not help overhearing and thought I should introduce myself. I am Miss Adrienne Beauvisage, your mother's companion. Lady Thomasina asked me to greet you in her stead, and I would like to assure you that she is in fine health and spirits."

Out came his quizzing glass. He raised it with gloved fingers and gave her a long, languid stare, from head to toe. "By Jupiter, what's a beauty like you doing rusticating with an eccentric like my mother?"

Her feminine self could not help noticing that, up close, he was indeed a very handsome man, with a face that reminded her of Greek sculptures. And, as Lady Thomasina had promised, his big brown eyes were quite beautiful. He removed his hat and bowed to her, revealing fashionably windswept golden hair. What could she say now?

Nathan intervened. His fingers touched the small of her back to alert her to his nearness, and then he spoke. "I also should make myself known to you, sir. I am . . . Nathan Essex, and—"

"Yes?" Harms snapped, glancing at the other man's modest clothing. "Whose companion are *you*?"

"There have been threats against Miss Beauvisage. Her family, in France, hired me to ensure her safety. I've been looking after Lady Thomasina as well." Considerably taller and more powerfully built than Huntsford, he consciously used his physical presence to assert himself.

The younger man's eyes darted away. "Why are you boring me with these meaningless details? My guests are tired and hungry." With that, he hurried his friends toward the massive doorway, servants scurrying in their wake.

Nathan and Adrienne stood alone together on the stone steps. After a minute of welcome silence, he muttered, "I despise that imbecile."

She strove for a cheerier note. "At least our situation here won't be dull any longer."

"Might I remind you that Walter Frakes-Hogg is lurking about and I must capture him—with your assistance? I wouldn't call that a dull situation."

Realizing that Nathan meant to be horrid and stubborn where Huntsford Harms was concerned, she made no further attempt to lighten the mood. "Be that as it may, I have more immediate duties. Lady Thomasina is upstairs at the mercy of her son, and I ought to go to her aid."

Nathan stayed behind. The last thing he needed right now was another view of Huntsford Harms ogling Adrienne. It created a strong dark twisting sensation in his chest that bore a suspicious resemblance to jealousy.

Harms Castle may have been too dusty and tarnished for the taste of its heir, but he and his friends made do all the same. Musty apartments were aired, and under the leadership of Huntsford Harms, common rooms were rearranged by the bestirred servants. The gallery was transformed into a portrait-lined billiard room, chairs were arranged along the walls in the drawing room and saloon to allow for dancing or other entertainments, and dropleaf tables were set up in the dining room so that the number of people dining could be adjusted easily.

Huntsford was supervising and explaining his wishes to Jarrow, while footmen moved furniture this way and that, when his mother appeared in the doorway of the dining room.

"I thought I must be hearing things!" Her massive bosom heaved from the exercise of walking the dozens of yards from her usual station in the library. Angus stood at her side, emitting a low growl. "Hunty, have you gone mad? What are you doing to my beautiful house?"

He chuckled and strolled to her side. "Dear Mummy, you have ever been a great one to tease. We both know that this old tomb could do with a bit of dusting up, hmm?" Coaxing a smile from her and a snarl from Angus, Huntsford continued, "Jarrow and I thought that these tables might make the eating arrangements more efficient. We fellows will doubtless be afield during luncheon, shooting and so forth, thus the kitchen need feed only Lucy and Clair at midday. You see?"

Lady Thomasina's mouth turned down again. "It is my house. You might at least ask."

"Now, now, give us a kiss. You mustn't worry about such nonsense, darling Mummy." Out of the corner of one eye, Huntsford noticed that Angus had discovered one of his prized powder-blue gloves under a cobweb-laced side chair. Glove in teeth, the terrier slunk toward the other door. "You there! Cur! Come here this instant!"

"His name is Angus, Hunty. After fifteen years, you might remember," Lady Thomasina called reproachfully as her son went scuttling after the little thief.

"Quick!" Huntsford shouted to Jarrow. "Someone close the door before he gets away!"

The nearest footman rushed to obey, and Angus dashed under an enormous sideboard. Huntsford, on hands and knees, peered at the terrier, who huddled against the wall and continued to hold fast to his glove while emitting the same disturbing growl.

"Mummy!" He looked back at her. "Can't you do something with this mongrel? I cannot begin to tell you how valuable that glove is. I mean, I have them made to fit only my hands, and it could take weeks to get another pair that color. . . ."

"Angus is very intelligent." His mother sniffed. "He must have sensed that you don't like him. He may have been waiting years to have his revenge!"

"Confound it, we're talking about a blasted dog!" Furious, he pushed his own face under the sideboard and glared at Angus. "Give it over, you bastard, or you'll be sorrier than you know!" Then, thrusting his arm toward the animal, he managed to just get hold of the edge of the glove.

"If you touch one hair on my darling Angus's body, it's you who will be sorry." Lady Thomasina had joined them at the sideboard.

"Your shadow makes it impossible for me to see a thing, Mummy! Do let me get on with this!" When Huntsford pulled at his corner of the glove, Angus sank his teeth into his enemy's flesh. The young man screamed, flailing, and felt the seam of his skin-tight coat tear all the way down from under his arm. Uttering a string of epithets, Huntsford withdrew.

Angus snarled, triumphant.

Lady Thomasina shook her head and sent a shower of gray powder over her son. "You really can be the most exasperating child. Do find something constructive to do with yourself, rather than causing problems throughout the house."

"The others are waiting for me in the billiard room."

"We don't have a billiard room."

"We've made the portrait gallery into one. A billiard table was brought from town." Still sulking, he got to his feet. "I ought to go and dust myself off a bit, change this coat, and so forth." Huntsford put on a false smile and strolled to the door. "Oh, Mummy—what's your new companion called? Annabelle?"

"Adrienne, silly child."

He laughed. "Yes, of course. I *am* silly, aren't I?"

Chapter Six

ONE OF THE MALE GUESTS, SIR BLAKE SMYTHE, HAD decided to pass most of his waking hours at Harms Castle painting. He could be found, with his paints and easel, at various sites outdoors when the weather was fair, and while indoors Sir Blake had taken to sketching cooperative human subjects.

Huntsford Harms was extremely put out by his friend's ill-timed show of independence. While it did mean that there were always just four of them for cards and other games, so one person was not left out, it also meant that no one else could be absent, including Huntsford himself. Barely a day had passed before Blake's pastime created the first crisis for the other guests.

"Where is Clair?" Alistair wondered as he, Huntsford, and Lucy assembled after supper at the card table in the drawing room.

Fresh candles had been lit and positioned in the round corners, the cards were prepared for whist, goblets of claret were poured, and the gentle lapping of the flames in the fireplace helped relieve the evening's damp. The only flaw in the scene was the empty fourth chair.

"I think Clair ate something that didn't agree with her," Lucy murmured, coloring. The two men fixed her with suspicious eyes. "Well, it might have been the champagne at luncheon. . . ."

"I saw her drink three glasses of her own, then two of mine!" Alistair, a romantically thin and pale young man,

72

sighed and shook his head. "We can't play whist without a fourth. Might not Blake join us this once?"

Hearing his own name, Blake glanced up in surprise. He was sitting nearby, absorbed in his work on a sketch of Lucy's dog, Peter. "What, me? I'd really rather not."

"Confound it, old man!" Huntsford pounded on the table and all their glasses jumped so that claret sloshed right to the rims before subsiding. "There—see what you nearly caused? Why must you behave so selfishly? Why can you not think of others rather than your own desires, night and day, day and night—"

"I say, leave off, will you?" Sir Blake eyed the claret decanter, wondering how much his friend had already imbibed that evening. "I hardly think that I am the villain in this piece. When you invited me here, you didn't mention *conditions*, such as doing your bidding for the duration of our stay!"

Oblivious, Lucy said, "I should like Blake to continue drawing my dear little Peter. That would mean much more to me than a common game of whist."

"Aren't we prosy! Have you forgotten who is the host here?" Enraged, Huntsford stood up and prepared to issue an ultimatum to Blake, when a cloud passed from his beautiful face. "I have the perfect solution. There is someone in the house who can take Clair's place in our little game."

He motioned to the page boy, who waited to obey any order Lord Harms might issue. "Do you know Miss Beauvisage, her ladyship's companion? Of course you do. Go to her room, or wherever she passes her dull little evenings, and tell her that Lord Harms and his guests desire her company in the drawing room. Immediately."

"May I confide in the two of you?" Lady Thomasina asked suddenly. She looked first at Nathan, then at Adrienne, then down at her cherry profiterole. "I hope that by unburdening myself, I may recover my appetite. I do love this dessert, you know. I'm particularly fond of Kentish cherries."

"Haven't I proven yet that I deserve your trust, my

lady?" Nathan wore a compelling expression that he knew to be particularly effective when combined with his spectacles.

Adrienne nodded agreement.

Sipping a generous glassful of port, Lady Thomasina grew teary. "Would you think me a very ridiculous old woman if I were to tell you that I am sometimes small-minded in my hopes for Hunty's future? That I occasionally worry that he might be ungenerous himself in his dealings toward me, his mother?"

"We would not think you ridiculous in the least," Nathan said carefully, "but I am not certain, exactly, what you mean, my lady."

Adrienne chimed in then. "Does this have anything to do with Angus and the blue glove?"

The terrier lay under her ladyship's voluminous skirts, with only his head exposed to the air. In his mouth he now carried, at all times, Huntsford Harms's ruined blue glove. Lady Thomasina bent to pat his little head before replying "No, I've tried to put Hunty and Angus's quarrel from my mind."

"Excuse me," Nathan interjected, "but am I to understand that your son and your dog have been *quarreling*?"

"Angus was merely teasing him, and Hunty wasn't very sporting about it."

"I see." He cocked a dark brow. "I think."

"Don't let him distract you," Adrienne said to the old woman. "You'll forget what it was you wanted to share with us."

"Thank you, Miss Beau. I find that I am growing fond of you!" Lady Thomasina's plump, painted face looked both wistful and garish in the leaping candlelight as she paused, considering her next words. "You see, my friends, I find that I don't want Hunty to truly grow up and be a man. I'm afraid that, if he marries, I'll be cast away—"

The door to her sitting room opened then, throwing a beam of light across the small table where the trio sat. One of Huntsford Harms's page boys marched to Adrienne's side.

"I've come to fetch Miss Beauvisage. His lordship says

you must come straightaway, miss. Lady Clair is—uh, ill, and they need a fourth for whist."

"How very peculiar!" Adrienne cried.

"That's putting it kindly," Nathan muttered.

"I couldn't be more pleased!" Lady Thomasina clapped her pudgy hands with delight. She told the page boy to wait in the corridor for Miss Beauvisage, and when he had gone, she leaned forward and explained, "It's just as I hoped. You see, that Clair person has her cap set for Hunty. Mothers know these things. I do not like her, even one whit. She is forever half in her cups, and that is a very bad omen. Now that she's ill from too much champagne, you can come to my rescue, Miss Beau! Hunty will find you far more entertaining, and soon he'll have forgotten about her entirely."

"And what if he transfers his attentions to Miss Beau?" Nathan demanded.

"Don't be silly, dear boy! Miss Beau is a servant, after all. Nothing to worry about, for any of us. And if Hunty should indulge in a mild flirtation, I daresay that Miss Beau would enjoy herself immensely!"

Sitting at the desk in his bedchamber, Nathan Raveneau lit a fresh candle with the nub of the old one and pushed it into the brass holder.

He treasured his nightly bits of solitude. These hours provided an opportunity to be completely himself without worry about stepping out of the role of Nathan Essex. He could forget about wearing spectacles and frayed clothing and once again become a whole person, with a past.

Reclining in an old stickback chair, he let his mind wander. It was too bad that the *Golden Eagle* wasn't docked a bit nearer, so that he could visit his ship, his crew, and his cabin, which contained the possessions of Captain Raveneau. The opportunity to soak up the atmosphere of his own truest home would be the best tonic imaginable.

For now, Nathan wrote nightly in the same ship's log that he'd kept for years. Bound in worn dark blue leather and stamped RAVENEAU in gold, it was crammed with not only the drier details of months at sea but also his own personal history. Here at Harms Castle, he kept the journal hidden in a locked chest under his bed. Often when Nathan opened the brass-bound chest he removed other belongings along with the ship's log. Tonight he wore his signet ring—engraved NR—and one of his own fine linen shirts.

August will be here soon enough, Nathan reminded himself.

Meanwhile, there were plenty of problems to keep both Raveneau *and* Essex occupied. He ran a hand through his shining black hair and dipped his quill in the inkstand. Writing in the log was a ritual that helped him find his own center before each night's sleep.

He had a great deal to sort out: Huntsford Harms, Walter Frakes-Hogg, Adrienne, of course. . . . The scratching of the quill was the only sound in Nathan's chamber until he heard a clock on the landing strike two. Almost immediately other noises commenced.

A man's shouts were quickly joined by a woman's voice, and then a second male chimed in. The shouts turned to wild laughter. Someone else broke into song. Was Adrienne still among the revelers in the drawing room? When Lady Thomasina's bell began to ring from across the corridor, Nathan opened his door just as Adrienne peeked from her room.

"I must go to her," she whispered. "Perhaps she's frightened by the clamor downstairs. They aren't very considerate, are they?"

"Quite the opposite." He couldn't help staring at her sleep-tumbled hair and the delicate lace collar of her nightgown. It was a great relief to find her safe from Huntsford Harms, in her own room. "I'll go down and have a word with them."

Adrienne couldn't resist giving him a shy smile before turning away and closing her door. Even though she was well aware of Nathan Essex's potent appeal, it had been a shock nonetheless to see him looking so devastating at two o'clock in the morning. With rakishly tousled hair, black-lashed eyes exposed without his usual spectacles, and his shirt half open to reveal a hard chest covered with crisp black hair, Nathan might have been a pirate emerging from his cabin on board ship. . . .

Adrienne tried to put him from her mind as she went through the dressing room to Lady Thomasina's bedchamber. She brought a candlestick, and lit the taper on the frightened woman's bedside table.

"Miss Beau! Where have you been? I thought you were still downstairs with Hunty!"

"Oh, no," Adrienne soothed. She pried the bell from Lady Thomasina's fingers and offered her own hand instead. "I began nodding off before eleven o'clock, which didn't make them very happy. But Lady Clair revived just in time to take my place, so I was able to escape."

"Escape? But you shouldn't have left him alone with her!" Lady Thomasina was wearing a sort of turban for a nightcap, and it tilted precariously to one side as she shook her head. "It's just as I feared when I heard them carrying on downstairs. I was certain I recognized that fortune-hunter's laughter! Bring me a glass of sherry. I must have some, or I'll be awake all night!"

"I don't think it's a good idea, my lady." She dared to adjust her employer's headdress, at which point Angus rose out of the nearby bedclothes, clutching his prized glove and growling. "It's only me, Angus. Nothing to fear."

"Get my sherry." Lady Thomasina pouted until her request was granted. "Don't think that you can defy me, Miss Beau. I'll sack you in the blink of an eye if you defy me."

"I hardly think it's fair for you to vent your frustrations at me, my lady. I have only been kind to you." She took her hand again and looked into her eyes. "Tell me now what is bothering you. That will help you sleep far more than sherry."

"I—I had a dream that Hunty and that creature were married, and they were simply horrid to me." All at once fat tears rolled down her cheeks. "I was turned out of my house in Cavendish Square, and that awful girl began tossing out all of my furnishings as well. When I came here, by mail coach, penniless, Jarrow and Mabel told me that I would have to live in an awful little dower house in the woods. It looked like a—a woodcutter's cottage!" Sobs overtook her, and she buried her face in a handkerchief that reeked of stale perfume.

"But, my lady, that was only a dream!" Adrienne said in sunny tones.

"Listen to them downstairs!" She paused, frowning.

"You see, they've already stopped. Mr. Essex went to ask them to be quiet, out of respect to you, my lady."

Lady Thomasina was not ready to give up yet. "But only imagine how I felt earlier! When I awoke, frightened out of my wits, all I could hear was the pair of them laughing and singing in the drawing room—and it was as if my nightmare had already come true!" Another siege of weeping sent Angus back under the covers. "Oh, Miss Beau, it is simply beastly to be old and useless, at the mercy of one's children!"

"I think that you'll see this matter quite differently in the light of day," her companion assured her. "Your fears have no basis in reality as far as I can tell. Your son hardly appears to be in love with Lady Clair, nor she with him."

"What makes you think that love enters into such matches?" But Lady Thomasina seemed to be relaxing. She lay back against her pillows and heaved a heavy sigh. "I suppose you think I'm an hysterical old wretch."

Adrienne felt her heart tug. "Not at all." She smiled with genuine compassion. "I am glad to understand you better, my lady."

"You're a good girl." Squeezing her hand again, Lady Thomasina let her eyes close. "Perhaps I'll rest for a bit now."

So much about this woman tried her patience. Her bedclothes were stained with jam and tea and littered with crumbs of every sort. She always smelled as if she were a week overdue for a good hot bath. She was tryingly eccentric, with her Systems, and unbearably spoiled. All too often Adrienne felt as if she were dealing with a slightly batty, gigantic baby who had gotten dressed in an ancestor's rotting clothes.

Yet tonight she warmed toward Lady Thomasina Harms. She felt protective toward her, and suddenly all the other annoyances faded into the background.

* * *

Huntsford Harms was sprawled in his chair at the card table, drinking claret out of the crystal decanter while Lady Clair dealt another hand of rouge et noir. On a nearby sofa, Lucy and Alistair, though slightly less inebriated, were engaged in a giggling display of physical affection that was dangerously over the line.

Sir Blake Smythe and Peter, the dog, were sound asleep together in a wing chair before the dying fire.

"You're not keeping track of my losses, are you, darling?" Huntsford demanded loudly.

Lady Clair's response was a high-pitched trill of laughter.

None of them noticed Nathan when he appeared in the doorway, and he was too angry to care. "I realize that this is asking a great deal of people in your condition," he said in clear, glacial tones, "but could you be considerate enough of Lady Thomasina to either go to bed or at least continue your drunken revels in silence?"

"And who the deuce are *you*?" Huntsford drawled, squinting through his quizzing glass.

"You remember, Harms," Alistair rejoined as he untangled himself from Lucy and stretched. "It's that man who's protecting Miss Beauvisage. Essex, I b'lieve. Good lord, look at the hour! Past my bedtime." He gave Nathan a sheepish smile. "No wonder I'm behaving badly."

"Not so badly," Lucy purred. When Alistair had left the room, she crawled to the edge of the sofa and stared at Nathan. "Are you certain your name is Essex? Clair, doesn't he look familiar without his specs?"

Lady Clair wore a suggestive smile. "If you say so, Lucy. I'd like him to be familiar!"

As the women ran their eyes over him, Nathan was aware not only that he'd left his room out of costume, so to speak, but also that Huntsford Harms was regarding him with growing animosity. It seemed wise to remove himself before any real damage occurred, and then hope that all of them were too foxed to remember in the morning that he'd been there. "I'll be going now. Good night."

Nathan had retreated only a few steps down the corridor when he heard Lucy cry triumphantly, "Now I know who he looks like! It's that wickedly handsome sea captain who was causing such a stir in London earlier this spring. Remember, Clair? They called him The Scapegrace!"

"What's that mean?" she rejoined woozily.

"Oh, you know—a reckless sort of rogue, or some such thing." Lucy waved a hand. "You know the type. Can't remember his given name, but my cousin Fanny was mad for him, not that it got her anywhere. Fanny told me that he only comes to London from time to time, and he refuses to fall in love with anyone, which just makes women want him more—"

"Perhaps he don't *like* women," Huntsford put in sourly.

"Don't be ridiculous. He likes them all right, for a few nights each! Fanny thinks there's some sort of tragedy in his past. A broken heart. I wish I could remember—"

"Don't bother. It don't signify because this Essex fellow is just a peasant," Huntsford argued. "He definitely ain't some fancy Scapegrace!"

Out in the corridor, Nathan froze. "Damn." He could barely whisper the word. As he traversed the stairs and passageways that would return him to his room, he continued to hear the echo of her words: "The Scapegrace!" During his last stay in London, people had taken up the name partly because he would not be coaxed into society and thus remained a mysterious figure to all but a small circle of friends. He wouldn't play by the rules of the ton, so he was seen as more dashing than ever.

He was spotted with women, which only made the others want him more, and he was seen gambling and drinking in the clubs, but few of the dandies seemed to know him well. People assumed, too, that Nathan Raveneau must be like his father, who had been a notorious rake in his day. Once the title Scapegrace was spoken, everyone adopted it, and Nathan himself only became more remote.

Londoners were notoriously fickle, however. No doubt The Scapegrace had been nearly forgotten after he'd disappeared this spring—until tonight, when Nathan made the mistake of turning up looking like Raveneau rather than Essex.

Of course, in the morning he would put on his unfashionable blue coat, and his spectacles, and he'd comb his hair a bit too carefully, and they would think The Scape-grace had been a claret-induced illusion. Nathan began to breathe easier as he approached the safe haven of his bed-chamber.

The door was ajar, and the tallow candle still burned on his desk, sending weak flickers of light through the opening. Safe. He pushed the door, entered, and was stunned to see Adrienne standing over his desk. Wearing her night-clothes and an expression of lively curiosity, she reached toward the open ship's log.

Nathan was momentarily paralyzed with shock, but his wits did not fail him. "What the devil are you doing in here?" he demanded.

Chapter Seven

ADRIENNE GASPED, LETTING THE LEATHER-BOUND volume drop back onto the desk. "Oh, you startled me! What's wrong? I was only waiting for you to return—"

"Haven't you ever heard of respecting other people's privacy?" He snatched the journal away and put it inside his armoire. One more moment and she would have seen RAVENEAU stamped on the cover!

"Why are you so touchy? I wasn't going to steal anything, for heaven's sake!" Frowning, she pointed to his spectacles, long forgotten against the back corner of the desk. "Has your sight suddenly been restored?"

"No. I just forgot to put them on." He reached past Adrienne before she could pick them up, look through the lenses, and discover that they were perfectly clear. "Everyone who wears spectacles isn't blind, you know." To underline the point that he didn't need the spectacles in order to function, he put them in a drawer.

She was studying with interest the fine silver inkstand and the handsomely bound books that were lined along the wall. "You aren't quite what you seem to be, Mr. Essex."

"I have no idea what you mean. Furthermore, I think it is you who should make explanations for your uninvited intrusion into my private sanctuary in the middle of the night—"

"I've never seen you wear that shirt before!" Adrienne touched the pleated front appreciatively. "Why, that's excellent fabric—and it fits you so much better than those others. Did you just have it made?"

"I'm not quite certain what you mean, unless it is an implied criticism of my usual wardrobe." It was a pleasure to see that he had caught her off guard. "Furthermore, why this sudden interest in my personal possessions?"

"No criticism was intended." Adrienne colored and dragged her eyes from the view of his chest. "It's just that you have appeared to be a man of modest means, but now that I've—"

"Invaded my privacy," he insisted.

"See here, I did not come here to pry into your affairs or to argue!" Drawing herself up, she recovered her spirit. It was alarming to realize that Nathan Essex was the only person who was able to daunt her, and far too easily. "I merely thought to inform you that Lady Thomasina is resting again." Briefly she described the old woman's dream wherein her son banished her to a woodcutter's cottage. "I hope that these fears of hers are not based in reality."

"I would venture to guess that dear Hunty is capable of all manner of evil. His friends are nearly as deplorable." At that moment, voices could be heard on the stairs. Lady Clair and Lucy had rooms in this corridor, and it seemed that they were at last retiring for the night. "Shh." Nathan stepped over to ease the door closed, then motioned to Adrienne to sit down.

She decided to join him on the edge of the bed, whispering, "If we must be quiet, we may as well be close enough to speak."

He did not reply at once, but listened, dark head inclined, until the softly giggling guests passed his door. Then Nathan murmured, "Shall I infer that you were not . . . tempted by your evening with Lord Harms and his friends?"

"Actually . . . I was mildly amused by it all, for an hour perhaps, and then I couldn't wait to escape. Except for Sir Blake, and Alistair, they all become very tedious the more they drink." Adrienne perceived just enough of a telltale glint in Nathan's eye to persuade her to add "I must own, however, that Huntsford Harms is not without charm."

He bit the inside of his cheek but released the bait. The

bed ropes shifted beneath them, tilting her closer to him. "You and I have another matter to discuss. We must formulate clear plans to capture Walter Frakes-Hogg. He will not tarry in Winchester for days on end, and with that in mind, we must act before he does. There really isn't an hour to waste."

"I have already told you that I will do whatever you ask. I love danger!" Her voice, though hushed, was charged with excitement.

Nathan thought that he had never known a woman with eyes as richly luminous as Adrienne's, but he was careful not to betray his weakness. "The object of this exercise is not to put you in danger, chit." One black brow arched. "That was not the service your father hired me to perform."

"You seem to invoke Papa's name only in moments of convenience."

"Perhaps I've been lax. We ought to remind ourselves of him more often."

She could feel the hard contour of Nathan's thigh through her nightclothes. When his grin flashed white in the flickering shadows, a chill skittered down her spine. Oh, how she longed to speak openly to him, beginning with the revelation that she'd been eluding her loving parents for as long as she could remember, and the more she was encouraged to behave properly, the more she felt the urge to run free. Instead Adrienne said, "My craving for adventure isn't related to my love and respect for my father and mother. But I'm not always certain they know that."

"I imagine your father understands you very well. And I hope that you know I will not put you in danger, however much you may beg me!" A twinkle lightened his eyes. "We may have to use you as bait to draw Frakes-Hogg into the open, but it won't go beyond that. You must promise to obey me, though!"

"You keep saying that, and I find it very tiresome."

"No doubt." He looked at her in a way that made her squirm.

"I should return to my room." When she started to rise, Nathan caught her hand and returned her to his side.

"Tomorrow we'll steal a few minutes after breakfast and

discuss this matter more fully. Between now and then we must think of an excuse for you to go into Winchester when the time comes to put our plan into effect, and I want you to consider the matter of Walter Frakes-Hogg's motives."

"Why on earth should I waste my thoughts on him? He's a beast!"

"This is important. I am not sure I fully understand what he wants for his revenge against you. Is it merely that he's angry that you dared to rebuff his advances, and so means to pay you back by having his way with you, against your will?" Nathan released her hand, leaning back on his elbows, and the tick crunched softly under his weight. "Or is the situation more complicated? Has his ego been sufficiently damaged that he wants to do you physical harm? Perhaps Frakes-Hogg has other concerns—like your deep affection for his daughters and your concern for their welfare. He may fear that you haven't given up. If he were not still worried that you could damage his reputation, why wouldn't he accept that you obeyed his threats and left London? Why has he followed you here?"

"Because he is the meanest sort of bully and enjoys tormenting those who are weak and defenseless!" Adrienne jumped up again, and this time Nathan let her go. When she looked back from the doorway, the sight of him lounging across the bed made her heart skip. The guttering candle flame only served to enhance the appeal of Nathan's long, ruggedly muscular body, the half-open shirt that revealed too much of his chest, the chiseled lines of his face, his glossy black hair, and the smoldering power of his eyes.

"But, Adrienne, if that is true," he inquired, "why has Frakes-Hogg chosen to torment *you*? No woman in England could be less weak or defenseless!"

She realized that it was another of his gently sardonic jabs but decided to turn the rapier back on him. Her hand on the latch, Adrienne glanced back over her shoulder and parried, "I am pleased that you have taken my measure so accurately, Mr. Essex. It will make for fewer misunderstandings in future! As for Walter Frakes-Hogg, I can only assume that he paints me in a rosier light than you. But he isn't the first man to underestimate me—or the last, I'll wager! Good night, sir."

When the door closed behind her, Nathan Raveneau flipped over on his back. A smile spread over his face and he whispered, "Touché, chit. For now."

"Very pretty village you have here, old chap." Walter Frakes-Hogg strolled along Winchester's High Street in the company of a nervous Huntsford Harms. "Very quaint."

"Better than quaint." Hurrying along the cobbles, Harms argued, "Used to be a Roman city, y'know, and after that the Saxon capital of bloody England, until those thieving Normans came along and upset a perfectly good system."

"I say, it's a bit late to cry over *that* spilled milk, isn't it?" He eyed the pink-skinned young dandy through hooded lids. "Afraid someone will see us together? You haven't done anything wrong, Harms!"

"I like to be discreet, that's all!"

"Ah, yes. Discretion is your watchword." His tone dripped sarcasm that was lost on his companion. "Let's find a pub where we can have a bit of privacy, then. I could use a spot of brandy."

They continued in silence past a mixture of half-timbered Elizabethan buildings and more recently constructed bow-fronted shops. Reaching an old gabled inn, its battered sign proclaiming The White Ostrich, the men peered into its shadowed recesses.

"I perceive that the lonely tapster is in need of more patrons," Frakes-Hogg decided. "Little chance that anyone will see us here, hmm?"

Huntsford Harms followed him inside, sniffing in distaste. "I say, awfully gloomy, don't you agree? I was hoping for more cheerful surroundings.

"I thought you wanted to be discreet." Frakes-Hogg had already taken a brace-back chair. "At least it's cool in here. Here comes the waiter. Order yourself a nice pint and stop complaining."

The younger man obeyed, and when the frothy tankard arrived, he drank. Then he took snuff. Finally, fidgeting under Walter Frakes-Hogg's intent gaze, he burst out,

"Confound it, you're staring as if I were a loose screw and you're waiting for me to climb on the table and make a cake of myself!"

"Not at all, Harms. In truth, my stare was admiring. I must have the name of your tailor; those pantaloons fit exactly as I would wish my own to do. And your walking stick—is it ebony? Very handsome. Every detail of your appearance is exquisite, including the arrangement of your cravat."

Huntsford swelled with pride. "Beau Brummell's valet showed this trick to Roland, my valet. It's deuced difficult though, and sometimes it takes an hour to get it right." Favoring his companion with a view of his profile, he added, "Do you know that, in London, they've taken to calling me the Tulip of Fashion? I did have a striking pair of powder-blue gloves, but my mother's wretched dog chewed them to bits and I can't get any more until I return to Town."

"A great pity." Frakes-Hogg leaned forward, his eyes as black as coal. "Let us speak of more serious matters. What do you know of Adrienne Beauvisage?"

"She seems quite charming, actually! Can't imagine what she could have done to you to make you go to all this trouble, even paying me to come down here and spy for you—"

"Do lower your voice!" Frakes-Hogg hissed.

Harms toyed nervously with the seals and fobs that dangled at his waist. "I just mean that it seems an elaborate and expensive plan, and of course I'm very glad for the chance to cancel my gambling debts, but I would hate to see any harm come to Miss Beauvisage."

"I don't give a damn what you think. Will you stand on principle and return to London—after returning the funds you have already received?" Frakes-Hogg paused for a sip of brandy, his face sharp as he waited for a response. "No? Let's get on with it then. Tell me about Adrienne. Does she keep to a regular schedule?"

He shrugged. "My mother's not exactly a model of punctuality. She's lazy, in a word. Adrienne just caters to Mummy's whims."

"What else?"

"She's been overseeing Mummy's mad plan to reorganize the library, and I know that she likes to read." Harms signaled for another pint of ale. "I'm rather taken with Adrienne myself. She joined my friends as a fourth for whist two nights ago, and she was bright and lovely. Quite a piece of audacity, in fact."

"If you harbor any romantic notions toward Miss Beauvisage, kindly dispel yourself of them," the older man replied coldly. "I have other plans altogether for that baggage."

"Do you know that they're on to you? Or at least they know someone's after her. She must be quality, or something like it, because her family's hired a hulking great fellow to guard her."

"What's his name?" The edges of his ears reddened.

"Essex, I b'lieve. Nathaniel? Perhaps."

"Black hair?"

"Very. Rather striking looks, but unpolished. Spectacles. And he wears clothing that appears to have been passed down from his father." Harms rolled his eyes. "Of course, what other sort of fellow would want that sort of employment? How could he be anything but bourgeois? I suppose we ought to be grateful that he can string words together."

"Does he appear to possess intelligence as well as brawn? And how does he get on with Adrienne?"

"I suppose he's passably intelligent, if arrogance is any indication. As for Essex and Adrienne, I really couldn't say. I have avoided him as much as possible." Harms drained his second tankard and yawned, deciding not to mention Lucy's outburst about Essex resembling the mysterious Scapegrace who had so intrigued London society. When she had taken a second look the next morning, with clear eyes, Lucy herself had agreed that it was laughable to imagine that the unfashionable, bespectacled Essex might be Nathan Raveneau, the Scapegrace.

"Kindly give me your attention," Walter Frakes-Hogg hissed through clenched teeth. Darkness was gathering outside and the tapster lit tallow candles. "I have better things to do than while away the days in this tedious hamlet. You were not sent to Harms Castle to drink and be merry, but

to help me devise a plan to be alone with Adrienne
Beauvisage. When you return today, you will turn all your
admittedly meager mental powers toward achieving that
goal." He stood up, looming above the Tulip of Fashion. "I
will meet you in the nave of the cathedral at two o'clock
on Thursday, and I fully expect you to be not only able to
answer all my questions but also to have devised the plans
I need."

Huntsford Harms slouched in his chair and stared at his
very white hands. They were trembling ever so slightly. He
thought of the two thousand pounds that Frakes-Hogg had
already paid him and the even larger amount that he'd receive when the other man's ends were met. It was hard not
to feel beastly about turning Adrienne Beauvisage over to
that villain, for God knew what purpose, but on the other
hand, the money would help Harms pay off the debts that
had been choking him for months. One awful cad had actually threatened to call him out if he didn't pay up, and he
couldn't aim a pistol to save his life.

The moneylenders already had half the valuables from
the house in Cavendish Square, and he lived in constant
fear that his mother would notice missing items. Furthermore, it was no good going to her for help, since she had
already cut her staff to the bone and had barely a pound of
accessible funds. Their fortune, such as it was, was in their
land, and the houses and their contents.

Sighing, Huntsford realized that he really didn't have any
choice but to obey Frakes-Hogg's instructions. The only
question remaining was how he could ever devise the plot
to deliver Adrienne Beauvisage. Would he have to knock
Essex over the head?

"Waiter," he called, "I'll have one more pint, and perhaps a meal as well, since evening's upon us. What have
you today?"

The next afternoon, the sunlight seemed burnished as
twilight approached. In the library at Harms Castle,
Adrienne finished her tea and looked over at Lady
Thomasina. The old woman was feeding a biscuit to An-

gus, who placed the treat on his blue glove, held it between two paws, and chewed.

"He's very spoiled, isn't he?" she said when she noticed her companion's amused gaze.

"You know that he is, my lady." Adrienne smiled. "Isn't it a beautiful day? Can you smell the fragrance of the garden?" She wandered over to the window and pushed open the leaded casement. There, below her, was Nathan Essex, strolling through the overgrown boxwood maze.

"June is my favorite month, I think," Lady Thomasina agreed.

"Why don't you rest for a few minutes, and I'll dash outside and pick up a bouquet for your sitting room. So many flowers have begun to bloom just in the past day!"

"I do feel rather sleepy. Where is Hunty? If he returns, send him to me."

"Yes, my lady."

Out in the corridor, Adrienne lifted her skirts and hurried down the broad staircase, pausing in the conservatory to get a basket and shears. For two days she and Nathan had been searching for a moment alone to talk, but fate had conspired to keep them apart ever since the night she had visited his bedchamber. Emerging onto the terrace, she saw that he had walked over to a small apple tree. A nest with eggs in it lay on the ground, and Nathan sat back on his heels and took it gently in one big hand.

"Poor little things," Adrienne murmured as she approached.

He glanced up. "At last. I thought you'd never see me and come out." Rising, he put the nest back into the leafy branches. "They're willow warbler eggs, ready to hatch. I think they'll be all right."

"Won't they die now that a human has touched the nest?"

"When I was a boy, my father showed me how to care for injured birds and animals, and none of them was rejected by its mother." He shrugged. "It's a myth as far as I can tell."

She inclined her head, eyes lively with interest. "Where did you grow up? What sort of family was it?"

"I don't really think that we have time for a chat about my childhood." Nathan began to walk rapidly away toward the garden maze, speaking over his shoulder. "Come on. We need to talk."

Adrienne hurried after him. Orange-tip butterflies were on the wing in the soft light, and she was delighted to see how many flowers were in bloom. Most were growing wild, even between cracks in the stone walkways, as if nature had found a way to triumph over Harms Castle's general state of dilapidation. "Oh, Nathan," she marveled, "have you ever seen a prettier twilight?"

Having already revealed more of himself than seemed wise, he hesitated before replying. "This is the gloaming, you know. One of those rare times when the light is brushed with gold."

Her heart beat in a way she now recognized. "How very poetic you are. Why don't you tell me your plans for Frakes-Hogg while I cut flowers to take inside to Lady Thomasina. That way, if anyone sees us, they'll think you're just keeping me company."

"I've just returned from Winchester." He spoke casually, strolling past her as she bent to snip ox-eye daisies and dusky cranesbill. "I've been paying the butcher's son, Dickie, to keep an eye on our quarry, and when I met him today, he had some interesting information. It seems that yesterday, Frakes-Hogg went into the White Ostrich Inn with a handsome young man Dickie couldn't identify. They had drinks and talked for a long while."

Adrienne moved on to a clump of honeysuckle while Nathan stared thoughtfully at the distant meadow. "Perhaps he's simply made a friend during the time he's been in town," she suggested. "Would that be so unusual? He's probably bored."

"Mmm. Yes, you're undoubtedly right. It's just that the other possibilities are so much more intriguing. A plot and all that . . ."

"I think you're giving Frakes-Hogg too much credit. What else did Dickie tell you?"

"He said that Frakes-Hogg has developed one regular habit. When the weather is fair, he goes for a walk at about four o'clock—past the cathedral, then around the wall of Wolvesey Castle that skirts the River Itchen." Nathan paused, waiting until Adrienne turned with a few bright buttercups in her hand. He held her gaze and continued, "I think that would be our best plan for putting you in his way. It would be outdoors, in broad daylight, so I'll be absolutely certain no harm can come to you."

She made a fetching picture in her high-waisted muslin gown, a wide basket of tumbled blooms anchored in the crook of her arm. As she considered his words, Adrienne's eyes slowly began to sparkle. "Yes. Yes, I think you're right! In fact, why don't I take the offensive and approach *Walter*? I'll march up to him and demand to know why he's been threatening me, and why he's in Winchester!"

"Dear chit, let us not forget that he is a large, evil man and you are a slight, though feisty, female. I think we'll have a better chance of getting him to misbehave if you pretend to be shocked to see him. He should think that he can take the opportunity presented to him to do whatever it is he's been dreaming of doing. I'll be armed and hiding nearby—you'll know where—and as soon as he lays a glove on you, I'll appear and that will be the end of Frakes-Hogg."

Her brow wrinkled. "What do you mean by that last bit? You aren't going to just kill him outright for accosting me, are you? You could end up going to the gallows yourself!"

"No, I won't kill him, though I wish I could. If he tries to harm you, it may come to that." A shadow seemed to pass across his face. "I do hope to have him taken into custody. I have all the evidence, including some of the notes he wrote you. I mean to make certain that Walter Frakes-Hogg won't bother you again."

"And then your job will be finished?"

Nathan regarded her delicate back as she reached down to cut red campion. The nape of her neck looked sweetly damp; soft chestnut tendrils had fallen loose to decorate her hairline. He felt a sudden throb in his groin and stepped backward. Have a care, Raveneau, he thought. She's more dangerous than she appears! When he spoke, his voice was husky. "I think that depends on the outcome of our adventure. I cannot leave unless I am satisfied that Walter Frakes-Hogg cannot harm you."

"Well, then," Adrienne said brightly, "for both our sakes, I will hope that you get your wish. If only there were a way to remove him from the lives of his daughters as well. . . ."

"Shall we agree to act on Thursday, then? Better to wait until market day is past—"

"Fine!" She put on a smile, dimpling for added emphasis. "I should go in now. Her ladyship will be looking for me. Ever since the night she had that dream, I've felt very sympathetic toward her." As they walked, Adrienne added, "I always get myself into trouble this way. I begin to care for people, like Frakes-Hogg's children, and everything becomes complicated. . . ."

"That reminds me—" He took the gathering basket from her as they emerged from the boxwood maze. "Do you have an answer for me about Frakes-Hogg's motivation in all this?"

"I told you already, he's a bully."

He sighed. "Would you be kind enough to enlighten me further?"

"It's as if he has no heart—and certainly no respect for women. When I rejected his more subtle advances, he felt challenged, as if it were some sort of game, like the fox hunts he so adores! He enjoyed stalking me, until he realized that all his methods were useless. He tried kindness, cajolery, then veiled threats, more insidious activity like rattling my doorknob in the middle of the night, and finally physical attempts to make me yield. It was humiliating for him to be bested by me in that situation."

"I don't suppose you're going to elaborate?"

She shrugged. "I was prepared. I had a knife, and I used it to lock him in my dressing room. And then I took the girls and escaped." The color ebbed in Adrienne's cheeks, but her voice grew stronger. "It sounds mad, but I think all of this—the time Frakes-Hogg has invested, the chances he's taken with his reputation, and the other risks—all of it is rooted in a compulsion to make me submit, to hear me beg for his mercy—"

Nathan reached for her trembling hand just as they were

about to enter the castle. "Don't. I never meant to put you through any more suffering ... but I do understand now." It came to him that she truly despised Walter Frakes-Hogg, and he was reminded of his own nagging hatred for Xavier Crowe. "What is it about evil men that drives them to try to bring down other people?"

Something in his tone gave her pause. "Jealousy, perhaps. And I *do* think that they are bullies. When they meet people who are strong and good, and who won't submit to their foul tactics, they're—driven, as you say, to break us. One hopes, in this case, that Walter Frakes-Hogg will die trying."

Just then Huntsford Harms came striding toward them through the gallery, his boot soles cracking on the marble floor. He wore his many-caped driving coat and beaver hat, carried his whip, and narrowed his eyes as he identified the two figures silhouetted against the sunset. "I say, are you going out or coming in?"

Nathan closed the glass doors to the terrace behind them and Adrienne gestured toward her flowers. "I was just picking these for her ladyship while she enjoys a brief nap. She has been looking for you, my lord."

"Isn't she always? What sort of flowers are those? They look awfully like weeds, don't they?" He laughed. "Lovely weather! I've just come from Winchester myself. Looking at the cathedral! Jolly little town, don't you think so?"

"Indeed," Nathan said affably, glad for the chance to begin setting their plan in motion. "In fact, we were just planning an outing to Winchester on Thursday afternoon. Miss Beauvisage is going to take some of her ladyship's worn books to the bookbinder's to be repaired."

"You don't say!" Huntsford blinked and began fingering his whip. "But, as it happens, I am going in myself that day. Let me stand in for you, old chap! I should like nothing better than to act as guardian to the beauteous Miss Beauvisage!"

Chapter Eight

"I RECEIVED YOUR MESSAGE." WALTER FRAKES-Hogg was clearly annoyed. "I hope it is momentous news that moved you to alter the plans I laid out yesterday. I must add that I am very unhappy that you chose to pay a messenger to fetch me today. The fewer people who know about the link between us, the better."

"That footman is just a dimwitted boy. I highly doubt that he remembers your name!" Flushing, Huntsford Harms looked around the White Ostrich and drank half his glass of madeira. "I had no choice, and I'm certain that you'll agree when you hear my news."

"Do lower your voice!"

Huntsford had never seen him in such foul temper. Stuttering nervously, he spilled out the story of Adrienne's plan to come to the bookbinder on Thursday, with Essex, and his own intervention. "I insisted that I be allowed to accompany her! Could any plan be more brilliant?"

"And how are you going to throw her together with me? Or did you think she'd come willingly to my rooms?"

"I—I—" He swallowed hard. "Must you stare at me so venomously, old chap? I'm on your side, after all!" Harms lifted his glass again, all the while racking his brain. "I happened to see Miss Beauvisage as I was leaving to come here, and she mentioned a yearning to go walking around Wolvesey Castle, along the river, when she's finished at the bookbinder's. Said she hoped I wouldn't mind, but she'd like to go alone. . . ."

Frakes-Hogg slowly lifted his head, arching his neck as if he were beset by sensations of intense pleasure. "How deliciously ironic! She won't need you to accompany her, my boy, because I shall be there. . . ."

Adrienne was at her wit's end as she went into Lady Thomasina's dressing room. She and Nathan had yet to find a moment to rearrange their plans, and now Hortie was ill and Adrienne had been enlisted to act as her ladyship's abigail.

"Which headdress do you want?" she called.

"I just told you, Miss Beau—the green velvet toque, with the silk roses! Do me the courtesy of *listening!*"

Muttering under her breath, Adrienne searched the dark, cluttered little room. To get more light, she opened the door leading to the main corridor and caught a glimpse of Nathan Essex as he entered his chamber.

"Psst! Come here a moment!" Adrienne could scarcely contain her excitement, but Nathan looked unconcerned. She pulled him into the dressing room and began whispering furiously. "*Now* what are we going to do?"

"Are you referring to Huntsford Harms's intention to accompany you tomorrow?" he inquired.

"Of course I am! Speak quickly!"

"I hope you'll be calmer tomorrow, chit." He gave her a measuring look, then continued, "You'll have to let him drive you, allowing time to visit the bookbinder well before four o'clock."

"I told him this morning that I want to walk along the castle walls. . . ."

"Did you? Good girl." His smile softened her mood. "Then it's fixed. I'll borrow a horse and come on my own, and I'll be there well in advance. There are some ruins of the old Roman wall along Riverside Walk. I'll be hiding in the lilac bushes nearby, watching—"

"Miss Beau?" Lady Thomasina's tone was querulous. "What's keeping you?"

"I'm coming, my lady!" She grabbed for the headdress. Limp silk roses hung precariously from the folds of velvet. "I really must go—"

"Don't worry," Nathan whispered. "Even if we aren't able to talk before tomorrow morning, there's nothing to worry about. I won't let any harm come to you; you have my word."

She tried to smile. "I do trust you, but perhaps I ought to carry some sort of weapon, just in case . . ."

By the time Adrienne emerged from the bookbinder's narrow shop on Parchment Street, Huntsford Harms was nearly mad with anxiety. The church bells had just chimed four, and his watch showed several minutes past the hour. Had Adrienne not said that she wanted to stroll Riverside Walk at four o'clock? Frakes-Hogg would have him drawn and quartered if this bit of muslin changed her mind!

Appearing quite unconcerned with the time, she approached the landaulet they'd driven from Harms Castle to Winchester with an eager stableboy hanging on the back as the tiger. It was hot, but Adrienne was calm and ravishing in a pale-blue walking dress topped by a short pretty spencer in a striking shade of canary yellow. Her bright curls spilled round her shoulders, and her face was framed by a chipstraw bonnet edged with a crisp frill. In spite of his state of near panic, Harms couldn't help salivating in Adrienne Beauvisage's company. She was exquisite.

"Why, Lord Harms, you're looking awfully pale," she teased as he handed her into the landaulet. "Or is that intentional?"

"The mark of a gentleman, *n'est-ce pas*? It's what separates me from plebeians like Nathan Essex." As he spoke, Harms consulted his watch once again. "I gather that you lost track of the time, my dear. You wanted to be walking along the river by now."

"Oh, yes." A pretty shade of pink washed her cheeks. "Perhaps you can drop me there, my lord. You won't mind if I walk alone?"

"No, no, not at all!" He couldn't suppress a burst of relieved laughter as the pair of chestnuts moved into the traffic on St. Georges Street. "I understand *completely*!"

The bells of Winchester Cathedral were marking the quarter hour when Harms reined in the horses next to the massive walls of Wolvesey Castle. Built in the twelfth century as a bishop's palace, the castle had been destroyed by Cromwell, leaving only ruins and the great walls that fronted the River Itchen. Today, in the heat of the afternoon, the river rushed past a brick and tile mill a short distance to the north, and a cornflower-blue sky was reflected in the sparkling water.

"I'll let you out here, then," Huntsford Harms said. He jumped down and hurried around to offer Adrienne his hand.

"I heard that there was part of the old Roman wall nearby. . . ." She looked around with a trace of worry in her emerald eyes. "Won't you show me?"

"Over there." He pointed. "I have to visit a sick friend. I'll return in a short while to get you." Then, before she could say good-bye, he flicked the reins and started away. Once around the corner, however, Harms came to another stop. He handed the chestnuts over to the tiger, slipped him a guinea, and charged him to guard the landaulet and pair with his life. Then he started up the nearest set of tower steps leading to the castle's wall walk. Once on top, Harms could watch everything that transpired between Walter Frakes-Hogg and the unsuspecting Adrienne Beauvisage.

It really was a shame that she had to be so lovely and charming—and so kind to his mother. . . .

There was nothing in her manner to betray the racing of her heart. In fact, to be certain that Walter Frakes-Hogg did not mistake her, Adrienne loosened the strings of her bonnet and let it fall backward so that her hair and face were fully revealed.

Her step was brisk upon the cobbles, and she breathed deeply of the fresh sunny air. Now and then she paused to gaze out over the River Itchen, or south to the water meadows that led to the medieval almshouse known as St. Cross Hospital. A casual observer would conclude that Adrienne Beauvisage was enjoying herself. Smiling slightly, she realized that, perversely, it was true. The scent of danger was intoxicating.

Of course, it was easier to savor the moment's thrill

knowing that Nathan was nearby, poised to rescue her from
the villain. . . .

Just then, as Adrienne was beginning to relax, a tall man
came hurrying silently across the stone bridge, his head
bent. He wore a voluminous gray silk cape and a tall hat.
His hands were hidden. Adrienne felt paralyzed, and it
came to her that Nathan's position near the Roman wall afforded him a view up and down Riverside Walk but none
back over the bridge.

She turned away, walking rapidly, suddenly quite terrified. It was difficult to breathe. Blood rushed to Adrienne's
head with each thud of her heart.

Footsteps approached behind her. She wanted to scream,
but no sound emerged.

"I am flattered that you recognized me, sweet," a low,
silky voice declared at her shoulder. "Stop now."

And she did. He had her elbow; his fingers pinched like
tongs. Waves of panic swept over her. What if Nathan
couldn't see them? What if Walter killed her outright, perhaps plunging a dagger into her heart, before he could
come? How silly she'd been to imagine that this was some
sort of lark, or that she might've had the courage or dexter-
ity to use the little paring knife fastened up her left sleeve.
Frakes-Hogg saw to it that her right arm was immobilized.

"I have a score to settle with you, sweet. Let us walk
into that tower, under the castle wall, where we may have
privacy."

Adrienne heard herself beg, "Please, can't you forget
about me? I'm far away from London now—"

"That's not enough, I fear, to make up for the indignities
I suffered at *your* hands. You were very audacious when
you believed I couldn't hurt you any longer, weren't you,
sweet?"

His voice was so calm, so deadly, that her fear escalated.
Perspiration dotted her brow. Why weren't there any pass-
ersby? Was no one going to help her?

They crossed the lane, walking away from the river.

"I have been so good to Ellie and Beth," Adrienne cried.
All the feelings of sick terror she'd known in his house

flooded back. The smell of his breath made her stomach lurch. "Please, they wouldn't want you to hurt me."

"If you cared so much for them, you would have done *anything* to stay in our home. I gave you many chances to remain with us. I treated you as a member of our family."

The castle wall filled Adrienne's vision, her arm burned where he gripped it, and then the arched entrance to the tower yawned before her, dark and forbidding. "What do you intend to do to me?" She tried to stop, but he pushed at her from behind.

"Too many things to list, sweet."

Another voice interrupted them. "Sorry, not today!" And then Nathan emerged from around the corner of the tower. The sheer power of his tall, strong, young body was accentuated by the pistol he carried. "Release the lady, sir."

"Mind your own business," Frakes-Hogg retorted.

"Miss Beauvisage is my business. Loose her." Nathan drew the hammer back and touched the trigger. "I realize that this weapon may not be very accurate, but at close range, I find that it is surprisingly effective."

Adrienne felt the pincers leave her arm. She was numb below the elbow. Blinking back embarrassing tears, she hurried to Nathan's side. "Oh—thank you."

He gave her a dazzling grin. "I'm pleased to be of service. Now then—go on. Wait for me in St. Cross Hospital. The brethren will keep you safe."

"No. I want to stay with you." She slipped the paring knife from the sleeve of her spencer and smiled. "I can help now."

"Adrienne, at least stand away." Nathan sighed. "You are still in danger. That knife is a toy."

Frakes-Hogg was weighing his slim chances to get away from this lithe, strong fellow, who was undoubtedly a fast runner as well. It hardly seemed worth the untidy scene that would ensue. "Now that you've rescued the fair maiden, I admit that you've won the day. Let us part friends." He bowed as if to bid them farewell.

"Don't be ridiculous. A crime has been committed, and I intend to turn you over to the authorities." Nathan could scarcely believe his good fortune when he saw a constable

crossing the bridge, coming in their direction. He raised a
hand to call him to their aid.

"Well, well, it's Frakes-Hogg, isn't it! I surely enjoyed
the pint you bought me yesterday," the jolly officer exclaimed as he drew near. His brow furrowed at the sight of
Nathan's pistol. "This fellow ain't bothering you, I hope,
sir!"

A benign smile spread over Frakes-Hogg's long face. "As
a matter of fact, he is. I think the man must be mad, or else
he and his accomplice mean to rob me, Constable! He accosted me, brandishing that pistol, and the woman drew a
knife!"

"That's not true!" Adrienne cried. "Walter Frakes-Hogg
accosted *me*! If you search him, I'm sure you'll find a
weapon!"

"Why on earth would I want to bother this young lady?"
he countered. "But, to prove my own innocence, I insist
that you conduct a thorough search of my person, my good
fellow."

"But, sir, you're a gentleman! I don't see how—"
Clearly embarrassed, the constable obeyed. No weapons
were discovered, and he turned accusing bloodshot eyes on
Nathan and Adrienne. "Perhaps I ought to take the two of
you in—"

"No, no." Frakes-Hogg waved off this suggestion. He
exuded an air of gracious forgiveness. "I am inclined to
hope that it was all an unfortunate error on the part of these
young people. Perhaps a case of mistaken identity, hmm? In
any event, I am late for an appointment. Will you walk with
me to the market, Constable? Good, good." He drew on
dark-gray gloves with a satisfied smile.

Adrienne stared, pale and disbelieving, as the constable
warned them to put their weapons away and obey the law.
Then the two men walked off down College Street and
turned north.

"I can't believe it," Nathan murmured.

"He is evil." Her voice wavered. "Oh, Nathan, I'm
frightened!"

He drew her into his arms, patting her curls. "No need
to worry. I didn't let any harm come to you, did I?"

"I believe he is capable of anything." She let the tears come. "He despises me and means to exact revenge beyond my worst nightmares. . . ."

Nathan held her closer, staring out over the river as his own jaw hardened with concern. Unfortunately, he feared that Adrienne may not have overstated the situation at all.

Above them, on the castle-wall walk known as the *allure*, Huntsford Harms saw and heard everything. He'd been shocked by his own protective feelings toward Adrienne Beauvisage. When Frakes-Hogg led her into the tower, he had been ready to go to her rescue himself, but then that damned Essex had interfered! How dare he come into Winchester on his own, to watch over Adrienne, when Huntsford had made it perfectly clear that *he* intended to be her protector today! It made him seethe now to watch them embracing from above, to hear Adrienne's sweet sobs and Essex's murmuring reassurances.

Somehow, Huntsford Harms would bring matters to right, so that one day he might be the man to rescue fair Adrienne and embrace her in the aftermath.

Huntsford rushed to bring the landaulet back to get Adrienne. However, she explained that she had encountered Mr. Essex on her walk and had been persuaded to let him see her home. It was his duty, after all. Huntsford had managed a stiff smile, seething inside, and proceeded to drive straight to the White Ostrich.

"No need to call attention to our vehicle," he told the tiger, handing over the reins. "Wait near the market."

Frakes-Hogg was waiting within. He was eating kidney pie and drinking brandy at a table deep in the shadows when Huntsford Harms approached.

"What are you looking so nervous about? Go on, sit down." The older man poured more brandy for himself. "Have you come to hear a report of my confrontation with Miss Beauvisage?"

"Well—uh—" The waiter arrived then with a glass of negus, and Huntsford drank. The sweet, warm concoction contained just enough wine to soothe his nerves. "As a matter of fact, sir, I saw most of what transpired on Riverside Walk. I was on the castle wall above you."

"Ah!" Frakes-Hogg's manner changed; he put on a smile. "Then you witnessed my skillful finesse of the unsuspecting constable! Not only did I extricate myself from the clutches of that insufferable thug who guards Adrienne, I managed to put the two of *them* afoul of the law!" He rubbed his thin hands together. "Congratulate me, young fellow."

"Yes, that was very shrewd of you, sir ... and I was frankly relieved that no harm came to Miss Beauvisage." Huntsford avoided his companion's piercing stare and took another gulp of negus. "I mean, she's been awfully good to Mummy and unfailingly pleasant to me and my guests. I really don't see why you bear her such ill will!"

"I don't think, given the financial arrangement you and I have struck, that it is your place to decide the merit of my intentions toward Adrienne." Frakes-Hogg's voice was low, but each word carried a sting. Pushing his plate aside, he drank more brandy and continued, "Don't tell me that you fancy her yourself!"

Huntsford scowled. "Of course not—but I don't see why you should find that notion so amusing. Not as if I'm a freak of some sort, or even the least bit unattractive to ladies! In fact, I'm known in Town to be a particular favorite—"

"My point has nothing at all to do with you, dear boy," he interrupted. "It's simply that Adrienne can't be enamored of you, because she's carrying on with that awful man—"

"Who? Nathan Essex? But that's *absurd*! You are funning, sir. Is that it?"

"Funning? *Hardly*. Remove your hat and gloves, old fellow. Have a nip of my brandy; it will steady your nerves." Frakes-Hogg watched him through narrowed eyes. Then, with exquisite timing, he delivered another blow: "I perceive that your feelings for the irresistible Adrienne run deeper than even you had realized. I am sorry. However, my news about her and Essex is not a vile rumor or merely conjecture on my part. You see, I saw them together. Late one night, before you arrived from London, I walked the grounds at Harms Castle, just to get a feel for the place."

"I'm not sure I like the idea of you lurking about in our garden," Huntsford protested.

"Oh, but I wasn't lurking there," he countered suavely. "I was among the stand of elm trees, and I saw them together."

"T-together? You don't mean . . . ?"

"I fear so. If not *quite*, something very near. They were interrupted by the gardener, who had spied me a few minutes earlier."

"This is—simply shocking!"

"Really? Come now, my boy, do you mean to say that your set don't go in for love play?" Frakes-Hogg winked. "As for Adrienne Beauvisage, I can assure you that she is hardly the virtuous lady she pretends to be. Perhaps now you can understand why she has driven me to seek justice in my own way. I have been badly hurt by that baggage."

Huntsford Harms stared at the man across the table from him. He would not give up longing for Adrienne, but this news about her and Essex deepened his feelings of jealousy. Perhaps she was simply smitten because of his role as her protector? If so, the first step toward having Adrienne to himself would be to usurp Nathan Essex's place in her life.

Fiddling with his watch fob, Huntsford muttered, "I can see now that I have misjudged both of them. And your revelation calls to mind something that was said about Nathan Essex the other night. I didn't give it any credence at the time . . ."

"*About* him? Hurry, damn it! What is it?"

Huntsford pursed his lips. "I think that this information is far too valuable to be *given* away. I think that this might be a good time for you to make another payment toward my gambling debts."

"Are you referring to the three thousand pounds I promised when our project is finished?"

"I think I should receive that, as planned, plus an additional two thousand tonight for the information I am about to pass along."

"The Tulip of Fashion would seem to be growing fangs and claws!" Frakes-Hogg stared hard, but he could not force one crack in the young man's smooth, handsome visage. There were already enough problems that could crop up at Harms Castle; it didn't seem wise to risk losing Huntsford as an ally. "By Jove, you're coming along magnificently, my boy! Learning well. I'm impressed, and pleased to give you the additional sums. You may come back to my rooms when we're finished here, and I'll pay you immediately. Ah, I see that I've made you smile. Good show."

"I'm glad that we are in accord, sir. And, you'll be glad when you hear what my guest Lucy Beauchamp had to say about Nathan Essex." Lounging in his chair, Harms began his tale. "One recent night my friends and I were in one of the common rooms of the castle, and Essex appeared. He'd apparently forgotten his spectacles, and when he left, Lucy remarked that he looked exactly like a certain roguish sea captain who had become rather mythic in London of late. The ton took to calling him The Scapegrace...."

"By God, I know about the sea captain you're speaking of! The Scapegrace's name is Nathan *Raveneau*, not cursed Essex!" Walter Frakes-Hogg's eyes were ebony flames. Other people in the taproom were turning to see what the fuss was about, so he made an effort to keep himself in check. "Could it *be*?"

"If it's true that he's in disguise," Huntsford mused, "then I wonder what the purpose might be. Why would a sea captain want to play nursemaid to my mother's paid companion?"

"It's quite inexplicable, but I do know now why I despised Essex at first sight." Sipping his third large brandy, red-cheeked, Frakes-Hogg seemed to forget that he was speaking aloud. "The bloody Scapegrace has been a thorn in the side of my business partner, Xavier Crowe. They both live in Barbados, and Raveneau is one of those insufferable men who feels duty-bound to impose his rules of conduct on everyone else. He has hounded poor Xavier almost from the day my friend arrived on the island."

"Barbados! I've always wanted to go there." Sighing,

Huntsford reasoned, "Perhaps if I tell Adrienne the truth about Essex, she'll simply send him away."

"Or, more likely, she'll want the dashing Scapegrace even more than she does the bourgeois Nathan Essex!"

Huntsford's brown eyes widened. He took snuff and bit his lip. "That's a good point. She might do."

"Lean closer, my boy, and heed me well." The skin tightened over Frakes-Hogg's cheekbones as he bent across the table. "There's nothing for it but to put him out of the way, perhaps even before I resolve matters with Adrienne. If you help me finish off Raveneau, I'll see to it that you not only have the means to pay off all your debts, but to travel to Barbados—to stay, if you like. Xavier has a grand mansion called Crowe's Nest, and he would be eternally grateful to you for helping dispose of his nemesis. Do you take my meaning?"

Huntsford gulped. "Yes. Yes, I do." The thought of murder turned his stomach. "I'll find a way, sir. I accept."

PART TWO

Come, woo me, woo me; for now I am in a holiday
humour, and like enough to consent.
—WILLIAM SHAKESPEARE

PART TWO

Chapter Nine

THE SIGHT OF NATHAN MADE HER ALMOST GIDDY. How odd it was for Adrienne to realize that she now gazed fondly at his worn top boots and dreamed of tightening buttons and mending the frayed places in his jacket.

"Who will have more soused herrings?" Lady Thomasina was looking at Nathan as she gestured at the array of silver breakfast dishes that lined the sideboard. "They're very fresh. I am also very pleased with the honeycomb. Isn't it delicious, Miss Beau?"

"Mmm. Yes!" Adrienne was glowing. The days since their run-in with Walter Frakes-Hogg had been rich with pleasure. Nathan was careful to stay close at hand, fearing that the villain would strike again, and the two of them decided on a joint project: an attempt to improve Lady Thomasina's lot in life. They'd made suggestions for small events like this morning's formal breakfast in the dining room, which would nudge the old woman to venture out of her rooms before noon. In some cases, her ladyship dug in her heels and clung to lazier habits, but she had made changes, and Adrienne and Nathan were hopeful.

"Have you given any more thought to an outing, my lady?" Nathan helped himself to more herring and poured fresh chocolate for Adrienne from a silver pot.

"You two are becoming rather annoying on this subject!" Lady Thomasina smiled as she spoke and finished her buttered eggs. "Besides, it's raining."

"Would you prefer to have people in?" Adrienne wondered. "We could arrange a reception for local neighbors. There must be people you knew in years gone by with whom you've lost touch. I am convinced that human contact would be a great tonic for you, my lady."

"I thought I had hired *you* to provide companionship! And we have Mr. Essex with us, and dear Hunty and his lovely friends. I don't need any other tonics."

Nathan passed her a scone with clotted cream. "I see a furrow in your brow, my lady. Why not give us one of your lovely smiles instead? Haven't you noticed the rays of sun breaking through the dark clouds?"

"If you're going to force me to go out or have people in, I shall choose the former. Perhaps we might visit Winchester's lending library and inquire exactly when we might expect Mary Shelley's *Frankenstein*. Alistair has read it and he says it is quite terrifying!" She scowled again, this time in the direction of the five extra place settings down the table. "I do wish those young people would make a little effort to placate me. They did say that they would join us this morning, didn't they?"

Jarrow sidled over from the doorway. "I beg your pardon, my lady, but I may be able to explain the absence of Lord Harms and his friends from the breakfast table. I believe that the time may have gotten away from them last night. The ladies are still sleeping—"

"What about Hunty? One expects a bit more from one's own son!"

"Quite so, my lady," the butler agreed, nodding his big head. "However, as you doubtless know, his lordship requires several hours to bathe and dress."

Adrienne couldn't resist interjecting "Would it be improper for me to ask if it is true that Lord Harms bathes each morning in water mixed with eau de cologne? I find that notion fascinating!"

"Indeed, his lordship uses imported eau de cologne," Jarrow confirmed. "His bath is a very involved process, followed by shaving, the dressing of his hair, and the arrangement of his cravat, known as 'creasing down.' His lordship's valet, Roland, works night and day to keep his possessions immaculate."

Lady Thomasina shook her head with a mixture of pride and annoyance. "I don't know where he gets it. All that fussing is a great waste of time, I'd say."

The sound of Nathan's decidedly sardonic chuckle caused Adrienne to take a different tack. "Speaking of new books—"

"Were we?" Nathan wondered. "I was hoping to hear more about the habits of Lord Harms and Roland."

Adrienne hiked up her skirt and gave him a slight kick under the table, smiling politely. "You jest, as always, Mr. Essex. Her ladyship expressed a desire to go into Winchester, in search of new books. I am a great admirer of Jane Austen—"

"Ah, Miss Beau, again we are in accord!" cried Lady Thomasina. "Are you aware that there will soon be two more of Miss Austen's books published?"

"I am! One, I am told, was written some years ago but was mislaid until now by her publisher, and the second novel, called *Persuasion*, was completed just months before Miss Austen's . . . death." Adrienne's expression changed from lively enthusiasm to sadness. "When I was in school, I saw her once at a millener's in London. I told her how deeply I admired her work, and she was so very kind; warm and genuinely modest. When Miss Austen died last summer, I grieved, truly. . . ."

"You do know that she was living in Winchester at the time of her passing?" Lady Thomasina asked softly. "Jane Austen now rests in the nave of our cathedral."

Adrienne nodded, bright-eyed. "The bookbinder reminded me during my visit to his shop. Oh, my lady, he told me that Miss Austen's house is located on College Street, just a short distance from the cathedral. I would love to make a pilgrimage there, and then to take flowers to her final resting place. Would you not come with me?"

"All three of us can make the journey," Nathan said. "And I know a nice inn where we can take luncheon."

"I must admit," her ladyship conceded, "that would be a meaningful outing. We can visit the lending library as well. Perhaps we ought to get out Miss Austen's other books and read them aloud. I have been missing the Bennet family."

"Oh, yes, let's read *Pride and Prejudice* first!" Adrienne got up, bent next to Lady Thomasina's chair and reached for her plump hand. It was an act of great fondness, given the stale smell of her perfume and powder. "And then next, shall it be *Emma*? I do so agree with her views on the respectability of old maids! How pleasant it is to discover more common ground between us, my lady."

"We may agree about Jane Austen, but not about old maids." She waggled a finger at the girl. "You're not fit to live without a man. There's a fire in you, Miss Beau, whether you realize it or not!"

Across from them, Nathan raised a teacup to hide his smile, but when Lady Thomasina glanced his way he gave her a fleeting wink.

"I despise that little beast," Huntsford Harms muttered to his friends.

Alistair looked up from the billiard table in time to see Angus the terrier enter the gallery, a scrap of blue glove dangling jauntily from his mouth. "I think he's delightful."

"Thank goodness that my little Peter is napping on my bed," cried Lucy. "He is frightfully upset by that other . . . animal." She was sitting on a gilt chair under two portraits of Lady Thomasina's Tudor ancestors. As Angus trotted near, Lucy bent down and hissed, "Go away, if you know what's good for you! Shoo!"

"Grrrr . . ." replied Angus, shaking his head for emphasis.

"You hideous rodent!" Harms thundered. "You're lucky to be alive!" He ran at the terrier, waving his arms, and Angus scurried away as quickly as his old legs would allow.

"I say, old chap! Wasn't that your glove in his mouth?" Alistair queried playfully. His friend gave him a dark scowl in passing, and he went on, "What's got you in such poor spirits? You've been spoiling for a fight all afternoon!"

"Can't a fellow enjoy a case of the sulks without having to make explanations? I'm not in the mood for billiards anymore. Think I'll go outside for a bit of air. Perhaps it's stopped raining." Harms strode away before anyone else could press the matter.

Alone in the central corridor, he felt as if the walls were closing in. All Huntsford wanted was a little time with Adrienne Beauvisage, to prove to her that he could look after her every bit as well as the bloody Scapegrace, but the other inhabitants of the castle continually got in his way.

If only Harms could expose that Essex/Raveneau character to Adrienne! It was supremely frustrating to know that the man was a fraud and that Adrienne was being duped, but to fear that she might find his real identity even *more* appealing!

It came to him that the library was around the next corner, and the object of his obsession was probably inside. Huntsford found a mirror. He checked his windswept blond locks, straightened his cravat (knotted à la Byron), and thrust his jaw out above perilously high shirtpoints. If Adrienne would only compare the way Huntsford's coat fit across the shoulders with that of his careless rival, she would have no doubt which man was worthy of her regard!

Bristling with determination, he advanced toward the library. Adrienne's voice drifted around the door:

" 'It is a truth universally acknowledged, that a single man in possession of a good fortune must be in want of a wife.' "

Harms entered with pleasure. "My dear Miss Beauvisage, might you be speaking of *me*?"

She was sitting opposite Lady Thomasina, who was in her usual tub chair. A book was open on Adrienne's lap. "Oh—Lord Harms!" She blushed slightly, as was her custom. "Actually, I was reading from *Pride and Prejudice*. Those were Jane Austen's sentiments, not my own."

"What's come over you, Hunty?" his mother cried. "This estate does not constitute a 'good fortune,' and even if it did, why would you say something so prosy to Miss Beau? Unless . . ." Her voice trailed off and she raised her quizzing glass, staring through the smudged lens as an idea occurred to her.

"Mummy, don't fly off into the boughs over nothing." It was his turn to color. "I was just attempting to put Miss Beauvisage at ease." Crossing to the windows, he spied Nathan out of the corner of one eye. The other man was perched high on one of the library ladders, sorting through books, apparently unaware of what was happening across the big room.

"Hunty, you may be interested to know that we have been planning an outing." Lady Thomasina continued to stare at him through her quizzing glass. "It seems that Miss Beau shares my admiration for Jane Austen. As soon as the weather clears, we will venture into Winchester and make a pilgrimage to her last address on College Street and to the cathedral where she was laid to rest."

Having reached the tall windows, Harms turned and looked back at his mother. She was leaning forward, glaring in a way that he was meant to understand. Perhaps he was not so unlike her after all. . . . "I envy you those plans." He watched Lady Thomasina's expression as he spoke. "And look outside, Miss Beauvisage. We have a rainbow!"

The beauteous Adrienne came toward him, smiling. "Really? I love rainbows but seldom see them."

When she was next to him, Huntsford dared to ask "Would you mind if I accompany you and Mummy to Winchester? I'm quite an admirer of Miss Austen myself."

Adrienne blinked. All morning she had been dreaming of the fun she would have with Nathan. Still, what could she say? "But, Lord Harms, what about your friends? I'm afraid you would find our company awfully dull."

"Are you putting me off, Miss Beauvisage? My friends are charming, but I long for the company of others."

"Well, then, of course you may join us." She smiled.

"Delightful. If I may be so bold, I will confess that I have been hoping for an opportunity to know you better." He saw, over her shoulder, his own mother nodding encouragement.

Speechless, Adrienne looked back toward the rainbow and hoped for a distraction. As if on cue a stranger on horseback cantered around the curve and approached the castle. "Goodness! Look. Someone's coming!"

"I don't recognize him," Harms said. He threw open the sash and let in a blast of warm, humid air.

"A stranger?" Lady Thomasina struggled to her feet.

"Nathan, come and help me. Angus is all tangled up in my skirts! I want to see who is outside."

He descended the ladder and crossed the room in seconds, glad for an excuse to inflict himself on Huntsford Harms. As Nathan and Lady Thomasina neared the window, Adrienne was leaning out and calling to their visitor.

"Excuse me, sir! Will you inform us of your business?"

Nathan was tall enough to see over her head, down to the drive where the stranger was in the process of doffing his hat. He was short in stature, and revealed a head of thick, bright red hair that gave Nathan a moment's pause.

"Yes, ma'am!" he called. "I am here to see Nathan—uh—" The fellow read from a scrap of paper. "Nathan Essex! Do you know him?"

Nathan took a step forward. He stared as his caller looked up toward their window, his sunburned face fully revealed. Unbelievably, it was Zachary Minter, the *Golden Eagle*'s first mate.

"Curse you, Zach! What the devil are you doing here?" Nathan demanded as soon as he had closed the door to his room behind them. "I distinctly recall giving you instructions *not* to show your face here, unless the circumstances were dire. Why do I feel that is not the case?"

"See here, guv'nor—"

"I've told you not to call me that!"

Zachary Minter's eyes twinkled with mischief. "Where's your ready wit, sir? I figured that you'd be missing me so much by now that you'd have changed your mind and would welcome me with open arms!"

"If we were on board ship, I'd tie you to the mainmast and lash you within an inch of your life."

Minter leaned toward him and whispered with conspiratorial delight, "We both know you'd do no such thing. I'm the best friend you have in the world, and you'll not convince me otherwise!"

"Am I going mad?" Glaring at his first mate, who was nearly a foot shorter than he, Raveneau pretended to tear out his hair. "If you're going to insist on torturing me, let us get to the point. Why are you here?"

"I came to tell you that the men are growing very bored and restless, and are taking to the pubs. Remember Crenshaw from Connecticut, the son of your parents' friends? He's enamoured of a—a lady of the evening! I do my best to watch over them, but I'm only one man! They signed on to go to sea, and instead they're up the Thames, expected to wait all summer—"

"You needn't beat me over the head with this. I take your meaning." Raveneau frowned as he thought of Franklin Crenshaw, who had come from Essex, Connecticut, to join his crew, and whom he had known since the boy's birth. Nathan's father, André Raveneau, was Franklin's godfather. "How was I supposed to know that this other matter would arise? I can't live two lives at once!"

"Clearly you're very busy here. I gather that your charge was the girl who leaned out the window and called to me?" Zachary watched him with a sly smile. "Very pretty indeed. I can see that you might enjoy playing her nursemaid better than captain of the *Golden Eagle*, but you did have a prior commitment to your crew. . . ."

"You're a wretched snake, Zach." Nathan poured himself a brandy from his private flask and drank. "You know very well that this is about obtaining that land in Barbados, to get at Crowe, and has nothing to do with Miss Beauvisage's beauty."

"Oh, of course not! You're the last person who'd notice a tempting morsel like her, let alone want a taste!"

"Are you trying to drive me to sack you?" Raveneau's face was dark and threatening. "Let up, or I will."

The smaller man replied cheerfully, "I'm shakin' in me boots, guv'nor!"

"I despise you. I rue the day our fathers pushed us together." Nathan stalked away. "Devil take it, there is a great deal at stake here, including Miss Beauvisage's safety!" Bracing one booted foot on the trunk beneath the window, he ran a hand through his black hair and sighed. "I simply can't leave, Zach. Not yet. In fact, I shouldn't even be away from Adrienne for this long—"

"Oh, so it's *Adrienne* now! I knew it, for I am never wrong about these matters!" He took a closer look at his friend. "I'll admit, though, that this is different from your usual dalliances. Usually, after a few days, you're itching to get away to sea. . . ."

"This is not a *dalliance*."

"I haven't seen you stay put with one female for this long since—" Zach paused, then said, "Eloise."

Nathan went white. "You know better than to mention her name, Minter! And, in any event, you are missing the mark altogether with Adrienne. Don't try to analyze my motives!" He glowered at him. "You can't stay here either. I'll have to invent a convincing story as it is."

"If you're going to send me back without one shred of advice, or better yet a plan, you may return to the *Golden Eagle* in a few weeks to find she has no crew. You and I can't sail a packet to Barbados on our own, nor can we recruit men on the London docks who could hold a candle to the ones you have already handpicked with such care." His well-rehearsed speech ended, Zachary helped himself to the brandy and waited.

"You know me too well."

"Someone must," he agreed with a grin.

"All right then." Nathan thought again of Franklin Crenshaw. He knew what his own father would advise. "We cannot leave for Barbados until my work here is completed, but perhaps we can find another way to occupy the men. You may bring the ship to the Isle of Wight, which you'll recall is just below the port of Southampton, not far from here. Drop anchor in Freshwater Bay and wait to hear from me." He paused, enjoying the plans. A grim smile touched his lips. "There isn't much on the Isle of Wight. I don't even know if there are any pubs there, and you'll be far enough from Southampton so that the crew should stay out of trouble. What do you think?"

"You're a crafty fellow, Captain Raveneau."

"Stop calling me that. Someone will hear you." Nathan shook his head, remembering Minter's recent memory lapse. "I was furious the moment I saw you today— reading my surname from a scrap of paper!"

"Better than getting it wrong altogether, eh? You've scolded me enough for now, don't you think?"

"Hardly."

"I'd like to say that I think you've hit on a fine plan, sir. The men will be overjoyed to be setting sail, even if they're only going into the channel a few miles. I'll tell them that you'll be joining us soon and that we must spend our days anchored off the coast preparing the *Golden Eagle* for the return of its captain!"

"Good." The two old friends shared a smile. Raveneau nearly confided his suspicion that this would be for the best, for he couldn't help wondering if he might one day need his ship unexpectedly. He had a vague inkling that there could be developments at Harms Castle beyond his control.

Adrienne was a strong force in her own right. However, other unpredictable characters were coming to the fore. Once Nathan had thought he could shape this adventure himself, keeping one eye on Adrienne and the other on the villainous Frakes-Hogg. Now there was no telling what might happen next.

"If you need me," Zachary Minter said, "you can send word to the ship. I won't have far to come from the south coast."

"Yes, that's true." Nathan's eyes softened. Minter's loyalty was a gift beyond price. "I shouldn't send you away so hastily. Let's go to the kitchen and have something to eat, and you can tell me about the crew. If you continue to know so much more than I, by the time I rejoin the *Golden Eagle*, the men might decide to mutiny against me!"

Zach puffed out his narrow chest. "Captain Minter . . . It does have a certain ring to it, I must admit!"

Laughing, they went out into the corridor together in time to see Jarrow marching up the staircase with a tray.

"Are you taking tea to her ladyship?" Nathan asked. When the butler nodded, he said, "I would be grateful if you could tell her, and Miss Beauvisage, that I am obliged to spend a little time with my—my cousin." Nathan gestured toward Minter, who could not have looked less like his relative. "He's from America. I thought I should have a bite of stew with him before he leaves for London."

The butler looked bored. "The weight of this tray prevents me from lingering to hear more of this fascinating tale, Essex. I shall give her ladyship your message."

The two men went in the other direction, toward the servants' staircase, and Jarrow continued on to the library. When he entered, Adrienne looked up expectantly.

"If you are anticipating the return of Mr. Essex," Jarrow announced, "I have been asked to inform you that he will not be coming. It seems that that redheaded fellow is his cousin from America, and they're going off together."

Noticing Adrienne's crestfallen expression, Huntsford said, "I find it very odd that Essex's own cousin had to consult a piece of paper to find his *surname*! Don't you think that's odd, Mummy?"

"Quite!" She stirred her tea. Her eyes were like little raisins as she studied first Adrienne and then her son. "I say, children, why don't we go to Winchester this very afternoon? It's so very pleasant outdoors under the rainbow. The sun is shining on all the droplets of rain that cling to the leaves."

"Why, Mummy, how poetic you are!"

"I don't think that Mr. Essex wants me to venture outdoors without him," Adrienne protested. "I agree that it's silly, but he is adamant."

Huntsford Harms took her arm with a commanding air and declared, "My dear Miss Beauvisage, I can promise you that I am every bit as capable of protecting you as that oaf! If Mummy wishes to travel to Winchester now, then we must do so, and I shall prove my mettle to you."

"It's not really necessary, my lord—" Adrienne's rebellious streak nearly took control, but she resolved to soldier through. "I mean, you don't have to prove anything to me, my lord. I never doubted your gallantry."

"Good, good!" Lady Thomasina clapped her plump hands. "Jarrow, send for the berlin and a team of horses. And, Miss Beau, do dash off and bring back my blue silk turban and whatever else one takes to town." She waved her away. "Hurry now!"

Her son was about to go off in search of his own hat and cane, but as he passed the tub chair, a hand clasped the tail of his frock coat. "Hunty, wait!"

"What? Why are you whispering?"

"I want to be certain that she's out of earshot," Lady Thomasina murmured. "Yes? Hunty, dear, don't you see that you and I are having the same brilliant notion about Miss Beau? Your regard for her is clear, and I approve most heartily. She would be the ideal woman for you, my dear!"

His brown eyes widened. "Let's not get carried away, Mummy. I mean, I don't think we ought to leap to conclusions."

"Why not? She puts your other bits of muslin in the shade. And, Hunty, I can see that, in order for you to woo her, you must have Nathan Essex out of the way. I adore him, but he's far too much of a distraction for that girl." Lady Thomasina wore a satisfied smile. "You see, I can help you. I am in charge, after all, and wield a good deal of power over both of them."

Huntsford tapped a long finger against his mouth. "Ah, yes. Point taken, Mummy." He might not have the same goal in mind as she did, but that didn't mean he would turn aside her efforts to help him win Adrienne. His mother was quite right; she could be very effective in aiding him to come between Adrienne and Nathan.

Chapter Ten

THE COBBLED STREETS OF WINCHESTER GLISTENED
with rain, though the sun now shone brightly. It was a market day, and the hilly town was crowded with people who had come from the green Hampshire downs to sell or buy wares.

High Street was the center of the market, so Adrienne, Huntsford Harms, his mother, and their coachman found that College Street was even quieter than usual. The creak of cartwheels and the din of voices were replaced by birdsong from nearby gardens and the gentle murmur of the River Itchen.

They had disembarked from the berlin near the castle wall by the river. Adrienne couldn't help remembering the scene of high drama that had occurred there, when Walter Frakes-Hogg had tried to force her into the old tower. Days later, it all seemed like a bad dream. With Huntsford on one side and Adrienne on the other, Lady Thomasina waddled west along College Street quite happily, pointing out landmarks to her companion.

"So much history here, Miss Beau! You French have no idea."

"I'm not really French, my lady," Adrienne hastened to amend. "My parents were both raised in Philadelphia and settled in France only after they were married. Our château was my great-grandmother's ancestral home."

"Hmm. Well, you weren't raised in England, in any event. That was my point. Look to your left, Miss Beau.

There is Winchester College! It was begun in 1382 by William of Wykeham, who also founded New College at Oxford. . . ."

Adrienne listened with one ear to her ladyship's speech about the history of the college. She could see the Gothic buildings beyond a particularly lovely garden that made her think of Jane Austen, whose home adjoined those grounds. How much pleasure she must have taken from those bright flowers during her final summer.

When they reached 8 College Street, Adrienne stared at the modest house. It was easy to imagine the invalid authoress sitting in the first-floor bow window and watching people walk where Adrienne now stood. "Do you suppose that she was happy here at all?"

"She was only in residence from May until July," Lady Thomasina said in gloomy tones. "Dr. Lyford told me that he hoped to cure her and that she did walk about the rooms during the day. She took a sedan chair outdoors at least once. . . ."

The medieval Kingsgate was nearby, at the end of College Street, and Adrienne felt a chill under its shadowed arch. It was difficult to understand why someone as young and gifted as Jane Austen should die. "I suppose that she must not have known the end was near. I mean, she did come to Winchester to be near her physician, hoping for a cure. . . ."

Huntsford spoke up at last. "I say, too much doom and death for one day, don't you think? Why don't we bundle into the coach and go somewhere for a nice spot of sherry?"

"I want to go inside the cathedral first," Adrienne said stubbornly.

"Whatever for? Just a lot of flying buttresses or some such!"

As they started north to the cathedral precincts, the berlin following at a distance, his mother whispered, "She wants to see her grave."

"Grave! Bloody hell! Whose grave?"

"Shh, Hunty!" Lady Thomasina gave him a pinch. "Show a little consideration for Miss Beau's sensibilities."

Those words broke through to him. Adrienne had paused
to wait for them in front of the cathedral, and Harms took
that opportunity to mend his image. He strode toward
Adrienne and said, "You're very considerate of Mummy.
She does like the security of one of us on each side."

Adrienne was looking particularly fetching in a lilac-
hued promenade dress with a matching bonnet lined with
white satin. Gazing up at the cathedral, she seemed oblivious to his words. "Isn't it spectacular?" She turned sparkling green eyes toward Lady Thomasina. "I am anxious to
know more."

"I find that I am growing tired, Miss Beau. My legs, you
know. I believe I'll take a seat on this bench, and you go
inside with Hunty. He'll be your guide."

"Oh, my lady, I couldn't leave you—"

"I *insist*. Hunty, do assert yourself."

He seized the moment, clasping Adrienne's hand around
his arm with authority. "Don't argue, Miss Beauvisage.
Mummy wouldn't send us off without her if she didn't truly
want it." Strolling into the great nave of the cathedral, his
mind went blank. Finally, he confessed that although he'd
heard the history of the grand building many times he remembered nothing.

Adrienne found herself quite taken with this uncertain
side of Huntsford Harms. He was usually so self-important
and vain, two qualities that she found terribly dull, but the
sight of him blushing and admitting that he was not a very
fit cathedral guide endeared him to her.

"Never mind, my lord. We'll learn together."

He basked in the light of her smile. "Call me Huntsford.
We are friends, are we not?"

"Yes, of course, and you must call me Adrienne."

As they rambled together through the long nave, she
gleaned bits of the cathedral's story by listening to other
visitors. "The transepts are Norman, of course," whispered
one man, while a tall young lady informed a group of children that the nave, with its intricate web of fan vaulting,
was the work of William of Wykeham.

"Did you hear that?" Huntsford murmured, bending

close to Adrienne's ear. "That fellow certainly was busy! Seems to me he was a bishop."

"There, you see," she teased. "You do remember something!"

They tried with limited success to stifle their laughter, since every sound was magnified to an appalling degree inside the cathedral. An elderly couple standing nearby gave them stern glances, and Adrienne bit her lip.

They found the slab marking Jane Austen's grave in the north aisle of the nave. Seeing his companion's solemn expression, Huntsford put on a suitably respectful attitude. His throat was dry, however, and he badly craved a drink. Moments later he guided her out into the sunshine.

"I had wanted to see the mortuary chests of the Anglo-Saxon kings," Adrienne said with a note of longing. "There is so much history in Winchester! I've heard that there is a Round Table displayed in the old Norman castle not far from here, and some believe it was the one King Arthur used. I don't suppose . . ."

"Dear friend, I should love nothing more than a visit to the Great Hall to view the Round Table, but I fear that we must save that for another day, when we are not accompanied by Mummy." Huntsford feigned disappointment. "Shall we have an outing of our own very soon? Perhaps on Tuesday? We'll do anything you like."

"Yes. I accept with pleasure." As they walked back toward Lady Thomasina, Adrienne continued to chatter about the legends of King Arthur, and Huntsford made charming replies. His eyes caressed her attentively, and it occurred to her that it was enjoyable to be treated thus. Nathan, on the other hand, was arrogant, cynical, and apt to behave as if she were a mischievous child rather than a beautiful, fascinating woman.

"Ah, there you are, you two!" Lady Thomasina could not have looked more smug if they'd appeared wearing wedding rings. "Clearly, you are getting on very well. I knew that Hunty needed more intellectual stimulation than those other gooseish girls could provide."

"Mummy, do try to contain yourself," he said, smiling through clenched teeth. "You'll frighten her away."

"Nonsense!" Adrienne's tone was cheerful. She took her ladyship's other arm and together they hefted her to her feet. "Shall we treat ourselves to tea at the Wessex? I hear they have lovely little cakes and sweets."

"Why not champagne?" Huntsford suggested.

The mood was nearly euphoric as the trio started down the footpath toward Kingsgate Street and their waiting berlin. Then Adrienne happened to look off across the cathedral grounds. A man was striding toward them, pushing aside the branches of a red oak tree that had grown across his path.

Could it be . . . ?

"Adrienne!" the man called. Emerging into the sunlight, he raised a hand to her.

"We mustn't dawdle," Lady Thomasina cautioned. The berlin was just a few steps away. The coachman opened the door as they approached.

"Nathan!" Without a thought, she released Lady Thomasina's arm and ran toward him, skirts raised. It was the most amazing thing—Adrienne's entire body was transformed by his presence. Her face was warm, her heart raced, and a certain joy rushed through her veins so that she tingled as she drew near to Nathan.

"How many times have I told you not to go off without me?" he scolded, his handsome face forbidding. He reached out and grasped her arm with one hand, as if to assure himself that it was indeed she, and that she was whole and safe. "I cannot turn my back for one hour—"

"Why are you so relentlessly horrid?" Adrienne tried to turn away from him, pouting. "How could I have imagined that I missed you today?"

Behind her, his expression softened. "Missed me, did you? What exactly did you miss?"

She felt his chest graze her back, and a jolting weakness overtook her. "Don't be impossible. I—I was simply looking forward to our outing. I had the mad idea that you and I would have fun, but clearly you were otherwise occupied with that suspicious fellow you call your cousin!"

"Devil take it, we weren't supposed to come into Winchester until tomorrow! If I'd guessed that you would go off and throw yourself in the way of danger—"

"Huntsford has protected me very nicely."

Nathan could scarcely refrain from picking her up and carrying her off. It was particularly maddening to realize that the Harmses were watching. "So, it's Huntsford now? If you are harboring any notion that *he* can be trusted to look after you, kindly dispel it immediately!"

"I think you are jealous!" Eyes flashing, Adrienne turned back just in time to see the exposed emotion in his face. Every nerve in her body ached for his embrace, longed to taste his kiss. . . .

Several dozen yards away, Lady Thomasina cuffed her son's arm. "Aren't you going to intervene?"

His thoughts were far away, with Walter Frakes-Hogg. It seemed that all the pieces had shifted since the night at the White Ostrich, when he'd promised to kill Nathan Essex. He had never had much hope of doing that, for there was an excellent chance that the bigger man would instead kill *him* in self-defense. It had seemed wise to agree, though, and stall as long as possible, for he didn't trust Frakes-Hogg to treat him fairly in any event.

Harms also feared that, after he'd been employed to murder The Scapegrace, he might be murdered himself just to keep the loose ends tidy. Frakes-Hogg had taken great pains to make certain no one knew he was even in Winchester, let alone associated with Harms. If Huntsford had an "accident," who would suspect Walter Frakes-Hogg?

Adrienne had been a happy diversion from these problems, and his new feelings for her were entirely unexpected. Now, watching Adrienne with Essex, his heart sank. The first step toward shifting the balance would be for Huntsford to prove to Adrienne that he could be just as strong and protective as Essex.

He took snuff and tried to ignore his mother's voice. Perhaps there was a way for Huntsford to correct Adrienne's image of him, drive a wedge between her and Essex, and eliminate the problem of Walter Frakes-Hogg, all at the same time. . . .

* * *

Adrienne allowed Alistair to pour more claret into her glass, and she drank it, then yawned. "I'm not much good to you tonight, I'm afraid."

Across the card table, Huntsford gnawed on a manicured fingernail. "It's all the same anyway. The games, I mean."

Alistair rolled his eyes. "I've known you all my life, Harms, and you've never been bored by gaming, drinking, or—"

"Did I solicit your opinion?" he snapped. "You've had too much to drink. Again."

"So have I," Lady Clair admitted. She propped an elbow on the table and cupped her chin.

"Would you mind if I bid you all good night? It's been a very busy day." Adrienne pushed her chair back.

Following her to the door, Huntsford hovered, wondering what she was thinking. "You haven't forgotten our engagement on Tuesday? I hope you won't change your mind—"

"No . . . although I don't know what Mr. Essex will say. As long as he believes I am in danger, he doesn't like to let me out of his sight."

"Didn't I protect you today?" Huntsford was agitated, but tried to censor himself. Soon enough he'd put his plan into action, and then the tables should turn.

"Yes, you protected me splendidly." Smiling, Adrienne added, "I am grateful, and so very sleepy. Listen to the clock; it is midnight! Good night, Huntsford." With that, she slipped out the door. Carrying a chamberstick, she let the tallow candle's sputtering flame guide her up the back staircase.

On the landing, a window was open to admit wafts of fragrant night air. The breeze extinguished Adrienne's candle but ignited the passions she'd kept in check all evening.

All her pulse points throbbed with anticipation. During the hours of cards with Huntsford and his friends, Adrienne had dreamed of what she would do later. And now, later had come. She'd been feeling wild all day, particularly since her scene with Nathan on the cathedral grounds, and the claret had emboldened her further.

Adrienne was tired of behaving herself, tired of reining in her passions. And, in her heart, she knew that Nathan felt the same. She'd seen the fire in his eyes that very afternoon, and his fingers had sent currents of heat through her body. Something had to give. Tonight.

Before he opened his eyes, Raveneau could smell jasmine, sweet and heavy on the warm air that lapped through the window opposite his bed.

He'd heard something, but perhaps it had come from outside. Years as the captain of his own ship had refined his ability to come awake immediately, with his senses alive.

What had it been? A dream? Nathan nearly let himself sink back into a cushion of sleep but managed first to open his eyes. Moonlight, silvery white and laced with garden scents, washed over his bed. Through the shimmery haze, Raveneau saw Adrienne.

Visionlike, she stood near enough to touch. Her hair was loose, the cognac-hued curls spilling over her pale shoulders, framing her exquisite face. She was wearing white lawn. Soft as gossamer, the gown was diaphanous. Nathan soundlessly drew breath at the sight of her body outlined against the moonlight, curving in a way that made his groin clench with need.

Adrienne hesitated, thinking. She had been about to steal into his bed, but now, clearly, he was awake and as moments passed, Nathan's eyes opened wider and he slowly rose on one elbow. It was a warm night; he was naked down to the white sheet that rippled across his belly and hid the rest of him.

Often she had wondered about his body, but it was more splendid than her virginal imaginings. He was dark against the bedclothes. The muscled contours of his shoulders, chest, and arms drew her eyes, and then mysterious feelings tightened inside Adrienne's body. Little hairs stood up on the back of her neck. Looking at his shadowed face, she found it hard to breathe, and the sight of Nathan's ruffled black hair caused her to stretch out a hand.

"What's wrong?" he said softly. "Are you in danger?"

She flushed. "No. I came—to be with you."

His voice turned rough. "You are mad."

"No." Kneeling on the edge of his bed, she slid her fingers into his shining hair. "Not mad."

"Go back to your own room. I am not a treat you can demand at will—like a hand-painted fan—"

Adrienne nearly laughed aloud at his audacity. Bending near his shoulder, she murmured, "If you imagine that you can deter me with insults, be warned that I am too smart for your tricks."

"No? They always worked before." He bit back a smile. "It's time for the games to end, don't you think? I have the feelings of a woman, and I want them resolved."

"Oh. Good God." She smelled enchanting. When Adrienne trailed her hand through the crisp dark hair covering his chest, Nathan groaned. It had been long weeks since he'd been with any woman, and more and more he hungered for this impossible minx. "Adrienne . . ."

"Oh." Inexplicably, tears crowded her throat. "Yes!" She slid into his open arms and found that lying against Nathan's male body was bliss in itself. He felt unyielding yet welcoming. It seemed that she belonged there, and both of them knew it. "Nathan, ever since that night in the garden—"

"Damn. I know." The words burned his throat. If she made him talk, he'd have to think, and that wouldn't do. "Shh." He caressed the lines of her back and bottom through the lawn nightgown. Adrienne, incurably impetuous, crawled higher, wound her arms round his neck, and began to kiss him. It was a bold experiment. With her tongue touching his and her breasts crushed against his chest, Nathan felt as if he were drowning in a sea of passion. He found the hem of her gown and pulled upward. She moaned.

Trouble, trouble, a voice warned Nathan from deep inside. Physical need had a louder voice, however.

"Oh, oh, you taste delicious," Adrienne managed to whisper. She found herself making little sounds that she didn't recognize, but they didn't seem to bother Nathan. He held her hard against him with one hand, while the other found its way under her nightgown and cupped her backside. Just the sensation of his powerful hand, inches from the source of her need, made her suddenly hotter and moister. She had an urge to push against him but didn't know what it meant.

"You're certain—" Nathan drew back for a moment, staring into her eyes, and the fire flared brighter between them. "If you're not, just say so."

"I want you. I want this more than anything in the world."

If he'd been in his right mind, Raveneau would have taken those words as a strong warning, but he couldn't think. He rolled Adrienne over into the pillows and tugged the gown over her head. His gaze was like a brand, searing the halo of moonlit hair around her face and the irresistible curves of her breasts and hips. He hardly dared look lower in search of the place he wanted to be so much it hurt . . .

"You are too, too beautiful."

"No," she argued, "you are." The sight of him braced above her was frighteningly stirring. Adrienne splayed her hands over his chest and felt her own nipples tighten in response. Her eyes strayed lower, and she glimpsed his manhood, poised in the shadows like a weapon. Indeed, she had never imagined—

Nathan kissed her slowly, savoring each sweet touch of their tongues. He used his lips like warm feathers, brushing the hollows of her face, her throat, her inner arms, and between her fingers. Adrienne's muted groans became less human-sounding. He feasted gently on each of her breasts, alternately suckling and teasing, until she arched against him and nearly climaxed without understanding. His own need was almost beyond bearing.

She opened her thighs to him in welcome. He touched her and she shuddered, panting. "Christ, you're wet—"

"Please, Nathan." She savored his name. "Nathan . . . Essex."

Raveneau had never wanted anything more in his life than to be inside Adrienne. He wanted something beyond mating, and the strength of that need, coupled with the sound of a false name, worked on him like a bucket of ice. Everything else rushed over him then: his obligation to protect her, his promise to Nicholai to keep his daughter virtuous until her twenty-first birthday, and the harsh realization that Adrienne might well be in love with him. No, not him . . . Nathan Essex.

What would the dawn bring? If he continued and met his immediate needs, Nathan would have a new set of problems on the morrow. Serious problems. Once a man's word was broken and his honor discarded, what good was he?

"I can't."

"Yes! I'll help you."

Her soft hand, reaching downward, was like a flame to be avoided at all costs. "That sort of help is *not* what I need." Nathan pushed himself away, out of danger. Lying beside Adrienne, he smoothed back her hair. She was staring at him in disbelief. "Thank God I came to my senses."

"Wh-what are you talking about? I don't understand!" She scrambled toward him, but he caught her wrists. For a moment, there was only the sound of her fierce breathing, and then she spoke sharply. "Have you taken vows? Are you a man of the cloth?"

"Of course not."

"Then what the devil do you mean? How dare you speak of coming to your senses!"

"Kindly lower your voice before the entire house hears us!" No longer apologetic, Nathan took Adrienne by her shoulders, pushed her on her back, and glared down at her, every muscle in his body taut as he crouched on the bed-clothes. "I am trying to remind you, Miss Beauvisage, that I am in the employ of your father, and it would be a breech of his trust if I were to plant my seed in his daughter! Perhaps you don't give these matters as much thought—"

"Ohh! I hate you!"

"Haven't we had this conversation before? Numerous times, in fact?"

"I'll say it again then! I despise you!" To Adrienne's fury, he silenced her by covering her mouth with his hand. She in turn sank her teeth into as much of his palm as she could get hold of, but he didn't budge.

"I'd quit that if I were you," he suggested. "Has anyone ever given you a good spanking? No? A pity. I wonder if it's too late?"

Adrienne began thrashing around, wildly, so he straddled her hips. "Beast! Scoundrel!" came her muffled accusations. It only increased her rage to realize dimly that he was far more attractive and desirable than she had ever imagined.

"Put your hands up. Come on." Nathan managed to drag the nightgown back over her head in an effort to restore her modesty. "For God's sake, be still, you little hellion! You are very fortunate that I am not a different kind of man, for you are trying my patience to the breaking point. If I didn't feel guilty for my part in this, I would gladly repay you now in kind."

Adrienne was horrified to feel tears burn her eyes. "I just don't understand!"

"Look—" He took a deep breath. His head began to throb. "It's not that I don't *want* you in my bed, but this simply cannot be. In this life, we are not able to have everything that we want. Hasn't anyone told you that?" The sight of Adrienne's face, turned sideways in the weak light, moved Nathan more than he cared to admit. Why was he so bewitched by her? The urge to take her in his arms and fulfill all her dreams was achingly powerful.

"Let me up." Her voice was raw. "I want to go back to my own bed. I never want to see you again."

He released her and covered himself with the sheet again. "Is it so difficult to believe that I could be doing the right thing for both of us?"

"Now? No, it's not difficult. Now I thank God that it didn't happen." Her heart hurt terribly as she gathered the shreds of her pride and left Nathan's room.

Chapter Eleven

"I'D LIKE TO KNOW WHERE YOU WERE LAST NIGHT, Miss Beau! I rang and rang for you." Lady Thomasina settled her bulk into a chair newly placed on the stone terrace. When Adrienne didn't reply immediately, she fumbled for her quizzing glass and sought the girl out, squinting. "Hmm? Have you nothing to say for yourself?"

Adrienne plucked her basket from a nearby bench and hurried away, down the shallow steps that led to the garden and the boxwood maze. It would be terrible if the old woman saw her bright cheeks. "There's nothing to tell, your ladyship!" she called back in a studiedly offhand tone. "I must not have heard you ring, being asleep—or else I was still downstairs, playing whist with Lord Harms and his guests. Yes, that was probably the reason I didn't answer."

"March up here, young lady. I want to have a look at you."

"Have I done something wrong?"

"I wish that you would tell *me*." She fixed her companion with a shrewd stare. Adrienne was looking particularly pretty this morning. Clad in a high-necked gown of French muslin, she had also wound her hair into a chaste braid, pinned to the crown of her head. Something was different, though, and it had nothing to do with the purity of her costume. In fact, it seemed to Lady Thomasina that Miss Beau was more womanly than she had been the day before. "What time did you leave Hunty and his friends?"

Why did she keep blushing? "You know, I am really not feeling quite the thing. I'm so awfully warm!"

"Indeed?"

"My lady, I really don't remember what time I retired last night." Adrienne tried a firm tack. "I confess that I drank a bit of claret, and my wits were rather muddled. I'm sorry I didn't hear you ringing. Do let us speak of something else."

Just then Nathan came through the doors to the castle. He carried *Pride and Prejudice* in one hand and a bowl of cherries in the other. At first, he seemed not to notice Adrienne.

"Why, Mr. Essex, you must bid Miss Beau a good morning," Lady Thomasina prompted. "She isn't feeling well. Do you see how flushed she is?"

He nodded to Adrienne. "Good morning. I hope your symptoms pass. Perhaps it's just the weather. Rather warm and humid after that rain."

She promptly felt the blood leave her face. The urge to glower at him was overwhelming. "I thank you for your brilliant observations, sir."

"My, my! What's this all about?" her ladyship cried. "I wonder if you're genuinely ill, Miss Beau. I wonder if your mood is a result of the claret you imbibed last night, the late hours you kept, and whatever you were doing that kept you from your own bed!"

Adrienne gasped. "My lady—I am shocked—"

"What do you think, Mr. Essex?" Lady Thomasina tied a lace cap over her powdered wig, watching him from the corners of her eyes. "No secrets among us, are there?"

He put the cherries in Lady Thomasina's lap and looked directly at her. "I think the sun is putting you in a temper, my lady. Why not forget about this other matter and let me read you a chapter about Miss Bennet and Mr. Darcy."

"I do like your reading voice best. No offense to Miss Beau, of course."

Fuming, Adrienne took her gathering basket and marched off into the stiflingly hot maze. She'd been making bouquets all week, so there wasn't much left to cut, but she examined each budding flower, shears poised, before deciding to wait a few more days. Just the sound of Nathan's distant voice, reading aloud in an insufferably entertaining manner, made her blood boil.

Was Nathan right? Had she been the one who had behaved like a madwoman, while he had been the defender of good and reason? Was he the better person?

An innocent pink rosebud climbed over the hedge and Adrienne cut it. "Take that!" she whispered fiercely. A bead of perspiration drizzled down her temple. Just then Nathan rounded an overgrown boxwood corner, and she jumped in surprise.

"What are you doing here?"

He held out her simplest chipstraw bonnet. "I thought you might need this. It's getting hot."

"Nothing you do can ever change the fact that I loathe you." With that disclaimer, she snatched the bonnet and put it on. "I suggest that you return to your reading before Lady Thomasina's suspicions are further inflamed."

"She fell asleep after three pages," he said, amused. "Angus and her ladyship are both snoring in the sunlight."

"Aha. Perhaps you are not so captivating after all!"

"I have never claimed to be." Nathan closed the distance between them, and Adrienne had no place to go except backward into hedge.

"Don't touch me! I still have bruises—"

"Hush." His blue eyes darkened until they resembled the ocean under storm clouds. Their bodies were so close that he could feel the heat coming off her, but Nathan was careful not to make physical contact. "I want you to behave yourself when others are present. You may hate, despise, and loathe me, but I must insist that you make an effort to conceal those emotions from Lady Thomasina and the others."

"Why shouldn't she know the truth?"

"You might want to reconsider what the truth *is*, chit. After all, I was not the one who came into your bed uninvited. Or have I got it wrong?"

Her face was burning. "Cad!" She longed to slap him, but her hands were full.

"Am I? I believe that a cad would have taken the—ah,

gift you offered so impulsively—and insistently—last night."

As Adrienne made another heated reply, Lady Thomasina was watching from the terrace, waiting for her son to appear in response to the message she had sent with Hortie. She couldn't see more of Nathan and Adrienne than the top of his dark head and the high brim of her bonnet, but she could hear enough of the tone of their conversation to arouse her curiosity fully.

"Mummy, why did you send for me?" Huntsford was clearly out of patience as he strode onto the terrace. Spying Angus, he scowled and the terrier disappeared under her ladyship's petticoats. "It took better than an hour to perfect this morning's cravat. We just finished, and I am *ravenous*. A magnificent breakfast arrived the very moment your gruesome lady's maid brought your summons. Do hurry!"

"How dare you insult poor Hortie? Sit down, and lower your voice. Essex and Miss Beau are in the maze, and they think I am napping, so let us not call attention to ourselves."

"What do you want?"

"Only to suggest to you that you begin to devote yourself seriously to the pursuit of Miss Beau. Something has caused a rift between her and Nathan Essex. She is angry with him but hardly indifferent. If you can manage to strike while the iron is hot, Hunty, you may be able to usurp his place in her thoughts."

He was admiring the reflection of his rigidly starched shirtpoints in the nearest window. "Tell me again why you are so keen on this match between me and Adrienne."

"Actually, my reasons aren't as devious as they might seem. I certainly think that she would be an excellent choice for you, and possesses a great deal more intelligence, goodness, and spirit than your other ladybirds—"

"For God's sake, Mummy, Clair is the daughter of an earl!"

"Well, it doesn't show. She's not real quality." Her ladyship popped an overripe cherry into her mouth. "I must confess, however, that the main reason I'm in favor of this match is my own regard for Miss Beau. She'd be good to me."

Had he heard his mother's voice catch? "I say, you needn't worry in any case. Aren't *I* good to you?"

"Hunty, darling, you had better get on with it. Every moment that Miss Beau is with Nathan Essex rather than you is a moment that might bring them closer."

"I have to eat. Jarrow brought me kippers and eggs and berries with cream. As soon as I've finished, I'll return to shower Adrienne with attention."

"Good." Lady Thomasina's puffy face softened further. "I'll think of another errand to occupy Nathan. Perhaps he can help me look for a lost book! I could make up a title."

Nodding absently, Huntsford started to leave, then paused in the doorway and added, "I can't stay here long today, however. If I'm to make any real headway with Adrienne, there's a task I must perform in Winchester. . . ."

"Whatever do you mean?"

"Never mind. It's nothing that concerns you, Mummy."

Puzzlement furrowed the old woman's brow, but then she noticed Nathan wending his way back through the garden maze. Just as Huntsford disappeared inside the castle, Lady Thomasina dropped her head to one side, closed her eyes once again, and pretended to snore.

After breakfast, Huntsford Harms dashed back downstairs in time to find Adrienne returning from the garden. His mother and Nathan had conveniently disappeared, so Harms took one look at the few meager buds in Adrienne's basket and volunteered to show her a place where dozens of roses were in full bloom. There followed an hour of pleasure that surpassed the camaraderie they had shared at Winchester Cathedral. This time Nathan did not intrude.

Huntsford took Adrienne to a ruined wall behind the stable. Old roses clambered over the stones in a sweet-smelling palette of softly faded colors. She held the basket, and he cut flowers until roses seemed to fill Adrienne's arms. They were laughing as they walked back to the castle, but then Huntsford was forced to leave her. With regret, he explained that he had an unbreakable prior engagement, adding a vague comment regarding an old school chum.

No sooner had Adrienne gone off to the kitchen to arrange vases full of flowers on the long worktable than Huntsford fairly vaulted up the stairs to his rooms. There he dressed himself in riding clothes, took another stairway back out of the castle, and returned to the stable to borrow a horse.

The afternoon sun was beating down by the time Harms emerged from the pastoral Hampshire hills into the town of Winchester. He made his way straight to the inn where Walter Frakes-Hogg had been lodging for weeks. Minutes later he stood outside the older man's door, knocking.

Huntsford had to try more than once before Frakes-Hogg finally cracked the door and peered out. "Who is it?" he hissed.

"It's Harms. Who else could it be?"

"What the devil are you doing here? How did you find me? I told you that you must never be seen in my lodgings!" Even as he spoke, Frakes-Hogg looked out, then right and left, and pulled Harms into the small, neat room. "What is it? You can't stay, you know!"

"Good God, how much have you had to drink?" Huntsford was shocked by the stench. "Surprised you can stand, sir."

"Yes, but I am a surprising fellow!" Frakes-Hogg returned to a wing chair by the window that overlooked High Street and picked up his glass of brandy. "I'd invite you to join me, but I haven't more than a few drops left, and I'm 'fraid I'll need those myself."

"No doubt." So this was how Walter Frakes-Hogg spent his time. No wonder he was such a repellant human being. "I've come to tell you that I've found a way for you to have Adrienne and for us to do away with Raveneau all in one sweep."

"Indeed? You have my rapt attention. Do proceed." Frakes-Hogg's bloodshot eyes were shuttered by grayish lids.

"Here is my question for you: How would you like to

enter Adrienne's bedchamber, well after midnight, when she is sleeping? I can arrange it, and I'll let you in. Can you imagine how utterly terrified, and helpless, she would be? I will go in with you and help you to blindfold and gag her—but of course she won't know it is I."

"Quite an intricate scheme, young tulip."

"Yes. I think it will work."

"I take it you will leave me alone with her then? We shall need our . . . privacy."

Huntsford cleared his throat, nodding. "Yes, in a manner of speaking, you'll be alone. I'll hide in the armoire near her door. After a bit, I'll open the door and pretend to scream or some such, as if it were Adrienne, to sound the alarm for Nathan. He'll come galloping to the rescue, I will come out of the armoire as he passes, and *voilá*—we'll be rid of him."

"It does sound plausible." Frakes-Hogg drank down the brandy. "What are you going to use to kill him? A knife?"

Harms began to sweat. "Yes. Don't you agree?"

"Perhaps it would be wise to club him first, to minimize the possibility that he might struggle."

"Yes." Huntsford looked at his watch. "Now that that is settled, here is the map I have made for you of Harms Castle." After taking it over to Frakes-Hogg's chair, he opened the sheet of parchment and pointed. "I've written the times and other instructions on the back, so there won't be any confusion between us. Here is the layout of the house. The room I have marked with an *X* is Adrienne's bedchamber. You can come up these back stairs to get there quickest. Over here you see Essex's room. He's very close, so there isn't any chance that anyone will come to save her except him."

"What then? What shall we do afterward?"

"I'll make certain no one hears or interferes while you make your escape. When you're gone, I thought I could just blame the dead man for everything. I'll untie Adrienne, remove her blindfold, and tell her it was Nathan pretending to be you."

"Really! Do you think it will work?"

"I'm quite certain it will. They've been quarreling. Why shouldn't she believe me, when I am the man who has saved her life? During the attack, Adrienne will be stunned and confused, so it should be easy enough to reshape her view of events."

Frakes-Hogg rubbed his reddening nose. "I don't know if this quite suits me. I want Adrienne to know that she is paying for what she did to *me*. If, afterward, Nathan Raveneau becomes the villain, what is the point?"

Since most of the plot Harms had outlined to Frakes-Hogg was false, designed only to get him into Adrienne's room, it was hard to find the patience to continue with their conversation. Huntsford rose and paced to the window. "Why don't I tell her, then, that Nathan was in league with you, helping you to tie her up and blindfold her? I'll explain that you escaped while I was fighting with Nathan. How's *that*?"

"Much better." A reptilian smile curved Frakes-Hogg's mouth. "Much. I should like her to believe she is still in danger. . . ."

"Fine then. I must be going. I suggest that you have a long nap to sober up, then a hot meal."

"You needn't worry, my boy." Frakes-Hogg followed him to the door, making every effort to appear dignified. "I pride myself on my clear head. I shall be at Harms Castle at one o'clock this morning."

"Excellent."

He gripped the younger man's arm with clawlike fingers. "You needn't worry," he repeated. "I have waited too long for this night to make any mistakes. I've dreamed of taking revenge on Adrienne Beauvisage, and I mean to make the most of it."

"I hope that you shall, sir. Good afternoon." As he spoke, only Harms was aware of the other layer of meaning his words held. He couldn't afford to let one drop of irony creep into his tone, for the ultimate success of his plan depended on Walter Frakes-Hogg trusting him.

Adrienne stayed up long after Lady Thomasina had fallen asleep. She sat by the window in her tiny room, reading and wondering what Nathan was doing in his own quarters across the corridor. It was so warm that both of them had left their doors ajar to allow a better breeze, and if she peeked out she could catch a glimpse of him sitting at his desk, writing in the mysterious book.

He'd told her to forget about him, and she wanted to, but when she tried to cast him from her thoughts, her heart would begin to ache. It was very confusing.

"Adrienne?"

Startled, she looked up, instinctively hoping that the male voice was Nathan's. Instead, Huntsford Harms was discernible through the partially open door. He held a candlestick in one hand and a vase of wild roses in the other.

"How kind of you!" Adrienne put her book aside and scrambled up from her chair to let him in. "You are very sweet, Huntsford."

He colored slightly. "It's very easy to be nice to someone as enchanting as you are, my dear Adrienne. I thought you ought to have your own bouquet of roses to remember our little outing this morning. . . ."

"They are more beautiful than ever. Thank you." She took the vase and buried her face in the fragrant, pale blooms. "I shall put them next to my bed."

"Perhaps they'll help you sleep. It's getting late, you know, and you need lots of sleep to help you contend with Mummy."

Over Huntsford's shoulder, she saw movement in Nathan's room. Was he listening? Was he jealous? Adrienne looked into Huntsford's eyes and wondered if she would not be better off caring for someone like him. Huntsford clearly adored her, and underneath all his pretensions, he seemed to be a good person. "You're very thoughtful, and I appreciate that."

Speechless for once, he wondered if her kind, steady gaze was meant to be an invitation. With trembling fingers, he touched her cheek, then dared to touch his mouth to hers. Adrienne did not avoid his kiss. In fact, her lips were soft—perhaps even responsive. If it wasn't midnight, and so imperative that Adrienne be sleeping by one o'clock, he might dare to go further. . . .

Just then there was a sound behind them and a hand tapped on Huntsford's shoulder.

"I beg your pardon, sir, but Miss Beauvisage is not permitted to have male visitors in her bedchamber."

Huntsford looked around to find Nathan Essex looming over him, his expression dark and threatening. "Kindly go away, old chap. I am Miss Beauvisage's host, as it were, and as this is my house, I won't have you instructing me as to where I can go!"

Enjoying the male rivalry, Adrienne exclaimed, "Mr. Essex, I shall entertain whomever I choose, whenever I choose—"

"The devil you will." His jaw was clenched.

"This is neither the time nor the place for this conversation," Adrienne retorted. "I am tired, and no doubt Lord Harms is, too." She turned to Huntsford. "I apologize for Mr. Essex's poor manners. Let us all say good night, shall we?"

"Whatever pleases you, dear Adrienne." Smiling into her eyes, Harms bowed, glared at Nathan, and sauntered off down the corridor.

Adrienne motioned for Nathan to leave her doorway. It was hard for her to look at him for fear he'd read all the emotions in her eyes. "Good night."

His own heart was in turmoil as he pivoted and returned to his room, pausing only to add "Do not imagine that I was jealous. I was only trying to save you from your own rash self and do the job your father has employed me to do."

More confused than ever, Adrienne closed her door and got ready for bed. The scent of Huntsford's roses seemed to envelop her pillow as she tossed and turned in the warm night air. By the time she drifted off, she'd pushed the sheet down past her hips and one slender foot peeked out into the moonlight.

Her dreams these days took her back to France. She would float, magically, above the Loire River, which wound like a silken thread through the golden valley of her childhood. Vineyards staggered up the hillsides, and at the top stood the Renaissance castle known as Château du Soleil. It was achingly beautiful, so much more beautiful now that she had chosen not to go home.

Tonight Adrienne dreamed that Nathan Essex was standing in the courtyard with her father and her brother, James. James was always a young boy in her dreams, although in reality he had passed his nineteenth birthday and was as tall as their father.

As the dream continued, Adrienne left the sky and descended the curving marble staircase inside the château. She could see the men in the courtyard through the gallery windows.

"What is Nathan doing here?" she cried.

Her mother appeared behind her. "Don't be silly, Adrienne. You brought him home. He is the perfect man for you, although his breeding and background aren't the best. . . ."

Outside, the men and young James laughed together, throwing their heads back, patting one another on the back. James seemed to lose years each time she looked at him. As the luminous sunlight shone down on the trio, Nathan hoisted the little boy onto his shoulders and turned back toward the château. Adrienne was confused. Was it James he held or their own child?

It was so warm. The scent of orange blossoms drifted up from the château's terraced gardens. Adrienne looked back to speak to her mother, smiling, and a hand came out of thin air to close over her mouth. Something cool and soft covered her eyes as well, but then it tightened painfully, tangling in her hair.

Gone were the sunlit château and all the people she loved. They had only been a dream. Struggling back to consciousness, Adrienne sensed very real danger and tried to scream, but her sounds were muffled by the scented hand over her mouth. It was hard even to breathe. She made little sobbing sounds as stark terror broke over her in waves.

What was happening to her? Who had invaded her room in the middle of the night? The first thought she had had was Nathan, but when he didn't speak, and the efforts to keep her quiet turned rough, another thought occurred to her. It was almost too horrendous to consider that her attacker might be . . . Walter Frakes-Hogg.

The person was tying her hands together, then her feet, grunting in response to her efforts to strike out blindly. At last he seemed to lose patience, gasping, and warned in an unrecognizable, guttural voice, "Be still or die, you strumpet!" Cold steel, terrifyingly sharp, touched the jumping pulse in her throat. Adrienne thought her head would burst from the pressure of the rushing blood. Still, she fought off tears and tried to think. Even though she was helpless, it was possible to remain alert, to assume that she would survive, and to try to remember that any detail might be the one she'd need to notice.

Now that she was awake, Adrienne heard the gentle groan of her door opening, followed by what seemed to be careful footsteps. Had someone else come in? She thought she could make out the distant sound of whispering, but the blindfold was tied over her ears, so it was difficult to be certain. Raw fear swept over her body, this time bringing a sickening sensation in its wake. Adrienne's stomach heaved.

She tried to turn on her side, to curl up protectively, but the hands returned, forcing her onto her back. When he touched her brow, her nose twitched. Was it the same man as before? The answer brought a harsh sense of doom.

"Ah, witch, how long I have dreamed of this night!" The hoarse voice was hideously familiar, as was its stench of brandy. "Don't worry, you needn't speak. I understand. You're overcome by my little surprise, hmm?"

Was Frakes-Hogg going to have the last word after all? How could she have imagined, even for a minute, that someone so wicked would give up and go away? His need for revenge would overpower all saner thoughts—even at the risk of his own life. If she could have spoken through her gag, Adrienne might have wondered if he were Satan incarnate, for Walter Frakes-Hogg seemed more evil than any mere mortal.

But Adrienne couldn't speak, or see, or escape. She raised her bound hands and struck out, which apparently pleased him. Moments later he was sitting on top of her, straddling her hips, holding her hands to his mouth. Bile rose in her throat.

"Sweet, what are you thinking? Regrets?" He leaned over, his wretched breath fanning her face, and kissed her throat. "So soft. I've dreamed of touching you again. Remember, many months ago, when we were still friends and you told me over tea that you believed life was made for dreams? You said that you intended to make all your dreams come true. I took your words to heart, sweet, and devised a few dreams of my own." Frakes-Hogg chuckled softly. Holding her wrists with one hand, he used the other to fondle her, tearing at the bodice of her nightgown until her breasts were exposed. "Oh, my. So lovely. What's that you say? Well, I don't mind if I do. Thank you for offering, Miss Beauvisage."

Shudders of pure revulsion swept over Adrienne as he crushed her breasts in his hands. She bit her own cheek as her pain mounted, and tears wet her blindfold.

Inside the armoire, Huntsford Harms held his breath and waited. It would heighten Adrienne's gratitude if her fear was at its peak when she was rescued, so he had to wait as long as possible. Harms felt quite mad, however, at the thought of Frakes-Hogg putting his hands on her, or spoiling her in any way.

Suddenly Adrienne managed to make a rather high-pitched sound that carried clearly through her gag. It was a sound of such fear and loathing that the hairs rose on Huntsford's neck. The time had come to act.

Dagger poised, he pushed open the armoire door, jumped out, and threw himself at the moonlit figure crouching on Adrienne's bed. Luckily, the element of surprise and his own youth and superior athleticism all worked in his favor. Frakes-Hogg fell over like a stone, his arms flailing. Choking him with one bent arm, Harms drew up the dagger with his other hand and plunged it into Frakes-Hogg's bony chest again and yet again. Moments later the villain emitted strangled gurgling noises, and blood poured from his mouth.

Harms let go, standing, and watched the other man go still on the floor. The awful sounds of his breathing had stopped.

His clothing torn and hair mussed, Harms hurried to free Adrienne of the bonds that he himself had secured just moments before Frakes-Hogg's arrival in her bedchamber. She had given way to sobs of shock and horror, and as soon as he pulled the gag from her mouth, she cried, "Oh, Nathan, thank God you heard—thank God you came!"

A fierce sense of triumph coursed through Huntsford's body. He untied her hands so that she could embrace him, then slipped the blindfold off. "Darling, are you all right?"

Her breasts were heaving; she had buried her face in his shoulder and clung tightly to him with both arms. Her state of shock was so great that a full minute passed before she realized that her rescuer was not Nathan at all, but Huntsford Harms. "Oh—I didn't know—" She looked up in confusion but could not bring herself to disengage. Nor could she bear to glance toward the floor, where Walter Frakes-Hogg lay contorted in death, his eyes staring eerily in the moonlight.

"I would do anything for you," Huntsford murmured reassuringly. "In fact, I couldn't be more pleased to have found a way to earn your favor."

Just then the door to Adrienne's bedchamber swung open. Nathan Essex crossed the threshold, clad only in a pair of breeches. He held a flickering candle in one hand and a pistol in the other.

"Adrienne—are you all right? I was awakened by a terrible noise. What the deuce is going on here?" Every inch of him was taut and guarded as he moved closer, taking in the sight of the dead man on the floor and the unlikely couple who clung together on the bed. "For God's sake! Will someone explain to me what's happened?"

"I've just killed Walter Frakes-Hogg," Harms announced calmly.

"The devil you have!"

"Yes," Adrienne confirmed, covering herself. She began to weep. "Huntsford has saved my life! How can I ever repay him?"

Stabbed by cynical disbelief, Nathan muttered under his breath, "Oh, I'm sure he'll think of something...."

Chapter Twelve

BEFORE LONG THE ENTIRE HOUSEHOLD HAD BEEN roused. Nathan lit lamps in Adrienne's room and called for footmen to remove the body. Hearing the commotion, Lady Thomasina sat up in bed and rang her bell. No one came, and so she put on a robe and turban, then trundled into Adrienne's bedchamber.

"I should like to know why my ringing goes unanswered—" Her querulous voice stopped the very instant she caught sight of Walter Frakes-Hogg's blood-soaked corpse. Nathan tried to turn her back, but it was too late, and she fainted dead away in his arms. Just then a quartet of footmen appeared with sheets and began to cover and wrap the body.

"Harms, take Adrienne out of here—" Nathan said to Huntsford, who continued to cradle Adrienne on the edge of the bed. "Then come back and help me with your mother. I can't hold her up for long!"

Finally, an hour later, Frakes-Hogg had been removed to an unused part of the stable and Huntsford's houseguests had been sent back to their beds. The parish constable would be summoned at dawn, after which the body would be returned to London for burial. Scullery maids scrubbed the bloodstained floor in Adrienne's room. Nathan finally dressed and sat down in Lady Thomasina's sitting room with her ladyship, Huntsford Harms, and Adrienne. Generous glasses of claret were poured and all four of them sipped in silence for a few minutes.

"I seem to be the only person who is completely ignorant of tonight's events," Lady Thomasina complained. "The moment there is any drama, I am forgotten."

"Hardly, my lady." Nathan took out one of the rare cheroots he had smoked since arriving at Harms Castle. He lit it with a candle and drew deeply on the strong smoke. "I know almost as little as you do. Adrienne, why don't you tell us what happened tonight in your room, before I came in?"

She sat close by Huntsford on a velvet chaise, dressed now but still trembling. Nathan's rather harsh demeanor only increased Adrienne's anxiety. Courage and strength had always come easily to her, but tonight she felt like a stranger in her own body. The only person she could depend upon, it seemed, was Huntsford, and she was enormously grateful for his devotion.

"You cannot expect her to talk right now! How can you be so insensitive?" Huntsford glared at his nemesis and slipped an arm around Adrienne. Then, when Nathan glanced away to tap the ash from his cheroot, Harms shot a look at his mother that she was meant to understand. Her ladyship appeared impatient at first, then, slowly, a kind of wonderment passed over her face. Her son continued speaking in a rush. "Perhaps I can tell what I know of tonight's events, to give Adrienne a chance to put the pieces back together." He gazed into her eyes and squeezed her hand. "Hmm? Will that suit you, my dear? Can you bear it?"

"Y-yes. Thank you."

Nathan watched the smoke curl up from his cheroot, brows arched, while under the surface he felt like a crazed beast. He wanted to charge the chaise, pluck Hunty away from Adrienne by his pretty shirtpoints, and send him hurtling face first through the leaded glass window. The thought of Harms screaming as he plunged three stories to the stone terrace was enough to bring a faintly wicked smile to Nathan's mouth.

"I beg your pardon, Essex," Huntsford exclaimed, "but I should like to know how you can possibly smile at a time when Adrienne is undergoing the greatest trauma of her life!"

Their eyes locked in a silent duel. "My expression had nothing whatsoever to do with Adrienne's ordeal."

"Then I suggest that you make an effort to turn your thoughts and attention to her, and away from other amusements." Before Nathan could say something to redeem himself, Huntsford hurried on. "We're all tired. Let me get on with my story, and then we can attempt to sleep a bit more before dawn brings the authorities with more questions."

"Yes, Hunty, by all means tell us!" Lady Thomasina's eyelids were drooping. "Poor darling Angus could waken at any moment in my bed, find me missing, and begin to cry!"

Her son choked back a rude remark about the dog and patted Adrienne's hand. "Really, Mummy, there are far more serious concerns tonight. You see, that dead man lying on the floor—"

"Walter Frakes-Hogg," Nathan supplied.

"Oh—was that his name? I had no idea. How did *you* know the villain, Essex?"

"He was the person who had been threatening Miss Beauvisage. Her father hired me to protect her from him."

"Indeed? What a shame that you failed at that task. It is fortunate, however, that I was able to do what you were not. You see, as I was passing in the corridor, I overheard a man's voice from Adrienne's room." Huntsford began to flush as he spoke, for it was difficult to remember all the details and to get them just right. If Nathan caught him in one mistake, all could be lost. "I had an uneasy feeling about the situation, so I gently pushed the door open. I saw that beast sitting on top of poor, dear Adrienne, who was bound, gagged, and blindfolded in her bed."

Nathan tried to catch Adrienne's eye. "Did Frakes-Hogg break into your room while you were sleeping? Did you hear anything that might give us a clue to how he got in, or how he found your bedchamber?"

Her chin began to shake. "No. I don't remember anything. I was dreaming of home, and my parents, and then I came awake because someone was covering my eyes. . . ." Tears closed her throat, and she curled closer against Harms's shoulder.

"See here, man, must you put her through hell all over again?" Her protector stroked her hair, even as he glared defiantly at Nathan. "As I was saying, I stole into the room, thinking that I would have to try to knock the fellow over the head with a basin or a chair, when I chanced upon a dagger lying on the floor. I picked it up, threw myself at him, and stabbed him to death."

"Oh, Hunty!" his mother shrieked. "I never knew you could be so recklessly courageous! It's the most terrifying yet *romantic* story I've ever heard!"

Nathan's simmering rage reached the boiling point, but he hid it expertly. "A dagger, you say? Miss Beauvisage, do you remember a dagger?"

"Someone held it to my throat at the beginning, when he was tying me up," she whispered.

"Someone?" Nathan seized on that word. "You mean someone other than Frakes-Hogg?"

"Why . . . it did seem so, but everything is a blur, looking back. Please, I am so tired. Can't this wait until tomorrow?"

"That's right, Essex! Have you no sympathy at all for this woman?" Huntsford's heart was pounding with sheer panic. "In any event, Adrienne is clearly confused by her ordeal, and your questions will only confuse her more. I can assure you that I was not blindfolded, and there was only one man in that room—Walter Frakes-Hogg!"

"You have an amazing memory, Harms," Nathan remarked laconically. He leaned back in his chair, legs outstretched, and watched the other man.

"Well—of course I do—but what do you mean?"

Nathan grinned and crushed his cheroot in a saucer. "Just that I am impressed that you would remember so unusual a name as Walter Frakes-Hogg, when you had never heard it before tonight, and I only said it once. It's quite remarkable. I also cannot help wondering what you were doing strolling down the corridor outside Miss Beauvisage's room, when your own apartments are in another wing of the house. What time was it? One o'clock or later?"

"What of it? It is my house, and I can walk anywhere I want, at any hour!" Huntsford swallowed. "Perhaps I was checking on my dear mother!"

"I don't think that's an answer, Harms."

"And I don't think I like your attitude! How dare you raise questions, when I am the person who came to Adrienne's rescue at the moment she needed me most. If I remembered Frakes-Hogg's name, it is only because I was paying close attention. I believe that you are jealous, Essex!" He couldn't resist the urge to stand up and point at Nathan, his voice rising dramatically. "Why not be a man and simply accept responsibility for your failure? Take it on the chin, old chap!"

"Has anyone ever told you that you are barking mad, Harms?" Nathan inquired in measured tones.

"I won't stand for this. I am taking Adrienne back to her room—"

"No," she cried. "I don't want to stay there alone. I never want to sleep in that room again!" The mere thought of Walter's blood pooled on the floor by her bed made Adrienne pale with revulsion.

"Perfectly understandable," Lady Thomasina agreed. "Miss Beau will sleep on the sofa in my bedchamber, with Angus and me for company. I'll give her a drop of laudanum to relax her." She heaved herself to her feet. "Now then, let us all attempt to sleep for a few more hours. Dawn will be here soon enough."

Only Nathan didn't rise. Instead, he pulled a footstool over for his feet and stretched out. "I will stay here. I do not intend to put any more distance between myself and Miss Beauvisage until we know for certain that there isn't anyone else involved. If Frakes-Hogg had an accomplice, that person may be loose in the castle, and I won't take another chance with Miss Beauvisage's safety."

Huntsford Harms opened his mouth to argue, but the expression on Adrienne's face told him that would be a mistake; she only wanted peace. So he pretended that Nathan didn't exist. Savoring the night's victories, Huntsford bade the fair damsel good night and took his leave.

* * *

At dawn, Nathan Raveneau stood in the tall windows of
Lady Thomasina's sitting room and breathed the soft air of
a new day. Sunrise was a pretty sight from any vantage
point, but lately he'd been craving the sugar-pink morning
skies of Barbados. The fiery hues had a way of melting into
the ruffled turquoise ocean, and the breezes were clean and
full of promise.

Now Nathan remembered why he never had been able to
stay long during his visits to London. There was something
about the English people that, in time, drove him over the
edge. He certainly felt that way now, trapped in this motheaten castle with the crackbrained Harmses and their
equally peculiar guests and servants. Every time Huntsford
Harms opened his mouth, Nathan's patience frayed a little
more.

To make matters worse, even Adrienne seemed to be giving way to the madness. How could it be that she no longer
shared knowing looks with Nathan, but sympathized with
that Town Beau instead? If it was only Nathan's own male
ego at risk, he could have borne it, but all his instincts
warned that there was more to Huntsford Harms than met
the eye.

A rustling sound made him turn just in time to see
Adrienne padding across the other side of the room. Clad in
her nightgown and a fringed silk shawl, she looked even
more vulnerable because she was barefoot and her hair
tumbled loose down her back. When she felt Nathan's gaze,
she stopped and turned her face toward the light.

"Good God," he muttered, closing the distance between
them, "you look terrible."

"And you grow more charming by the moment," she replied in a tone edged with weariness. "That's why I don't
want to see you. My nerves can't bear it."

He'd only meant to remark on the way that her shadowed eyes stood out against the dead white of her face; to
let her know that he was worried, that he cared. "Dearest
chit," he murmured tenderly, "I am concerned for you. Perhaps I should have said that no romantic heroine has ever
looked more beautiful in her moment of tragedy."

Adrienne shook her head. "You don't understand what

I've been through. There's simply no room for levity, however well meaning. And now you'll have to step aside. I
must find Hortie, so that she can help me find another bedroom nearby." Her expression was haunted. "Perhaps she'll
be good enough to move my things for me. I just don't
think I can go back in there yet."

"Why don't you ask me for help? What do you think I'm
doing here?"

She looked at him in mild surprise.

"You sit down, and I'll take care of everything." He
gently took her arms and guided her into Lady Thomasina's
favorite chair, which reeked of her powder. "Just rest. Close
your eyes, and when you open them, I'll have your new
quarters arranged and a bath ordered."

"Oh—that would be . . . lovely." Adrienne's face clouded
then. "Has the constable arrived?"

"No. I only sent a messenger within the last hour, so it
will be later in the morning before he arrives. Do you remember who it will doubtless be? Frakes-Hogg's friend, the
beefy fellow who intervened on his behalf in Winchester."

"Oh, well, I suppose there's nothing we can do. At least
Frakes-Hogg is dead now, so there's no more danger. All
the constable can do is record the facts, and they couldn't
be more straightforward, could they? Then he'll go away
and leave us alone. I just want to sleep, on clean sheets, for
days. . . ."

"A fine idea. Meanwhile, rest, and I'll return in a few
minutes."

There was so much he wanted to say to her, but clearly
there were other matters that must be arranged before
Adrienne could listen. As Nathan chose a new room for her
(next to his own) and moved her belongings, he mulled
over all the events surrounding Walter Frakes-Hogg's death.
It just didn't fit together properly. Returning to her tiny
bedchamber to be certain he hadn't left anything behind, he
found himself staring at the horrible stain that was still visible on the floor, despite all the maids' efforts, and then he
looked at Adrienne's bedclothes. Her pillow was wedged
between the bed and the wall, and the sheets were torn

away from the mattress. The linen strips that had been used to bind and silence Adrienne were scattered about. Dear God, how much did that monster put her through before Harms interrupted?

It galled Nathan to think that a supercilious dandy like Huntsford Harms could have been a hero, while he himself had slept in ignorance across the corridor, but it was easier to swallow when he realized how desperately Adrienne had needed rescuing. The realization that Frakes-Hogg might have raped and even murdered her if he'd been allowed to finish sent a chill down Nathan's spine.

He ought to rise to the occasion and thank Harms, but he knew that he simply couldn't get the words out. His gut insisted that there were secrets yet to be told. He just hoped that he could uncover them before anything else happened. . . .

"I thought you might be napping," he said to Adrienne upon reentering Lady Thomasina's suite. She stood in the same window where he had watched the sun rise a short while ago. "Are your feet cold? Come, I'll take you to your new room. I think you'll like it better." He was the picture of kindness as he guided her toward the door. "It's on the other side of the corridor, where the sun is better, and you're just far enough now from her ladyship that you'll have a good excuse for not coming when she rings!"

Adrienne smiled automatically at this sally, but her eyes were distant. "I'm very fond of Lady Thomasina, you know. I feel rather guilty for the laughter we've shared at her expense."

"You're beginning to sound too good for this world, chit. Soon you'll decide to join a convent, and your father will think I've driven you to it." Behind his humorous tone was concern. What would it take to restore Adrienne to her old, headstrong, infuriating self? Had Walter Frakes-Hogg's assault beaten down all her feelings? "Dear Adrienne, do not forget that I am your friend. And remember, too, that all days will not be as dark as this one. You must struggle to find your way back to the light."

After they passed into the corridor, Lady Thomasina

opened the door between her bedroom and sitting room and
peeked out. "Did you hear that, Angus? He is trying to
come between Miss Beau and Hunty!" She glanced down
as the terrier trotted over with a food-stained glove finger.
"I am quite determined in the matter, you know. Nothing
else will do except a marriage between Hunty and Miss
Beau. It will be wonderful for me, of course. I've decided
that I'll call her Addie when she is my daughter. We'll read
together all day long, and she'll give me exquisite
grandbabies, and Hunty won't dare to put me out in the
dower house as long as Addie is his wife." Smiling dreamily, Lady Thomasina waddled over to her dressing table and
found the little cache of old chicken bones she kept for Angus. "Here you go, darling. I do hope you aren't sick again!
Now then, I must listen for Hortie, when she carries the
hipbath to Miss Beau's room. She's been very cross with
me for ignoring her lately, but I'll find a way to win back
her trust, beginning this very morning. There's no one else
who could take my secret warning message to Hunty, and
there's no time to lose!"

Angus wasn't listening. As her ladyship opened her ink-
well, dipped in a worn nib, and began scrawling madly on
a sheet of foolscap, the terrier curled up on her skirts and
gnawed at the spoiled chicken bone.

Adrienne looked around her new bedroom with a wan
smile. "I do like it. I think it will be more cheerful, though
it needs a good cleaning. Thank you for your help, Nathan." She opened the door further, waiting for him to
leave.

It would have been easy to leave this conversation for a
time when she was stronger, but the future was too unpredictable. "I know how tired you are, but I really think we
should talk. Will you sit with me for a few minutes? I'll
leave when Hortie comes with your bath."

"You've sent for her?"

"Yes. God, Adrienne, you're so pale. Every time I look
at you, I am so sorry." He shook his head, searching for
words.

Taking a chair near the window, across from his perch on a high trunk, Adrienne sighed. "There's no point in dwelling on it, is there? None of us can change what happened. I am telling myself that I must be grateful I'm alive and Walter is dead. I'm safe now, and shall remain so."

"Thanks to dear Hunty," he muttered in acid tones.

"Yes, that's right!" At last Adrienne found a reason to raise her voice. "I owe him my life, whether you like it or not, and I cannot allow you to castigate him in my presence any longer. I will not tolerate any more of your mean remarks."

"You . . . won't . . . *tolerate*?" His voice dripped disbelief. "What the deuce has he done to you? Cast a spell?"

"How many times do I have to remind you that Huntsford saved my life? That would be reason enough to feel loyal toward him, but I must add, in all honesty, that we have been forming a friendship for some time. Once I had an opportunity to know him, away from his frivolous friends and *you*, sir, I discovered that he is a nice person. And he treats me like a precious jewel."

"Oh, for God's sake, don't tell me that you've fallen for a lot of flattery! I would have thought that a woman so clearly beautiful and intelligent as you are wouldn't need to be fawned over."

"There, you see? You have a streak of unkindness in you, Mr. Essex." Adrienne turned to stare out the window, her eyes sad. "All women need to receive kind words and compliments. I begin to think that you were right about . . . the other night. The situation between us has resolved itself for the best."

Nathan seemed to be running into a wall at every conversational turn. Perhaps it was time for simple honesty. He took a step toward her and dropped to one knee. "Adrienne, I'm sorry."

"That's good, but I'd really rather that you just leave me in peace. In fact, now that Walter is dead, you can go back to London—or wherever you come from. . . ."

"You don't mean that." He took her hands in his and tried to capture her eyes as well. "Look at me. Please. I'm

sorry if I've been too hard on your ... friend Huntsford.
Perhaps I'm jealous—"

"I wish you would just let it go and be glad that I'm no
longer in danger." Adrienne tried to keep her hands from
shaking, and her cheeks from turning pink. "Oh, Nathan,
why must you make everything so difficult?"

"Because that's what life is with you, my dear. Don't
you know that yet?"

She couldn't stop the smile that tugged at the corners of
her mouth. "Well, maybe I've grown up a bit in the last
day. If you are going to stay here, you'll have to make
peace with Huntsford. However ... you still haven't given
me a reason why I need your protection."

"The reason is that I am not satisfied that you are out of
danger."

"What on earth does that mean?"

"Did you hear any of the questions I asked Huntsford
last night? Much of what happened is quite murky, to put
it kindly—"

"Walter Frakes-Hogg was a murky person! What else
could you mean?"

As Nathan rose to his feet, he considered his next words
carefully. "I am in complete agreement with you about
Frakes-Hogg. He was an evil man. However, I don't understand how he gained access to the house and found his way
to your room. Furthermore, why was Huntsford Harms
passing down our corridor at an hour when he knew that all
of us were asleep? I can't recall seeing him in this part of
the house once before, but he was here twice last night."

"What difference does any of this make? Why should I
care what he was doing there, as long as his presence guar-
anteed my rescue?"

"Didn't the explanation he gave for having the dagger
ring a bit ... false?"

Mounting confusion wore down Adrienne's nerves.
"Where is Hortie? I don't understand why this should take
so long! Perhaps she's waiting for me to come after my
own bath." Adrienne jumped to her feet and tried to pass
by Nathan, but he caught her wrist. Their bodies were mere

inches apart as she demanded, "Why are you saying those things? I don't understand. If you have any regard for me at all, you would try to soothe me this morning, not increase my torment!"

Something seemed to give way inside of Nathan. Admitting that he cared felt rather like weakness, but her pain pushed him beyond that. "This may be hard to understand, but I'm saying these things because I am . . . fond of you—"

"Oh! You have a very odd way of showing it!" Still, it was wrenching to recognize the openness in his eyes and to feel her own heart leap in response. His fingers were warm against her wrist. "Look—Nathan, I simply—"

"Miss Beau? So, here you are, you minx!" It was Lady Thomasina, swathed in old velvets and brocaded silks.

Adrienne quickly backed away from Nathan, and he released her arm. "Your ladyship! I hope you don't mind that I claimed this room for myself. Nathan said it seemed to be unused."

"Mind? Nonsense." All benevolence, the old woman entered, panting a bit. "I am rather surprised to find you here alone with Miss Beau, Nathan dear. I'm not certain that it is entirely seemly, in view of all that's happened. However," she pressed on, waving off his protests, "be that as it may, I have come to give you important news. I was so distraught last night after seeing that gruesome corpse that I didn't speak up when Nathan quizzed poor Hunty about his movements leading up to the heroic rescue of Miss Beau."

Thoroughly suspicious, Nathan waited. "And what was it you 'forgot' to tell me?"

"Why, that Hunty was with me, of course! He had come to my rooms for a sweet mother-son chat, and he had just bade me good night when he passed Miss Beau's room." She met his eyes. "It was just as he said."

Adrienne was flooded with relief. "There, you see?" She whirled on Nathan. "Are you satisfied?"

"For the moment, perhaps." It was pointless for him to argue. The only chance he had to sway Adrienne would be the existence of proof that Huntsford Harms was not all he appeared to be. "I imagine that the constable will be arriving at any moment. I believe I'll go downstairs and wait for him."

"Look for Hortie, will you?" Even as Adrienne spoke, the peevish abigail came through the doorway carrying a hipbath. She was trailed by footmen with containers of hot water. "At last! I have been yearning for a bath ever since . . ." Her voice trailed off.

Seeing the flashes of pain in her eyes, Nathan wavered. Before he could reach her, however, the already crowded room had another visitor. Huntsford Harms squeezed past his mother and went straight to Adrienne.

"My dear, I have been so worried about you." He had toned down his garb, leaving out the elaborate cravat, the fobs and seals at his waist, the chin-scraping shirtpoints, and the polished Hessians. Instead, Harms wore simple riding clothes and his hair was brushed casually. "How are you feeling this morning? Are you bearing up?"

Lady Thomasina joined the pair, and she and her son exuded caring concern toward Adrienne. Watching them, Nathan burned with renewed frustration as he realized that there was no easy solution.

But he couldn't give up either—for more reasons than he could admit, even to himself. "Adrienne?" He looked forbidding as he spoke her name from the doorway. "I'm going down to wait for the constable."

Huntsford interjected, "No need for that, old chap. I knew that it would be difficult for Adrienne to speak about last night, so I went down early and met the constable when he arrived. He understands that our situation was unique, and the outcome was unavoidable."

Stunned, Nathan said, "Harms, you knew that I wanted to speak to the constable. You had no right to interfere."

"Once again we differ in our important choices. You insist upon searching for crimes where there are none. I, on the other hand, am concerned only for the welfare of this fair flower. As long as you harp on this subject, her torment will continue." He warmed to his speech and pointed an accusing finger. "I insist that you stop inflicting pain upon dear Adrienne!"

Nathan took a step toward Huntsford, eyes glittering with rage. "You are nothing but a self-serving, devious—"

"No!" Adrienne stepped between them. Tears filled her voice and spilled onto her cheeks. "Nathan, just go away! I don't need or want you near me!"

Chapter Thirteen

"I WONDER IF THAT FELLOW IS NOT UNBALANCED," Huntsford Harms remarked, poking his head around the doorframe to make certain Nathan was not in the corridor. "I mean, really!" He grimaced at the two women and rolled his eyes. "Can you believe that anyone could behave so abominably?"

"I—I think he means well—about me, that is," Adrienne said.

"You are too trusting, my dear. What do you really know about him, after all? Your father could have hired him in desperation, and we might be harboring the worst sort of criminal in our midst!"

"Gadzooks!" Lady Thomasina tottered over to the narrow bed and collapsed. "Hunty may be right! Nathan's charm may have been a ruse to win our trust!"

"I just don't think so." Adrienne shook her head stubbornly.

"Well, my fair flower, it might be worthwhile to take a grain of doubt to your future dealings with Essex. It occurs to one that he might be slandering me in order to deflect attention from *himself*. . . ."

Adrienne stared at him in horror, unable to speak.

"Darling Hunty!" His mother opened her fan and swung it to and fro until her cloying scent filled the room. "Could it be?"

He shrugged. "Just a thought. I mean, mightn't Essex have been the person helping Frakes-Hogg bind you,

Adrienne? Oh, dear, I've upset you. How thoughtless of me! Do, please, forget everything I've said. I promise never to mention it again, as long as he does as you've ordered and will pose no further threat."

"As—I've ordered?" she repeated in confusion.

"Why, yes. You told him to go away, didn't you? I suppose I assumed he'd be leaving in any event, since Frakes-Hogg is dead and you don't need to be protected any longer."

"Oh. Yes." Adrienne was dazed. "I must ask you both to leave now, before my bath is cold. Thank you again for your many kindnesses, my lady." Nodding toward Huntsford, she felt her cheeks warm. "And thank you, too."

He seized the moment and bent to kiss her hand. "It has been an honor, my dear."

With that, Lady Thomasina let her son help her to her feet, and she leaned on him as they left Adrienne's bedchamber. Hortie, who had been pouring the bath, testing the water, and adding a bit of rose-scented oil, joined them. She wiped her hands on her apron and looked back before closing the door.

"I expect that's what you need, hmm?" For once, Hortie spoke with a hint of kindness and perhaps even sympathy.

Adrienne gave her a wry smile. "I wish that soap and hot water were enough to wash away all my troubles and confusion."

She seemed on the verge of saying more, but the Harmses were waiting. Once all three were on their way down the corridor, Hortie went ahead, and Lady Thomasina and her son lagged behind, whispering.

"That was a stroke of genius, darling boy!"

"Casting doubt on Essex, you mean?" He looked smug. "I thought so too, Mummy."

"I have another idea to draw dear Miss Beau farther into our fold, and I'll put it into practice shortly." Lady Thomasina watched until she saw Hortie turn down the servants' stairs. "I don't think we can afford to dawdle, you know. Miss Beau is feeling weak and confused right now, and Nathan is definitely out of favor. The tide could turn in his direction at any time."

"If only I could think of a way to get rid of him!" Huntsford complained.

"Well, darling, you never know. Now that you've sharpened the point of Miss Beau's insistence that he leave, I daresay he may not have a choice."

"If he has half a brain, the big oaf will realize that he's fighting a losing battle and, furthermore, that he's simply not wanted!"

"Just so. Come in and have tea and scones with me, and we'll firm up our plans."

Lady Thomasina started through the doorway to her sitting room, while her son hesitated, loath to endure any more of her company that morning. Since Lady Clair had been threatening to go off to Brighton if he didn't give her more amorous attentions, Huntsford wanted to squeeze an interlude in her bed into his morning's schedule. "Mummy, would you mind terribly if—"

She looked back with a piercing glare. "I suggest that you remember what is important. I am not a person you can treat with frivolous disregard, Hunty."

For years she had been conniving to bind her adult son to her. Now that fate had delivered a way, Lady Thomasina could not afford to take chances by loosening the ties. She went into her sitting room and he followed.

For the first time in his life, Nathan Raveneau had problems he couldn't solve. He didn't know what to do with Adrienne or the scheming Harmses, and he wished that Nicholai Beauvisage lived near enough so that Nathan could just take her home to the safety of her own family.

Of course, then he wouldn't be able to see her any more. And, since Adrienne was not yet twenty-one, he wouldn't get the land on Barbados if he took her home now.

After the awful scene in Adrienne's room, he paced the castle corridors like a caged panther. The air inside seemed dead, and he was starved for the sunlight and wind he was used to on the decks of the *Golden Eagle*. So Nathan walked to the stables and persuaded one of the boys to let him borrow a wild slate-gray stallion.

It was tremendously liberating to gallop across the soft

green hills, a bit too fast for safety. The stallion jumped streams and stone walls, and Nathan yelled as they sailed through the air, his hair and the horse's mane flying. When the time came to turn back, he felt much improved.

"What's his name?" he asked the stable boy when he'd dismounted.

"I don't think he has a name. The coachman found him runnin' loose on the road to Southampton."

"Really." Nathan was struck by the irony of that. "He's not my horse, but since no one else has cared enough to give him a name, I shall. I'll call him Runaway."

Before the stable boy could reply, Hortie stepped out of the shadows. The expression on her usually pinched face was oddly complacent. "Mr. Essex? I don't mean to interrupt, but I can't stay long. They'll miss me at the castle if I don't hurry." Clearly he couldn't imagine what that could possibly have to do with him, so Hortie continued, "I have important news to tell you—alone."

He would accept assistance from any quarter. Telling the boy that he'd return to help with Runaway, Nathan led the way out the back of the stable, to the ruined wall massed with old roses. "Well? What is it, Hortie?"

"I heard some things I thought you should know."

"And why would you want to help me?" He watched her face carefully.

"I'm tired of being treated like a piece of furniture, after all my years of service. No sooner did you outsiders come in than I was forgotten!" Hortie wagged a skinny finger at him. "It ain't right, sir! No offense, of course."

"None taken, I assure you."

"No offense to Miss Beauvisage either, but I don't want her here. If I help you, maybe you'll take her away, and things'll be the way they were before. If she stays, the way her ladyship and his lordship are talking, I'll never regain my rightful place."

"What's all this about Miss Beauvisage staying?"

"That's what they're planning. I heard 'em, but they thought I wasn't listening—"

"Perhaps you'd better start at the beginning," he suggested crisply.

Hortie nodded. "Yes. Well, when you left her room, and I was fixing the bath, his lordship said that he didn't trust you, and mayhap you were trying to cast suspicion on him so that no one would think you'd had a part in the crime!"

Nathan blinked, then slowly rubbed his eyes. "Good God, he's even more devious than I dreamed. . . ."

"Yes, sir. And it was a shame, because I could see that Miss Beauvisage was more confused than ever by what his lordship was saying. He was reminding her that she'd ordered you to leave, pressing her about it."

"Something happened after that?"

"Well, I should add that her ladyship didn't lift a finger to defend you, which surprised me, since she's been so fond of you. But when we were in the corridor, and I was at the far end, I heard them talking, and it all made sense. She wants her son to marry Miss Beauvisage, so I guess she wants to get rid of you."

Nathan was stunned. "*Marry* her? Hortie, have you been into the sherry? I really don't think—"

"I know what I heard!" She drew herself up and thrust out her bony bosom. "Her ladyship was whispering that they'd have to work fast, while you're out of favor and Miss Beauvisage is in this weakened state. His lordship wishes he could just get you out of the way!"

"Hortie, how can I ever repay you?"

"Well . . ." She turned coy, batting her stubby lashes at him. "I can think of a few ways. . . ."

"I'm afraid that I'm hopelessly faithful, and my affections lie elsewhere." He managed to touch her cheek and smile. "However, let's think of something else. I might be able to scrape together a few guineas—"

"I suppose that might do," she allowed, then grinned. "After all, we both stand to gain, right? I'd better go, then. Good-bye, sir."

When she was gone, Nathan perched at one end of the tumble-down wall and looked away from the afternoon sun. With both Lady Thomasina and her odious son plotting against him, it would be more difficult than ever to regain Adrienne's trust. Perhaps the answer lay not in opposing them and arguing endlessly with Adrienne but in playing into their hands.

Certainly it was time for a shift in strategy. What did he have to lose?

The next morning Adrienne was awakened by the warbling of birds in the great elm outside her window. Already sunlight spilled into the new bedchamber. The walls might be cracked and the paint peeling, but the light was much better than in her old room, and her mother had always maintained that sunshine could perform miracles on one's spirits.

Turning on her side with a sigh, she wished for a miracle. It seemed that a great weight was pressing on her chest.

"Miss Beauvisage?" Hortie's voice was followed by a sharp knock. "Aren't you awake yet? It's past eight o'clock!"

"Come in, Hortie." She sat up in bed to greet Lady Thomasina's abigail.

"You're asked to join her ladyship's party for breakfast in the dining room at nine o'clock."

"I suppose it would do me good."

"Yes, miss."

Adrienne rose and dressed in a round gown of cream sprigged muslin, thinking that she would welcome the assistance of a maid to help with the fastenings on her gowns. She was growing weary of independence. Perhaps her parents were right. For all her bravado, it seemed that she wasn't as strong as she'd insisted.

If only the situation with Nathan could have turned out differently. Not long ago Adrienne could easily have imagined taking her troubles to him, weeping into his shirtfront, and allowing him to carry her through this dark patch.

Approaching the dining room, Adrienne encountered Huntsford Harms. He greeted her warmly, arms outstretched.

"My dear, how good it is to see you up and about! Would you like a walk outdoors later?"

"That would be very nice." And it *was* nice to receive attention from Huntsford. He never said anything troubling to her, and his only concern seemed to be her welfare. At the moment, he was the ideal friend.

She took his arm as they entered, but her smile faded at the sight of Nathan sitting in his usual place beside Lady Thomasina.

"Surprised to see me?" he murmured. "Don't I belong any more now that Huntsford has deigned to make an appearance?"

"Why must you be so difficult?" Adrienne asked.

"That's right, my boy," Lady Thomasina remonstrated. "Have a little consideration for Miss Beau's sensibilities. She's not feeling at all the thing at the moment."

He fell silent then, rising to fill his plate with the overcooked dishes on the sideboard. The eggs tasted salty and the sirloin was leathery, but Nathan chewed without complaint as the others chatted about the latest *Racing Calendar* and the new blue gloves Huntsford was having made in Winchester.

"I decided that it might be months before I return to London," Huntsford was saying as he gazed into Adrienne's eyes. "Why not have the new gloves made here, I thought! It's no good stomping about in a temper at Angus. Mummy assures me that he is extremely fond of the color blue, so it's not as if he *meant* to upset me by taking the gloves!"

Nathan couldn't help interjecting "You don't sound completely convinced, old chap!"

The other man narrowed his eyes from across the table but laughed for Adrienne's benefit. "How amusing. Oh, Mummy, before I forget, I must tell you that my guests will be leaving this afternoon for Brighton. It seems that Prinny is hosting some sort of assembly at the Royal Pavilion. He's been rather listless since the death of Princess Charlotte, so everyone is taking this as a good sign that he's recovering."

"They aren't coming back?" her ladyship wondered.

"No. No, I don't think so." Huntsford turned to Adrienne again. "I have other concerns these days. Their interests seem quite frivolous to me."

Nathan had eaten his fill, and now he leaned back in his

chair and dabbed the corners of his mouth with a napkin. "It would appear that we have all reached a fork in the road, as it were. I too am leaving this afternoon."

"What!" Adrienne couldn't help gasping.

"You did ask me to go, if you will recall, Miss Beauvisage." Slowly he arched a black brow. "And I have realized that you are quite right. Now that Walter Frakes-Hogg is dead, there is no reason for me to remain here. Besides . . ." Standing, Nathan pushed his chair back under the table and bowed. "You all are carrying on very well without my interference, hmm? I begin to perceive that four is a crowd."

"You are a wise fellow, dear Nathan." Lady Thomasina extended her plump beringed hand to him. "I shall miss you, however."

"I have truly enjoyed my time in your home, my lady." Clasping her fingertips, Nathan bent to kiss the back of her hand. "Perhaps we will meet again one day."

Adrienne stood up without thinking. "I will walk with you a ways. To say good-bye." She only knew that she must say something, and couldn't in Huntsford's presence.

When they were in the corridor, Nathan stopped and fixed her with a bittersweet look of longing. "Never let it be said that I wore out my welcome."

"I didn't really think you'd go."

He was surprised to feel a tightness in his chest. His eyes stung. "I've grown weary of arguing and of being told that I'm unkind. I have to remind myself that you are a grown woman and ought to be able to look out for your own . . . interests."

"Yes." Something seemed to be choking the words in her throat. "I ought to."

"I have a long ride before nightfall. I would have left already, but I wanted to make a proper farewell." Then, gently, he caressed the side of her face and let his hand drift down to cup her chin. "For God's sake, have a care, chit. *Try* not to do anything you'll regret later."

Adrienne could only nod, aching. All the things she wanted to say were impossible, so she whispered, "Safe journey."

"I don't believe in good-byes, actually." His eyes were tender, and the temptation to take her in his arms and kiss her was strong.

"But—" Adrienne plucked at his sleeve, unable to speak, and only nodded. As Nathan turned and walked away, she tried to memorize the shape of his shoulders, the appealing lines of his booted legs, the way his hair curled at the back of his neck. There wasn't room for any more pain in her heart, so she tried to pretend he'd be back, that it wasn't over.

Just then Huntsford Harms came up behind Adrienne, chewing a last bite of sirloin. "That's one person I'm delighted to see depart. Won't our lives be pleasant from now on?"

During the next two days, more farewells were made. The departure of Lady Clair, Alistair, Lucy and Peter the dog, and Sir Blake and his paintings was attended by a great deal of fanfare. When they were gone, the house seemed unnaturally quiet. Adrienne tried to busy herself by returning to the library Systems, but by now the footmen knew their work so well that she felt redundant.

Huntsford was glad to take over the task of keeping her amused. He taught her every card game he knew, but she thought them dull. On the second evening, as Adrienne nearly nodded off in the middle of an intimate game of macao, they were both roused by the sound of Lady Thomasina's bell ringing madly from the top of the stairs.

"Confound it, what's that all about?" His voice was tinged with irritation, for he'd been just about to call for a bottle of champagne and suggest that he and Adrienne share it in the moonlit conservatory.

As they ascended the stairs, Adrienne wondered why she wasn't more content with the new arrangement. It was true that she keenly missed Nathan, but she was determined to forget him, and the Harmses were doing all in their power to make her happy. Lady Thomasina behaved as if Adrienne were a guest rather than her hired companion, and Huntsford had been showering her with charm, exotic food and fine wines, and sweet consideration. In a strange way, she felt more at home with each passing day, yet the fit wasn't entirely right.

"Thank heavens you've come!" Hortie met them on the top stair, wringing her hands. Her face was even whiter than usual, and her eyes threatened to pop out. "Her ladyship has had a terrible spell!"

"Bloody hell!" cried Harms. "What sort of spell?"

"I suppose it's apoplexy, or worse."

Adrienne's heart jumped. She hurried ahead of the others, suddenly flooded with guilt for not taking better care of Lady Thomasina these past days and for leaving her alone this evening. Oddly enough, she'd become very fond of the bizarre old woman.

She feared she'd find her sprawled across the worn Turkish carpet, perhaps in the throes of uncontrollable seizures, but instead Lady Thomasina was propped up against two perfumed pillows in her bed. A branch of candles burned on the table beside her, she was wearing her silver brocade turban, and her cheeks were freshly painted.

Adrienne rushed to her side. "My lady, can you hear me?"

Her lids fluttered. "Miss—Beau?" She groped toward her with one hand. "At last, you've . . . come."

"Of course! Oh, I'm so sorry that I haven't been a better companion to you these past days. Perhaps I would have noticed signs. . . ."

"I noticed them . . . myself, but I didn't want . . . to worry." She managed a feeble smile. "Such a—bother."

Huntsford came up behind Adrienne and put a hand on her waist. "Thank God she's alive!"

"I don't think . . . I have much time . . ." Lady Thomasina croaked. In the background, Hortie began to weep loudly. "I am so very grateful that . . . Miss Beau is part of our family now."

"I'm honored that you should say so," she replied, touched.

"I think of you . . . as a daughter. Would you mind if I called you . . . Addie?" Her ladyship peeked enough to see her nod, and then she patted the edge of the bed. "Sit beside me, Addie."

"Is there anything I can do to help you now?"

"Yes. Hunty . . . be a good lad and sit here with Addie. And, Hortie, get me a glass of sherry."

"Sherry?" the servant repeated. "Do you think that's a good idea?"

"Yes, I do! Kindly obey me!" Lady Thomasina snapped, then pasted on a smile as she returned her attention to the young couple. "My, what pleasure it gives me to see the two of you sitting together like this. . . ."

A flush warmed Adrienne's cheeks. She felt odd, but then suddenly her ladyship widened her eyes in alarm and pressed a hand to her huge bosom. "What is it? Another spell?" Instantly Adrienne reached for her hand and looked back at Huntsford. "It is terrible not to be able to help!"

He was watching his mother. "Perhaps there will be something we can do."

"Yes . . ." Another beatific smile curved her ladyship's mouth. "Addie, nothing would make me happier during my last days than for you to be my daughter. Oh, to see my darling Hunty married and starting a family with you, in the homes I've loved! I want to spend whatever time I have left in the company of my children . . . Hunty and Addie."

She was stunned. "My lady, are you quite lucid? Perhaps the apoplexy has impaired your . . ."

"My mind?" Lady Thomasina was tart again. "Not a bit. I've been hoping that you two would find each other in your own time, but now we may not have that luxury. I must add that you might have developed a *tendresse* for my son earlier, if not for the interference of Mr. Essex. Might you agree?"

Huntsford spoke up first. "I would agree. Of course, I cannot speak for Adrienne, but in my own case, I felt drawn to her the instant we met on the steps outside." Very softly he touched her arm. "Do you remember?"

"I remember, and I do care very much for both of you, but—I am not certain I am ready to think about marriage!" The sight of Lady Thomasina going pale again was frightening. Adrienne squeezed her hand, then impulsively kissed it. "I have been through a great deal recently, and if I marry Huntsford, I want to be certain that I am able to make that decision with a clear mind. That does not mean I refuse. On the contrary—" Adrienne glanced up in time to see Hortie scurry out of the bedroom. "I will give your words very careful consideration."

"We shall have to woo her, Mummy," Huntsford said.

"I suppose." Pouting, her ladyship glanced away, her chins trembling. "I am tired now."

"I should go to bed myself," Adrienne agreed. "Please don't be cross with me, my lady. I want very much to make you happy."

When she had gone, closing the door in her wake, Lady Thomasina Harms glared at her son. "I don't know where Hortie went, so I assume that she will return momentarily. There's no time to waste."

"That was quite a performance, Mummy."

"Yes, well, someone had to grasp hold of the situation before the opportunity slipped away. When I mulled over all the elements, it seemed that a deathbed request had the best chance of success. I'll stay near death for days if necessary! Of course, I don't doubt that you might have been able to bring her 'round to marriage on your own, but who knows how much time we have? Besides, Miss Beau isn't searching for a husband. It will take special circumstances to push her to the altar."

"She's not quite herself now, since the . . . incident. Not as strong and independent as usual."

"Exactly! And we must take advantage of that weakness!"

As his mother droned on, Huntsford Harms realized how well pleased he was with the turn of events. The notion of marrying Adrienne was attractive for many reasons, not the least of which was her arm's-length attitude, the resulting lust generated in him, and the probability that he'd have even more access to his mother's assets once he became a husband to the right woman.

However, Huntsford was hatching a plan of his own that he couldn't share with her ladyship. Now that Frakes-Hogg was dead, he intended to sail to Barbados on the pretext of delivering the news of his death to his business partner, Xavier Crowe. Then Harms would explain that Frakes-

Hogg had been planning to send Huntsford to work with Crowe but hadn't had a chance to write the letter before his untimely death. After arriving on the island with his bride, Huntsford would be harder to turn away, and Adrienne would not only add to his own luster, but her presence on Barbados would drive Nathan Essex/Raveneau utterly insane. . . .

Hortie carried a lit candle as she felt her way along the dark corridors of the servants' quarters. Once all the rooms had been filled, but the staff had been cut so much in recent years that now most were empty, collecting dust and cobwebs.

The next-to-last door on the left was closed tightly. She knocked twice, paused, then added another sharp rap. Inside, the bolt slid across, and the door opened perhaps one inch.

"It's Hortie!" she whispered. "Let me in. I haven't much time!"

A strong male hand reached out of the gloom and pulled her inside. "Finally! I'm going to go raving mad in here!"

Through the shadows, she made out the now-familiar figure of Nathan Essex. Clad in a loose white shirt, snug breeches, and top boots, he seemed more romantic than ever and even a bit savage. His dark face was unshaven, and his hair was in attractive disarray. The tray of food she'd brought earlier perched on a stool in the corner, scarcely touched.

"You should have eaten," Hortie scolded.

"Easy for you to say. What was that on the plate? Scraps the cook was saving for the dogs?"

"I could hardly assemble a proper meal for you, could I, without arousing suspicion? You're supposed to be two days' journey away from Harms Castle, after all, not hiding in—"

"This godforsaken cell!"

"I'll thank you to show a bit of gratitude, sir! What would you do without my help?"

Nathan had the good grace to be serious for a moment. He smiled in the darkness and touched the abigail's face, admitting "You're quite right. I am deeply in debt to you, Hortie, and I'm still endeavoring to find another way to repay you."

"You've given me more than I dreamed—"

"But that's just money. I mean something of substance."

Hortie's face colored. "Well, sir, you'll have plenty of time to think about that, but for now I must hurry! I wanted you to know that Lady Thomasina is pretending to be on her deathbed in order to force Miss Beauvisage into marriage with his lordship! She put on the most amazing performance tonight, and even I was taken in for a while."

"And Adrienne?" he asked hoarsely.

"She's still rather in a daze, and that's what they're counting on, I know it! And, of course, she thinks she's lost you. The girl has a kind heart, and she's awfully fond of her ladyship. If she thought she could make her last days happy, there's no telling what might happen!"

"I don't believe it. The girl I know vows she won't marry any man!"

Hortie put her hand on the latch. "Why should I argue with you? I only know what I heard. Her first instinct was to say no, but then she began wavering, and her ladyship started swooning. If I was you, sir, I wouldn't sit in here with the rats and wait for the right moment to make your move. Before you do, Lord Harms might convince her to elope!"

Adrienne was a devoted nurse to Lady Thomasina. She even picked up where Nathan had left off in *Pride and Prejudice* and tried to read with as much lively humor as he had, but her ladyship would not be cheered. Hour after hour she lay on her pillows, refusing food. Even Angus found the mood too depressing and removed himself to the library. There he curled up in Lady Thomasina's tub chair with his scrap of blue glove and a chicken neck, growling at anyone who dared approach.

"Nothing seems to be working," Adrienne said to Huntsford. The clock had just struck nine, prompting the old woman to proclaim weakly that it was her bedtime.

"You can't sit here all night, my dear." He sighed. "Let

Mummy sleep, and you and I will repair to the library for some madeira and a nice chat."

Her ladyship opened one eye. "Yes, Addie. Go with Hunty. That's what will make me better. Hortie can look after me."

Outside in the corridor, he turned liquid brown eyes on her. "Don't you see, Adrienne, that only one thing will revive her?"

"I can't talk about this right now." Wondering if she were going mad, Adrienne walked quickly down the stairs to the library where she and Nathan had passed so many happy hours. When had it all begun to go wrong? Now that the shock of Walter's attack and death was wearing off, Adrienne simply ached for Nathan. The more hours that passed without him, the greater her pain became. Adrienne thought that she would do anything for another hour of banter with Nathan—and one more inexpressibly arousing kiss . . .

Huntsford followed her into the library. He had already lit candles and poured glasses of madeira for them. Adrienne didn't question this, but picked hers up and paced the long room, drinking and staring at the monochromatic rows of books. In her mind's eye she saw Nathan again, high on the ladder, searching out bottle-green volumes.

"Tell me what I can do to win you, and I shall obey," Huntsford said in a low voice, coming up behind her.

"You are too kind." Was it possible that she would never see Nathan again? She had no idea where he came from, or where he had gone. "The events . . . of the past few days have left their mark on me, I think. I've always prided myself on being resilient—"

"And you shall be again. I can help you. I'll care for you and give you anything within my power to make you happy." He turned her in his arms, reminding himself that Adrienne had liked Nathan's masculine forcefulness. "Perhaps there is more to me than you imagine, my dear!"

"I'm certain you are right." It was a relief to lean against him. Huntsford offered unwavering support, unlike the prickly, mysterious Nathan Essex. If Nathan had truly cared, wouldn't he have stayed and fought for her—as Huntsford continued to do?

"Oh, Adrienne, I want you so much." Slipping his arms around her, he searched her beautiful face for a sign. She didn't struggle, but passively closed her eyes and turned her mouth up to him. Desire broke over him in waves. "My darling!" he cried in a deep, commanding voice, then took possession of her lips.

She tried to lose herself in his kiss, but felt only an odd sense of awkwardness, as if their mouths didn't quite fit and their rhythms were different. There was none of the euphoric, tingly liberation Adrienne had known in Nathan's arms. Perhaps her recent ordeal was to blame, however. She might need more time to thaw from the shock she'd sustained. . . .

"I feel terribly warm." She gave him a tremulous smile and slipped free of his embrace. "I don't know if I'm ready for this—"

"Adrienne," he muttered, "I adore you. I've never felt this way about a woman in my life." He could still feel the pressure of her breasts against him, and lust surged through his veins. She seemed unattainable! "One word from you, and Mummy and I will both be the happiest people in the world. You know that is the only thing that will enable her to recover, don't you? I'll pamper you, and take you on a tour of Europe—every year if you like!"

Panicky at the thought of another kiss, Adrienne reached for her goblet and drank. Perhaps Huntsford was right. Would it be so terrible to become Lady Adrienne? If Nathan were coming back, it would be different, but he was gone forever.

And if she refused and Lady Thomasina died, how would she feel for the rest of her life?

"Please," Huntsford coaxed. "Let me kiss you some more, and we'll see how we get along, if you take my meaning. Would you guess that I am a skilled and tender lover? Your pleasure will be my only goal. . . ."

Wavering, Adrienne set down her glass. She had taken one step toward him when, suddenly, the tall windows burst open with a crash and a man jumped lightly into the room.

He wore a white shirt, breeches, top boots, and a wicked smile.

"That was a pretty speech, Harms!" Nathan walked toward them, brandishing a sword. "I sympathize with your plight, but sympathy is all you'll get tonight. You will never be Adrienne's lover as long as I live."

"What the deuce are *you* doing here?" Huntsford shrieked.

"Why, I've come to abduct Adrienne," he replied coolly. "Come over here, chit."

"Nathan, this is madness," she said. Her heart raced with giddy excitement, a feeling she'd nearly forgotten in his absence.

"Do you see this sword? It means that we don't argue. You must do as you're told." He gestured neatly with the weapon. "Come over here."

Adrienne obeyed, and Huntsford went scarlet. "She doesn't want you! We are betrothed!"

"If that's true, it's all the more reason for me to remove her from this place." Nathan drew her firmly against him with his free arm. "Her father would definitely not approve of such a match."

Adrienne looked up at his rakish face, captivated and furious at the same time. "Where did you come from? Are you mad?"

"Perhaps. Are you?" To further inflame Harms, Nathan forcefully pressed his mouth to hers. "You see, kissing can still be fun. Come with me and I'll convince you further."

As she allowed him to hoist her onto the waist-high sill, and thence to the balcony, Adrienne wondered if she truly was losing her mind. "Lady Thomasina is ill—"

"No, she isn't. Not a bit. Hold on." Without sparing another word for Huntsford Harms, Nathan tossed his sword to the ground and carried her over the railing. Conveniently, there was a sturdy trellis attached, and they were on the lawn in moments.

"Huntsford will follow us. He is very determined," she warned.

"I doubt that. You see?" Laughing, Nathan retrieved his

sword and pointed with it to the figure in the window above. "He hasn't the nerve even to come out!"

Adrienne did as he bade and mounted the waiting stallion. A moment later Nathan was behind her on the beast's back, one powerful arm round her waist.

"Say hello to Runaway," he whispered in her ear, his several days' growth of beard tickling her in a way that was maddenly provocative. "The moon is full, and it's a wonderful night for adventure, hmm?"

The stallion threw his head back and snorted. As they galloped off across the grounds, Huntsford screamed wildly from the open windows.

"This will kill Mummy, y'know! You'll both pay! I'll hunt you down, mark my words!"

"I'm shaking with terror," Nathan murmured into the wind.

PART THREE

Once more upon the waters, yet once more!
And the waves bound beneath me as a steed
That knows his rider! Welcome to their roar!
Swift be their guidance, whereso'er it lead!
—George Gordon, lord byron

Chapter Fourteen

It seemed to take hours to reach Winchester. Jouncing along on the back of a horse ominously christened Runaway, Adrienne experienced a total lack of control. Her slim gown forced her to keep both legs on one side, and she constantly felt on the verge of hurtling into a ditch or hedgerow. Nathan held the reins, so she could do no more than cling alternately to Runaway's mane and her kidnapper's body, and pray. With only the moon to light their way, they thundered so recklessly along a hilly, winding road that Adrienne was certain each moment would be her last.

"Please!" she yelled after an especially terrifying brush with death. "Slow down!"

"A search party led by Jarrow is doubtless in close pursuit!" Nathan replied with mock horror. "He would not be merciful if he overcame us."

"Jarrow?" she echoed, laughing.

No other words passed between them. Adrienne had no wish to distract him, and in fact, she was secretly quite thrilled. When coherent thought became possible, she decided that tonight Nathan epitomized all her girlhood fantasies. It truly was a delicious adventure—in part because Adrienne trusted her abductor.

In time, as it became clear that no one was chasing them, and Runaway began to tire slightly, Nathan drew back slightly on the reins. The River Itchen was a molten silver ribbon, following the road to the west. An owl hooted from a tree, and rabbits scooted about in the meadow. Adrienne

could scarcely keep her eyes open. When Nathan gathered
her against his chest with his arm, she snuggled in and
dozed. The night air was cool, and she had sorely missed
the familiar touch and scent and sturdy warmth of him.

Was it her imagination, or did he kiss her hair after a
while?

Adrienne awoke in Winchester, as they drew up outside
the porter's door at St. Cross Hospital. For centuries, needy
travelers had received a portion of bread and a horn of ale
known as the Wayfarer's Dole. Adrienne was shocked that
Nathan would come here for food, but realized that he
probably thought it was the one place they could be guar-
anteed safety.

When they had eaten, she stood shivering next to Runaway and gave Nathan a faltering smile. "I've been
thinking—"

"No need for that yet," came his cheerfully sardonic reply. "We must make haste."

"No, Nathan, I mean I have been thinking about what
we're doing. I appreciate your concern for my welfare, and
part of me was relieved to escape from Harms Castle, but
I have realized that I cannot go. Not yet."

"Too late, I fear. We've already gone."

"I mean, I ought to go back."

"Sorry."

Adrienne stuck out her chin. "I am not making a request,
Nathan. This is my *decision*." She spoke slowly, weighting
each word with conviction. "I can't just run away. All my
things are there, and I must resolve my affairs with Lady
Thomasina . . . and Huntsford as well."

"No." He shook his handsome head. "I'm afraid that's
out of the question."

Her patience was ebbing rapidly. "How can you behave
this way? You have no right to make these decisions for
me. If you won't take me back, then leave me, and I'll hire
a chaise in the morning."

"Your father hired me to make these decisions, I'm
afraid, and this matter is fixed. We will continue."

Adrienne's rage increased. She threw herself at Nathan,
but he simply grasped her wrists, easily subduing her. "I

hate you! You can*not* bully me in this manner! I won't allow it!"

"Just when we were beginning to have fun, you turn on me. Ah, well, I'm used to it." He threw her onto Runaway's back, swinging up behind her in the next instant. The horse started forward and Adrienne let out a yell of panic. "You don't want to ride that way until dawn, do you? I'll let you sit, and leave your wrists untied, if you promise to behave yourself."

Runaway was cantering over the bridge as Nathan drew his captive into an upright position. She promptly spat in his face, but he would not let his temper snap. "Try to act like a woman, not a brat," he advised coolly. "We have a long ride ahead."

"This time you have gone too far. When we reach France, I shall tell my father, and then you'll be sorry you didn't listen to me."

"Oh, we're not going to France."

"London, then!" Adrienne snapped.

"No, not London either."

Her sense of panic mounted. "*Where*, then?"

"I'm not ready to divulge that information yet, my dear chit. Just relax and enjoy the night air."

"I am going to kill you," Adrienne ground out, but her words were drowned out by the sound of Runaway's hoofbeats. They had gained the south road, and the stallion stretched out his legs in an even gallop.

Above Adrienne's head, Nathan Raveneau smiled grimly to himself. She had a lot of surprises in store, and he doubted that she'd be pleased by any of them.

Morning was breaking when the stallion and his two riders reached the outskirts of Southampton.

"Just a little farther, Runaway," Nathan soothed, stroking his neck. "We're nearly there."

Adrienne awoke, aching all over and immediately craving a bath. It seemed that her entire body was bruised and dusty. "Have we reached our destination?"

The land portion is nearly over. We're going just below

Southampton, to a tiny place called Hill Head. Soon enough
we'll be able to get some rest."

"I must say, I'm fed up with your air of mystery! It's my
life you're trifling with, and I don't appreciate your high-
handedness one bit!" She wriggled in front of him, trying
to achieve a measure of comfort.

"Hold still before you send us both into the road," he
warned.

Adrienne craned her neck to look at him, and suddenly
it dawned on her that something was missing. "Where are
your spectacles? How is it that you can see?"

"Actually ... I don't wear spectacles."

They reached the top of a hill overlooking the jade waters of the Solent, which separated the mainland from the
Isle of Wight. As they descended into the tiny village of
Hill Head, Adrienne was distracted from the beauty of her
new, dawn-gilded surroundings by Nathan's admission. If
he didn't actually need to wear spectacles, why then had he
done so for many weeks? Deep inside, she had always
sensed that he was not who he pretended to be, but now
that stranger was holding her captive!

Her voice was more hesitant than before as she asked,
"Has it all been a masquerade?"

"I suppose you could say that."

Adrienne's heart thudded. "Who are you, then?"

He was looking around as they came up in front of an
old Tudor inn called The Anchor. "I'd really rather not discuss it at the moment. I'm looking for Dickie, the butcher's
son. Do you remember him?"

Always, she had trusted him, in spite of everything. Had
she been right? "What would Dickie be doing here?"

"I sent him ahead to make the arrangements for us. Ah,
good, there he is!"

The lad emerged from the inn in the company of a short,
redheaded fellow who looked oddly familiar to Adrienne. As
soon as he called a greeting, she remembered. "Look! It's
your cousin!"

"What? Oh, him. No, he's not my cousin."

"Have you spoken one true word since the moment we
first met?" Her voice rose with frustration.

Nathan was jumping to the ground. As he reached up to help Adrienne down, he held her close to him and gazed into her uncertain green eyes. "Adrienne, you already know everything about me that really matters. As for the rest, the answers you seek will have to wait a bit. If it's any comfort, your father knows *all* about me." He brushed her cheek with the backs of his fingers and smiled.

It was maddening to feel herself succumb to his spell, as always. The redheaded man was watching them with a knowing look in his eye, and it felt like a slap in the face to Adrienne. "I'll thank you to keep your distance, sir!" she told Nathan tartly. "Believe it or not, I am well able to resist your conceited attempts to charm me!"

His eyes widened, and then he threw back his head and roared with laughter. "Of course you are, my little spitfire!"

Zachary Minter sidled up beside them and winked at Adrienne. "Well, well, I think I am going to like you, Miss Beauvisage!"

"If I tell you that I am being abducted against my will, would you help me to escape from this brute?"

His face fell. "Oh." Zach turned quizzical eyes on his oldest friend. "Is she having me on?"

"See here," Nathan thundered, "I must ask Miss Beauvisage to stop these stalling tactics, and I must ask Minter to stop making foolish remarks! I am the captain, I'm tired, and I want to get on with the day's plans!"

"Captain of what?" Adrienne exclaimed.

"Just be silent until I tell you to speak!"

"Oh, guv'nor," Zach protested, "that's a bit harsh, isn't it?"

Nathan ignored him and turned to Dickie, smiling at the lad with an effort. "Do, please, pardon my friends. Miss Beauvisage has been without sleep, and she's not herself. Now then, Dickie, I want to thank you for your help; we couldn't have done it without you."

"My pleasure, sir!"

"I want to make a present to you of this beautiful stallion called Runaway. Will you give me your word to treat him with the utmost care? Here, take these guineas and spend some on yourself, and keep the rest to pay for his food."

Dickie's eyes shone with wonder. "It's a fortune! Me grandfather has a fine farm just outside of Winchester, sir. I can stable him there and visit every day. Would that be good enough?"

"Perfect." He ruffled the boy's hair. "Stop at the coaching inn a ways up the road and have Runaway watered and fed. And buy yourself a hot breakfast. Godspeed."

When Dickie had ridden away, up the cobbled street on the stallion's back, Nathan turned toward the water with a bittersweet sigh. "If there had been a way to take Runaway with us, so he'd be comfortable, I would have done it. I love that horse."

"You did the right thing," Zach assured him. "Now then, let's go. The long boat is waiting at the dock, and your crew is frothing at the mouth to see you, Captain!"

"God, what a horrific thought."

Adrienne had decided to keep quiet, to just listen and watch. Since Nathan wouldn't tell her anything anyway, she would probably learn more through careful observation. Still, the urge to ask about the ship and its destination was strong.

What sort of power had her father bestowed on this man? How could Nathan possibly presume to carry her off to an unknown destination against her will?

If she had thought it would do a bit of good to ask him, she would have done so.

Zachary Minter was kind to her as they rowed in the direction of a magnificently rakish packet that swayed gently in the ruffled waters. The ship was a stirring sight, particularly for someone like Adrienne who so keenly adored adventure and romance. A vessel like that was the stuff of her dreams.

"We aren't going to *that* ship, are we?"

It was Zach who puffed out his chest and answered, "Yes indeed, Miss Beauvisage, that is the *Golden Eagle*, and I am her first mate. I couldn't be prouder of my association with this ship and Captain Raveneau."

"Who is Captain *Raveneau*?"

Nathan threw the smaller man a menacing glance.

"Uh ..." He cleared his throat. "That is, actually, my name."

They were drawing alongside the sharp hull, and a rope ladder was lowered. Stunned to the point of numbness, Adrienne said nothing but let the men help her ascend. Zach went first, and Nathan came behind, both watching for any misstep she might make, given her attire. However, she made the climb safely and swung her slim legs over the rail.

The crew was assembled on the quarterdeck, each man neatly outfitted and standing at attention. It was evident, even to Adrienne, that they were overjoyed to have their captain back on board. Nathan shook hands with each man, pausing to make a personal comment that let the seaman know that he remembered and valued him.

Finally, when the greetings were finished, Captain Raveneau stood before the crew and said, "I cannot express the joy I feel this morning. During my weeks away, I have realized as never before how closely bound I am to this ship, you men, and this way of life. The prospect of a good long ocean voyage fills me with pleasure. Are you all ready?"

As one, they shouted, "Yes, Captain!"

"Good. Oh, by the way, this is Miss Beauvisage. She'll be sailing with us, and I expect every one of you to treat her with unfailing courtesy and respect. Is that clear?"

"Yes, Captain!" All the men were smiling from ear to ear.

"I suggest that we prepare to set sail, then. I am going below, and Mr. Minter will carry on." Nathan paused then and whispered something in Minter's ear before leading his captive below.

The atmosphere on the ship was tremendously stimulating for Adrienne. As she followed him toward the hatch that would take them to the berth deck, she decided that there really wasn't any adventure as thrilling as a sea voyage. She'd sailed on handsome ships like this before, but the captain had been her uncle or her father ... not the mysterious Raveneau. Even his corrected name was provocative. The notion that she might not know what to expect, now that Nathan had stripped away his disguise, sent a chill through her.

Still, Adrienne couldn't let him know any of this.

"Mind your head coming down the ladder," he cautioned before jumping to the gangway below. "It's dark."

"Are you taking me to the hold? Will I be clapped in irons?"

Raveneau laughed. "Not at all." He led the way along the shadowed passageway, past the galley and the crew's quarters.

"The *Golden Eagle* is bright and shining in spite of your absence, Captain!" She ran a finger over the oiled teak bulkhead and a polished brass railing. "Perhaps they don't need you after all."

"In case you were not aware of it, ships' captains have more important functions than overseeing the housekeeping," he replied in astringent tones. "And Minter knows what my standards are. He's a sterner taskmaster than he looks." After passing the galley and the crew's quarters, he paused in front of a paneled door. "Well, here's your new home—at least for a few weeks."

Adrienne stared at the spacious cabin revealed when he threw open the door. "But—these are your quarters!" Awash with sunshine that poured through the transom, the built-in carved bunk was big enough to sleep two comfortably, and the other furnishings were handsome. Slowly she went forward and ran her hands over the dark wood of the table that folded down from the wall, the heavy chairs, and the specially made chests that held all of Nathan's personal belongings and navigating gear.

"All the furnishings are made of Barbadian mahogany," he explained. "I love the stuff."

Questions crowded inside her. Had she known him at all, truly, during their weeks at Harms Castle? But she bit her tongue, remembering that he couldn't think he'd won. "You are so arrogant! How can you imagine that I would care about such matters at a time when I have no control at all over my destiny? I have been abducted and dragged over the countryside, through the night, on horseback, and now you have taken me to sea and locked me in your private cabin—for God knows what purpose!" Warming to the drama, Adrienne paced back and forth in her tattered gown, eyes ablaze. She waved a fist at him. "Sir Pirate, I demand that you release me!"

He dropped into a sturdy bowback chair, pulled off his boots, and rubbed his eyes. "Why don't you sit down and rest for a while?" Then, unfastening the latch that secured a deep drawer, he opened it and took out a bottle of cognac and a pewter cup. "You'll pardon me, I hope. It's early, but then I haven't been to bed."

Adrienne watched him pour a small portion and drink. "Rude. You're so rude! Will you not offer me a drop?" When he shrugged and proffered his cup to her, she marched over, took it, and swallowed. The liquor didn't burn as badly as she'd imagined it would. In fact, the warmth that spread through her body was soothing.

"Have a care. Too much and you'll be sick." Nathan caught her arm and drew her into the chair opposite his. "Minter's arranging for us both to have hot baths as soon as possible. Don't worry." He held up a defensive hand. "I'll take mine in the galley."

"Where are you going to sleep?" Adrienne spoke innocently, then watched as an unnerving glint crept into his aquamarine eyes. "You wouldn't dare! I forbid it!"

This made him laugh again. "Do you? Who bestowed such power on you? My dear, I hate to spoil your fantasy, but times have changed. No longer am I the hired lackey, the bourgeois oaf who could find nothing better to do with my time than traipse after you and Lady Thomasina. On this ship I am in command, and you must do my bidding."

The familiar tingling started at the base of her neck. Still, she glowered at him. "One would think that simple breeding would dictate that you—"

"Give up my cabin? You jest, Miss *Beau*. But, of course, if you would prefer to sleep with the rest of the crew . . . ?"

"There must be somewhere else!"

"If there were, you would be there. Do you imagine that I am sharing my only private space by choice?"

"Take me home then! To France!"

"If you continue this campaign to try my patience, I may.

We'll discuss all of that in greater depth after we have both washed and rested." Nathan stood up to go in search of Minter. "You see, I not only don't have time to go cavorting across France with you, I gave my word to your father that I would take care of you until your twenty-first birthday. We have an agreement, and I intend to keep my part of it."

"But why? If you explain to him the circumstances—"

Minter, Crenshaw, and a procession of lowly seamen filed in then. Two carried a large tin bathtub while the others lugged buckets of steaming water. Raveneau watched them from the doorway, conscious of Adrienne's question hanging in the air. He met her eyes over the heads of his crew members and flicked both brows up. "Let's just say that the reward for me is great enough to persuade me to put up with you, dear chit."

For once she failed to respond.

It was the best bath Adrienne had had in weeks, perhaps since the last time she'd gone home to Château du Soleil. To soak in a big tub was heaven, and there was plenty of hot water and a lovely piece of lilac-scented soap. Adrienne scrubbed every inch of her body, then washed her hair, ducking under to rinse away the froth. While submerged, she blew bubbles. When she finally popped out, hair and water streamed over her face and down her breasts.

"You scared the devil out of me!" Nathan Raveneau stood over the bathtub, freshly washed and dressed and looking as if he'd seen a ghost. "I was about to reach in and grab whatever I could find of you! What the hell were you doing in there?"

Belatedly Adrienne put a hand over each wet, round breast. "I was . . . playing. Like a fish."

"Oh, for God's sake!" He retraced his steps to the doorway and gathered a pile of lacy clothes off the floor. The diversion provided a good opportunity to catch his breath, for even he had been caught off guard by the sudden attack of panic.

"I won't be made to feel guilty for frightening you, since

you had no right to come in while I was in the bath—
naked, after all!"

Nathan stalked back, towering over her, a bundle of feminine garments spilling awkwardly from his arms. "I'll have
you know that I knocked first. When you didn't answer, I
called to you, then only opened the door an inch or two.
Can you imagine my reaction when I saw no sign of you
in the bathtub and bubbles rising in the water?" He narrowed his eyes and clenched his jaw for emphasis.

"I suppose I can, since you wouldn't get your fantastic
reward from Papa if I drowned!" Her catlike green eyes
strayed to the gowns he carried. "You make rather a silly
sight with all that muslin and lace framing your face, sir.
Before you leave me, perhaps you should explain."

"I brought you some clothing that ought to fit. If you
think me too *silly*, I can toss them out and you can wear the
gown you arrived in—"

"No!" Chilled by now, Adrienne slid down in the tub. It
was faintly gratifying to note that Nathan's eyes skimmed
the water, searching for a blurry glimpse of her nakedness.
"Put them on the bed. Thanks to my abrupt departure from
Harms Castle, I own less than a beggar!"

Nathan dropped the clothing on the bed on his way to
the door. There he glanced back and said in parting, "You
know that you're a baggage, don't you?"

"Of course." In spite of herself, Adrienne gave him a
spellbinding smile.

"They're cooking a meal for us. I'll join you shortly to
eat, and then I intend to sleep, possibly until tomorrow."

When he had closed the door, Adrienne got out of the
bath and dried herself thoroughly. Her skin felt silky and
her hair luxuriant as it fell over her back in a damp mass
of chestnut curls. The clothing beckoned from the bed, and
she examined each garment with mounting curiosity. There
were gowns of soft muslin and silk, spencers and cashmere
shawls and gauze scarves, and the underclothes were sensu-
ously exquisite. Adrienne's eyes widened as she found
beautiful petticoats, chemisettes, white cambric pantalettes,
and silk stockings of the finest quality. Whoever had owned
them had confidence in her body, for the garments—while

flawless in taste and quality—were designed to display every inch of their owner's charms.

Who had left these clothes behind with Nathan? A spark of jealousy caught fire in Adrienne's heart. Had he had this wardrobe made for his lover? Her cheeks flamed hotter with each thought.

Slowly she donned fragile pantalettes and a stylishly simple round gown of gauzy cream muslin. It dipped low, revealing half her breasts, with only some lace edging to distract the eye. The morning sun was warm, and Adrienne decided to go without a fichu. Dressed, she glanced at the other garments on the bed and imagined another woman wearing them, clinging to Nathan and enjoying the admiring caress of his gaze. Her heart beat faster.

Adrienne's hair was still damp and her cheeks pink when Nathan returned. While stewards set a table and carried in the meal, she noticed the change in his own garb. No longer did he wear frayed clothes that looked as if they'd been in his wardrobe for a decade. Now his shirt was snow-white linen that set off an expression more relaxed and confident than Adrienne had ever seen on him. Gone were the old-fashioned breeches, replaced by sleek nankeen pantaloons that were the color of fine champagne. His freshly washed hair gleamed blue-black in the wide beam of sunlight.

"So much makes sense now," she whispered to herself.

His gaze flicked in her direction. "Does it? I'm glad."

When the other men had gone, Nathan gestured for her to take a chair at the table that was now set with white linen, china, and silver. "We won't always stand on this much ceremony; things break too easily at sea. But, navigating the Solvent, the waters above the Isle of Wight, takes time and care. It should be steady going for a few hours."

Adrienne watched as he poured champagne for them. She badly wanted to ask where the clothes had come from but sensed that it would be a mistake. When Nathan handed her a goblet across the table, his eyes fell on her bosom, and she knew a moment of pleasure that did not need to be shared with the gown's previous owner. What did the past matter, after all? The ghosts were gone, and she was here with him now. Even the most dedicated rakes could reform. . . .

"The food smells wonderful!" she exclaimed. "It seems days since I last ate."

"Have a taste. This morning is all about meeting basic needs." There was a hint of wickedness in his smile.

"Do those needs include my desire to be set free?"

"No." Nathan pointed to her plate. "Eat now, talk later."

Compelled to obey, Adrienne turned her attention to a fairly good beef chop with gravy, warm biscuits, stewed peas and lettuce, and a generous serving of potatoes. At intervals, she felt thirsty, and the cold champagne tasted delicious. When both of them began to feel sated, Nathan refilled their glasses and leaned back in his chair.

"I think my cook has grown lax in my absence. If this is the best he can do on the first day of our voyage, what will the fare taste like a month from now?"

Her eyes widened above the rim of her goblet. "A month! See here, I do not want to be trapped on this ship for a month! I'll go mad!"

"Perhaps not when you reach your destination. It's worth the long voyage." There was a subtly persuasive note in his voice. "Believe me, it's not that I want you, but I don't have any choice."

Dessert was a bowl of sublimely ripe sliced peaches drizzled with cream. Adrienne spooned one into her mouth and made a small sound of appreciation. She adored the prospect of sailing across the ocean with a lot of men to an exotic destination. What could be more romantic, especially compared to the two alternatives of Harms Castle and her family home in France? And, although she could hardly admit it to herself, Adrienne was captivated by Nathan.

Of course, all her secrets had to be kept from him. Their eyes met across the table. "Perhaps you ought to start at the beginning and explain everything, such as your real identity and your bargain with my father!"

"My name is Nathan Raveneau, just as you heard today. I was born in Essex, Connecticut, in America, but my father is French. He built ships and traded with China and the

West Indies, so I dreamed of having a ship of my own since childhood."

"You took the name of your town: Essex!" The champagne made her feel reckless. "Raveneau ... Why does that name sound familiar to me?"

"Perhaps because our parents are old friends. When I was a lad and my father was still trading, we used to sail to Europe as a family. I clearly remember your mother, Lisette Hahn, coming on board in Philadelphia, in 1793." It warmed him to see the pleased astonishment in her eyes. "She may have been the first female I appreciated, if you take my meaning. We took her to England to find your father, Nicholai, and they were married not long after that. And my family still socializes with your uncle and aunt, Alec and Caro Beauvisage. Those ties are more easily maintained since they all live in America."

"You're American, and yet you have a British accent—" It was hard to reconcile this new Nathan with the image she'd nurtured for so long, of Nathan Essex, a working-class man who'd probably been raised in a modest row house in London, or on the docks in Liverpool, or perhaps on a small farm.

"I've lived away from America most of my adult life, so accents tend to stick to me after a bit." Smiling then, he broke into a flat New England voice. "But, you see, I can still sound American when I want to!"

A long minute passed before she replied, "It's as if my entire point of view is suddenly tilted, and I can't gain my balance. To think that you knew my mother before I was born! Nothing about you fits anymore!"

"Or does it fit for the first time?"

"Perhaps." Musing over the past weeks and Nathan's bold masquerade, Adrienne remembered all the insults she'd hurled at him. It was amazing that he hadn't walked away. "I've been awfully uncivil to you at times—but then you were very bad to tell me so many lies about yourself. That was wicked."

"Let's call a truce then." He speared a juicy slice of peach with his fork and ate it, chewing slowly. "Hmm?"

"How can we do that? You've kidnapped me!"

"Odd. You don't appear to be feeling particularly abused at the moment." It was growing more difficult with each sip of champagne not to stare at her lips, for they looked even riper than the peaches she ate with such enjoyment. An adorable dribble of cream clung to her chin, while a smaller droplet had fallen to the bare swell of her breast. Nathan felt an unsettling twinge in his groin.

"Explain your bargain with my father," she demanded. "And you must tell the truth!"

"I was at White's Club, just a few hours after my run-in with you in Oxford Street over that dashed fan!" There was laughter in his eyes. "It seems a long time ago, doesn't it?"

"A lot has happened." Adrienne felt her eyes mist. "You were odious, you know. Unpardonably rude."

"Perhaps, but you were worse! No, no, let's not argue. To return to that night at White's Club: I was feeling out of sorts, and so was your father. He told me about his recalcitrant daughter, and I told him about the spoiled chit who had caused a colossal spectacle over a *fan*—"

Adrienne opened her mouth to protest, but the hot flush creeping up her cheeks said what words could not.

"Ah, you see the irony of the situation. We didn't know then that we were speaking of the same person!"

"Me," she supplied softly.

"Exactly!" Warming to his tale, Nathan sipped champagne and stretched out his legs. "Your father and I supped together. I mentioned my home on the island of Barbados, where an enemy seeks to make my life as difficult as possible. It developed that your father owns land there that adjoins the property of that villain. I need that land to catch him at his crimes, but I haven't had the money to buy it. Your father and I found a way, then, to help each other."

Her quick mind began fitting the pieces together before he could elaborate. "You promised to look after me in return for his land! But Walter Frakes-Hogg is dead and you have removed me from Harms Castle, which I still consider to be an alarmist maneuver on your part. In any case, why don't you take me back to Papa now and simply claim your reward?"

Nathan deftly toyed with the fluted goblet, staring at the

champagne's golden bubbles for a long minute. "Our agreement was that I would protect you and keep you, ah . . .
chaste until your twenty-first birthday on August first. According to my calendar, it is barely June." He couldn't
bring himself to look up at her, bracing instead for the
storm he knew would erupt.

"You are *lying*!" Cold fury drained the blood from her
face, leaving only a pink nose as evidence that Adrienne
had drunk too much champagne. She ran at Nathan, throwing herself onto his lap and grabbing the front of his shirt.
"My father would never do such a thing to me! Take back
your lies!"

Calmly he met her eyes, gripping her wrists at the same
time. "I am not lying, and your father wasn't a villain to be
concerned for your welfare. Perhaps you're really angry at
yourself, for all the rash things you've done to cause him to
worry that much? You know I have spoken the truth, for he
traveled all the way to London to try to persuade his headstrong daughter to come back to France with him. He loves
you, and feared that you might do something foolish while
too young to know better—something like climbing into
my bed that night at Harms Castle and demanding that I
make love to you."

She softened slightly against him and saw the involuntary desire in Nathan's eyes. So, that was why he had re-
sisted so fiercely that night! He'd been afraid of losing the
bargain with her father, of losing the land he coveted more
than love or honor. "You are a beast."

"So you've said. Get off me now, chit. I'm tired and I
want to go to sleep." The sight of her in that gown was
driving him mad.

Adrienne rose and watched as he assembled their dishes
and put the tray outside the door. Then Captain Raveneau
walked over to the big, inviting bed, sat down on the edge,
and gestured to her.

"Be a good girl and take off my boots." He extended a
leg.

She could still smell him on her cheek, and faintly on the
warm curve of her breasts. It was a terrible thing to lust after a man so much. Approaching with studied reluctance,

Adrienne pretended to pout as she pulled off first one boot and then the other. The sunlight glinted on his hair. "Surely you do not intend that we should *share* this bed?"

"Haven't we already had this conversation?" He yawned and began to remove his snug pantaloons. "I think we know each other well enough to dispense with the usual niceties, don't you? At this point, wouldn't modesty be misplaced? However, if you feel that strongly about it, you may lie on the carpet. . . ."

Adrienne was blushing furiously. She turned her back until he'd disrobed completely, and she sensed that he'd gotten between the soft sheets. "I suppose that there is room enough for both of us."

"Quite." He lay on his back and arched his brown arms over his head. The sheet fell midway down his chest.

"May I wear your shirt as a nightgown? The woman who left these other garments behind doesn't seem to have owned any."

A naughty smile curved his mouth, but he didn't open his eyes. "Whatever pleases you."

Her own smile was wider. *I'll remember those words!* Adrienne thought as she struggled with the fastenings on her gown and prepared to join him. If she could have designed her own fantasy, it could not have been better than reality.

Even the ridiculous bargain Nathan and her father had struck to keep her virtuous was just the sort of challenge she loved best. After sliding the shirt over her head, Adrienne climbed into bed beside Nathan Raveneau and wondered what would happen next.

Chapter Fifteen

IN THE DEPTHS OF TWILIGHT, ADRIENNE OPENED HER eyes and tried to remember where she was. The movement of the ship, the creak of the masts, and the voices of seamen on the deck above righted her memory.

She was turned on her side in the mahogany bed, looking out over the shadowed cabin. Her hair, scented with lilac, spilled over her shoulder and then across the white sheets. A down-filled pillow cradled Adrienne's cheek; the shirt she'd worn to bed was hitched up to her waist, and the bedclothes felt like silk on her bare limbs. Waves of deep contentment washed over her.

And then, as if even in sleep he sensed her thoughts, Nathan rolled toward her. He nuzzled her neck and slipped an arm around her waist.

She was hungry for the taste of his mouth, hungry to touch him and to feel his masculine hands on her body. But . . . how? Was this all she would be allowed: an occasional, tantalizing brush with him while he slept? All the moments of growing closeness Adrienne had shared with Nathan at Harms Castle came flooding back. As he snuggled against her, naked, she remembered the time she'd fallen from the library ladder into his arms, and his kiss the evening they'd nearly made love in the moonlit garden, and the night she had slipped into his bed after drinking too much claret.

Perhaps even more meaningful were the words and deeds that had helped to strengthen the bonds between them. Each interlude of shared understanding was a rose pressed in her

memory. Even their arguments were stirring; the sparks
they made added to the distinctive flavor of their relationship.

"Mmmm." Nathan's sound was born of bliss, and of
deep sleep. "El-o-ise . . ."

Adrienne froze, sensing that Eloise was more than a
dream. Had she shared this bunk with Nathan? Did the
beautiful clothes belong to her? How much had he loved
her?

Now, heart pounding, eyes stinging with tears of jealousy
and fresh resolve, Adrienne moved her body closer to Nathan's. She waited, expecting him to roll away. Moments
passed. It seemed that the beating of her heart echoed in every corner of her being, telling her that the past was gone,
and she was here with him now. Holding her breath, she
turned onto her back and searched for his face.

Nathan was awake now; alert, looking into her soul. His
eyes were an expression of everything Adrienne felt inside.
Both of them knew what the other wanted without speaking
a word. His mouth covered hers, hot and sensual, and his
strong arms embraced Adrienne's slim form. She was almost gasping with suppressed desires.

Holding fast to his shoulders, she opened her mouth and
was thrilled to feel his tongue circle her own. Nathan made
a low, primitive sound, touching every corner of her mouth,
then teasing her full lips with the edges of his teeth.

He was on fire; engorged, it seemed, for every time he'd
held back and denied himself. Every fiber of his being
thrummed with desire for this one woman: Adrienne. There
would be no going back, and yet it hardly seemed real. Perhaps later he would awaken, sated to the point of bliss, and
find that it had all been the safest of dreams.

"I want you." Had he spoken? God, how sweet she was,
so soft and responsive. Even her uncertainty was arousing.
Somehow, as Nathan felt her try to kiss him back, he realized that he must make the effort of his lifetime to hold
back once more, to make this an experience Adrienne
would treasure.

"Please," she whispered, "don't stop this time." She
couldn't help it. The need was so ravenous that she thought

she might die if he changed his mind. Nathan's simplest touch was excruciating: his fingers in her hair, tracing the column of her neck, brushing her breasts through the fabric of the shirt that tangled round her. Her nipples puckered, tingling, and a hot, congested feeling spread downward to smolder between her legs.

Gently he opened the buttons on the shirt she wore so fetchingly, while Adrienne gazed at every detail of his face. She kissed chiseled cheekbones, expressive brow, proud nose, hard jaw, while Nathan smiled into her emerald eyes. Their union felt so natural that it banished his last doubts. There was something between them, and perhaps this was the way to put it to rest.

Her coltish legs twined around him so that their hips came in contact. Adrienne started with shock when she felt him, fully erect, brush against her belly and her gently parted nether lips. Her eyes suddenly were huge, and she was flooded with a mixture of apprehension and intensified passion.

"Never mind," he reassured gently, drawing back. "Relax." And then, as he opened the shirt, his eyes ran leisurely over Adrienne's beautifully rounded breasts, the hollow her tummy made beneath her rib cage, her gracefully arched hips, and the sweet auburn-hued V of curls that beckoned to him. "You're gorgeous."

"You don't think—"

"I wouldn't change an inch of you, my darling."

She gloried in the endearment and in the irresistibly roguish smile he gave her before gathering her close and beginning to kiss her all over again. It was almost too much pleasure to bear.

As Nathan's mouth scorched her shoulder, she explored his body with her hands. His flesh was warm yet unyielding beneath the surface, and his muscles were sculpted exactly to her taste. Strong and defined, he had a wide, smooth chest in proportion to his lean hips and sleek flanks. Her touch was tentative, then daring as she ran her fingers lingeringly over the light mat of dark hair on his chest and said, "I love the way you are made—like a big cat."

He kissed her again, murmuring appreciation, and tugged

the shirt from her arms. Now, with tightly leashed control, Nathan turned her this way and that, nibbling, tasting, caressing, drawing surprised moans from his lover. He pushed away her mane of hair and nipped at the back of her neck, then down her spine, stopping when she squirmed. His mouth ministered to her tender inner arms and midriff, then, with exquisite slowness, cupped one breast and circled the nipple with his tongue.

"Oh!" Adrienne cried. "It—I—"

"Shh." The pink crest was hard when he took it into his mouth, suckling rhythmically, gently kneading both swollen breasts, until her thighs opened again and she arched upward.

If he didn't succumb soon, Nathan feared he might burst. A self-deprecating smile touched his mouth. He let her wrap her arms around him but slid a hand lower to touch her. Adrienne flinched. She was moist and puffy, pulsing just as he was. Blood pounded in his temples. If he caressed her very long there, it might be more than she could bear, and God knew it was already too much for him.

"If I hurt you, speak up and I'll stop," Nathan said.

"No—no—" Thanks to his careful preparations, she was in a state of complete readiness and wanted nothing more than to mate with Nathan in the truest sense. She felt wonderfully protected in the strength of his embrace.

He entered her tentatively, and Adrienne drew breath. "Mmm," he breathed. When, he wondered, had he felt such torturous bliss? The entire universe seemed centered there, where her body tightened around his.

"Help me," she urged.

Nathan cupped her buttocks with his hands and slowly went in to the hilt. The barrier was slight. There was no going back, so he rocked her against him a little, thrusting as gently as he could. Their bodies were both damp, and there was a musky scent in the air.

Instinct took over for Adrienne. She clung to his back and pushed up to meet his thrusts, pleasure and pain mingling. At last Nathan bit his lip, groaned, and she felt him pulse inside her.

"I felt you," she said against his shoulder.

"Did you?" Smiling, he kissed her. Already the pangs of doubt were starting. The sun had set and he was grateful for the grayish shadows that helped conceal his expression from her. "You must be thirsty. Let's have another glass of champagne."

Adrienne lolled on the pillows, and Nathan drew the bed-clothes up to cover her nakedness. She was happy—glowing with a sense of completion—and it made him distinctly uneasy. Feeling her eyes on him, Nathan pulled on a pair of breeches. He was pouring from the second bottle of champagne they'd opened that day when his head cleared.

His agreement with Nicholai Beauvisage had been violated! Adrienne would not be virtuous when she reached her twenty-first birthday, and he would not receive the land in Barbados! Why was it that his brain always seemed to be out of commission during crucial moments of decision—like the one he'd reached when Adrienne came up against him in bed? Nathan's face was stormy and distracted as he returned to her with their cups.

"What is it?" she asked, concerned.

He'd be a worse beast than he already felt if he brought up this selfish issue just minutes after making love to her. So he tried to smile again. "Nothing, sweet Adrienne." He ran a hand over her hair, rather in the manner of a fond brother. "I'm tired."

"Mmm. So am I." She drank down the champagne, then lay back on the pillows to savor the afterglow. "I think I'll go back to sleep for a bit."

"Good. You may need to sleep until morning." Realizing that she was waiting for him to join her, Nathan removed his breeches and climbed back into bed. Darkness slowly covered the cabin as the ocean rocked them.

"I'm glad you don't have to go on deck and be the captain," Adrienne murmured drowsily. She snuggled close, her cheek on his chest.

"Well, even captains must sleep, or I'll be no good at all. I have complete trust in Minter."

"Can I tell you a secret?"

He felt as if a heavy weight were pressing on him. "You won't regret it later, I hope. . . ."

"Don't be silly. I just wanted to tell you that I'm not so sorry to be here as I said I was. In truth, I don't want to go back to France or to Harms Castle anymore. I want to stay with you and continue this marvelous adventure."

Nathan felt queasy. "The champagne's gone to your head, my dear. Close your eyes now, hmm?"

Soon she did sleep, but he could not.

Zachary Minter gave the night watch to a seaman named Braddock. When he rose at dawn and went above, there was Captain Raveneau, pacing on the quarterdeck as if he'd never gone away at all. The sight of him did Minter's heart good.

The dawn sky was the color of English roses, but the coast of Britain was fading from sight as the *Golden Eagle* sailed deeper into the Channel. Once again all was right with the world as Minter hurried to join his captain and friend.

"Good morning, sir!" he exclaimed as he approached. "I don't mind telling you that it's truly fine to see you back on your quarterdeck where you belong!" His smile faded, however, when Raveneau turned. His eyes and cheekbones were shadowed. There were furrows in his brow and the scent of brandy on his breath.

"No need to scold me, Zach. Yes, I've been drinking, but I don't think it counts as before breakfast since I've scarcely slept." Nathan went to the rail and stared out over the choppy water. "I'd like to say that the simple joy of being at sea again kept me awake, but that wouldn't be quite true."

Minter's task, always, was to discover the real problem Raveneau inevitably tried to disguise. "What's causing you such torment?" As he spoke, a cloud of suspicion gathered over him. "I hope it isn't that wench! There's been nothing but trouble since the day she came into our lives!"

"*Our* lives?"

"I've been inconvenienced as much as you, Captain! Maybe more."

"Well, cheer up then. Our involvement with Miss Beauvisage may be at an end after all." He looked utterly miserable as he spoke.

As the sun rose higher, more men appeared on deck, and that made Zachary nervous. "See here, old friend, I must insist that you stop telling riddles and lay this matter out before me. Perhaps I'm dim, but quite frankly, I don't know what the devil is going on!" He caught Nathan's sleeve and tugged at it. "Look at me and tell me the truth. You know you will sooner or later, so let's get it over with."

Nathan grimaced as if he were in pain but met the other man's penetrating eyes. "I explained to you the terms of my agreement with Adrienne's father?"

"You were to keep her out of mischief and danger until her twenty-first birthday in August, and in return, Beauvisage promised you the land adjoining Xavier Crowe's estate."

"Right." Nathan cleared his throat. "Did I mention the part about my responsibility to see to it that she reach her birthday with her virtue intact?"

"I don't remember." Zach peered at him, eyes narrowed. "Yesterday you said that we had to keep her with us in order to fulfill the twenty-first birthday rule. Now you're hinting that the bargain may be off and Miss Beauvisage may part ways with us. Don't tell me that *you* . . ."

Raveneau looked guilty. "It's a complicated situation."

"God's foot! I—I'm speechless!"

"It's no use shouting at me. I can't believe it happened either, and I've been heaping condemnation on myself for the past dozen hours. To think that I put myself through endless ordeals at Harms Castle, all so that I could obtain that priceless land on Barbados—and then, when I finally escape to the haven of my ship and my crew—"

"Were you drunk?"

"No. But I *had* been sleeping." He added hopefully, "Perhaps I thought it was a dream. Might that excuse me?"

"No. If you ask me, which you haven't, I'd venture to guess that there's more involved here than pure mindless lust. You just won't admit to it yourself! I'm not blind, sir, and I can see quite clearly that there is a bond of some sort—"

Raveneau clapped a hand over the smaller man's mouth. "Don't say that! Adrienne Beauvisage is the last woman on earth I would choose to be bound to—let alone—" He paused to swallow. "—*love*. She's a hellion! Unmanageable, headstrong—"

"Sounds to me like a match made in—"

"Hell," Nathan insisted grimly.

"So, now that you've had your way with her, we're taking her home to France and admitting defeat to her father, who trusted you to protect her from scoundrels of your ilk? Then we'll sail on home to Barbados and forget we ever knew Miss Beauvisage?"

Nathan closed his eyes. "I will despise myself for the rest of my life if I let that land, and the opportunity to finally do in Xavier Crowe, slip through my fingers—simply because I—"

"I'm growing bored listening to you scold yourself. What is Miss Beauvisage's current view of the situation?"

A steward appeared with two mugs of strong hot coffee, and they paused to drink for a few minutes. "God, I'd forgotten how vile this coffee is," Nathan said, then drank some more. "There's nothing like the taste of boiled, bitter coffee mingled with a gust of salty sea air." He took a deep breath and grinned. Zachary only stared in response, waiting. "Oh, yes. Adrienne. Well, she seems to have thawed a bit toward me."

"She's no longer begging to be rescued from this abduction?"

"Uh—no." A slow flush crept over Nathan's face, giving him a boyish look. "In fact, she has confessed that she's rather fond of me and would rather sail to Barbados with us than do anything else."

"I see! No wonder you're in this state."

"Have I ever told you, Zach, that sometimes you behave like my mother?"

"Someone must." Looking around, Zach saw that there were men who needed direction and tasks to which he should attend. "See here, Captain, the morning advances! I'll give you one choice piece of advice, all right?"

"I am listening."

"It seems to me that you can still have the land you covet on Barbados. Nicholai Beauvisage is a friend, is he not? If his daughter is a hellion who has sworn off marriage, it seems highly likely to me that he'd be overjoyed to see her wedded to *you*. He would doubtless view you as just the son-in-law he'd choose, and he would be delighted to give you that land." Minter watched his comrade's expression carefully. "Of course, Miss Beauvisage could decline your proposal and decide to return to France after all."

"*Proposal?* I can't believe my ears! Are you suggesting that I actually marry that little spitfire?" He strode across the quarterdeck, then back again. "You are mad, Zach!" Nathan stopped, and his brow cleared. "But wait. This is another of your jests, isn't it?"

"Oh, no, I'm quite serious. Haven't you ever heard of a marriage of convenience? Of course, she probably won't agree to such a risky scheme. . . ."

Nathan put a hand to his thudding heart. "Have I not told you that risky is Adrienne's favorite word? I would like to know why you don't mention my feelings on this subject? Why do you assume that Adrienne is the only participant who would need convincing?"

Minter shrugged. "I know you love these sparring matches, Captain, but there is work to be done. Look at that inept seaman in the ratlines!" Turning away, calling to the boatswain, he looked back one last time at his oldest friend. "We both know that you've never had time or the inclination to search out real love. So why not marry for more practical reasons? Can you think of a better reason than the land you yearn for? Besides, Miss Beauvisage is hardly spinsterish. She'd give you beautiful children."

With that, Zachary Minter went off to oversee all the details on board the *Golden Eagle* that the captain was too preoccupied to bother with.

Nathan, meanwhile, stood gripping the quarterdeck rail, his entire being in turmoil. He was exhausted, frustrated, and more confused than he could ever remember feeling. In fact, confusion had visited him rarely in the past. Even as a child, he'd always known his own mind and had been certain of his needs and abilities.

Until Adrienne. Damn her!

There seemed to be nothing for it but to go below and talk with her, even though Zach's plan seemed too ludicrous for words.

Walking along the shadowed gangway, Nathan recognized Franklin Crenshaw approaching from the other direction, an empty tray in his hand. The sight of his captain made him go scarlet.

"I—I've just taken breakfast to Miss Beauvisage, sir," he stammered when they were face to face. "She requested it."

"That was good of you, Crenshaw." He stared hard at the young man, wondering why he looked so embarrassed. "I trust that nothing was amiss?"

"No, sir, I don't think so! Miss Beauvisage could not have been more charming."

"I see." He arched a dubious brow. "Thank you, then. Back to work."

Moments later Nathan entered his own cabin and found Adrienne sitting up in the sunlit bed, wearing his shirt and happily buttering a muffin. At least her bare legs were safely tucked under the covers, but that was little consolation given the rest of her appearance.

"Good morning!" she called, beaming at the sight of him. "Goodness, you look more and more like a real pirate. Will we bury treasure on your island?"

Her glossy hair was still long and loose. One curl drooped appealingly over her eye. Nathan couldn't help feeling alarmed by the strength of his attraction to her. "Couldn't you have scraped together a little of your celebrated breeding and gotten dressed before you called for breakfast? You'll soon have my entire crew in a lather!"

Adrienne laughed, pink-cheeked. "Have a bite of my muffin. It's surprisingly tasty." She was so terribly happy that nothing he said could dampen her spirits. "You have that stormy look. I know it can't be anything I've done, because I've been sleeping ever since we kissed good night. Come and sit down and tell me what's wrong."

Disarmed, Nathan did as she bade. He perched on the edge of what had been his very own bed and was taken aback when Adrienne leaned forward and kissed him.

"Mmmm. Even after brandy and a cheroot, you still taste good." Her eyes sparkled with daring. After long weeks spent trying to conform to a prescribed role at Harms Castle, she was finally able to give free rein to her true self. Nathan had certainly approved of her impetuous streak in bed last night, and the tenderness and closeness they'd shared had allowed Adrienne to open her heart at last. "I've missed you. How long have you been awake?"

"Hours." In search of a distraction, he sampled a piece of muffin. "I . . . have had a great deal on my mind."

Instinct made the little hairs on her neck prickle. "Please don't tell me you're speaking of regrets." She took her hand from his arm and moved back into the pillows.

"This isn't about regrets, or even sentiment," he said coolly. It took real determination to steel himself against feelings that would only get him further into trouble. "I lost my head last night and I've been trying to straighten this matter out ever since, with little success."

"This *matter*?" Adrienne repeated. Her heart began to ache.

"For God's sake, can't we simply discuss this as two grown people, perhaps even as friends? We've been through a great deal together, after all. Just this once, try to lead with your fine intellect rather than your fiery emotions!"

She jumped out of the bed, set the tray of breakfast dishes on the table, and began dressing. "Obviously you and I were differently disposed last evening. Let me restore my shattered modesty, and then we'll sit down and untangle our affairs."

It was impossible not to hear the throb in her voice. When she had slipped on a simple muslin gown and couldn't reach to fasten the back, Nathan walked over and assisted. Both of them were aware that his strong fingers were trembling slightly.

Adrienne pulled her hair back with a ribbon, took a seat at the table, and folded her hands. "Now I am ready."

"Well, this is all very simple, actually. Or it can be."
Somehow he found himself wandering over to the cellaret,
where bottles were fitted into niches and securely stop-
pered. This was thirsty business. After pouring himself a
small glassful of brandy, Nathan drank, but he felt no better.

"Anything would seem simple to a man who freely in-
dulges in strong spirits at dawn," Adrienne observed politely.

"Just once would you let me have my say?" He began
pacing, moving with the motion of the ship. "Perhaps, as a
woman, you do not understand that men are created differently when it comes to . . . uh, mating."

"Kindly instruct me."

He paused near the table, aware of her cutting look, and
refolded his left cuff. "Well, when a man has an opportunity to—be with a woman, it seems that that urge overrules
all civilized impulses. His mind, his reasoning power, and
his sense of discipline are swept away by a powerful ancient instinct that women will never be able to compre-
hend."

If she hadn't been so furious, Adrienne would have
laughed. "Fascinating! And women don't have such instincts?"

Swallowing hard, he offered, "As a man, I really
couldn't say, but I have always been told that ladies are
more concerned with more delicate matters—like romance
and marriage."

"This has been an informative lesson indeed, sir!" Her
hands were clenched. "And what bearing might it have on
me? Could you be telling me that last night you were in the
grip of 'ancient instincts' too powerful for you to control?
That your need to 'mate' rendered you temporarily *sense-
less*?"

Nathan glanced at her under his lashes. "Something like
that," he muttered.

"Which means, of course, that I mustn't delude myself
that you care for me." Adrienne caught the back of his shirt
as he turned. "If you are such a big brave man, why can
you not sit down and look me in the eye?"

He did so. "All right, I admit it—I'm ashamed of my

own behavior toward you. At Harms Castle I was able to maintain a semblance of honor, but that's gone now." The sight of her pale face and bright eyes made him straighten his shoulders. "We both should face facts and admit that neither of us is suited to the sort of romance our parents have enjoyed in their marriages. You and I are both stubborn and fond of our independence. We like to take risks and dislike compromise—"

"So last night was just another adventure for us?"

Nathan leaned toward her with a tentative smile. "You might say that, yes! If you look at it that way, it will be easier to store our . . . interlude away in your memory and not expect me to become someone I am not."

"Oh, I understand perfectly. You're a rogue."

He grinned. "And you're a gently bred vixen. We're not cut out for romantic love. As long as we understand each other, we can manage quite well."

"What did you have in mind?" Adrienne inquired.

Now he was really skating on thin ice, particularly with a woman as perceptive as Adrienne. Longing to jump up and resume pacing, Nathan instead held her gaze. "I've been cutting myself to ribbons this morning—over my failure to live up to my bargain with your father. He trusted me to protect you."

"I was the lamb, and you the wolf in sheep's clothing?"

"It's not as if I plotted your seduction, for God's sake, or took you against your will!"

"That's true. And now what do you intend to do with me? Does your honor, or lack of same, allow us to carry on as if last night never happened? My father wouldn't know, and I wouldn't tell."

"Then you suggest that we both deceive him?"

Adrienne tossed her chestnut curls. "I've been doing it all my life and Papa is used to it, though I do think deception is rather a strong word. I call it managing my own life."

"You really do want to go to Barbados?" He watched her, but her usually expressive face was closed.

"Yes. Have I not told you so? I'm looking forward to it."

"Believe it or not, I am a man of honor. I would *not* consciously deceive your father, especially in this case. I could not accept land I hadn't earned. However, there is one possible solution—if you, and then your father, agree."

Hope fluttered inside Adrienne's heart like a little bird, but she couldn't let him see. "Yes?"

The words caught in his throat. "I—well, it seems to me that there is a way for both of us to have what we want, but it strikes even me as rather coldblooded." She didn't encourage him except to hold his eyes, waiting. "We could marry."

Chills ran over her body. "What, exactly, are you proposing?"

"Neither of us has wanted to marry for love. Why not join our houses for more practical reasons? You'll have the life of adventure you desire in wild Barbados, and I'll have that land I covet." He smiled jauntily. "It would solve my problems with all the mothers of marriageable daughters as well!"

"You are speaking, then, of a marriage of convenience?"

"Yes."

Adrienne lifted her chin. "I accept."

Chapter Sixteen

THE *GOLDEN EAGLE* WAS SPARED THE CALAMITY OF hurricanes or attacking ships, and the trade winds sped her four-week voyage to Barbados. During that time, Captain Raveneau immersed himself in all the duties he'd neglected for so long. Every waking hour was spent poring over charts or on deck, overseeing the ceaseless activity of the crew. At night he slept in a hammock at one end of the cabin. Nathan explained to Adrienne that since his hours were so erratic, it was best that he not take the chance of disturbing her.

Besides, their interactions had reached a new stage. No longer bantering and bickering as in the past, they now behaved as a cordial betrothed couple. Nathan asserted that he had already broken enough rules; until they were married, he would be the soul of propriety.

Adrienne knew it was all an excuse to avoid her, but told herself that she could afford to bide her time. There were dozens of fine books to lose herself in, and when her thoughts wandered to Nathan, she allowed herself the luxury of fantasy. Most of the time this tactic worked. She would imagine their exotic life on Barbados, coloring in the details of a fine manor house and a deep feather bed where she and her husband would pass the sultry nights in conjugal bliss. On the evenings when Nathan was especially short with her, she sometimes lay in her bunk in the shadowy cabin and let the sea rock her until images of their beautiful, laughing babies lulled her to sleep.

Yet, when Adrienne wore the other woman's clothing, unwelcome questions about the mysterious Eloise, whom Nathan had called in his sleep, crept into her mind. At last she firmly reminded herself that whoever Eloise had been, she was gone and now Adrienne was with Nathan. And that was that.

The afternoon that land was first sighted, her world grew rosier still. Nathan took Minter's suggestion to invite her on deck for a look through the spyglass.

"The ocean is breathtaking," she marveled. When they'd first sailed from England, the Atlantic Ocean had seemed dark and dramatic. Now the tropical waters dazzled. The sea, a brilliant azure, seemed friendly with its silvery flying fish, warm breezes, and heartbreakingly stunning sunsets.

Nathan said nothing, but watched from a distance as she looked through the spyglass. Secretly he felt that the beauty surrounding them was no match for Adrienne. Her afternoons spent reading on deck had lent her skin an appealing golden-peachy glow, and her eyes were vivid in contrast. Many a night he had lain in his hammock aching for her.

Sometimes Raveneau wondered if Adrienne was a curse.

"Look!" she exclaimed with a radiant smile. "Is that really Barbados? It's not at all what I expected—"

"It's shaped rather like a pear with a lower half that swings out toward the east," Minter said. "You're looking at that side of the island, which also happens to border the Atlantic Ocean. The west coast is gentle; the east is wild, even treacherous. Bridgetown, the main port city, is on the western coast."

"I'll have to study a map, to learn more," she mused.

Minter pointed toward the shore. "That particular craggy-looking landscape is called the Scotland District. You'll find that nearly every village, city, house, and road is named for something English. Even Barbados itself is lovingly referred to as Bimshire."

Adrienne was already infatuated with her new home. "Bimshire? How charming!"

"Charming isn't the word for the Atlantic side of the island," Nathan informed her. "Farther down the coast is Cobbler's Reef, where the surf is treacherous and Xavier

Crowe watches at night from his house for unsuspecting ships. He and his henchmen use false lights to fool the ships into thinking they've reached Bridgetown. Then his wrecking parties plunder the cargoes."

"How terrible! No wonder you despise him!" She peered to the south, fascinated in spite of herself. The water was exquisite, layering in shades of vivid blue and turquoise as it became shallower toward the shoreline. It was difficult to reconcile such beauty with danger. "Xavier Crowe lives on the southeastern side of Barbados? Where is your own estate? And where is Papa's land?"

"My home is called Tempest Hall, and it's more northeast, inland a bit." His brow arched with familiar cynicism. "Your father's fifty oceanfront acres adjoin Crowe's northern border." Nathan took a step backward. "If you two will excuse me, I'll check on the navigation. I know that you'll keep Miss Beauvisage amused, Zach."

She watched him turn away, then pause for a moment to speak to an old, gnomelike surgeon's mate. Next to her, Zachary Minter spoke in a tone of grudging sympathy.

"I know Captain Raveneau hasn't been very kind to you of late, Miss Beauvisage, but he's really not a bad sort. Do you see that ancient fellow he's chatting with? Tarpeck was a crewmember on the *Black Eagle*, the privateer that André Raveneau sailed during the Revolutionary War in America. The old fellow isn't much use anymore, but we found a place for him." Minter watched her face.

"I suppose your captain can't be all bad." Adrienne felt that it was better if Nathan thought that she was every bit as cool about their marriage as he was. If he knew that she felt giddy every time he drew near, all would be lost.

Even now the sight of him in biscuit breeches that skimmed his lean hips and the muscles in his thighs made her heart pound. All his gestures were etched in her memory, along with each detail of his harshly handsome face. . . .

"Miss Beauvisage, are you all right? Is it the heat?"

Adrienne discovered that Minter was looking at her, puzzled, and she smiled. "Actually, I adore this climate as long as there is a breeze. If I don't take care, I'll be as brown as

Nathan before long." Slowly she began to stroll along the deck rail, and Zachary Minter followed, quite spellbound. "If I looked preoccupied, it was because I was considering your words. I realize that you are very loyal to Nathan, and I know that he is loyal to you and all his men. But I am a lady. Will I ever be accepted?"

The first mate's perpetual sunburn disguised his guilty blush. "I confess that I had my doubts about this arrangement right from the start. I didn't want him to go to Harms Castle, even if it meant getting that land on Barbados, and I sure didn't want you on this ship. But," he hastened to add, "that's not quite true anymore. I'm beginning to think that there might be something to this."

"That's rather cryptic." Adrienne glanced at him sideways, under her thick lashes. "You're telling me that you have begun to accept me, yet your captain seems to be pulling back more and more since we agreed to marry. Are you aware that in England we were friends . . . after a fashion?"

"I can see that." Zach cleared his throat. "It isn't my place to discuss Captain Raveneau with you this way. We've known each other all our lives, so I sometimes forget and say more than he'd want. He guards his privacy with a vengeance."

"And he keeps his heart tightly locked?" Adrienne suggested wistfully. "You must know all the . . . people in his past."

"That's . . . true. Look—" Zach glanced left and right, then leaned closer to confide, "I hope you'll try to be patient with him. He's just like his father was—wild as the sea, and fighting instinctively against any woman who would tame him. Do you know what they called him in London?"

"No." There were so many new pieces to the puzzle of Nathan. "What?"

"The Scapegrace."

"Oh! But—of course I've heard of The Scapegrace! He was said to be a libertine! I heard shocking stories about his conquests. . . ." Her eyes widened.

"Never mind those. All you need to understand is that he has always been used to his freedom. If he behaves badly toward you at times, it is not because he doesn't care, but because of his inner struggle with his nature."

"His reputation darkens by the moment." Adrienne wondered again if she could have misjudged him so perilously. "You said he's like his father . . . yet even André Raveneau learned to love, didn't he?"

"God, yes!" Minter laughed for emphasis. "Once he finally surrendered to loving Devon he went right off the edge. Nathan's parents have been happily married for thirty-five years!" He paused. "But he hasn't any desire to emulate his parents."

"I see . . ." Her heart sank even as she gathered the courage to ask Minter about Eloise. How could she explain the way she'd learned the other woman's name?

"Minter!" It was Captain Raveneau, shouting from the quarterdeck. His face was dark. "You are amusing Miss Beauvisage a bit too well! Leave her now and return to your duties."

Adrienne put one hand on her hip and shielded her eyes with the other as she challenged him from halfway across the ship. "Is it a crime for someone to befriend me?"

To her chagrin, Nathan did not respond, but presented his back to her as if she had not spoken at all.

The *Golden Eagle* sailed around the top of Barbados, then leisurely skirted the western coast, bound for the prosperous port of Bridgetown. At dawn, Adrienne was completely packed and ready to disembark from the ship, even though they hadn't reached land yet.

Standing at the rail, she gazed out at the aqua water that lapped against sugary beaches lined with slim palm trees and lush flowering plants. This was the side of the island that bordered the warm, gentle Caribbean Sea. To Adrienne, it was like a dream, wrapped in the glow of sunrise. Everything about Barbados seemed exotic, and the unpredictable newness of her future was thrilling.

"Second thoughts?"

She heard Nathan's voice over her shoulder and felt his breath on her cheek. A familiar, euphoric feeling tingled her scalp and traveled down to the tips of her toes. Given the mounting evidence of her fiancé's rakish past, Adrienne had spent much of the night worrying that her cause was hopeless and that she might be just the latest woman to wear the silky underclothes in his cabin. Still, when Nathan was near, hope swelled within her again.

"No second thoughts," Adrienne murmured. She didn't turn to look at him, but allowed the corners of her mouth to curve upward. "I think I may have been born to live here."

"Indeed?" Nathan reminded himself that even marriage needn't be permanent—particularly not *this* sort of arrangement. He didn't care to ponder his aversion to true love but supposed that it could be traced to his parents. Their marriage was so perfect that Nathan felt that anything less would be failure.

He also might be avoiding real romantic entanglements because of his own bitter history. Not only didn't he like to hear Eloise's name spoken, he tried not to think of her. It was easier to focus on Xavier Crowe and direct his hatred toward him. Meanwhile, it seemed likely that Adrienne would grow homesick on Barbados, and he would generously grant her a divorce.

"Is it your belief," he inquired, "that we are being guided by the hand of fate?"

Recalling Zachary Minter's cautionary words about Nathan's matrimonial jitters, Adrienne laughed. "Oh, no, nothing as serious as that, sir! I anticipate only a good adventure."

His brow cleared. Slowly he nodded, smiling. "That's good. Very good. We are of one mind, then."

"Are we?"

The *Golden Eagle* was coming around Needham Point, headed for Carlisle Bay and the port of Bridgetown. Sails were furled. Nathan went off with Minter to bring the ship in safely, and Adrienne stared in surprise at the bustling city of stone buildings that curved around the bay.

The slow voyage of imagining was over. Adrienne's dreams were turning swiftly to reality. She hadn't expected Bridgetown to look so civilized. Tarpeck was wandering the decks, getting in the way, and Minter sent him to

Adrienne's assistance. The old man was half blind, but he'd
sailed this route countless times.

"That upper part of the harbor is called the Careenage,"
he explained, pointing with a misshapen finger to colorful
rows of vessels lining the quays. "They turn the ships on
their sides and scrape the hulls there. That's 'careening.' "

Adrienne used Tarpeck as her guide then. He identified
St. Anne's Barracks, which surrounded a neat square. At
the other end of town was Fontabelle, now empty, where
the governors of Barbados had once lived, and Pelican Island, covered with lovely palm trees. "The town's burned
twice and survived some dreadful hurricanes," Tarpeck
said. "Plenty o' wooden buildings and great plantations
houses have been lost to fire and storms. It's the coral stone
ones, with the thickest walls, that survive."

Again Adrienne was struck by the extremes of life in this
paradise. How could a place as idyllic and beautiful as Barbados be so dangerous? It was unnerving to think that one's
home could be standing one day and be blown away the
next. . . .

"Those hills out yonder are part of other parishes,"
Tarpeck growled. He stuck his gnarled finger out again, in
the direction of low, undulating hills in the distance beyond
Bridgetown. There were houses here and there, and an
abundance of feathery palms. "Pardon me, miss, but I see
that I'm needed. I have duties to perform, y'know."

"I deeply appreciate your assistance, Mr. Tarpeck!"
Adrienne gave the grizzled old seaman a glowing smile and
was rewarded by a dip of his head, accompanied by a gruff
sound.

When the *Golden Eagle*'s anchor was dropped, tiny native boats circled the ship. The boats' occupants offered services of every sort, from clothes-washing to baggage
transport. Adrienne had seen very few Negroes in France or
England, so she couldn't help being curious. She was relieved to discover that they weren't frightening in the least.
Dressed in light, brightly colored clothing, these people
were friendly and welcoming.

It wasn't necessary to make good-byes to the ship and
her crew. The *Golden Eagle* would remain anchored off

Barbados until her captain rearranged his life and decided what his next voyage would be. The men saw Adrienne off with warm smiles and whispers of good wishes, which made her wonder how many of them knew that she would soon be Mrs. Raveneau.

Their luggage went to the docks first, and then Adrienne and Nathan, with Minter, descended the accommodation ladder and found places in the longboat that would take them to shore. Dressed in a simple muslin promenade gown with green ribbons to match her eyes, Adrienne was becoming more and more aware of the heat as the morning advanced. There was a nice breeze, but the humidity was a condition she had never experienced.

"I feel rather silly with my parasol," she confessed to the men. "Everyone will think me a spoiled Englishwoman."

"I don't doubt that you'll be an unladylike shade of golden brown in no time at all," Nathan replied, "but I would advise that you use your parasol, or a bonnet, as often as you can bear it. Too much sun too quickly will make you ill, and very red!"

"Besides," Zachary chimed in jovially, "the Bajans, as the islanders call themselves, will expect you to act the part of a wealthy planter's wife. You ought to—" He broke off under the fire of Raveneau's stare. "Did I say something amiss?"

"Your captain doesn't like to contemplate his approaching nuptials," Adrienne said tartly. "I daresay he'd like to lock me in my room after the wedding so he won't have to admit to anyone on the island that he's gotten married at all!"

Nathan gave her a menacing stare. "I was hoping you had left that acid tongue in England!"

Meanwhile, Zach tugged at his collar. "God's foot, isn't it getting hotter by the minute? And I think this boat is shrinking! Ah, here's the quay, and not a moment too soon!"

If she hadn't been so furious with Nathan, Adrienne would have laughed. As it was, she caught sight of Minter's reassuring wink and gave him a tiny smile in response.

Nathan was looking around as he jumped onto the dock

and took the luggage Minter handed up to him. "What a relief. There's Philip, reliable as ever. Thank God some things
don't change."

An old white-haired Negro gentleman made his way
through the people, barrels, crates, and coils of rope that
covered the quay. Somehow, perhaps because of his direct
gaze and dignified bearing, Adrienne guessed that he must
be Philip, the person Nathan was so happy to see.

"I be happy to be findin' you, Captain," he said in a low,
melodious voice.

"Philip, you are a sight for sore eyes!" Nathan's temper
was replaced by high spirits. "Look at that handsome waistcoat! Did Orchid make it for you?"

A warm smile creased the older man's face. His ensem-
ble of loose beige trousers with a white shirt was crowned
by a vest of tangerine and lime striped silk. "You do be a
kind man, sir. Sorry to say dat Orchid feelin' weak dis pas
season. We daughter, Lily, make de waiscoat for me."

Nathan looked concerned. "Orchid will be all right,
won't she? I've been away too long. I want everything to
be unchanged when I come home, but how can that be
when I am at sea for so many months?"

"I wonder dis too, sir," Philip murmured with a nod. His
brown eyes wandered toward Adrienne.

"You must be curious about this young lady." Nathan
took Adrienne's arm in time to save her from being
knocked over by a passing sailor. "This isn't the place for
conversation, but I should perform an introduction. Philip
Smythe, this is Miss Adrienne Beauvisage." As they exchanged smiles and greetings, Raveneau grew paler.
"I—uh—I should add, Philip, that Miss Beauvisage is
my—uh—intended."

"Sir! It can be so? Dear Lord, we do have blessing! Orchid be so happy. She t'ink dis day not come in she lifetime!"

Adrienne gave her betrothed a sidelong glance, imitating
his own arched eyebrow. "My darling, why would Philip
and Orchid think that you would not be the marrying sort?"

His grip on her arm tightened. "I haven't a clue. Let's go
before we're pushed into the water."

Minter helped them transport the baggage to a waiting wagon, then took it upon himself to hand Adrienne into the neat little carriage that Philip referred to as a sulky. As she took her seat under the sheltering hood, the small man leaned closer.

"Good luck, miss. I mean that sincerely." He gave her another wink. "Try to be patient with him, even though he won't deserve such mercies."

His words made her smile, but her face fell as she realized Zachary wasn't coming with them. "Must you stay with the ship?"

"Don't look so terrified. He won't gobble you up, no matter how loudly he may growl." On impulse, Minter reached out and patted her creamy cheek.

Nathan was climbing in on the other side, and Philip perched in front, gathering the reins. "Zach," Nathan warned with a satirical undercurrent, "don't grow too attached to Adrienne. It's not seemly."

Minter blushed. "I'd better be getting back to the *Golden Eagle*. I wish both of you good fortune."

"But, wait—surely you'll be coming to our wedding?" Adrienne cried suddenly, remembering.

"I don't think it will be that sort of wedding," Nathan said. He leaned forward and tapped Philip on the shoulder, signaling that they were ready to proceed.

Adrienne's world was whirling with a mixture of confusion and delight. As they clattered over the narrow, cobbled streets of Bridgetown, Nathan acted as guide. It seemed that everything had an English name, from Trafalgar Square, just south of the Careenage, to the main thoroughfare called Broad Street. However, Bridgetown looked nothing at all like London. There were people of every color and class, and animals ranging from donkeys to monkeys, and vendors selling a variety of bright, exotic fruits and flowers. The shops, inside the sturdy stone buildings, had small windows that showed no goods to the curious newcomer. Perhaps, Adrienne decided, the last hurricane had convinced the merchants to keep glass to a minimum.

"I don't think I realized," she said softly, "that there would be so few white people and so many . . ."

"They prefer to be called colored," Nathan supplied, "and, yes, the slaves and free colored people far outnumber the rest of us. Five to one, I'd guess."

She made a little sound of surprise. "Slaves! I—I don't think that had even occurred to me! I suppose I thought it was only the Americans who engaged in such barbarism."

"Not all Americans; just in our South," he corrected. "And, yes, unfortunately, the plantations here and on other West Indian islands are staffed mostly by slave labor."

"I cannot tell you how shocking I find that. I don't know if I would have come had I known."

"Indeed." Nathan flicked up an eyebrow and lounged against the upholstered seat. "Would it be easier to tolerate if I tell you that the slave trade was abolished here twelve years ago?"

"You mean the slaves have been freed?"

"No . . . we just can't bring any more to Barbados. That doesn't mean that there aren't already enough, or that the children of these slaves won't be slaves themselves." He shrugged. "It's a fact of life, I'm afraid—although I do think that we may see emancipation on Barbados in my lifetime, which is more than I can say for America."

"Nathan . . ." Her pretty chin was set in an unforgiving line. "Surely you do not own slaves? You, as an American from the northern states, could never be a party to something so cruel and degrading to your fellow human beings!"

"No one has ever challenged me on the subject in quite those terms," he allowed. His own expression took on a stubborn hardness. "I have never purchased a slave, and I have offered many their freedom. When I bought Tempest Hall, I got everything, including its slaves, and it hasn't seemed wise to tamper with the workings of the plantation when I am scarcely home as it is."

"Then you *do* own slaves!" Adrienne spoke the words as if she were accusing him of torture and murder.

"For God's sake, keep your voice down! Yes, I suppose I do, but it was never a conscious choice. Many of my workers are free now, but frankly, I can't afford to pay them all a wage yet."

Philip's head inclined a bit in their direction. "You do have debt aplenty as it is, sir," he interjected.

"Surely you are not going to defend this man, are you, Philip?" Adrienne cried. "How can you defend someone who has the audacity to claim ownership of your being?"

"Oh, Captain Raveneau don' own me," the old man replied cheerfully. "My wife an' me be free one score and ten year. Master Graves give we de gift when he die."

"That was thirty years ago—and you chose to remain at Tempest Hall?"

"Yes, Mistress. We have nice life an' work dere. We t'ink, why leave we home?"

Nathan reached for her hand and gripped it hard. "You have a lot to learn about life on Barbados, my dear. You might be wise to hold your tongue until you are better informed."

The road they traveled up the western coast offered views of the placid, aqua Caribbean Sea, plantation houses set inland on high ground, and some swampland in between.

Nathan was glad for the chance to change topics. "We could have sailed north to Speightstown on the schooner that travels back and forth, but I was anxious to set foot on the island and have a look around. Unfortunately, the roads here aren't good." He gestured toward the ruts. "Barbados was once covered with palm trees and shady forests, but when the English arrived two centuries ago, they cleared the land, drained the swamps, and began building homes and planting crops. Roads were put in to get the goods to the ships, but they aren't useful for much else."

"So many great stone windmills!" Adrienne exclaimed, pointing at a handsome plantation as they passed. "What are they for?"

"The sugarcane is ground in the mill, but that's just one step in getting sugar. I'll show you our buildings tomorrow and explain the process. It's very involved and mysterious!"

"You know that I'm curious, and I love to learn. Before you know it, I'll have devised a better method!"

Philip turned all the way around to stare at her, eyes wide, and Nathan began to laugh. "De lady not like any we know!" exclaimed the old man, which elicited more laughter from his employer.

The road dipped low through a long gully, with tree roots protruding all around them, and Nathan explained that the wildly beautiful trees above were called bearded figs. "Actually, the island is probably named for those trees," he said. "Barbados means 'bearded ones' in Portuguese. Most likely the settlers were referring either to these ancient trees that look as if they have beards—or to bearded tribesmen." He paused, then added, "You see, my dear bluestocking, you are not the only one who likes to study."

"Is Nathan Raveneau as much a scholar as Nathan Essex was?"

"More."

The drive to Tempest Hall took hours. Adrienne asked about the groves of mahogany trees they passed and the cavorting green monkeys she glimpsed from the sulky, and Nathan explained that both had been imported by early settlers. "Even we Bajans sometimes forget that many of the things we take for granted aren't indigenous, like the mangoes I eat every morning!"

Finally, after stopping for a midday meal in Holetown, Adrienne was overcome by drowsiness. She dropped off and slept for most of the afternoon. When she awoke, she found that her cheek was resting on Nathan's shoulder. Both of them were damp with perspiration, but he smelled clean and wonderfully masculine to her, and the sensation of his warm, hard body touching hers was bliss.

"Ah," he murmured, sounding both tender and amused, "she stirs."

Adrienne didn't want to move. Daringly, she snuggled into his chest, and he allowed it. "I'm so tired. It must be the climate. Or that spicy food!"

"Or perhaps it's lack of sleep *last* night? Here, sit up, chit." He cradled her near for a moment, then propped her up. "We're nearly there."

"At Tempest Hall? How can that be?" Suddenly Adrienne was alert. Rosy-cheeked and sleepy-eyed, she looked enchanting as she leaned out the side of the sulky for a better look. "We had so far to go—"

"You sleep many hours, Mistress," Philip informed her with a broad smile. "You look like a baby girl."

The horses crowned the top of a high hill and Nathan pointed out the jagged east shore of the island in the distance below them. The Atlantic Ocean was periwinkle blue, its ruffled white breakers edging the beach. To the south, in a valley, lay a tiny village of weatherbeaten wooden houses. Before Adrienne could turn to look in another direction, Philip guided the sulky down a hill through a gloriously dark mahogany forest. The dramatic trees met high above the road, their gnarled branches intertwining to make a cool canopy.

"It's so beautiful!" Adrienne cried, awestruck. "It's the last thing one expects on a tropical island."

"We love our mahogany trees. Most of our furniture is made from trees grown right here on Barbados." As he spoke, Nathan looked down a bare hillside to the mill and outbuildings of his own plantation. There was little human activity to be seen. The mill wheel didn't move at all. "What's going on, Philip? Don't tell me Horner has let things go in my absence?"

Philip looked uncomfortable. "I do be taken up wit' Orchid's illness. I t'ink you bring Mr. Horner to manage de plantation, and I not go in de middle."

"Who is Mr. Horner?" Adrienne asked.

In distracted tones, Nathan explained that he'd been trying to revive Tempest Hall, even though he was away so much. Deciding that an expert plantation manager would be an ideal solution, he had imported Owen Horner from England that very year, and had expected to see great progress upon his return from sea.

They had turned down a narrow lane lined with great hedges of sweet lime. Wood doves cooed from a row of tamarind trees, and a pair of monkeys ran across their path and crashed into the bushes. Adrienne couldn't help laughing at the scolding sounds they made. Then, just as she was about to ask the names of the brilliant blue and magenta flowers that spilled over a nearby stone wall, the towers of Tempest Hall came into sight.

"I never thought to see towers on a plantation here," she murmured.

"Dey not towers, Mistress," Philip replied. "Dey chimneys! Englishmen come here long ago an' bring plan for house, but he confuse 'bout de Bajan climate!" And he laughed, delighted, at the old joke.

"No, I don't suppose there is much need for a fireplace," she agreed.

"We have four," Nathan said dryly. His attention had already wandered, and he hopped to the ground as the sulky rolled up before the gates opening onto the gardens in front of Tempest Hall. "Do my eyes deceive me, Philip?" He pointed to the fancy blue-trimmed chaise waiting nearby.

"No, Captain." The old man looked embarrassed. "De man is who you t'ink."

"I take it this isn't the first time he's visited in my absence?" Instead of growing louder with anger, Nathan's voice turned colder.

"No. I tell you, but we have a nice day, wit' de lady and all. . . ." Philip saw that his employer was waiting for more, so he climbed down and went to stand before him. "Mr. Horner and he be friendly. I warn Mr. Horner dat you do not like dis. . . ."

Adrienne was warm inside the sulky and overcome with curiosity. Through the open gates, she could see a courtyard with flowering trees on either side of the walkway that led to the house. What little was visible of the front of Tempest Hall was keenly enticing: an arcaded verandah supporting a great stone balcony along which marched six shuttered windows. The tiled roof was gabled, and studded with four ornate chimneys. Adrienne thought, This will be my married home! She could hardly wait to go inside.

A moment later she had lifted her skirts and joined Nathan and Philip out in the fresh air. "Will someone tell me what is going on?" she demanded. "Whose carriage is that?"

Just then two men came out of the house, laughing as they strolled into the garden, each carrying a glass of golden liquid. Upon catching sight of Nathan Raveneau, the taller, heavier man looked as if he'd like to find a place to hide, and his bald head turned pink.

"Let me guess," Adrienne tried. "That's Owen Horner, yes?" After receiving a short nod from Nathan, she continued in a hushed whisper, "And who is that with him? The owner of the chaise? He *looks* very friendly! Goodness, he's coming toward us as if you and he are long-lost brothers!"

The man strode confidently through the garden, heading straight for the newly arrived trio. "Ah, Raveneau, you've arrived earlier than Philip predicted. And I see that you've returned with more cargo than usual!" Short, but compact and fit, the fellow had thick, wavy brown hair, deeply tanned skin, penetrating pale-blue eyes, and a charming smile. "Shall I introduce myself to the lady, or will you do the honors?"

Adrienne could feel the dark energy emanating from Nathan's body. His features were taut and he seemed to forget that she even existed. It came to her then who this man must be, and she shivered with apprehension in the heat. "You are Xavier Crowe, aren't you?"

He bowed low before her and lifted the glass to his lips, as if toasting her with Raveneau's best Bajan rum. "Your humble servant, my lady. I am flattered to be recognized. And you are . . . ?"

"None of your damned business!" Nathan ground out. Tendons stood out in his neck, and his hands were clenched at his sides. "Get out. You knew that I'd kill you before I'd let you in my house, and yet you came behind my back anyway. I'd like to kill you still now, but that would be too easy. Get off my land and never come near us again!"

Crowe shrugged, smiling, and finished his rum. "Testy, aren't we?" He waved to Horner, who was lurking inside the verandah, and walked to his chaise. There he turned back and stared directly into Adrienne's eyes. "I'm not a beast, Miss Beauvisage. You mustn't be afraid of me when next we meet."

A moment later Nathan had gripped her arm and was literally dragging her away toward the house. "Horner!" he

yelled. "Pack your things and get out. I don't want to see
your traitorous face again!"

"You can't just sack me without a dime to my name!"
the Englishman protested loudly. "I came halfway 'round
the world to work for you. Where will I go?"

A voice called from the drive. "You may come to
Crowe's Nest, my good fellow. I should be glad to hire a
man of your many talents." Looking toward Raveneau,
Crowe added, "Shall I take your regards to Eloise?"

Nathan didn't speak but stared daggers back at Xavier
Crowe, who finally did climb into his chaise and start off
toward the mahogany forest. Adrienne could only watch,
Crowe's parting words echoing in her mind.

In the next moment, Nathan had crossed the verandah
and gripped the front of Owen Horner's sweat-stained shirt.
"I'll know where to find you, then, if I discover a discrep-
ancy of even one pound in the plantation ledgers."

The manager was trembling visibly. " 'Twould seem that
I have another haven on this island, though you mustn't assume that I have been in league with that man—"

After wresting the glass of rum from Horner's fist, Nathan poured it over his head. "Get out."

When he returned to Adrienne's side and grasped her
arm, she could feel the raw power of his fury. Horner scut-
tled away toward his quarters and Adrienne allowed Nathan
to pull her along, but as soon as they were inside the cool,
shadowy house, she made a noise of protest. "Loose me!
You are hurting me!"

Instantly he released her arm, startled by his own behavior. As he paced across the spacious sitting room, Nathan
raked both hands through his hair. "You don't understand
how evil Xavier Crowe is. You can see that he managed to
suborn my plantation manager in my absence, and who
knows where that would have led if I hadn't caught them
together?" He drew a harsh breath. "But it's not just what
he's done to me. He's murdered and stolen and ruined
countless lives, and all of it amuses him. Perhaps I
shouldn't have brought you here."

"We mustn't be irrational." Adrienne straightened her
slim form, trying to appear composed while her heart was

throbbing with the memory of Crowe's taunt—about Eloise! She badly wanted to ask Nathan who the woman was and what part she played in his grudge against Xavier Crowe, but he was already too angry. Instead she said, "I'm not afraid of Xavier Crowe . . . but I do wonder, how did he know my *name*?"

Chapter Seventeen

"What do you mean? Crowe *doesn't* know your name. I refused to introduce you." Nathan stopped in the middle of the room, waiting for her response.

"Don't you remember? Just after he walked to his chaise, he told me not to be afraid of him, and he called me 'Miss Beauvisage'! There was the most unnerving gleam in his eye."

"I haven't been back on the island for one day yet, and already I'm compelled to play this familiar game of cat-and-mouse with Xavier Crowe!" He strode into the dining room, opened the celleret, and poured himself a glass of the same rum Crowe and Horner had been drinking. "You'd think he'd have had better things to do these past months, wouldn't you? It's as if he has written a play and has arranged all the characters on stage, just as he desires, right down to Owen Horner. All that was needed for the drama to begin was my arrival. . . ." He drank, thinking. "Or shall I say, *our* arrival. It's eerie that he could know your name before I'd even gotten you to Tempest Hall."

"I'll have sherry," Adrienne volunteered with a note of irony.

"I was just about to ask." Nathan held out a goblet for her, his expression pensive. They drank without toasting, silent except for the incessant creaky-honking calls of guinea fowl in the gardens. At length, Nathan mused, "Perhaps Crowe had a spy at the Careenage."

"How did the spy reach Mr. Crowe before we did?"

"Devil if I know. Perhaps he was on horseback."

"A great deal doesn't make sense."

"I've told you, he's a demon! For all we know, Satan himself whispered your name in his ear. Let's forget about it, hmm? That's the only reason he did this, to make certain we'd torture ourselves trying to puzzle it out for the rest of the day!"

Adrienne found herself gazing around the two big rooms that spanned the front of Tempest Hall. "Tell me about the house, then. It's lovely!"

He seemed to focus on the condition of his home for the first time, and frowned. "It looks as if my entire staff has been on holiday for months! Not only are the field slaves apparently napping in their huts instead of working, but my house looks like hell!"

Secretly Adrienne agreed. The furniture, which consisted of fine dark mahogany pieces in styles ranging from Sheraton in the dining room to Georgian in the sitting room, needed polishing. Some of the caned chair seats were broken or frayed.

The rooms were painted light tropical colors: pale melon in the dining room and lime in the sitting room. Adrienne thought they were refreshing choices, but noticed that the paint was peeling high on the walls and in the corners, as well as on the jalousie shutters that framed every deep casement window. The beautiful wide-board floors were dark with grime, and the priceless Turkish carpets were dusty.

"You have critical eyes," Nathan remarked sarcastically. "At least there aren't any draperies to rot and smell."

"Better still, there are window seats! I love any house with window seats." She tried to sound lighthearted. To show disappointment at a time like this would be horribly rude, but Adrienne did feel just a little let down. So far, Tempest Hall bore little resemblance to the splendid manor she'd imagined during their voyage.

"This place is a wreck," Nathan insisted. "It wasn't much before I left, and now it's worse." He watched her. "Your part of the bargain is losing its luster."

"Don't talk nonsense." She had wandered over to study the set of English Coalport china displayed behind glass in the dining room. "You have made far too much of the expressions on my face. Goodness, these dishes are exquisite! It's the Imari pattern, isn't it?"

"The china, crystal, and silver were gifts from my parents when I purchased Tempest Hall. My mother thought that the Imari pattern was a good match for Barbados. 'Savage, elegant, and lush' was her description, I believe." He smiled suddenly, openly, at the thought of his vivacious mother.

"It sounds as if she and I would get along."

"That's what I'm afraid of." Nathan glanced away. "The Sheraton sideboard used to be in my family's Connecticut house. Most of the rest of the furniture was already in place. The Barbadian mahogany seems fitting."

Adrienne moved to the sideboard to touch the tall, curving glass shades that surrounded every candle in sight. "What are these for?"

"The windows are open all the time, and there is, one hopes, a constant breeze. Those globes keep the candles lit. Some people call them hurricane lamps."

She smiled, looking to the fireplace in the sitting room corner that had never been used. "Your mother is right. I can already tell that life here is a fascinating mixture of the familiar and exotic."

"That's precisely the reason I love Barbados." Nathan tossed back his rum. "This was a grand estate in its day, and I mean to restore it." It killed him to acknowledge that he cared about Adrienne's opinion. "I hope that you'll . . . be patient. Don't judge my home too harshly on the basis of this first look."

"I love a challenge, and I want to help, at least indoors."

"You'll have a staff, Adrienne, but of course you must tell them your wishes. Unless they've all been bribed by Xavier Crowe, they should obey you." Conversations about their marriage made him nervous. "Once we're rid of that blackguard, Barbados will be paradise."

Another voice spoke from the doorway leading to the back of the house. "Don' you talk dat way sir. Sound suspicious like murder you dream 'pon."

He turned to see Orchid Smythe taking a step into the

sitting room, and went immediately to greet her. "Damn, but it's good to see you, Orchid!" His eyes ran over her, making a worried assessment. Small and thin, with great expressive eyes, sharp cheekbones, and a full mouth, she wore the lovely garb favored by free women of the West Indies. Her head was covered by a high, intricately tied blue-and-white-striped turban and a shawl of Madras plaid cotton crossed over the front of her low-necked, laced bodice. The full apron that covered most of Orchid's blue skirt was immaculately white, as if she had just tied it on for the first time.

"I happy seein' you home, Mas—" She caught herself before the word "master" was out. "Captain. Sir. You belong here."

"Tell me the truth. How are you feeling?"

A peaceful smile warmed Orchid's face, which was nearly the color of rich mahogany. "I t'ink I go to God pretty soon, sir. I know dat seem sad, but I rejoice when I go. I jus' wearin' out, plain and simple." She was still smiling when Philip came up behind her and wrapped a supportive arm around her waist. "De tragedy is I not much good to work, Captain Raveneau."

"Sit down, Orchid." He motioned to Philip to help her into a nearby rocking chair. "My only concern is your comfort. And if you think a physician could do you any good, we'll send for one immediately."

The old woman waved a hand at him as her husband gently lowered her into the chair. "No, sir. An' no more talk 'bout me. I wan to meet dis pretty lady."

"I am Adrienne Beauvisage, and it is an honor to meet you, Mrs. Smythe." Adrienne drew a chair up close to Orchid's and took her frail hand.

"You actin' too nice, Mistress," the older woman scolded. "Bad 'nuff I can' work much, but makes me feel worse if you carry me 'round like I already dead." Orchid looked up at Nathan, smiling again. "I like she. When you have marriage?"

He cleared his throat. "I—ah—"

"Soon, yes? Here in de garden, so I can watch. Make me happy 'fore I die." She was beaming now.

"All right then, Orchid. If that's your wish, consider it granted," Nathan said.

Adrienne smiled along with the rest of them, but inside she felt odd. It was bad enough that he'd proposed to get her father's land, but now it seemed that only Orchid's deathbed request was causing the wedding to take place in a timely fashion.

"So much work need doing in dis house!" Orchid was saying. "Make it ready for guests."

"I don't think we need to bother with guests," Nathan replied. "I mean, wouldn't it be simpler, and more dignified, to have a quiet ceremony?"

Orchid looked stricken. "Oh, sir, I sorry de house look so bad. You walk inside, look 'round, an' I t'ink you are angry wit me."

"Nonsense. Philip had already explained to me that you hadn't been well." Nathan paused. "But, Orchid, why didn't you organize some of the other workers to do the tasks we discussed before I left? The painting, and reupholstering, and—"

"Mr. Horner not give me de money, sir! He say dere not enough for househol spendin', an' I say, one bellyful don' fatten a hog!" As her voice rose, her breathing quickened. "An' Mr. Horner take mos' of de house girl and make dem work in he field! Only Retta help me cook."

A muscle jumped in Nathan's cheek. "Damn him. I begin to wonder if he was in Crowe's employ from the first—perhaps even before I hired him in England. . . ."

Philip spoke up. "I glad he gone. Time for new start."

"Yes. Clearly our situation can only improve." What Raveneau left unsaid was the question of how the plantation would function from now on.

"I'll show you the rest of the house," Nathan said in a tone that indicated he had countless other matters on his mind but would do his duty.

"Show me my room, and I'll freshen up." Adrienne gave him a crisp smile but inside felt lost, lonely, and disappointed. How long would it be before she had her bearings in this strange world?

Nathan conducted a cursory tour of an impressive library that was located behind the sitting room, then pointed out the narrow gallery that traveled all the way around one side of the house. It had plenty of windows and places to sit and dream and stay cool. Nathan explained that early settlers had learned that galleries not only made good breezeways, but they kept the inner walls of the house cooler and gave an added layer of protection against hurricanes.

"The only reason Tempest Hall has survived for nearly two centuries is that there is coral stone under the plaster facade. The outer galleries and the verandah across the front were added later, I've been told."

Adrienne learned that there was a serving room behind the dining room and that the actual kitchen was detached, to prevent fires. They went upstairs via a magnificent white Chinese Chippendale staircase. On the second floor, Nathan walked Adrienne through various open bedrooms. There was his own, which was largest, and was painted pale lemon and furnished with splendid mahogany pieces, including a massive testered bed. He took her right into his spacious dressing room, pushed open a door on the far wall between an armoire and a chest of drawers, and pointed.

"That will be your bedchamber. I'll . . . uh, make room for your clothing in here. And I suppose we ought to find you a maid. Perhaps there will be someone among the house slaves whom you'll like well enough."

"I can fend for myself for the time being. The house is in enough disarray right now without giving anyone added duties." Adrienne went into the room slowly, taking in the details one at a time. It seemed likely that this had originally been the bedchamber of the lady of the house, but since Nathan's ownership, it had languished unused. The walls were light coral, peeling near the ceiling, and the Kuba rug was worn nearly to the floor in places. The furnishings were lesser versions of those in Nathan's room: liberally carved pieces in dark Barbadian mahogany.

"God," he said flatly. "Everything in the house looks worse than I remember."

There were dead cockroaches here and there on the floor, and the room smelled of mildew and sultry air. Adrienne ran a finger through the thick layer of dirt that coated a dressing table. "I begin to think that you need a wife more than you care to admit!"

Nathan stared at her. In spite of the rigors of the day, she looked so appealing that he felt alarmed. Long ago he'd decided on not to try to measure up to the standard of his parents' blissful marriage. He'd chosen a different sort of life and had carried it off with dashing ease—with the exception of one situation. That incident, and the residual memories, had only hardened Nathan's heart further against illusions of romance.

Now he was about to marry for reasons that had nothing to do with love or devotion. Surely that was better, wasn't it?

"I'll leave you to do whatever it is women do at times like this," he said, his voice slightly choked.

The dressing room door closed behind him and Adrienne was alone. Thick, confusing feelings rose up until she thought she must sob. She sat down on the bed, afraid to bury her face in the old woven spread. Covering her mouth with her hands, she let the sounds come, and felt burning tears spill from her eyes.

After a few minutes of such despair, Adrienne shook herself. Enough of that. She'd chosen to come and would get used to this place. It wasn't a prison. She could go back to France if she chose to, since there were no legal ties between her and Nathan. If she stayed, it would be of her own free will. She wasn't gooseish enough to have come so far and plunged into such deep water simply for adventure's sake.

No, it was for the sake of love. She loved Nathan Raveneau.

There it was, the real truth. It was unnerving to face up to it because it would also mean facing her hurt if he never returned that love, but Adrienne was too honest to shade her eyes from the bright light.

Love. Adrienne wrote the word on her heart, then whispered, "I love him. I want to be his wife."

It was as if a weight had been released. The dead cockroaches were meaningless, as was the dust. This was the home they would share as a family, and transforming it would be just one aspect of Adrienne's grander project.

Might Nathan love her too? Could he ever make peace with such an emotion and all that it implied? Joy and determination joined to give her hope.

A knock sounded at her door and she slipped down from the high feather tick to answer it. A young black woman stood in the hallway, head bowed deferentially. She held a basin filled with water and a cake of soap, and there were linen towels over her left arm.

"How kind you are! Let me help you." Adrienne tried to take the basin from the girl, but she held tight. "I'm Miss Beauvisage. What is your name?"

"Retta," she replied softly, and carried the basin and towels to a washstand near the tile-lined corner fireplace. Retta had thick, curly lashes and great full-moon eyes. Her hair was hidden under a green-striped kerchief that wasn't as tall as Orchid's, and Retta's loose white dress hid a body that appeared to Adrienne to be too thin for good health.

"It's nice to meet you, Retta. I admired Orchid's headdress, and now yours. What is it called here?"

The servant put a hand up to touch the starched cotton. "We call dis 'headtie.' Women tie it certain ways to show if dey married or not. Orchid wearing a turban, 'cause she a free colored lady. De free Creole ladies, born in West Indies, have fanciest turbans."

Adrienne thought that the fashions here weren't so different from those in Regency England. Women would always find ways to enhance their beauty—and indicate their social standing!

"I think your headtie is lovely, Retta!" She gave her a warm smile. "And thank you for the water. It reminds me of how much I'd really like a proper *bath*!"

"Bat'house in back," Retta whispered. Seeing Adrienne's quizzical look, the girl led her across the hall to a window overlooking the gravel yard behind the house. There were various stucco, tile-roofed outbuildings there, but Retta pointed to a pair at one end. "You take de bath in dere."

"What's the other one for?"

The girl dropped her eyes again and muttered what sounded like "Earth closet."

Adrienne didn't press the matter. Retta headed toward the servants' stairs at one end of the hallway and turned back before descending. "I bring somet'ing to eat an' drink. Supper at eight o'clock."

"Don't bring anything upstairs. I'll come down. I'd like to look at Mr. Raveneau's library."

Retta looked surprised by this announcement, but made no protest before she hurried soundlessly down the narrow staircase.

Alone, Adrienne set to work in her new bedchamber. After bathing as best she could, she brushed her hair until it shone again and pinned it back up, loosely, with tortoise-shell combs. Already the tropical air was making her hair curlier, and the effect was charming. Finally she donned clean undergarments and another gown from the trunk on board the *Golden Eagle.* This one was fashioned of light jaconet muslin, and the bodice was just a bit too snug, displaying rather more of her breasts than Adrienne would have preferred. However, since she had no wardrobe of her own, it would have to do.

She was feeling much fresher when she went downstairs to the library. Retta was coming in the back door from the kitchen just then, carrying a tray with a plate of cakes and sliced fruit and a pitcher of something that looked like fruit juice.

"You ready now?" the girl inquired. "De Captain do know you going in dere?"

Realizing that this must be her title for Nathan, Adrienne drew herself up. "He doesn't need to know. This is my home now too."

Retta shrugged. She gestured for her new mistress to precede her into the big library, then busied herself laying out the dishes from the tray, pretending not to notice that Raveneau was sitting at the desk.

"Ah, Retta, is that my planter's punch?" he asked without turning. Ledgers and account books were spread before him, and he had rolled up the sleeves of his shirt. "I can taste it already."

"Yessir." Retta poured a tall glass from the pitcher and hurried over to the desk. "I bring you pawpaw an' piece of lime, an' cake."

The moment he glanced up, he saw Retta's nervous backward glance and swiveled in his chair. There was Adrienne, fresh and lovely, pouring her own glass of planter's punch. With an effort, Nathan kept his voice even. "Adrienne, what brings you into my library?"

"I try to tell her, Captain—" Retta blurted out, then bit her tongue.

"Tell me what?" asked Adrienne.

"Retta, you may leave us." When she had gone, Nathan watched through the window until the girl entered the detached kitchen outdoors. Then he put down his quill and stood up. "Perhaps I failed to explain that this is not only my library but my study as well." He waited, brows raised.

"You stress the word 'my' in a way that makes me wonder if that arrangement will continue even after our wedding. Will all of the house be yours except *my* bedchamber?" Adrienne's cheeks were turning pinker as she sipped the fruit-flavored drink. "Am I to ask permission before entering one of *your* rooms?"

"You're talking nonsense."

"Am I?" Boldly she slipped one of his treasured volumes of Shakespeare from its place on the shelf and sat down in a strange-looking chair that forced her to recline. "Then you won't mind if I stay?"

"I am trying to go over the books to see how much damage Owen Horner has done."

"I won't bother you. I'll be quiet as a mouse." Adrienne squirmed. "What sort of chair is *this*?"

Nathan couldn't help laughing. "It's called a planter's chair; designed for the master of the house to enjoy on a hot afternoon, while sipping a bit of grog." He drank from his glass of punch and walked closer. "You see, there are these extensions under the chair's arms. . . ." He demonstrated, folding out what looked like long, flat wooden paddles. "Some men rest their legs up on these to cool off in the heat. Others use them when they want their boots re-moved."

"Planter's punch and the planter's chair," Adrienne mused with a note of irony. " 'Twould seem that the planter imagines himself a man of leisure!"

"Keep that in mind when you're sipping the punch," he parried. "There's more rum in it than you'd guess. Too much and you'll be reclining unconscious in that chair, just like one of the planters it's named for." With that, Nathan returned to his desk. He ate slices of papaya drizzled with lime juice, shuffled papers, wrote notations in the ledgers, and made a special point of ignoring Adrienne.

"You haven't told me how you will take possession of my father's land," she said after a few minutes of silence. "How will he know the outcome of your agreement?"

"We dropped two crew members on the northwest coast of France, near Brest, the same night you and I . . . reached this arrangement." Nathan couldn't bring himself to say the word "marry," it seemed. Slowly he turned again in his chair to look at her. "I thought I told you, but perhaps I forgot—"

"Quite possibly," Adrienne agreed sweetly. "Following your romantic proposal of marriage, you barely spoke to me for the rest of the voyage."

He gave her a chilly smile. "I sent Duffy and Keane to your parents' château, carrying a letter from me that ex-plained our . . . plans. I requested, if they approve, that your father send me the deed to his land and that they also allow my men to transport any possessions of yours that you might want."

"Wasn't it rather coldblooded to just write to them, with-out sending a word of reassurance from me? They've al-ways expected to be with me on my wedding day, to know my husband and to share in our joy."

"Then, given our situation, isn't it just as well that they won't be here?"

Adrienne told herself he was purposely being difficult and tried to shake it off. After all, she had free will and could write to her mother and father without consulting Nathan. "How will your men get from France back to Barbados, when we have sailed on without them?"

"There are plenty of ships sailing to and from French ports, and I gave Duffy and Keane plenty of money to buy passage. One of my own family's ships might be taking on cargo at Nantes, if I have the schedule right." He turned back to his ledgers. "We should have word soon."

"At least I'll be glad to have my own clothing, so that I won't have to continue wearing hand-me-downs from your lover's trunk."

Nathan declined the bait. "I've made other arrangements as well. A dressmaker from Bridgetown's best shop will visit you tomorrow. You may choose as many gowns and other garments as you like."

"Are we going to wait to marry until we have word from my father? What about your promise to Orchid?"

"See here, I simply don't have time for this!" Nathan rose again, advancing on Adrienne in her planter's chair and lifting her to her feet. "I told you that I had work to do, but you insisted on invading my privacy anyway." He led her into the long, breezy gallery and firmly deposited her on a mahogany-and-wicker chaise. "Here is your book."

Stung, Adrienne lifted her chin as he started back into the library. "What about my glass of punch?"

"I'll have Retta bring you some tea instead." With those parting words, Nathan closed the door between the library and gallery and leaned back against it, his heart thudding. He could never let her know that it wasn't her chatter that maddened him so, but his own gnawing attraction to her.

It was terrifying to consider the chaos that would ensue in Nathan's well-ordered existence if he ever lost his head over that woman.

It was simply unthinkable.

Chapter Eighteen

"IT NEED TIME," ORCHID ASSURED ADRIENNE AS SHE poured her breakfast tea and admired the breathtaking view from the balcony that opened off her new mistress's bedchamber. The guinea fowl were calling from the gardens, and the air was scented with the flowers of ylang-ylang trees. "You make new life."

"I had such hopes when we arrived, but this is our third day at Tempest Hall, and I feel more lost than I did then." She spread guava jam on bread, sighing. "I never see Nathan. . . ."

"He go away on he ship so long, dere too much work now. You have sugar, Mistress?"

"Orchid, you shouldn't be calling me that, or waiting on me! Won't you sit down and chat for a little while? Part of my problem is plain old loneliness."

"Custom is best," the old woman declared, but she needed no further urging. She took the other chair and lowered herself into it. "Maybe I break one custom wit you, Mistress. De captain is a fortunate man."

"You are ill and you can do anything you please. You certainly shouldn't be climbing stairs, Orchid! If Retta is busy, I can come down. Here, have some tea."

She held up a hand. "No." A wry smile curved her withered mouth. "You scare me off, talking like dat, Mistress."

"Tell me, is Nathan always away so much? Even when he's not out on the plantation, he's locked in that library, and he's made it clear that he doesn't want me to bother him." Adrienne turned her scrubbed profile into the morning breeze and sighed again. "I must tell you, Orchid, that I don't take naturally to a subservient role. If that's what he'll expect of me as a planter's wife, perhaps I should go back to Europe after all."

"No!" Orchid looked alarmed. "Mustn't say such t'ing! He need you. Men slow to learn, but Captain he have fine spirit. You believe Orchid and wait. If greedy wait, hot will cool. It need time."

She smiled, growing used to the proverbs that Orchid sprinkled through her conversation. "I'm impatient by nature."

"Some reward wert de wait, Mistress."

"You're very cryptic." Suddenly Adrienne's appetite flickered and she took a bite of bread with jam. "Zachary Minter said something like that to me—that I must be patient with Nathan."

"Very true. He like a wild horse dat need taming wit' patience . . . and oder t'ing." Wearing her secret smile, Orchid closed her eyes for a moment, as if resting. "You have a visit from de dressmaker, Sally Ann? She make you pretty, pretty gown."

"Yes. And she brought some things that I was able to keep."

"Ah. Good. Captain not so bad, den." Orchid opened her eyes. "And you have a visit from people up de road?"

She made a face. "The Harrisons and the Terrills? Those men were just what I feared planters might be—overfed and supercilious! And their wives were terribly pretentious. That's what happens to people who think they can *own* other people."

"What you mean, Mistress?"

"It turns them, I think, like curdled milk. All their good instincts are replaced by habits like gluttony, vanity, and selfishness. How else can they live with themselves?"

Orchid shook her head slowly. "Don't judge too harsh. People bend to de way of de neighbor. Slavery part of life here."

"It will be if no one ever speaks out," Adrienne asserted.

"Let me ask you something else—about one of our other neighbors on the island."

"Who?"

"Xavier Crowe." When Orchid began to turn away instinctively, Adrienne put a hand on her thin arm. "Is it a crime to speak his name?"

"He a bad man!"

"Orchid, tell me, isn't there another reason Nathan hates him so? Something more . . . personal?"

She pressed her lips together. "Could be. But I not say. Talk does make talk."

Before Adrienne could reply, she heard hoofbeats emerging from the shelter of the mahogany forest, followed by the sound of a familiar voice that carried up to the balcony.

"Miss Beauvisage!"

Her heart lifted. "Hello, Mr. Minter!" Happily, she stood up and waved to the red-headed figure on horseback as he approached the open gates to Tempest Hall. There was someone else riding behind him: an older man with white hair and sun-darkened skin. "I'll be right down!"

Orchid insisted that her impulsive mistress take the time to choose proper attire and to fix her hair, and Adrienne reluctantly agreed. She slipped into an airy high-waisted gown sprigged with tiny flowers and trimmed with a froth of lace. Her hair was upswept into a cascade of chestnut curls fastened with pearl combs. The effect was enchanting.

"Will I do?"

Orchid nodded, managing a tired smile, and Adrienne insisted upon helping her down the stairs. They were just emerging into the cool hallway next to the library when Nathan appeared, his tanned face a shade paler with shock.

"Yessir," Orchid confirmed before he could speak. "I know who be here."

"I thought perhaps I was having a sunstroke," he muttered. "We'll have to have refreshments, Orchid."

Adrienne spoke up. "She's in pain, Nathan. I think Orchid should lie down for a few hours. Shall I go and help Retta?"

"No!" He caught her arm. In his open white shirt, biscuit breeches, and top boots, Nathan exuded masculine appeal.

He hadn't shaved that morning, and his black hair curled over his collar. "You'll have to come with me to greet our guests, though God knows I'd like to hide you somewhere."

"What are you talking about?"

"Minter's brought my *father* with him! Only he could manage to turn up at this cursed moment in my life!"

Adrienne peeked into the sitting room, to find André Raveneau looking around curiously as he stood chatting with his son and Zachary Minter. Weatherbeaten and lean, he so closely resembled an aged version of Nathan that a chill ran down her back.

And indeed, if Nathan did look like his father when he neared seventy, he would be blessed. André Raveneau had wavy white hair that made a striking contrast to his tanned skin, his smile was still dazzling, and his body still lithe. A thin white scar marked his jawline.

"When did you intend to invite your mother and me to see Tempest Hall?" he was asking Nathan in a tone edged with fond sarcasm.

"Why should I send an invitation when you weren't waiting for it?" his son replied in kind. "You do as you please."

Minter was squirming as he stood between the taller men, and a fleeting glimpse of Adrienne provided him with a welcome diversion. "Look who's peeping round the door frame!" he cried. "It's the beauteous Miss B—"

"Allow me, will you please?" Nathan cut in with a quelling look. Walking to meet her, he whispered, "Please, for God's sake, make an effort to behave yourself."

André watched with keen interest as a green-eyed, piquant beauty entered the sitting room on his son's arm. "I perceive that it was more fortunate than I guessed that I decided to visit Barbados."

"Father, I would like to present Miss Adrienne Beauvisage, the daughter of your old friends, Nicholai and Lisette Beauvisage." Nathan spoke as if he were under duress. "We are . . . uh, betrothed."

André blinked in disbelief. "Can this be possible?"

"I fear so," his son muttered.

"It is a pleasure to meet you, sir," Adrienne said sweetly. "Or have we met in the past? Did you not visit Château du Soleil during my childhood?"

"Indeed. You must allow me a few moments to gather my wits, Miss Beauvisage. This news is wonderful, but quite a shock to a man of my advanced years." He took her hand, kissed it, and gave her a wicked smile. "Uniting the Raveneau and Beauvisage families might be the beginning of a new dynasty!"

Retta and another girl named Dolly appeared wearing matching kerchiefs and pushing a tea cart. Orchid watched nervously from the dining room as they served refreshments to the guests who now took seats. Once the ceremonies had been performed and everyone had sipped hot tea with sugar and taken a few bites of coconut bread, Nathan turned to his father.

"You still haven't explained what brings you to Barbados. I hope you haven't brought bad news?"

"None. I was simply bored. Lindsay and her new baby, Bridget, were visiting Connecticut, and there is only so much I can do as a grandfather." He shrugged in exactly the same way Nathan did so frequently. "Your mother was busy, and I needed an . . . outing."

"And what are you here to do?"

André felt the familiar undercurrent of his son's independent will, and his own similar nature was engaged. "Don't imagine that I'll intrude on your life, Nathan. Clearly, you have other things to do—"

"It's not that. However, I've just returned from England, and I have the devil's own problems to deal with here. Xavier Crowe has been visiting and corrupting my plantation manager, so I've had to sack Owen Horner—and he's gone to work for Crowe!"

"Xavier Crowe . . ." André repeated thoughtfully. "Wasn't he the fellow who . . . ah, swept Eloise Sinclair off her feet in London?"

Feeling reckless, Adrienne spoke up. "Eloise Sinclair? The name is familiar. Who is she? Have we met?"

"I highly doubt it, my dear," Nathan said in an acid tone,

then glanced at his father. "Yes, Eloise married Crowe. How tactless of you to mention it."

André's eyebrows went up at this, but he made no reply. Nathan, meanwhile, turned to Minter. "It is a piece of good fortune that you happened to ride up today. I need your help."

"Won't Mr. Minter stay here with us?" Adrienne implored.

Nathan spoke without looking at her. "Adrienne, would you leave us alone? I would like privacy to discuss some business matters with Zachary."

Hot blood rushed up her cheeks. "Is it really necessary that I go?"

"That's right, son. Don't send her away." The elder Raveneau leaned over and patted him on the shoulder. "You'll have to get used to hearing your wife's opinion if you mean to marry a Beauvisage!" Genially he turned to Adrienne. "Don't worry, my dear. Nathan's mother is even more unmanageable than you, so he's used to strong women. No doubt that's why he fell in love with you."

The betrothed couple stared anywhere but at each other, and the air was thick with tension. Finally Nathan leveled his gaze at his father and said, "You don't have any idea what you are talking about, but if you would allow *me* to request privacy in my own home, I might be able to explain!"

Tears burned Adrienne's throat. Humiliated and furious, she stood up, bit her lip while smiling at the guests, and left the sitting room.

Zach pulled at his collar and complained to his old friend, "Damn, but I sure do sweat a lot when you and Miss Beauvisage get together. I hope you don't kill each other after you're married!"

Before Nathan could reply, his father spoke again. "I know you don't want advice from me, but I am shocked to see you treat your future wife in such a manner."

"According to the stories I've heard about your own courtship—if it could be called that—you were hardly the ideal suitor!"

André fell silent, stunned to realize that his son was ab-

solutely right. In those days, he'd been a scoundrel to his
beloved Devon. "Touché. But that doesn't mean that you
have to repeat my mistakes."

"Look, Father, this has nothing to do with you or
Mother. If you must know, it isn't a match made for the
usual reasons. I am marrying Adrienne in order to gain possession of her father's land. It adjoins Xavier Crowe's estate, and when I have access to him, I'll be able to bring
him to justice."

"This is going to be an arranged marriage? Is there no
love at all between you?"

Out of the corner of his eye, Minter tried to give André
Raveneau a hopeful glance. Nathan, meanwhile, replied,
"There is a contrary bond between us—and I do find her
attractive—but it's not love. However—he drained his teacup and sat forward—"as Zach has pointed out to me, I'm
past thirty and it's time that I marry and have children.

It was hard for André to listen to his son and realize that
his own hard lessons could only have been pounded into
his head and heart through experience. "I can't help wondering how much of your grudge against Xavier Crowe has
to do with Eloise. I haven't forgotten how much you cared
for her. . . ."

Minter began choking on a bite of coconut bread. Since
Nathan's mood always darkened if Eloise's name was mentioned, Zach waited now for the explosion. "Perhaps I
ought to leave you—"

"No!" Nathan glared at him. "I have to talk to you about
something relevant to the present, unlike the dusty subject
my father has raised." He glanced back at André. "What
happened between Eloise and me was a long time ago. If
Crowe managed to woo her away from me through the
same underhanded tricks he uses today, perhaps it was
meant to be. I wish her joy. I can only assume that Eloise
was not the person I imagined her to be in my state of
youthful idealism."

"And you no longer idealize women—or love?" his father murmured.

"You could say that. I might add that my hatred of
Xavier Crowe is based on the *other* lives he's destroyed,

and on the fact that he has gotten rich through piracy and deceit."

"Fair enough." André rose and wandered across the sitting room, pausing to light a cheroot. "I gather that you haven't told Adrienne about Eloise?"

"No, nor had I thought of her myself until you arrived!"

André held up a hand in surrender and disappeared into the dining room to admire the Imari china.

"As for you, Minter," Nathan said, relieved to be rid of his prying parent, "I want you to come to work here as my plantation manager—at least until I can find someone new whom I trust."

"God's foot, you can't be serious!" Zach exclaimed. "What do I know about such things?"

"Enough to cooperate with me for the next few weeks to get this estate in working order. I can't do it all myself, but I could manage with your help." He linked his long fingers around one knee. "I can't go to sea until this mess is all straightened out, so it makes more sense for both of us to concentrate our energy here."

"If that's what you want, I'll do it," Zachary said warily, "but what about the *Golden Eagle*? What about the crew? We can't just walk away—"

André Raveneau came striding back across the Kuba rug, fragrant cheroot smoke curling upward in his wake. "Let me take her to sea. I'll take care of the ship until the two of you are able."

Nathan stood up to meet him. "If you think Mother will forgive me for keeping you here so long . . . I accept." He clasped his father's hand. "With gratitude."

The rest of the day was a blur for Adrienne. After learning that both Zachary Minter and her future father-in-law would be dining at Tempest Hall, she and Orchid began planning the menu and gathering ingredients. It was clear to Adrienne that, in view of Orchid's failing health, new house and kitchen maids must be trained, but she had no idea how to choose those girls from the field slaves, or exactly how to train them.

"Thank goodness Retta and I have already done so much

of the cleaning these past two days," Adrienne remarked as she and Orchid washed mangoes to make into a pudding. "At least the most obvious problems, like the dusty shutters, are remedied."

"Captain never allow it if he see you scrubbing de house," Orchid replied. "If I feel better—"

"It's my house too. I don't need his permission to clean it." She smiled. "There is so much I don't know how to do yet that it was a relief to dust and wash and see the improvement. Orchid, will you teach me about taking care of a house like this?"

The old woman nodded. "De new broom sweep cleaner, but de ole broom know de corners!"

Adrienne felt a wave of longing for her mother. Seeing André Raveneau reminded her of the joys and frustrations of parents. She was as stubborn as Nathan when it came to listening to her parents' advice, but impending marriage softened her views.

"I like Nathan's father," Adrienne said. "And he mentioned a name that made me curious. Orchid, have you heard of a woman named Eloise Sinclair?"

"I—uh—what you say?" She was spared then by the appearance in the kitchen doorway of Philip and a tall, heavyset woman. "Ah, here is Lily!" Orchid opened her arms. "Lily, this Mistress Beauvisage. I tell you 'bout she." She looked back to Adrienne, beaming. "Lily we daughter. She just have two baby boy, but now she work again. Captain say dat she may learn to be housekeeper."

Lily bore little resemblance to her parents except in her perceptive, intelligent eyes. After exchanging greetings with Adrienne, she said, "I am free, so I don' have to work, but Mama say dat you need help. She and Captain need help. He is good to us, so I help." She tightened the knot on her green-striped headtie and smiled at her mother. "Papa promise to watch me babies. What we fix to eat?"

Retta and Dolly were enlisted to peel and chop fresh fruits and vegetables, and once every decision was agreed upon, Orchid sent Adrienne up to her room for a bath and a nap.

"You mus' not be in de kitchen, Mistress. Lily do see dat

I am safe an' well." She pointed to the doorway. "We all have a place here, and you do be mistress of de house."

Wandering out into the yard, Adrienne felt strangely lost again. Orchid was the one person she knew liked her here, besides Minter, and she liked staying close to the frail old woman. The heat was oppressive, even in the shade of a gigantic sandbox tree that had a snakelike mass of exposed roots. Guinea fowl scurried along in the dust, searching for food, and across the yard, female slaves carried tall terracotta jugs on their heads. They were laughing together as they disappeared into an outbuilding.

What was their life like? Adrienne longed to visit their huts and discover the truth, but if she hadn't belonged in the kitchen, she certainly wouldn't be allowed in the slave village.

At the other end of the yard was the bathhouse. Adrienne wandered over for a look. The tile-floored building had three different tubs in it, including a hipbath. There was a pump nearby, and Adrienne decided to see to her own bath rather than bother the servants to bring one upstairs.

The cool bath proved invigorating, but it was over too soon. Back upstairs, Adrienne let her hair dry in damp, long curls and lay down on her bed. She wore a white cambric chemisette and pantalettes and stretched out, barefoot, with the shutters pushed out to let in the breeze.

The ocean was distantly visible from Adrienne's bedchamber, and she dreamed of visiting that wild east coast and plunging into the surf. If only Tempest Hall were a little closer to the beach, so that she could swim, endlessly, on steamy-hot afternoons like this one. . . .

Adrienne drifted off after a while, then was awakened by noises behind the door to the dressing room. Suddenly there was a knock at that door, and it flew open. Nathan stepped into her room.

"I'm looking for my favorite tan, wide-brimmed hat. It isn't here."

"Why would you suspect me of taking it?" Annoyed, Adrienne slipped off the bed and went to meet him. "You have no right to just burst in here, you know. Perhaps I ought to bolt my doors since you cannot wait to be invited."

"Don't you dare bolt any door in this house. I won't have it, and I won't allow you to talk that way." Nathan tried not to look, but his eyes strayed over her skimpy attire of their own volition. Her damp hair smelled of lilacs, and the inviting curves of her breasts peeked above the lace that edged her chemisette. He turned away. "I need my hat. The heat is punishing today, and I've loaned one to my father. We are touring the cane fields, checking on the harvest that's just finished and planning for the next crop."

Adrienne followed him. "I am furious with you, you know. If you think you can misbehave and then expect me to pretend to forget about it, you have chosen the wrong woman."

"I didn't exactly choose you," he muttered. There were hats on shelves and on hooks, but the light was dim, and most of them were the wrong shape to provide protection against the sun. "However, if you are going to pout, I apologize for entering your room without your permission."

Spotting a tan, wide-brimmed hat in the middle of his bureau, Adrienne tapped him on the shoulder and pointed. "Is that what you're looking for?"

"I knew that you must have hidden it!" Nathan grabbed the hat and went through the open door to his own bedchamber."

Adrienne was right behind him. "That is ridiculous, and you know it. I wouldn't touch your filthy hat if I were in danger of heat stroke. Furthermore, your failure to wait to be admitted to my room is the least of it."

"See here, they are waiting for me downstairs."

"Then they can wait a few minutes longer." She crossed her arms in front of her slim waist and tapped a bare foot. The realization that her state of undress was bothering him gave her a delicious feeling of power.

"You are the most aggravating, demanding chit I've ever known." Nathan perched on the edge of his bed and opened another button on his muslin shirt. "Have your say, and be quick. It's too hot up here."

"I am angry about this morning! About the way you treated me in front of your father!"

"Too much has happened since then. I can't remember every word I spoke hours ago." He made a dismissive gesture with one lean hand. "However, if I was rude, I'm sorry."

Infuriated by his offhand tone, Adrienne was further outraged when he started to rise, heading toward the door. "No! Sit down!" Her eyes flashed as she grabbed Nathan's arms and pushed him back onto the bed. She was amazed that he allowed it. "I am not finished, sir!"

The line of his jaw hardened. "Indeed?"

"Do you have any idea how it feels to be dismissed, as you dismissed me this morning? I have agreed to be your wife, but that does not mean I will be kept off to one side, or sent from the room when it is time for adult conversation."

"Marriage should not mean the termination of personal privacy."

Her eyes stung. "This is all about the land, isn't it? You really don't care for me at all." Walking away, proud and vulnerable in her underclothes, Adrienne turned at the door to the dressing room and said, "All I am asking for is respect. If you mean to hide me, and be embarrassed that you are married, I would rather go home."

From her balcony, she watched the men ride away over the brow of a lush green hill. If it was too hot upstairs for Nathan to bear, why should she? It was still early in the afternoon. Orchid had banished her from the kitchen, and the rooms downstairs looked perfect for the evening meal. Perhaps, Adrienne reasoned, if she got away from Tempest Hall for an hour or two, her mood would improve.

Still, it seemed better not to announce her intentions too publicly. She put on some of Nathan's old clothes, adding another of his wide-brimmed planter's hats over her pinned-up hair. Then Adrienne walked downstairs and out the door. No one seemed to notice her. At the stable, she had to divulge her identity to get a horse, but her confident manner carried her through.

The stable boy directed her to the road that would take her down to the ocean. "De horse, Ben, do know de way," he added.

Adrienne let Ben walk past the numerous outbuildings that ringed the sugar mill. There was a great deal of activity around the windmill itself, which was built of stone and crowned by a massive wooden spindle driven by four rotating arms. Nathan had told Adrienne that the windmills were introduced to Barbados by Dutch Jews who had conceived the idea of cultivating sugarcane on the island.

Now that the crop was in, the race was on to grind the sugar, and it was a long and arduous process. None of the mill gang noticed Adrienne and Ben as they passed by and disappeared into the trees.

The road leading downhill toward the sea was rutted, but Adrienne didn't mind their uncertain progress. The sensation of the warm soft breeze, the scents of salt air and lush vegetation, and the sounds of chattering birds mingling with the crashing Atlantic waves were a feast for her spirit. She needed her freedom every bit as much as Nathan did, and he would have to understand that.

When they came to a fork in the road, Adrienne spoke to Ben. "Do you know which way we should go to the ocean beach?"

He set off, starting toward a nearby village that appeared to be comprised of free blacks. Before they'd gone very far, however, Ben searched out an overgrown path that branched off from their route. Adrienne had to hold onto her hat with one hand to keep from losing it as they struggled past shrubs and trees that crept over the lane. What would Nathan say if he could see her now? Did Ben really know where he was going? Her heart began to pound.

Just as they emerged into the open, on a cliff lined with windblown whitewood trees, Adrienne caught sight of a woman getting onto her horse's back. She wore a proper gown and bonnet, and carried a sunshade. A young black man wearing fancy livery waited for her a few dozen yards away.

"Hello!" Adrienne called, elated. Was it possible that she might make a friend out here today?

The woman turned for an instant, then urged her horse forward. She looked both frightened and strikingly beautiful.

"Wait!" Adrienne cried. "Don't be afraid. I'm not a man, I'm a girl!"

The other woman slowed, then wheeled around and came closer. "You are very foolish if you are female and riding out alone. Even I am not that foolish. This island is more treacherous than it appears. The ocean kills cheerfully. Take the advice of someone wiser and go home to your husband." With that, she turned and started south toward her waiting companion.

"But—who are you?"

The only reply the woman made was to wave her hand in the air, glancing backward momentarily before she and her horse cantered into a grove of coconut palms and disappeared from sight.

Adrienne thought that she had glimpsed something in the stranger's beautiful eyes, but how could that be? The distance between them had been too great. Who could she have been? Adrienne was consumed with curiosity, and immediately the mystery took root in her mind. While Ben took her down the path to the beach, she imagined a variety of tragic pasts for the nameless woman.

The beach was a long ribbon of white, broken occasionally by big rocks overgrown with sea grapes, and the water was intensely turquoise, turning cobalt blue farther out. There was no sign of human life as far as Adrienne could see, and it was easy to pretend that she and Ben were on a deserted island. Mesmerized by the rhythmic pounding of the waves, she dismounted and walked barefoot through the warm sand. The water rushed toward her, lapping over her toes, and Adrienne felt a surge of joy.

The strange woman's warning about the ocean couldn't have pertained to a situation like this. As Adrienne waded out a little farther, she realized that the pull was too tantalizing to resist.

Nathan had sent his father and Minter back to Tempest Hall for a wash-up, rest, and tea. As usual, he had an urge

to ride alone, to burn off some of the dark energy that made
him so cynical. There were now four people on this little
island who could get under his skin: his father, Adrienne,
Xavier Crowe . . . and Eloise. Either Nathan would have to
find a way to make peace with his demons, or he'd be
forced to sail away in order to escape.

Riding along the hills that rose above the beach, Nathan
caught sight of a horse and a young man on the sand below.
The fellow looked very small and thin in his loose clothes.
He was white, but Nathan didn't recognize him at first
glance. Bringing his gray gelding, Compass, to a halt, he
took out his brass telescope and had a look.

"Christ Almighty," he muttered in disbelief. It wasn't a
skinny man at all, but his own bride-to-be. She was doing
a little dance on the beach, all the while shucking off men's
trousers and a shirt as if this were the most natural behavior
in the world. Poor, dutiful Ben looked on uncertainly.

Nathan was shocked to find that his sense of angry out-
rage was tempered by a frisson of euphoria. Adrienne had
a quality that gave him joy when he opened himself to it—
and that could be terrifying for a man who had decided to
live without such heady passions. If he was going to be
reckless, he'd do it on his own terms, at sea or on the back
of a horse, or making love to a married woman.

Down on the beach, Adrienne was wearing only her
lawn chemise and pantalettes, with their bits of satin ribbon
and lace. The fabric was so thin in the sunlight that he
could see the swell of her derriere. Nathan bit the inside of
his lip. What was it about her body that drove him mad?

Now she'd started into the water. It was folly for her to
put her toe into the Atlantic Ocean, and he'd told her so.
And yet there she was, flirting with death. If she didn't go
in beyond her knees, she'd be all right, but—

A wave came crashing in and Adrienne went to meet it,
diving into the curl of froth. She emerged laughing, dark
hair streaming down her back. The soaking underclothes
now were completely transparent against her bare skin. Nathan was on fire with desire and fury and terror that she'd
drown before he could reach her.

He left Compass on the brow of the hill and went scram-

bling down the tangled path on his own. His breath burned
in his throat. By the time he gained the overlook to the
beach, he was covered in sweat. Adrienne had grown more
daring by the moment. She was swimming out beyond the
first wave even then, and Nathan guessed that a hint of fear
was creeping into her heart.

"Adrienne!" he shouted. "Be careful! Don't go any farther!"

He could see her hair and the occasional flash of her
round bottom, but she didn't give any sign that she'd heard
him. The waves picked her up then, and when she tried to
stay on the crest, she was pulled under. Nathan instinctively
found the path downward and reached the sand in mere
moments. Adrienne had disappeared from sight. A procession of waves had formed behind her, and their power was
even more awesome than their beauty.

Yanking off his boots, he plunged into the water. Almost
immediately she was flung against him by the ocean and he
carried her out to safety. Adrienne was gasping and cough-
ing up saltwater, and there was a scrape on her pretty nose.
Shaking, she clung to Nathan.

"You little fool!" He sat down with her in the sand, cra-
dling her against him. "You could've been killed!"

"No—I was all right—" As her senses returned,
Adrienne realized that it would never do to admit to him
how terrified she'd been in those last moments when the
waves had pushed her down, down, squeezing the breath
from her, pinning her against the ocean floor until he'd rescued her by some miracle. "The wave had to go back out,
didn't it?" She gave him a winsome smile. "I'll own that it
was very exciting!"

"You will, will you? Well, I'll own that I'm going to
whip you within an inch of your life when I get you home,"
he said grimly. Meanwhile, her wet body was stirring up
other feelings even more intense than his anger. "What the
devil am I going to do with you?"

"I don't know," Adrienne said in a tiny voice. "At least
we're not bored." She paused. "I did have a grand adventure today."

"Well, thank God for that! Now get into those clothes and let's get home."

As it turned out, Adrienne and Nathan had plenty of time to recover from her adventure before the evening meal. The only challenge was pretending that nothing was amiss in front of the others.

Adrienne was tentative in her new role, especially with Lily, who didn't have Orchid's kind nature. When her new mistress came down the stairway and peeked into the serving room, Lily was waiting for her chance to speak her mind.

Adrienne beamed at the sight of platters of fragrant food already laid out on the long table. "It all looks wonderful, Lily! I can't thank you enough for coming to our rescue."

"We need a cook, or we need a housekeeper, but I am not two person, Mistress."

Adrienne blinked. "I realize that today was a difficult day, but how has your mother managed in the past?"

"Dat is different. Now Captain has a wife. Everyt'ing change now."

"Well . . . I suppose you have a point. I'll speak to my, ah, that is, Captain Raveneau."

Entering the dining room, Adrienne was elated by the sight of the table. Orchid had just stepped back to admire the large arrangement of red and white hibiscus that graced the center of the table. All the china, silver, and crystal were laid out, and the effect, by candlelight, was stunning.

"Those flowers are beautiful!" Adrienne exclaimed.

"Hibiscus," Orchid replied. "Dey live only one night."

At the dinner table, Adrienne noticed that Nathan was warming up to his father. She and Minter said little as the two men talked about the future of the sugarcane plantation.

"Change is in the wind," Nathan predicted as Retta served a second course of rock lobsters. He squeezed lemon over his and sampled a bite. "I can really see the results of the new Bourbon sugarcane we've been planting for the past few years. Captain Bligh introduced it to the West Indies twenty years ago, and it is simply the finest. Now, if I can just get my rat population under control. . . ."

Zachary turned to Adrienne, anxious to include her in the conversation. "Planters brought the mongoose to Barbados, hoping they would prey on the rats. Unfortunately, the mongoose sleeps by day and roams by night, and the rat's habits are the reverse!"

Everyone laughed, and Adrienne began to relax, though she was still nervous about meeting Nathan's eyes. The combination of their quarrel upstairs with their tempestuous encounter on the beach had left them both unnerved and confused. Adrienne sensed that they were closer now . . . and perhaps that was the reason Nathan seemed to be holding her at arm's length again. Perhaps it was hopeless to imagine that she would ever understand him.

Yet, as they ate roast pigeon with string beans, yams, and delicious honeyed biscuits, Adrienne saw his pride in Tempest Hall. Would he recognize that she was partly responsible for this night's success? Would he remember how different these rooms had looked when they had arrived just a few days ago?

Later, after mango pudding and cordial, the group strolled the gallery and listened to the chorus of tree frogs and the far-off rush of waves. Candles flickered under their hurricane globes; the night air was soft and mild. When the tall-case clock on the landing struck eleven, André Raveneau looked startled.

"This island is spellbinding. I had no idea it had gotten so late." He turned to Adrienne, smiling. "I must start back to Bridgetown if I'll be any good to my new crew on the morrow. It has been a distinct pleasure to meet you, my dear, and I trust that I'll see you again—soon, I hope."

"Oh, yes. Certainly, when we—"

Nathan spoke over her. "Of course, Father, we'll be coming to Bridgetown soon. Adrienne will be longing for the sight of civilization, and we'll both enjoy a visit to the ship."

She had been going to assure his father that they would meet again at her wedding to Nathan, but now that seemed less certain. Feeling strangely sad again, Adrienne slipped away while Zachary and Nathan were discussing the means by which Zach would be sent his possessions from the *Golden Eagle*.

Upstairs, she undressed in the darkness and climbed into bed. The sheets were faintly damp with the humidity, with a whiff of mildew. She could hear insects scurrying on the floor and saw a lizard cross the balcony in the moonlight. Adrienne heaved an aching sigh. It was such a strange place. Could she ever be happy here without love?

Now when she looked back at her afternoon's adventure, the memory was tinged with foreboding . . . and the danger of her brush with death. She'd forgotten to mention the strange woman to Nathan, and a new instinct told her not to. Who was she and what had her cryptic warnings meant?

An hour later, Adrienne was still looking at the peeling walls when a soft tap came at her door.

"Adrienne? Are you awake?"

His voice sounded almost gentle, but she didn't answer. After one more try, Nathan went away.

Chapter Nineteen

ADRIENNE AND NATHAN WERE MARRIED UNDER THE rose arbor in front of Tempest Hall, the day after word arrived from France that Nicholai and Lisette Beauvisage granted their blessing. Lisette had sent a trunk filled with her daughter's favorite clothes, books, and other keepsakes, and Nicholai had enclosed the deed to fifty acres of oceanfront land adjoining Xavier Crowe's estate on the southeastern coast of Barbados.

Not until she came into the garden and saw Nathan, a vicar, Orchid, Philip, and Lord and Lady McGrath from the next plantation east did Adrienne realize that Nathan had meant it when he said he thought a small wedding would be best.

There was no sign of either André Raveneau or Zachary Minter.

Still, standing under the arbor in a whisper-soft gown of white lawn, a garland of bright, exotic flowers decorating her hair, Adrienne tried to think only of Nathan. He looked fantastic, clad in cream pantaloons, a crisp white shirt and cravat, and a perfectly tailored swallow-tail coat of dark-blue broadcloth. His black hair was wind-blown and his deeply tanned face lent him an air of danger. Adrienne had the rare opportunity to gaze into Nathan's sea-blue eyes while the vicar was speaking, and what she saw there both thrilled and unnerved her.

"Do you, Adrienne, take this man . . ."

Her hands began to perspire in his. Of all the risks she

261

had embraced in her lifetime, this was the greatest. Heart pounding, Adrienne whispered, "I do."

As Nathan repeated his vows, he had to look away from his bride. He still couldn't believe this day was real. He had certainly tried every trick he could think of to minimize the significance of the wedding, including finding excuses to exclude his father and his best friend. If they could have married by post, Nathan would have done that.

One thing he would not do, however, was postpone the ceremony once the deed to the Beauvisage land arrived. Nathan couldn't consider the land his own until he fulfilled the rest of his bargain with Adrienne's father, and he was, with all his flaws, an honest man.

His own hands were cold as he found the carved gold band and slipped it onto her finger. "With this ring I thee wed, and with all my worldly goods I thee endow."

"I now pronounce you man and wife." The vicar, a gaunt man who read the words without expression, had not met even the groom until today. "You may kiss your bride, Captain Raveneau."

Something in Nathan's eyes made Adrienne take an involuntary step backward. Immediately, like a cat, he closed the distance between them and captured her in a hard embrace. Startled, Adrienne couldn't breathe for a moment. His arms seemed more powerful than ever and when he kissed her, his demanding mouth evoked sensations that made her shiver in the heat.

In the background, Orchid was weeping and clapping. Lord and Lady McGrath stiffly offered congratulations, then she said something about being under the weather.

"Good of you to ask us," Lord McGrath muttered, "but we must go."

His wife was watching Adrienne closely. After a moment she looked at Nathan and said sweetly, "Oh, Captain Raveneau, I happened to see Eloise Crowe at the milliner's yesterday. She was having the most fetching chipstraw bonnet made; I think she grows younger by the year." Still smiling, Lady McGrath tried to pretend she didn't notice that a rivulet of perspiration was drizzling down her pudgy, powdered cheek. "I mentioned your impending nuptials, but she hadn't heard. She begged that I convey her sincere wishes for your lasting happiness. . . ."

Lord McGrath was scarlet with embarrassment. "My dear, I really don't think—"

"My lady," Adrienne interjected in cheerful tones, "if you should see Mrs. Crowe again, do thank her for her kindness. I look forward to meeting her at last when Nathan and I are finished with our—" She rested her cheek against his shoulder and gazed dreamily up at him. "—honeymoon."

"Quite, quite," McGrath blustered. He gripped his wife's arm and led her off toward their landau before she could say another word.

Adrienne felt slightly dizzy and wondered if she would be ill. As they went into the house for a light celebratory meal, she lingered at the edge of the dining room.

"What's wrong?" Nathan asked. Retta came toward them with glasses of champagne on a tray, and he accepted one for both Adrienne and himself.

"I don't feel well." She managed a weak smile. "Perhaps it's all the excitement. I think I ought to go upstairs and lie down for a while."

There was so much work to be done on the plantation, as the new crop of sugarcane was planted, that the new bridegroom went back out into the fields. The ground was covered with shallow holes, and slaves were putting cane cuttings into them. Zachary Minter stood sweating in the afternoon sun, talking with the overseer.

"For God's sake, what are you doing here?" Minter exclaimed upon sighting Raveneau.

Nathan had changed into light biscuit trousers and a loose white shirt, and gave no sign that he was now a married man. "Adrienne wasn't feeling well. She went upstairs for a rest, and I thought you might need me out here."

"Did you explain to her why I wasn't at the wedding?" He shaded his eyes against the sunlight. "I think we're both beasts for deciding that I couldn't spare the time to be a witness—"

"I think it was just as well. Lord and Lady McGrath

came to sign the papers and, I expect, to have a look at the new Mrs. Raveneau. They're doubtless making a tour of the island this afternoon to spread the word."

"Nothing wrong with that." Zachary watched his friend's rakish profile, but it gave nothing away. "Did it go well? Are you . . . happy?"

Nathan shrugged. "Well enough. But I should be asking you how this work is progressing." His gaze traveled over the lines of slaves, laboring in the punishing sun. "It's hard to watch, isn't it? Now I remember why I chose to be an absentee planter."

"Believe me, I would do this only for you. It's hell to watch the slaves sweating like this."

"I suppose we ought to change the system one day."

"In the meantime, we are behind with the planting. It was a wonder that the last crop was harvested and processed at all, given Horner's poor performance. Now time is of the essence."

"There have to be three thousand holes for every acre of land, yes?"

"Yes. And a cane cutting placed in each hole, then covered with mold." Zachary began rolling up his sleeves. "The ground is showing signs of overuse, you know. There are plenty of problems to address when you have a moment."

Nathan drew a harsh breath and replied ironically, "You make it sound so inviting. We'll sit down together and discuss your concerns—but first I suppose I ought to visit my bride."

"Wait." Zach touched Raveneau's sleeve. "I haven't any right to interfere, but I have known you all my life, and—"

"Yes, yes, go ahead," Nathan retorted tersely.

"I just want to say that I think your new wife is a splendid woman, and you are a fortunate man. I know that you both are stubborn and proud, but now that you're married, couldn't that be put aside? Adrienne cares for you, you know. She could make you a damned fine helpmate, if you'll let her."

Nathan nodded slowly. "Yes . . . well, we shall see." He

patted his friend's shoulder, then started back to Tempest Hall.

His hair still wet, Nathan came from the bathhouse into the shadowed back hallway. Through the door to the serving room, he could see Orchid, sitting in an old chair, watching Lily and Retta clean a batch of flying fish.

"Captain?" she called, and leaned forward so that he couldn't slip out of her view.

"Hmm?" Nathan moved toward the doorway but did not enter. "I was just going up to see if Adrienne is awake yet."

She pursed her lips, obviously making an effort not to say everything that was on her mind. Instead she muttered, "I never see a wedding day like dis."

"Yes, it was a shame that Adrienne didn't feel well." Nathan stared Orchid down, then added, "I'm not hungry. I ate enough for the whole day at the wedding meal."

"I send a tray up to Mistress Raveneau." Orchid nodded toward the empty dishes. "She seem better. Some way, at leas'."

"As always, I deeply appreciate your tact and restraint."

"You miss me when you go away!" she reminded him as he moved out of sight. "Goat head every day better dan cow head every Saturday!"

"Words to live by, I'm sure."

Ascending the stairs, Nathan realized that the house was slowly changing. When he had first come here as the new owner two years ago, Tempest Hall had been run down, and since it was already furnished, it felt like someone else's home. Nathan had been away most of the time since then. Each visit had strengthened his bond with Orchid and Philip, and he'd slowly come to know the names of other slaves. The seed of a desire to stay and make Tempest Hall his real home began to take root—and now it had happened, almost without his realizing it.

Adrienne's subtle touches were everywhere, from the newly washed and painted shutters, to the floors that smelled of polish, to the bouquets of flowers, large and small, that seemed to grace every room and corner. Nathan felt a twinge in the area of his heart as it occurred to him that he had backed into marriage just as he had backed into residing full time at Tempest Hall.

He was deep into a new life but unable to look at it squarely ... yet. Part of him still wanted to bolt, to swing onto a stallion's back and gallop down the coast to Bridgetown, back to the sure escape the *Golden Eagle* had always afforded. At sea, Nathan was master of all he surveyed, and there were no realities except the water, the next adventure, and the distance from conventional existence.

He stood in front of Adrienne's door and wondered how it could be possible that he now had a wife. He knocked.

"Adrienne? Are you awake?"

"Yes" came her muffled reply.

"May I come in?"

A full minute passed, and then the door opened. Adrienne had changed into a plain chemise frock, and in the distance Nathan glimpsed the wedding gown she'd worn earlier in a pile on the floor. The garland of flowers that had graced her chestnut curls now lay forgotten amid the folds of white lawn.

She stared at the floor. "I don't have anything to say to you right now, and I certainly do not intend to consummate our marriage tonight."

"Indeed?" He tried not to smile. "I suppose I shall have to content myself with memories, then."

"Don't be crude." Adrienne turned away and walked barefoot to look out on the balcony.

Although she appeared to be dismissing him, Nathan chose to close the door and follow her across the room instead. "I gather that you are disappointed ... with me. Are you going to make me guess what I've done wrong?" He touched her shoulder. "Was it the wedding?"

She fought the power of her attraction to him and tried not to smell his freshly washed skin. More tanned and lean-muscled with each passing day, Nathan was nearly impossible to resist.

Adrienne's will prevailed, however, and stirred the embers of her anger. "You were never this dimwitted in England, sir! How do you think I felt when you invited no one of meaning except two beloved servants to our wedding? I expected to find at least my father-in-law and Zachary among the guests, but instead there were two strangers who treated me as if I were an interloper!"

He frowned. "My father can't be riding back and forth between Tempest Hill and Bridgetown every day! And Zach had to oversee the work in the fields. You have no idea how far behind we are. Why, I had to go back out myself this afternoon!"

"What a terrible hardship that must have been!" Adrienne shouted sarcastically, whirling on him. "Do you take me for a fool? You would have grasped at any excuse to separate yourself from me today!"

"You are the one who rushed away to your room before I could even propose a toast to my new bride!" he shot back.

"Don't imagine that I can be confused. You know me better than that." To her horror, Adrienne felt her eyes pool with hot tears. "Today I felt as if I were some dirty little secret that you were sweeping under the rug. Your planter friends imagine that you have only married me because you couldn't have Eloise!"

Nathan looked stunned at first, then furious. "You—you—Oh, for God's sake, stop crying! You don't know what you're talking about."

"Why don't you explain, then."

Running a hand through his hair, he muttered, "I haven't worked it out yet in my own mind."

"You mean you don't want to tell me about her."

"No, it's that I'm not certain what to say yet." The anger seemed to drain out of him at the sight of her anguished face. "Adrienne, it's not that I'm ashamed of you. Never that. It's marriage that worries me."

Her stomach hurt. "Leave me alone."

"This is a damned odd way to have a wedding night," Nathan complained. He opened the door to their shared dressing room and looked back at her. "A lot of women marry men much worse than I, you know."

"And you're modest as well," she parried sarcastically.

"You jest? Perhaps you have forgotten that you belong to me now."

"I curse your bloody men's laws! I belong only to my-self. Get out!"

He stared back at her, eyes flashing. "I trust that you re-member where to find me, my dear."

"Snow will fall on Barbados before I come to your bed!"

"An empty threat." A hint of a smile played at the cor-ners of his mouth, and Adrienne blushed. As he made his exit, Nathan added, "Good night, for now . . . Mrs. Raveneau."

Lonely and hungry, Adrienne lay awake in her bed and wondered what time it was. Moonlight made luminous pools across the sheets. Was it past midnight? Hours seemed to pass as she tried in vain to fall asleep.

How had their relationship come to this? Could this be the same man who had once worked at appearing so earnest in his spectacles and unfashionable clothes? Adrienne's heart ached for Nathan Essex and the carefree humor and antagonism that had existed between them at Harms Castle.

She closed her eyes and imagined that they were in Lady Thomasina's library again, laughing and laboring together over her ridiculous Systems. Then they had walked together in the garden maze and eaten side by side in the servants' kitchen. And in spite of Adrienne's protestations, he had helped her contend with the eccentricities and hidden dan-gers at Harms Castle.

Nathan had always been an enigma, yet she had instinc-tively trusted him. Their lives had been entwined since the moment of their meeting on Oxford Street, when they had stopped traffic.

We are married! Adrienne thought. Whatever the reason was for Nathan's difficulty in opening his heart and giving up his freedom, she knew that he was not really a cold man. She'd seen gentler emotions in his eyes too many times. Sighing, she sat up and slipped her feet over the edge of the bed. A small lizard darted out, just grazing her toes, and disappeared onto the balcony.

Adrienne smiled. She slipped a circassian wrapper over her nightgown, brushed her hair, and went into the dressing room with a pounding heart. There was a faint strip of light under the door to Nathan's bedchamber, and as she raised her hand and knocked, Adrienne felt a warm surge of joy.

"Nathan! A gruesome-looking reptile has just come out from under my bed!" She did her best to sound frightened. "Can I come in?"

"Yes—the door is open."

Adrienne entered slowly, brimming with mixed emotions. The room's lemon-hued walls were burnished with candle-light and shadows, and the big four-poster Hepplewhite bed was empty, its sheets in disarray. The room smelled faintly of cheroot smoke.

"Here I am."

She looked around the door and found him seated at his desk near the window, writing in the same dark blue leather volume she had seen at Harms Castle. Mahogany shelves, brimming with books, lined the wall behind him. There was a small glass of brandy at Nathan's elbow, and although he was still clothed, his shirt was open and his dark chest exposed.

"It must have been a lizard that you saw—hardly huge, my dear. I find it hard to believe that this was your first glimpse of one. They're as common as crickets on Barbados."

"Well . . . this lizard looked bigger to me."

He drew on his cheroot, eyes narrowed. "They are both harmless and helpful; they eat the insects. Were you really afraid?"

"Now that you put it that way . . . perhaps not. He must have startled me in the darkness." Pinned by her new husband's gaze, she swallowed. "I can't sleep."

"Would you like a drink?"

"Please." Adrienne was giddy to have received such an invitation. She hurried over and took the cane chair near his.

Nathan poured a little brandy into another glass, handed it to her, and toasted with a sardonic flourish. "Well, here's to our wedding night. And here's to our marriage. It's going awfully well so far, don't you think?"

His razor-sharp tone brought tears to her eyes. "I—gather that you blame me? I can speak only for myself, but I am feeling sad . . . about today. I expected to see your father, and certainly Zachary, at our wedding. Their absence seemed to be a way for you to let me know that this marriage is not—valued by you."

"Well, that's clear enough." Nathan was at a loss. Now what should he do? If he let his own heart open in response to her eloquent appeal, what would happen? "I do see your point. I suppose I thought that we had a different sort of arrangement and that you understood." He felt like the worst sort of cad, especially when he saw her exquisite green eyes swimming with tears.

"I did agree, but I don't know if I can fulfill that part of our bargain." Her lower lip trembled. "I am a real person, not a hollow shell. I know that I adored the idea of coming to this wild, exotic place and entering into another adventure with you, but I find that I am . . . lonely."

"I regret to hear it." Tentatively Nathan skirted the edges of emotion. "Perhaps you are right, and I am at fault for this botched wedding day. I—ah, haven't been very nice to you, have I?"

"Well, we have both been unkind. I sometimes wonder if our relationship has changed into a battle of wills."

Emboldened by the brandy, Nathan felt a sense of relief as they talked. "Adrienne, I am sorry if I have done a bad job of making you feel welcome at Tempest Hall. Zach and my father have both been at me about it, but I've found it keenly difficult to let someone else into my life . . . especially someone like you."

"I am grateful for your apology." It made her heart pound harder to look into his eyes without glancing away and to recognize the embers there. "If I were a different sort of woman, you'd have an easier time of it, wouldn't you? You should have married a bit o' muslin who would content herself with managing the house, picking flowers, doing needlework, and plotting the takeover of Barbadian society." Adrienne's dimples winked invitingly.

"Yes. I could ignore her except for the interludes of conjugal bliss."

She blushed under his suggestive gaze. "Why didn't you marry someone like that, then?"

"I didn't want to marry at all, and as I recall, neither did you! It's one thing to care for one's friends and relations, but quite another to have a woman in my dressing room, at my table, and in my bed, daily, for the rest of my life!"

"And in your library," Adrienne added impishly. She sipped the brandy and luxuriated in the sensation of happiness gently creeping back into her heart. All was not lost after all. "You seemed to think it would be worth marrying me to have my father's land. Didn't you? Or did you imagine that you could put your wife off to one side and tend your marriage at intervals, the way you've been handling other parts of your life—like Tempest Hall?"

"I admire the subtlety with which you ply your rapier, my dear," he murmured, all irony. "You find the mark when your victim least expects it."

"I am only speaking the truth. I know you better than you think, Nathan. And I like you, when you aren't trying to build a wall between us." A tide of emotion rose in her again. "I—I have missed my friend."

He nearly put his hand to his heart, for she had struck deep with those last innocent words. "We have shared many good times, I will admit."

"Are we never to laugh again? Will pride, or fear, keep us from enjoying the camaraderie of months past?"

"Well . . . Adrienne, it is more complicated than that. We have shared much more than laughter, if you will recall."

She dared to reach her hand out toward him, her fingers slim and pale in the candlelight. A tear spilled onto her cheek. "It is only as complicated as we choose to make it. Nathan—we could be happy!"

His heart pounded in his ears. Every fiber of his being yearned to be close to her again. He reached toward her outstretched hand with his own dark fingers, captured it, and brought her onto his lap. Slowly he enfolded her in his arms, and a shudder ran through him. Nathan couldn't remember ever feeling anything as powerful, not even when he had battled for his very life, for this delved into his unacknowledged, deepest needs.

Adrienne took the liberty of resting her cheek against his hair, basking in the sensation and scent of him. For once, she didn't want to ask about Eloise. "While lying awake in my bed tonight, I was thinking about our walks in the garden at Harms Castle. Do you remember the time, at dusk, when you introduced me to the gloaming?"

"Yes." It was hard to speak. Memories rushed through the cracks that were opening in his heart. "You know, I'll have to show you our gloaming here on Barbados. The golden light is even richer and more magical . . . and then the sunsets over the ocean are beyond belief."

"I long to walk on the beach again. And swim."

"I might be able to arrange that, if you promise me that you won't wander off alone again!" He couldn't be angry; she smelled too sweet, too achingly familiar. Her wrapper and nightgown were tissue-thin, and the warm outline of her breast pushed against his chest. There was an insistent tightening in his groin.

"I remember the first time I saw that ship's log, open in your room at Harms Castle. I had a feeling then that there was much more to Nathan Essex than met the eye."

"It was stifling to pretend to be someone else," he reflected. "The only time I could bring out a few of my own things was late at night, in that room. I was horrified to see you there, peeking, dear chit." Nathan smiled. "You never could keep your nose out of other people's business. Why do I find that so charming?"

Adrienne ran her fingers over the hand she loved so well. "You aren't being nice to me just because—"

"No. But—" His tone was playful. "—it is our wedding night. What better time could we choose to make peace?"

"You're sly."

"Don't you want to seal our truce by making this a real marriage?"

"I—" She melted when he traced the curve of her throat with his lips. "Yes. But . . . you must promise me that you won't turn away from me in the morning. Nathan, can we strive to be husband and wife?"

He blinked. "I'm not certain how much I'm capable of. I'm bound to make brutal mistakes—"

"I don't expect anything as deadly dull as wedded bliss!"

she rejoined, laughing. "All I ask is that you not shut me out again."

"I'll need courage," he admitted. "I'd rather fight a duel than trust my own cursed heart."

"Then be my friend. Fight with me if you must, but be my friend again." She blinked back more tears. "I prize my independence too, you know, but there have been times when I have looked into your eyes and have seen the best friend of my life."

Fear stabbed him again. It was a lot to ask of him, to be her best friend—*and* her lover *and* her husband! "I'll try. That's all I can promise." Gently he gathered her closer and stood up. "My father said the first step is the hardest."

Adrienne wrapped her arms around his neck and gave herself over to the moment. The feeling of this tall, strong, raven-haired man carrying her as if she were a child was the stuff of her dreams. Every aspect of the bedchamber was romantically masculine, including the mosquito netting he'd tossed over the canopied four-poster. With infinite care, Nathan set his bride down on the edge of the feather tick and slowly drew back the rumpled sheet, watching for her reaction.

There were brightly colored flower petals strewn across her marriage bed. It was a lavish invitation to love. Adrienne made a sound of delight. "Nathan! How—" Slowly her catlike eyes narrowed. "Did you know that I would come to you?"

"How could I know that, unless you imagine that the lizard was in my employ?" He was smiling. "All right, I had an idea that you might come."

"And . . . you wanted me to?"

"What man would not?"

"Some men would have forced the issue, as you reminded me earlier this evening. It is your wedding night, after all." She cuddled against his chest. "Thank you for waiting for me."

"I may have faults, but taking a woman against her will is not one of them." As the hunger began to build within him, Nathan stripped off his shirt and boots before sitting down behind her and sliding his hands around her waist. "I do have one question for you, my bride."

"Yes?" She leaned into him and felt his heartbeat on her back.

"Was there really a lizard?" His tone was amused.

Adrienne gasped. "Of course! What sort of a schemer do you take me for?" When he only laughed in response, she admitted, "I might not have really been afraid of him, though. It just seemed a good excuse to knock on your door."

Nathan's manhood stirred and the blood surging through his veins grew hotter. "Oh, my sweet, I have missed you. I've missed your audacity." He drew the ribbon from her hair and buried his face in the fragrant cloud of her curls. "I've missed your laughter and the sparkle in your eyes, and the way your little chin sets when you have made up your mind and mean to convince me."

She could have wept. "I was with you all along."

"I know." His voice was ragged. It was hard to remember what he'd been fighting against all these weeks.

When Nathan's mouth touched the side of her neck, Adrienne jumped a little at the sheer intensity of sensation. All her nerves were deliciously on edge. He slipped her wrapper off, then untied her nightgown so that it fell open across her shoulders. His hands were on the bare flesh of her back, touching lightly, and suddenly the place between her legs felt warm, then congested.

"Mmmm." As she sighed, her breasts tingled. So much longing had been stored up, locked away until the needs of her heart could be satisfied.

He kissed her shoulder blades and the nape of her neck, while his hands slipped inside her nightgown to graze the curve of her lower back. Unconsciously, Adrienne nudged her bottom back against his crotch, starting a bit upon encountering the hard ridge of his manhood through his nankeen breeches.

"You see what you do to me?" Nathan whispered, his breath hot on her ear.

She shivered again. "How can it be me? I'm melting."

It took every ounce of restraint he could muster to hold

back, when he wanted to just draw her down into the flower-strewn sheets and ravish her. It was Adrienne who let down the front of her nightgown, reached back for both his hands, and covered her taut breasts with them.

"Please, touch me."

Clearly, his bride would not be passive during lovemaking. When he recovered his powers of speech, Nathan said, "I can never believe that one woman can be so exquisite."

Her musical laughter filled the bed. "Don't be too charming. I won't trust you."

"It's true." He felt her nipples burning the palms of his hands. "Oh, God, so true."

"I ache." She moved his hand lower. "Here."

His control snapped. "You're driving me mad." Turning her in his arms, Nathan brought his mouth down over hers in a hot, insistent kiss that left her breathless. Rough and tender by turns, he caressed the satiny curves of the body he'd dreamed of nightly.

And Adrienne returned his kisses and ran her own fingers over Nathan's rugged form. She couldn't get enough. Finally, panting, her desire beyond bearing, she said, "Make love to me. Please. It's time."

The rest of her nightgown was stripped away along with his breeches, and then Nathan pressed her back onto the feather bed. Pink, white, and coral flower petals clung to her hair, and as he lay down over her, he thought that she was more beautiful than the most exotic blossom on Barbados.

Adrienne craved the feeling of Nathan's big body covering her. She loved the sensation of his chest crushing her breasts and his lean-muscled flanks pinning her slimmer legs—and the shaft of his manhood pressing between her thighs in a way that was pleasure beyond description. Her arms wound around his neck and she opened her mouth to his demanding kiss. Had God ever created a more splendid male animal than her husband?

Her face was so warm, and the air around them was heavy with the scents of flowers and their aroused bodies. Crickets chirped, night birds called, and the softest of moonlit breezes wafted through the open shutters. Adrienne understood at last what drove animals to mate. She opened her thighs, aching for release, and arched upward. Nathan came into her, trying to go slowly, but she pushed to meet him and took him in to the hilt. Little groans escaped from her lips. Clinging to his back, her limbs pale in contrast to his bronzed body, Adrienne met each thrust, reaching farther and higher each time their bodies fused.

In her heart, she whispered, *I love you.* Now they were one.

Consumed by the impending moment of his release, Nathan wondered if he was dying. What else could such excruciating pleasure mean?

PART FOUR

Stand still, you ever-moving spheres of Heaven,
That time may cease, and midnight never come.
—CHRISTOPHER MARLOWE

Chapter Twenty

THE CLOCK WAS CHIMING TEN WHEN ADRIENNE reluctantly opened one eye to the sunlight that intruded through the open jalousie shutters. The air was already warm, and it came to her that she was not only naked, but uncovered, lying on her side.

A strange, panicky excitement broke over her, and then she felt a fingertip touch the back of her neck. As Adrienne held her breath, the finger slowly traveled down the curve of her spine, past the last inch of her backbone, teasing the shadowed crease of her buttocks. Warm breath fanned her shoulder. The exploring hand crept back up to push her hair aside, and then the nape of her neck was being kissed in a way that sent a jolt of fire to the core of her womanhood.

It wasn't a dream.

As Nathan's arms enfolded her, she rolled back so that their faces were inches apart. The very sight of him filled Adrienne with joy and desire. His hair was ruffled, and in the sunlight she glimpsed a few white strands among the ebony. There was a pillow crease on his tanned cheek, and she could see all the shades of blue and turquoise that gleamed in his black-lashed eyes.

"Good morning, Mrs. Raveneau," he whispered huskily.

Her cheeks grew warm at the sound of his voice speaking her new name; words failed her. Had Nathan truly accepted their marriage? Could the walls have tumbled down so completely? She put a hand up, touching first his hair and then the roughness of his jaw, and smiled shyly.

"My blushing bride." His tone was playful now, perhaps even sardonic. "Have marriage vows tamed you?"

Adrienne rose to the test. While wrapping her arm around his neck to bring him down for a kiss, she reached lower with her other hand and boldly clasped his stiffening member. Nathan's eyes opened in surprise, and she drew back long enough to murmur "Tamed? On the contrary. I blush because I am shocked at my own thoughts."

He loved the study in contrasts that was Adrienne. He knew how soft and vulnerable her heart was, and yet she had a core of steel that would not be vanquished. Even now, when he realized that she needed gentle reassurances he couldn't quite give, she wouldn't betray her weakness.

And his body loved her as well. Nathan couldn't remember ever losing quite so much control during lovemaking. He had urged her to trust him, to let herself go at the moments when she'd wanted to hold back, and it had seemed proper to set an example. It hadn't been too difficult to cross over into unguarded territory as the night deepened along with their passions. Now he was astonished by her daring.

"You're a hellion, do you know it?"

She nipped his wide shoulder with her teeth and smiled. "Do you mind? Would you rather have a prim wife?"

He couldn't speak. Her hand was driving him over the brink. Reaching down, he caught her wrist and pinned it with its mate above her head. Adrienne squirmed, eyes flashing, and demanded that he let her go. Instead, Nathan covered her open mouth with his and kissed her ravenously. He was hard between her legs, and she was equally aroused, so wet and warm that he could have pushed inside her right then with ease. Her breasts were more beautiful than ever in the morning light, inviting his touch and then his lips—

"Captain Raveneau?"

They both looked up, frozen with surprise. Incredibly, the uninvited caller proceeded to knock loudly on the door. Nathan saw that his bride was panic-stricken, struggling out from under him and scrambling to find a sheet with which to cover herself.

"Devil take it," he muttered darkly, then shouted, "Who is it?"

More firmly, the voice replied, "It's me! Zachary!"

"In that case, go away."

"I wouldn't be here if it weren't important. Please, give me just a moment—" He paused, adding hopefully "I have a *tray* for you as well. Retta has sent up hot coffee and pawpaws and little raisin cakes. . . ."

Clutching the sheet to her breasts, Adrienne smiled. "Raisin cakes! I'm starved."

Nathan gave her a withering glance. "So was I, but not for cursed raisin cakes." A moment later he was out of bed, pulling on breeches and yanking open the door. "You can't come in," he told Minter. "Say whatever it is from the doorway."

The smaller man goggled. "You don't mean—" He tried to steal a peek around Raveneau's back and saw a familiar figure in the big bed, and a mass of chestnut hair that shone in the sunlight. She waved, just for an instant.

"Why do you look so bloody shocked?" Nathan growled. "Did you forget what's involved in a wedding night?"

"Oh. Well, no—but, I thought—I mean, you two didn't seem to be quite the usual newly married pair—" Bright red with embarrassment, Minter summed up: "I didn't think she was even speaking to you!"

"I'm giving him another chance," Adrienne called irrepressibly.

Raveneau snatched the breakfast tray out of his friend's hands. "If you don't mind—"

"Wait! I didn't come up here just to deliver the raisin cakes!" Zach put his foot in the door. "You have a visitor, and I agreed to bring her to your room since she's been waiting downstairs for two hours—"

"We're not entertaining today," Nathan interjected firmly.

"I think you will want to see this lady." Minter looked around the corner and motioned to someone. "Here, wait—here she comes—"

Exasperated, he put the tray on the nearest table and returned to look out into the corridor. A plain, thin woman was emerging from the shadows, and at first he had no idea who she might be. Then, as she came closer and looked shyly into his eyes, the truth hit him like a bolt of lightning.

"My God," Nathan said. "It's *Hortie*."

"Yes, it's me."

"What the devil are you doing on Barbados?" he asked, stunned.

"I came with Lord Harms!"

"You can't mean—old Hunty?" If Nathan hadn't been so astounded, he would have laughed.

"Yes, I am referring to Lord *Huntsford* Harms, Mr. Essex."

"He's not in my house as well, I hope?"

"No, sir. He doesn't know where I went, though he certainly might guess."

Thoroughly confused, Nathan realized that Hortie needed more than a hurried interview in the corridor. He could hear his new bride whispering loudly from the bed in an effort to gain his attention and he turned back to wave her off. Then, facing Hortie again, he said, "Look, we should have a proper conversation. Would you mind waiting for a few minutes while my wife and I dress? We'll join you in the library."

Ever mindful of his captain's needs, Minter stepped forward to escort the woman. Nathan had nearly closed his door when Hortie stopped halfway to the stairs and looked back.

"Wait! You are married? I didn't know!"

He gave her a valiant smile. "It's a very recent development." And then he disappeared into his room to escape the questions that were about to follow.

Adrienne wore her husband's shirt, but it did little to disguise her loveliness. When she ran into his arms, Nathan couldn't refrain from slipping his hands under the shirt tail and clasping her bare bottom. The scent of her hair alone was enough to drive him mad.

"I should have sent Hortie to the kitchen to wait for us— until tomorrow, perhaps," he said hoarsely, kissing her.

Adrienne was torn between passion and curiosity. When at last she could speak, she drew back and searched his face. "What on earth can it all mean? Why would Huntsford come to Barbados? He couldn't possibly know—"

"No, I shouldn't think he could." He turned pensive, picking over memories. "There was a night at Harms Castle when Lady Clair saw me without my spectacles. She said that I resembled The Scapegrace, who had been such a man of mystery in London. They all laughed at the notion that Nathan Essex could be anyone of real importance, and I prayed that her words would be forgotten." Nathan moved away from her and went to the window to stare out over the gardens and, farther out, the cane fields. "Harms turning up here is too incredible to be a coincidence. Somehow he must have ferreted out the truth."

"What could he want?"

"You, of course!" he shot back with a harsh laugh. "Hunty has doubtless come to Barbados to *rescue* you!"

Adrienne had an absurd urge to laugh herself. "Well, we won't find out the truth by staying upstairs. Let's hurry and dress and go down to meet with Hortie." She paused to sigh. "I never liked her. She was horrid to me."

"Not to me. She made it possible for me to abduct you, you know. Hortie was my spy at Harms Castle."

Halfway through the door to the dressing room, Adrienne turned back, a gleam in her eyes. "Indeed? It sounds, then, as if she has come to Barbados to find you! I shall have to set her straight."

"Silly chit." He let her go. There wasn't time for more banter; he had to find a clean shirt. Still, when the door closed behind her, Nathan felt an unexpected pang, as if the air had gone flat without Adrienne in the room. The last time he'd had similar feelings about a woman, the object of his affections had been Eloise Sinclair. When she suddenly married Xavier Crowe, Nathan had felt as if he'd been poisoned, and the effects had gone on for months. Perhaps they were still going on.

It was hard to consider opening his heart again and taking such a risk, but then Adrienne was his *wife*. And she was nothing like Eloise.

Back in her own room, Adrienne wondered what the future would bring. Would she and Nathan have separate rooms, sharing intimacies only when he came to her bed?

After hurriedly washing and pinning up her long hair, Adrienne slipped into a round gown of thin cambric muslin, newly arrived from France. It was lovely to have a trunk filled with her own things ... but where would she put them? Looking around her own bedchamber again, the closeness she and Nathan had shared so recently began to seem like a dream. Adrienne's own parents had never bothered with separate rooms. When she was growing up, sometimes she would stand outside their door in the morning, wondering whether they were awake yet, and always there would come the sounds of their mingled whispers and muted laughter. Their bed had been the center of their life-long love affair, and from it radiated the successes of their marriage.

Why was it that the kind of closeness her parents had achieved seemed just out of reach for Adrienne and Nathan? Just as a wave of uncertainty rose within Adrienne, the dressing room door opened and Nathan appeared.

"Are you hiding from me, my little dove?" he teased. "Here, let me fasten your gown. One of a husband's more enjoyable duties, I perceive."

She was embarrassed to have doubted so soon and to be so relieved that tears crowded her throat. As he came up behind her, kissed her neck, and then began to close her gown, Adrienne cast her eyes down.

"Thank you," she whispered. Turning in his arms, she put her face into his shirt front.

"Are you all right?" Nathan tipped her chin up. His intuition provided the answer. "While we're downstairs, Philip and Retta will move your clothes into the bureaus in my—*our* dressing room. And I'll make space for you in my bedchamber as well. I thought we could make a reading nook for you in the corner opposite my desk. There is a bookcase in Horner's old office that we can move up here. . . ."

The tears began to flow now and, liberated, she let them soak into his shirt. "Oh, Nathan—"

"That is, unless you'd rather have a room of your own—"

"No!" Adrienne shook her head so forcefully that a curl fell over her brow. "I want a proper marriage."

"Last night I did promise to try, didn't I? Did you think I was having you on?"

"I—I thought perhaps I'd dreamed it all."

"No, darling." He held her close against him, soaking up the warmth and the imprint of her body. "It was quite real."

"Let's go downstairs now and see what Hortie has to say."

Nathan kissed her, wiped her eyes, and tucked her hand through the crook of his arm as they went down together. Orchid met them in the doorway to the library, looking agitated.

"Some maidservant in dere! Mr. Zach tell me you ask for her, but I don' understand, Captain." Lowering her voice, she hissed, "She has to do wit' Xavier Crowe, I suspect!"

"Mrs. Raveneau and I knew Hortie in England, Orchid, so there's no cause for concern. You've had breakfast brought in? My wife is hungry."

"Yes, sir." Orchid liked the sound of that speech. Her face lit up as she beheld her mistress. "Good morning, Mrs. Raveneau! You look happy."

"I am, thank you, Orchid." She beamed, and their eyes met in understanding. "And I am starving."

As they passed the old woman, Nathan murmured to her, "Don't forget to send Retta and Philip upstairs."

"I glad to do dat!" Seeing Captain Raveneau and his bride looking contented with one another was almost enough to offset Orchid's concern about Hortie.

Inside the library, Hortie was sitting on a long settee of Barbadian mahogany, a plate of raisin cakes and sliced fruit on her lap. Her sallow complexion and pinched features made her seem more unattractive than ever against the backdrop of West Indian lushness.

"Hello, Hortie," Adrienne said. "Don't get up. Sit and eat, and we'll join you." She walked over to the dishes spread over a table and made herself a plate of toasted and buttered plantain, sliced papaya, and raisin cakes.

"You—are his wife?" The words were spoken, in shocked tones, before she could think. "Were you both having all of us on from the first? Did you know his real identity?"

"The answer to both questions is no," Nathan said. He fixed himself a dish of food and poured coffee, then took a chair beside his desk. "Adrienne's father was afraid she wouldn't accept my protection at Harms Castle if she knew my real identity."

"We didn't decide to marry until after Captain Raveneau took me on board his ship," Adrienne added with a note of finality. She didn't think that they owed Hortie any further explanations.

"Lord Harms says that people call you The Scapegrace," the maidservant pressed Nathan.

"Let's talk about you, Hortie" came his reply. "Tell us how you and Lord Harms came to Barbados, and why—and what brings you to my home now."

"'Twasn't long after you abducted Miss Beauvisage—I mean, Mrs. Raveneau—that he decided to set sail. I heard him talking to Lady Thomasina about his plans, and he said that he had a message to deliver to someone called Crowe, on Barbados. He wanted his mother to come with him, and that meant that I came as well."

"What on earth could Huntsford have to do with Xavier Crowe?" Adrienne exclaimed.

"He said he had met a business partner of Crowe's, and that man suggested Lord Harms might find opportunities for the future here." She poked her fork at a piece of plantain and frowned. "It was that business partner who told Lord Harms about your real identity, Mr. Es—I mean, Captain Raveneau—and your home on Barbados. I would wager that he came as much to seek revenge, or to save Miss Beauvisage, as to form a business alliance with Xavier Crowe."

"The only real business Crowe's involved in is piracy." Nathan scowled. "Thievery and murder."

Adrienne was pondering all the new information she'd just heard. "Hortie, did you say that Lady Thomasina is on the island?"

The servant bobbed her head. "Yes'm. She'll do anything her son asks, but I don't like it. Her health is failing, and he's too busy drinking rum with that Crowe fellow to pay any attention to his own mother."

Adrienne imagined her former employer out of sorts in a strange house: swathed in velvet, perspiring heavily, and ringing her bell to no avail. Perhaps she was sitting in a planter's chair, legs elevated, and unable to get up. "Poor Lady Thomasina!"

"And why have you come to Tempest Hall?" Nathan asked. "To warn us?"

"No, sir. There were too many servants at Crowe's Nest. I wasn't wanted. I've come here to ask for work."

Adrienne nearly gasped. "But, Hortie—what about Lady Thomasina?"

"She wanted me to leave, so that I could save Angus from Xavier Crowe's beastly hounds. They kept poor Angus cornered under the bed day and night, and I think Lord Harms rather hoped they'd get him in their massive jaws and murder the poor pup."

Nathan and Adrienne exchanged glances. "Do you mean that you brought Angus with you?"

She colored. "Yes. He's tied to a chair out in your gallery, sir. Philip has given him a bit of roast pigeon."

"Oh, for God's sake." Nathan walked to the glass door opening onto the gallery and spied Angus pacing in the sunlight, his pink satin tether stretching to the limit at each stop. When he saw Nathan, the frizzy terrier bared his teeth and emitted a low growl. "Simply splendid. Just what we needed: a devious, mean-spirited, gluttonous cur."

"I rather like Angus," Adrienne offered. "Besides, we owe Lady Thomasina that much."

"I sense that we're going to be drawn into another *situation*," he muttered ironically.

"You are already in a *situation* with Xavier Crowe" was her tart reply. "As for Hortie, don't you see that her arrival here is the answer to our prayers? We've been needing a housekeeper to help Orchid, and Hortie would be perfect! Lily will be the head cook, Retta the maid, and Hortie can pick some other girls to train." She gave the Englishwoman an apologetic look. "You know, they have slaves here. I find it appalling, but there's nothing I can do—not yet, at least."

"I should be honored to become the housekeeper for Tempest Hall, Captain and Mrs. Raveneau." Her thin lips curved in a droll smile. "You see, sir, it was meant to be. You told me at Harms Castle that you wished to repay me for my help, and now that has come to pass."

"Hmm. Yes. And, I shall always be grateful to you, Hortie. I'm glad you're here, but . . ." He cast a dark glance toward the gallery, "I don't recall being indebted to Angus."

Adrienne's laughter lightened the mood. Standing, she smiled at Hortie. "Would you like a tour of the house? I'll introduce you to the rest of the staff, and we'll decide on a room for you."

"Can Angus stay with me? I promised her ladyship that I'd look after him."

The two women left the library then, leaving Nathan to pour himself more coffee and stare broodingly out the windows. Honeybees swarmed over the yellow tube flowers of a Lucky Bean tree growing near the bathhouse. Already it was hot.

Hunty and Xavier Crowe! Could it be? Even more unbelievable was the realization that he and Adrienne had only been married one day and already they were being drawn into another dangerous predicament.

Needing some fresh air, Nathan went outside to tell Zachary that he was going to ride south to inspect his new land. It was time to have a look at the fifty acres that would position him right next to Xavier Crowe, Huntsford Harms, and Cobbler's Reef, where so many unsuspecting ships had been lured to their doom.

Standing on one of Crowe's Nest's balconies overlooking the beach, Huntsford Harms wondered if it was possible to bake to death in this climate. Everything about Barbados seemed extreme to him, especially this lavish estate and the brilliantly blue surf that pounded against the sand below. When they'd first come to the eastern side of the island, Harms noticed that most of the trees and shrubs arched in the wind. Later he discovered that they remained bent over even when the air was calm.

Xavier Crowe had laughed when Huntsford mentioned this. "Yes, the wind has shaped them, just as we English learn to bend to the rigors of life here. Bimshire's not England, I fear, for all its delusions of grandeur!"

Indeed, Barbados was a study in contrasts. For every spectacular view of the ocean, sunset, or tropical flowers, there was an equally vivid image of acres of scrubby land where nothing would grow, or unpainted slave shacks being thrashed by the wind. Huntsford had discovered that he couldn't even swim in the ocean to cool off without being nearly killed by the treacherous waves.

"What do you think?" inquired the voice of his host as he walked onto the balcony.

"I think that it's not quite paradise after all."

Crowe regarded Huntsford, then touched a finger to his sunburned cheek. "Tsk, tsk. There's nothing quite as fragile as English skin, hmm?" Then he took snuff and looked out over his domain. "The rest of the island is rather more what you may expect; greener and all that. But I love my little corner all the more because of its wildness. No one bothers me, and my home is all the more splendid in these surroundings."

Huntsford wanted to ask about the shipwrecks he'd heard whisperings of during the voyage from England, but there was always a steely glint in Xavier Crowe's cerulean eyes that gave him pause. Sometimes it seemed that the glint hardened as Crowe's smile intensified.

"Your home is certainly splendid, sir, and my mother and I are grateful to be here." Huntsford was intensely curious to know the source of his host's money, for he didn't seem to grow crops, and although there was talk of a shipping business, Crowe didn't appear to work at all. "I am eager to be of service to you. As I've said, our mutual friend Frakes-Hogg felt that you and I could deal famously together."

"Are you, dear boy? I am glad to hear it. How grateful I am that Walter convinced you to come to Barbados before his death." He put on an expression of melancholy. "I have always trusted his instincts about people, and I have been needing an . . . assistant."

As they walked out into the corridor, Huntsford wondered whether he dared ask exactly what he would be assisting with, and decided to continue to keep silent and wait. "I am eager to help, sir, and I am a hard worker."

A cynical smile made Crowe's mouth twitch. "Come with me, my friend. There is something I want to show you."

They traversed the spacious corridor, stopping along the way to peek into Lady Thomasina's bedchamber. The old woman had the shutters tightly closed and lay snoring in her net-draped bed.

"How dear is her ladyship," Crowe purred kindly. "I am terribly fond of her."

Huntsford could find no reply. His gut told him that Xavier Crowe was even more interested in getting his hands on Lady Thomasina's assets than he, her son, was, but he had yet to discover the reason. So, he smiled and nodded, and they went on to Crowe's own magnificent suite of rooms.

When they came through the door, Eloise Crowe gasped and turned from the shuttered window. "Oh—Xavier—you frightened me! I thought you had gone out—"

"What are you doing in here?" he said curtly. He looked around as if checking to see if she had tampered with his things. "Are there workmen in your own rooms?"

"No, of course not. I . . . thought I heard a noise, and so I came in here to look outside, where the view is best."

Huntsford was fascinated by this glimpse of their real selves. Downstairs, at meals, they were all polite chatter, but it seemed to be an act that was familiar to any English noble. Their marriage was as empty as most. Eloise, however, reminded Huntsford of an elegant butterfly caught in an invisible net.

They had no children of their own, but had taken in the orphaned son of Xavier's dead brother. The ten-year-old boy, Martin, seemed to have bonded with Eloise. Xavier pretended to be nice to him, but Martin looked at him the same way Eloise did. It wasn't so much fear in their eyes, Huntsford supposed, as trepidation.

"May I have a word with you in private?" Crowe's voice was glazed with frosty charm.

She went into the corridor, willowy, pale, and sable-haired, and her husband followed. Gripping her arm, he murmured, "Have you taken Lady Thomasina's special tea to her?"

"Oh, Xavier, must we? It grieves me to see her so groggy—"

"Haven't you learned yet not to argue with me?" It pleased him to kiss her until she began to recoil. "Do my bidding and you may have a brief ride up the coastline, as long as you don't go too far north again. One hour, do you understand?"

Her huge eyes lit up. "Oh, thank you!" She swallowed, then said slowly, "I'll get the tea."

Crowe returned to his houseguest, closing the door and shaking his head. "I must apologize for my wife. She comes in here to watch the road for her lover."

"Wh-what?" Huntsford gaped.

"Oh, he never actually does come, but she imagines she hears him. Nathan Raveneau. She wishes she'd married him instead of me." He shrugged and took snuff. "I pity her."

Huntsford could scarcely breathe. Was it possible that Crowe had uttered the name of Nathan Raveneau? If he was going to confide one of his real reasons for coming to Barbados, now would be the time, but Huntsford was still wary of his new mentor.

Instead, he asked, "Have you been married long?"

"Nearly four years. I confess that I married her to thwart Raveneau, and it may have been a case of cutting off my nose to spite my face." His laughter was low and sardonic. "It was one of those mad things one does in London. I already knew and disliked Raveneau, and when I saw him there, courting Eloise, the temptation to go to his weakness was too strong to resist."

"How did you do it?"

"I plied her with charm and expensive gifts, then I lured her onto my ship and we set sail before Eloise could protest. By then she was beginning to guess that I wasn't quite what I'd seemed." Crowe showed his white teeth in a grin. "It was grand. Raveneau gave chase and ran us down at sea, demanding that I hand over the poor damsel. However, Eloise already knew better than to speak the truth. She paid enough heed to my threats to assure him that she loved me and wanted none of the dashing Raveneau!"

Huntsford chuckled. "I wish I could have seen his face."

"A priceless moment, I can assure you." Pausing, Crowe savored the memory. "However, I made a bad bargain. My wife is barren."

"How sad for . . . you both."

"I find what consolation I can elsewhere, and I amuse myself by bending her spirit to suit my purposes. Meanwhile, Eloise dreams of Raveneau and showers love on Martin, who is soft and spineless as a result."

"He seems a nice lad to me."

"Enough. I didn't bring you here to talk about them."

Looking around the grand, airy room, Huntsford wondered how the gigantic wardrobe had fit through the doorway. Hanging on the wall nearby was a massive gilt mirror. Xavier Crowe motioned for his guest to follow him to the mahogany four-poster bed, which was so high that in order to reach the mattress, its occupant must climb a set of three steps. When Crowe lifted the top step, he revealed that it was actually a box, its lid formed by the step.

"Have you ever heard of Stede Bonnet?" Crowe asked softly.

"The Gentleman Pirate? Yes, I've read about him. He was from Barbados, wasn't he? If memory serves, he was in partnership with Blackbeard a century ago, off the coast of Carolina."

"Excellent, dear boy. You're brighter than I dared hope." He reached inside the stairstep-box and took out two pistols. Sensing Harms's shocked stare, he explained, "A fellow never knows when he might be attacked in his bed." Then he opened what appeared to be a narrow secret compartment located under the pistols and drew out a tattered piece of parchment. "I have reason to believe that this belonged to Stede Bonnet."

Huntsford's brown eyes were wide with amazement. "Why, it looks like a treasure map!"

"Do moderate your tone." Crowe turned the paper away from the younger man's view. "Now then, to continue, Stede Bonnet was indeed born on this island, the son of a planter. He inherited the family plantation, married and became a father, and then rather abruptly decided to pursue a career as a pirate. For a long time, I gather than Bonnet's wife thought he was simply away on business!" He laughed with gusto.

Watching him, Huntsford commented, "Quite a man, hmm?"

"Indeed! Men like Stede Bonnet are the stuff of legends!"

"But didn't they hang him?"

"Yes. In Charles Town, I believe. Perhaps he let his guard down."

"Are you implying that one might learn from his story?"

"I learn from everything I encounter. It's the key to my success." His shrewd gaze fastened on the map.

"Might I inquire how you came into possession of such an ... artifact?"

"I—uh, discovered it in the captain's cabin of a wrecked ship." Crowe fussed with a loose button on his coat. "Cobbler's Reef is notoriously treacherous, you know. But that's a story for another day." He opened the map on the silk counterpane and gestured to Huntsford to step closer for a good look. "Do you see? It says 'Bonnet, 1718' in the bottom corner, and the location is clearly spelled out."

Huntsford stared. It was a crude map, smudged in places, but he could see that it showed the southeastern quadrant of Barbados, and St. Philip's Parish was labeled in ink. "Where is your estate on this map?" he asked.

"Here," Crowe replied, pointing to a spot near Long Bay. "And here ..." His finger traveled a few miles north, to a spot labeled Cave Bay. "Here on this beach is the buried treasure! Do you see how he's marked the spot? I surmise that when Stede Bonnet was in danger of being caught, either by the authorities or perhaps his erstwhile partner, Blackbeard, he sailed back to Barbados—to the far side of the island from his home—and buried his valuables. He made a map so that he could find it when he returned . . . but unfortunately for *him*, that day did not come!"

"Doesn't someone else own the land you're pointing out?"

"Oh, yes, but he's almost never here. The fellow lives in France. I ride all over that property at will."

"But . . ." Huntsford was about to point out that any treasure recovered on that land would belong to the Frenchman, not to Xavier Crowe, but it dawned on him that his host had no intention of conducting himself honorably. Little hairs rose on the back of Huntsford's neck, and he smiled. "If I help you, will I receive part of the . . . booty?"

Crowe laughed loudly. "You are talking like a pirate already! Yes, of course I'll share the treasure with you, my boy! Shall we say one-quarter?"

"Splendid!" Huntsford Harms's eyes lit up. "I can't tell you how pleased I am that I took Walter's sage advice and came to Barbados!"

"No less pleased than I am. Now then, let's ride up the coast and try to find the location marked on our map, shall we?"

"Lead on, sir! Do you know any pirate songs?"

Crowe closed the stairstep-box and glanced back over one shoulder. With an effort, he maintained his composure and replied softly, "No. Why would I?"

Chapter Twenty-one

✿ SQUARING HER SHOULDERS, ADRIENNE FACED HER husband across the library with arms akimbo. "If you are going to inspect our new land, then I want to come with you."

"I'd rather that you stay here until I've seen it once—"

"Why?" She narrowed her eyes. "Do you expect me to believe that you haven't ridden down there since we came to the island? I know you too well, Nathan! You have seen it, and now I want to see it as well." Trying another tack, she stepped closer and took his hand. "Is it very beautiful there?"

"Magnificent. And you are sly as a fox. All right, I'll take you, but it may be dangerous."

Adrienne's eyes sparkled as she started upstairs to dress. "Don't move. I'll be right back!"

Of course, Adrienne was right. Almost as soon as they'd first arrived at Tempest Hall, Nathan had slipped away on his own to have a look at the property he'd own after the wedding. He was giving up his freedom in exchange for that spot overlooking Crowe's Nest, and the urge to see it and gauge its usefulness was overwhelming.

Now that Nathan and Adrienne were married and the land was rightfully his, he knew a heady sense of confidence that good would prevail. Huntsford Harms's presence on the island only reinforced that feeling. Everything was coming together.

The Raveneaus rode on Compass and Ben, south along the rugged east coast, following the road that came and went along the cliffs overlooking the ocean. Occasionally they galloped through a small village or skirted a struggling plantation, but their fifteen-mile journey was speedy.

It seemed to Adrienne that the water grew even more impossibly bright as they went farther south. Such blazing blue and turquoise tints could not truly exist in nature, but there they were. The splendor of the scenery was staggering. She slowed her horse to stare at a ruined plantation house that perched all alone on the edge of the cliff. The faded coral stones of the hollowed-out house made a striking contrast with the dazzling blue ocean below.

Ahead of her, Nathan reined in Compass and looked back toward Adrienne. Then he pointed to the solitary house and the scrubby land around it and nodded, smiling.

Adrienne could not have been more thrilled. As they dismounted and tied the horses inside a hidden grove of cannonball trees, she looked up at her husband with wide eyes. "It's wonderful! But I wonder what happened to the house. Does it have a name?"

"I think it's called Victoria Villa." They went in through the classical arched gallery that ringed the house and saw that the structure was beyond saving. The floors were rotten and the ceilings gaped so that they could see right through to the sky. "Someone probably left years ago, and it simply fell into disrepair. The sea air destroys quickly."

Adrienne stared under a coral archway to the ocean and shivered. "Victoria Villa . . . How romantic! Do you suppose it's haunted?"

"I'm more interested in the rest of the property." Nathan reached back for Adrienne's hand and drew her out into the sunlight. "Look to the south. Around that bend in the cliffs lies Crowe's Nest. I brought my telescope today to see just how much is visible from our southern border. And there," he continued, leading her to the edge of the cliff, "is Cave Bay. Can you see why I wanted it?"

"Indeed," she whispered. The cove that lay beneath the ruined house was nothing short of breathtaking. "It belongs in a romantic novel, I think!"

Cave Bay consisted of a great semicircular beach. The dark, sheltering cliff walls rose vertically above the white coral sand, which was covered with coconut palms and masses of sea grapes. The cliffs extended out into the pounding surf on both sides, so that the little bay was tucked away like a bowl.

"Let's go down there and see if there really is a cave!" Adrienne urged. Something in the sea air and the rhythm of the great Atlantic rollers filled her with wild energy. It had to do with Nathan as well, for there had always been a glint of daring in his eyes and his spirit, calling to her.

Drawing her into his arms, he felt the curves of her body beneath her thin gown, and he caught a whiff of musky lilac from her skin. Desire welled up in him without warning. White sand and the turquoise water beckoned. Steps were carved into the cliffs. Nathan imagined making love to Adrienne with the water lapping over them and the sun on his back. . . .

Just then the barest hint of voices touched his ears. Was he imagining it? He pulled out his brass telescope, scanned the edge of the cliffs, and there were Xavier Crowe and Huntsford Harms, scarcely visible but headed toward Cave Bay.

"Unbelievable. Crowe and Harms are coming," he whispered. "Go in the house and find a hiding place, preferably one with some view of the bay. I'll hide too, where I can watch and—I hope—hear. If anything goes wrong, you take Ben and ride for Tempest Hall, understand?"

"Yes, but I'm not afraid of them, and neither are you."

"Don't argue, chit. Just once blindly obey."

Adrienne agreed, but she knew she'd never leave without him. She watched Nathan climb halfway down the cliffs and tuck himself into a big clump of sea grape bushes before slipping inside the villa. There was one tall hurricane shutter clinging to an inner door, and Adrienne folded it back so that it made a corner hiding place for her.

Down on the cliffs, Nathan opened his telescope and watched as Crowe and Harms used the stone steps to descend into the cove.

"I say," Huntsford cried when he'd gotten halfway down, "is this quite safe?"

Crowe waited on the sand below, rolling his eyes. "If you're going to live in Bimshire, old boy, you'd better learn to keep up."

A gray plover flew overhead, giving its plaintive cry, and the breeze fluttered saucer-shaped leaves against Nathan's face. It couldn't be going better if he'd planned it. Now that Huntsford had gained the beach, the two men were walking, moving in his direction across the sand. They both wore white shirts that caught the wind, and Huntsford's face was dark pink from too much sun. Crowe was opening a large sheaf of parchment, pointing.

"How on earth can you expect to locate the exact spot?" Harms's voice rose in frustration just enough to allow Nathan to make out the words. "Your map is a century old!"

"My dear chap," Crowe rejoined forcefully, "don't you trust me? A map like this, in Stede Bonnet's own hand, is worth a fortune. We would be *mad* to dismiss its importance." He paused. "What difference does a century make in this place? 'Tis not as if a city has sprung up over Bonnet's hiding place!"

Nathan blinked. They were talking about Stede Bonnet, the gentleman pirate. What sort of ridiculous treasure-hunting scheme was Crowe trying to trick Hunty into swallowing?

"But, sir," Harms whined, "don't you have better things to do than dig holes all over this beach?"

"Indeed I do," came the stern reply. "That is why I have agreed to share this treasure with you when *you* find it. Old boy, I fail to understand your plummeting enthusiasm. Surely a strong fellow like you isn't put off by a bit of physical labor?" Again Crowe paused, then drove in his point. "What do a few holes matter when you will be discovering a treasure that will provide tremendous wealth for the rest of your life?"

"But—what if someone else has already found it? Or what if it isn't as grand as you think?"

Raveneau couldn't make out the speech that Xavier Crowe delivered in response, but whatever he said, it seemed to work. Huntsford's blond head was bobbing up and down amid the trees.

"Yes, yes, I am honored that you chose to share the map with me," he exclaimed. "I'll do my best."

"You do come with the recommendation of my esteemed colleague Frakes-Hogg," Crowe intoned. "I would hate to think that he underestimated your mettle."

"No!" Harms cried. "I'll find the treasure and prove myself to you, sir. We have more in common than you know. Actually, I had another reason for coming to Barbados, besides the matters relating to Walter Frakes-Hogg."

"Yes . . . ?"

"It's Nathan Raveneau. You are not the only one who hates him. He kidnapped the woman I love and brought her to this island." Huntsford's voice grew even louder. "I mean to rescue her!"

"How terribly noble you are. I must confess that I have met Miss Beauvisage, on the day she arrived at Tempest Hall."

Listening from the crest of the hill, Nathan wondered again how Xavier Crowe had known her name. Had he employed spies? Perhaps Walter Frakes-Hogg, whom Nathan hadn't realized was acquainted with Crowe, had written him letters?

"If you've met Adrienne, then you know how exquisite she is."

"Indeed. Far too lovely to be wasted on that lout Raveneau." Crowe took snuff, then added, "I'll do what I can to aid your cause, but you may be too late. I've heard that they are betrothed."

"What?" Huntsford made a choking sound, then pounded his fists on the trunk of the nearest coconut palm. "I cannot bear to think of her purity being besmirched by one such as he!"

Crowe looked bored. "I may know a way for you to see her. Major Carrington, who owns a fine plantation in St. James Parish, has invited us to a ball six days from now. There's a quaint festival among the slaves known as Crop-over—a time when they celebrate the end of the harvest. The Carringtons apparently have decided to join in, in a more civilized manner of course, and they are calling their party a Crop-over Ball."

"I was under the impression that you don't usually attend such gatherings. I thought that the people of Barbados had been spreading lies about you, and—"

Crowe interrupted. "Perhaps the best way to dispel such rumors is to show them that I am a man like any other. Besides, Eloise would doubtless like to go, and Bajan society will be clamoring to meet our houseguests!" He gave a mirthless laugh. "You see, I'm not a bad fellow!" Consulting the map again, Xavier Crowe pointed to a spot a few feet away. "I believe that is where you ought to begin digging, old boy. Shall we get the shovel?"

Nathan and Adrienne didn't have a chance to talk during the ride home. The wind increased, clouds gathered, and a warm rain began to fall, drenching them as they rode.

"I'm so anxious to hear your news!" she exclaimed when their horses slowed momentarily behind a wagon stacked with puncheons of sugar syrup. "Did you hear anything that they said?"

"We'll talk at home," he shouted over the wind. "I'm glad for this thinking time."

Adrienne was too, for she had seen someone herself: the mysterious, beautiful woman who had warned her away from the ocean much farther north had ridden past today. From Adrienne's hiding place behind the hurricane shutter, she had watched the woman ride past Victoria Villa, then circle back and pause for a moment on the edge of the cliff. Could she be the ghost of Victoria?

Minter was waiting for Nathan when they reached Tempest Hall. The squally wind had caused all sorts of problems with the sugar mill, and Minter didn't know what to do. Adrienne went inside on her own, and no sooner had she washed and donned dry clothing than Hortie appeared and requested the tour she'd been promised.

"It's a very different world from England, ma'am," Hortie decided a half hour later, pursing her lips. "I don't think I shall ever feel comfortable."

Adrienne paused in the midst of opening a door. "Are you bothered by the climate—or the slaves?"

"I will admit," Hortie whispered, "that I don't care to live with heathens. There are many more at Crowe's Nest, and that's one of the reasons I left. How do you think it feels, ma'am, to be given orders by a black girl?"

Nearly biting her tongue, Adrienne managed to consider her reply. "I have a great deal of respect for Orchid and Lily and Philip and Retta, and many of the slaves here. In fact, I feel very sorry that they are not all free people. I also understand that you are unaccustomed to being with people of color. I believe that you will come to share my views, Hortie, and in the meantime, you must treat everyone here with courtesy and respect." She stared into Hortie's pale eyes. "Do we understand one another?"

"Yes'm." She grew paler. "I heard, at Crowe's Nest, that there was a terrible slave rebellion on this island just two years ago! Cane fields were set afire, and—"

"Not one plantation owner or family member was harmed by any slave, although several hundred *slaves* were killed!" Adrienne said. "I'm certain that the slaves feel their circumstances are very unfair, and I understand that that uprising came about because they'd been led to believe that their freedom was at hand. My hope is that their rebellion helped spur their cause, hastening the day of their emancipation."

Hortie tightened her mouth again. "Yes'm."

They went into Nathan's bedchamber, and Adrienne showed her the way the dressing room was arranged. It pleased her to discover that the changes Nathan had promised had been carried out while they were out. Her things were interspersed neatly with his, just as her parents had shared space throughout her lifetime. They went into the room where Adrienne had slept until last night and out onto the balcony. Tropical flowers scented the warm breeze.

"I do understand some of what you're feeling, Hortie." Adrienne gave the woman a smile. "This is a very strange place in comparison to England, and you didn't even choose to come. I have felt lost myself, but I'm getting better now. I'll do whatever I can to help you adjust as well."

"Our lots in life are a bit different though, aren't they?"
The servant's expression said what she could not about her
dreams of Nathan Raveneau. "I'll be all right. I'm glad to
be here, rather than at that awful Crowe's Nest. Not one
nice person in the entire house except for Mrs. Crowe."

"Her name is ... Eloise?" Adrienne's heart began to
pound.

"Hmm? Oh, yes, I suppose so."

"I would have expected her to be unpleasant, if she is
married to a villain like Xavier Crowe."

"Men like that always marry women like angels. I've
seen it over and over again."

"Is she that lovely? And kind?"

Hortie gave her new mistress a long stare. "She's no
lovelier than you, if that's what you mean. And yes, Mrs.
Crowe is kind, but she has that air of sadness I've seen so
often among titled folk." Her thin nose pointed a little
more. "Wealth is rarely a guarantee of happiness. Just the
opposite, I believe. I've seen a lot of wretched marriages—
thoughtless men and lonely women."

"Well, we're not wealthy, so there's no need to worry
about us," Adrienne replied distractedly, her mind on Eloise
Crowe.

"Is it Lady Thomasina you're concerned about?" Hortie
asked. "Mrs. Crowe has been very nice to her, but Lord
Harms is always off with Mr. Crowe, and so she spends
most of her time in her bedroom. They keep the draperies
closed, and she was sleeping nearly all day when I left
there...."

"But that's terrible! Poor Lady Thomasina!"

Hortie nodded, as Nathan came into the bedchamber
through the dressing room.

"I thought I heard voices! Ah, good, you are showing
Hortie around. We want her to feel at home." How lovely
Adrienne looked, felt, sounded, and smelled to him.

"It's very different here from England," Hortie offered.

"Yes, that's true," Nathan agreed. "But change can be a
good thing. And you are here now, so let's make the best
of it." The housekeeper seemed in no hurry to leave them
alone, so he walked to the door and opened it. "Perhaps

you can go downstairs and have a chat with Orchid about her methods for running the house." This didn't seem to inspire her, so he added, "I think Angus is looking for you as well. You'd better make certain he hasn't escaped from the gallery, or relieved himself on our furnishings!"

"I had nearly forgotten poor Angus!" With that, Hortie fairly dashed out the door and it closed behind her.

"At last we are alone," Nathan murmured. They met each other halfway and enjoyed a heartfelt embrace. "This is not the way I had envisioned our honeymoon."

"Sharing it with Hortie, you mean?" Laughter crept into her voice. "I don't think she wants me to be alone with you. Perhaps she believes she can stop us from consummating this . . . union."

"Fortunately, she's much too late for that." He kissed her lingeringly. "You taste better than anything in the world. It's amazing."

"You are silly. Now tell me everything that you overheard in Cave Bay! I was worried that Crowe and Huntsford might discover you and challenge you to a duel!"

Nathan laughed. "Can we talk while I change out of these clothes?" He led the way into the dressing room and began stripping off his soiled riding garb. His bride perched on the edge of a low stool, waiting. "I learned that Hunty is afraid of heights and has a nasty sunburn." Naked, he reached for a clean shirt and felt her eyes wandering over him. "Are you listening to anything I've said?"

"Hmmm?"

"Take heed! I'll take you to bed and make love to you quite forcefully if you don't stop staring at me like that."

"You *will*?" Adrienne squeaked hopefully.

"Well—just as soon as I've had something to eat. I'm famished." Fastening up the shirt, Nathan saw that he had her attention again and turned serious. "I don't think it was a coincidence that we saw Crowe on our land today. I had the feeling that he's been treating your father's property as his own, since Nicholai lived half a world away. And I'm in no hurry to let him know that he's being watched by the new owners."

"What did they say?" Adrienne hopped up and followed

him into the light of their bedchamber. They sat down in the chairs by Nathan's desk while he pulled on his boots. "I am fairly panting with suspense!"

"I know. I like it." He gave her a wicked grin. "All right. They were talking about a counterfeit treasure map that Crowe has invented to keep Hunty out of his hair."

"How do you know it's counterfeit?"

One of his black eyebrows arched. "Crowe maintains that it belonged to Stede Bonnet, the gentleman pirate who plied the waters between here and America a century ago. He was from Barbados, so Crowe has persuaded Harms that he buried his stolen riches on our property."

"You don't think that's possible?"

"I didn't entertain that thought for a moment," he scoffed. "In the first place, I don't believe that it is remotely possible that a map like that could have remained undiscovered and unused for a hundred years. Second, I know Xavier Crowe. This sort of scheme smells of his methods." He stood, then took Adrienne's hand and drew her into his arms. "I hate talking about him. He's a blot on our lives."

"I know, but do finish your explanation." She kissed him for encouragement, then they wandered toward the door. "I'm not sure I quite understand."

"Crowe will find a way to use Harms, but he isn't ready to divulge the details of his secret raids on ships. So, he's keeping him out of the way—digging holes all over Cave Bay cove!"

"Did you learn any more about Huntsford's reasons for coming to Barbados?"

"I heard them talking about Walter Frakes-Hogg, who apparently had business dealings with Crowe. It seems that it was Frakes-Hogg who told Hunty about Xavier Crowe—and that confirms my suspicion that those two were in league back in Winchester."

"The possibilities are frightening!"

"Including my favorite: that Hunty *planned* to kill Frakes-Hogg that night."

"Why would he want to come to Barbados, though?"

He opened the door to the upstairs hallway and replied in

a softly ironic voice, "I only know what he told Crowe today—that they share a common hatred of me, and that Harms intends to rescue you from my evil clutches." After a brief pause, he added, "And of course, money is always a valid motive. Hunty longs to accumulate wealth without working."

Adrienne guessed that her husband meant to end the conversation then, since anything further that they might say could be overheard. "Wait!" She caught the front of his shirt. "I saw something very odd today, when I was inside Victoria Villa. Do you think there could be a ghost? Of Victoria, perhaps?"

"Honestly? No. God, I am ravenous." He looked distracted.

"Do you have more news about Crowe?" she prompted.

His grin flashed white in the late-afternoon shadows. "We are going to a ball next week. Major Carrington and his wife are having a party to celebrate Crop-over. It's usually a festival that's held by the slaves, when the last bit of cane has been cut and processed, but apparently Carrington has decided to enliven the summer for the rest of us...."

"What does that have to do with Huntsford and Xavier Crowe?"

"They plan to attend, along with other members of their household. Ordinarily, I wouldn't consider subjecting myself, or you, to a night of Barbadian society, but we can't miss this. Crowe has promised Hunty that he'll see you at the ball. Can you imagine a better drama? I don't think they know we're married." Nathan led her toward the stairway, enticed by the aroma of slow-cooked pepper pot wafting up from the dining room. "Besides, although I may have shunned proper society in the past, I realize that I ought to change some of my ways now that I am a married man. And I should show you off."

"Don't change too much," Adrienne cautioned, half in jest. "If you turn into a stuffy pillar of society, I'll never forgive you!"

They were laughing until they turned at the landing and saw Angus waiting for them at the foot of the stairs. One

of the green lizards Adrienne had come to like so much
was dangling from the terrier's clenched jaw.

"Grrr," Angus growled.

Before Nathan could speak, his wife cried, "You don't
need to say it! I'll tell Hortie that she *must* keep Angus in
her room."

"That spoiled beast has probably murdered my favorite
lizard." Nathan glared at Angus, who lowered his head and
growled louder. "I never thought I'd say this, but I begin to
empathize with Hunty."

"At least you don't have any blue gloves!"

They both started laughing so hard they had to sit down
on the stairs, and Angus dropped his lizard and began to
bark.

Northmont, the plantation house belonging to Major
Edward Carrington and his wife, Honoria, was situated on
a hill near Speightstown. Thick-trunked fan palms and
enormous bearded figs sheltered the grand house, which
was built in the Georgian style except for the open verandah on three sides. Standing at the front door, guests could
look out over the Caribbean Sea that lay far below, and the
addition of the fiery setting sun made for a breathtaking
view.

Adrienne, flanked by Nathan and Zachary Minter, was
dreamily admiring the gilded ocean when the door opened
and a handsome black footman bowed before them.

"Welcome to Northmont."

The sight inside the house was almost more spellbinding
than the sunset. They were ushered into a marble-tiled en-
tryway, but Adrienne stood on tiptoe to peek into the rooms
beyond. Nathan whispered that the entire ground floor of
Northmont was taken up by formal rooms, including the
magnificent ballroom, a spacious dining room, and the biggest library on the island. Adrienne could almost pretend
that she was back in Europe, attending a royal assembly.
However, the sultry air, the scents of spicy native foods, the
all-black staff, and the countless flickering hurricane lamps
reminded her that this was Barbados, not Gloucestershire or
the Loire Valley.

Wandering into the airy stairhall, they heard music: harpsichord, violins, flutes, and more, playing together exquisitely. Richly garbed guests were dancing under glittering chandeliers, and servants were carrying huge trays and dishes of food into the nearby dining room.

"You're glad we came, aren't you?" Nathan whispered in her ear.

A wide, radiant smile spread over Adrienne's face. "Yes." She lifted the satin-and-pearl-edged hem of her gown and showed him her white satin shoe, which was tapping in anticipation.

Minter spoke up. "You're too young to be locked away with an elderly fellow like Captain Raveneau."

She giggled. "I sometimes forget that my husband is more than thirty years old! No wonder he doesn't waltz with me." She extended her hand to Minter, who was wearing an ill-fitting suit and whose red hair was sticking up rebelliously in back. "Do you dance, Zachary?"

Nathan snatched her away then. "You're a married woman. People will talk if you continue to throw yourself at bachelors!" The corners of his mouth twitched, but he tried to look stern, and the effect was impressive. Clad in evening clothes that included a waistcoat of cream striped silk and an immaculately cut frock coat, Nathan was the image of a civilized pirate. His sun-darkened face was roguishly handsome, his eyes were brilliantly sea-blue, and his black hair looked as if it had been blown into place by the wind.

Adrienne splayed a hand possessively over his shirtfront. A week after their wedding, she was more captivated than ever by him. "How could I ever throw myself at any other man but you? You look simply delicious."

"So do you, Mrs. Raveneau." His gaze wandered from her upswept chestnut curls threaded with damask roses, over her expressively lovely face, down to the elegant ballgown of white corded silk and pearls that showed her shoulders and most of her arms and bosom. The gown had been made by Sally Ann, the dressmaker from Bridgetown, and there were even long gloves to complete Adrienne's new image of refinement.

"Ah, there you are, Captain Raveneau!" A tall, pink-cheeked old gentleman with a number of ribbons pinned to his coat came toward them. "I'm sorry that my wife and I have so many guests tonight that we weren't able to greet you when you arrived."

"But we have just come in, Major Carrington," Nathan assured him, and introduced his wife and Zachary.

"Raveneau, you are a fortunate man to have persuaded this ravishing woman to come to Barbados!"

"I can be quite persuasive," he agreed.

"My husband was so romantic, I couldn't refuse. I'll never forget the sheer poetry of his marriage proposal," Adrienne informed their host, eyes twinkling with mischief. "It was so kind of you to invite us tonight, Major. Your home is beautiful."

"Come in and dance for a bit before the food is served, won't you?" As they started into the ballroom, Carrington made idle conversation with Nathan. "I must confess that it becomes confusing to address you as Captain Raveneau on nights like this, old chap."

"I beg your pardon?"

"Your father's here, you know! Sometimes I forget which one of you I'm talking to!"

Nathan blinked. "I wasn't aware that Father was invited—"

"Of course! André and I have been acquainted for years. I've known him since the American War for Independence, when we fought on opposite sides, and I was delighted that he could come tonight!" Carrington pointed across the ballroom to the open doors leading to the verandah. "I believe you might find him out there, in need of rescue. The last time I saw Raveneau, he had been waylaid by Lady McGrath. She was telling him all about your wedding. He seemed to find it rather odd that she had attended and he hadn't." The old man waggled his bushy white eyebrows.

"Nathan," Adrienne exclaimed, "you'd better go and talk to him. His feelings may be hurt that he wasn't invited!"

"Just so," he agreed, nodding. "Perhaps Zach will dance with you until my return."

"Don't worry about me; I am quite able to amuse myself!" She gave him a bright, reassuring smile and watched as he started off around the edge of the ballroom. When she turned back to speak to Zachary, she noticed that he was smiling at a pretty girl who was standing nearby with her mother. "You must ask her to dance, Zach!" she whispered.

Blushing, he shook his head, but allowed himself to be persuaded. When he'd gone off, Adrienne backed up closer to the wall and opened her fan. She moved it back and forth in time to the music, smiling as she watched the dancing guests, until someone spoke.

"Pardon me—"

Turning, Adrienne looked into the big dark eyes of a lovely young woman near her own age. "Good evening!" In spite of her embroidered ballgown and the ostrich feathers in her upswept hair, the lady looked awfully familiar to Adrienne.

"I hope you won't think me too bold," she said, "but I had to tell you that yours is the most beautiful fan I have ever seen!"

"Do you like it? I am so pleased! The fanmaker in London told me that Marie Antoinette received the silk as a gift and commissioned the fan herself!"

"How fascinating!" Her new friend's eyes grew bigger than ever, and her mouth made an O. "Why, this is a treasure, then! How proud you must be to own it!" She leaned closer, whispering "Tell me, is your fanmaker Eugene Ralna? My mother adored his creations."

"Yes! I think he is a funny little man, but there is no denying his skill." They laughed together, and it came to Adrienne how much she had missed the company of a female friend her own age.

"It's been a long time since I have met someone like you," the young woman was saying. "Life on Barbados can be awfully lonely."

"I am rather new to your island," Adrienne said. "Did you come here from London, then?"

"Yes, more than four years ago." She sighed. "I miss England . . . and all my friends."

"Well, perhaps you and I can become friends." Adrienne put out her hand. "I would like that very much. Do you know, I have a strong sense that you and I have already met. Is that possible?"

A shadow passed over the woman's face. "No. I haven't met anyone for a very long time."

Her expression unlocked Adrienne's memory. She was the woman who had warned her on the beach. She was Victoria's ghost! "Wait! We have met! I remember—it was that day on the beach near Tempest Hall. I only saw you from a distance. You told me not to ride alone, that the island could be treacherous. . . ."

The woman had gone as white as her gown. "I'm confused—"

"And the other day you were riding past Victoria Villa! I thought you might be a ghost, but my husband assured me that I was being overly romantic!" Laughing, Adrienne put a hand on her arm. "Please, tell me your name."

Before the other woman could answer, Zachary returned from his dance and stood off to one side, staring in consternation. When Adrienne glanced his way, he said, "I guess you two have met then?"

Both of them shook their heads, then looked at each other. Since Zach didn't seem to be able to find his voice to perform introductions, the dark-eyed woman spoke.

"I was about to say that my name is Eloise Sinclair Crowe, and I am pleased to meet you, Mrs. . . . ?"

Adrienne nearly gasped aloud, and feared that her shock must show on her face. "I—I am Adrienne Beauvisage—" Her voice dropped to a whisper. "Raveneau."

Eloise looked confused. *"Raveneau?"*

"Yes. I recently married Nathan Raveneau."

"I was afraid that you might say that. In my heart, I knew." Tears filled her beautiful eyes. "And you are happy, are you not?"

"Yes." Adrienne was sorry to hurt the other woman.

"Of course you are happy." Eloise's smile was bittersweet. "How could it be otherwise?"

Chapter Twenty-two

As André Raveneau followed his son back into
the crowded ballroom, he remarked, "You were pigheaded
on your wedding day, and rude, but at least I can take comfort in the knowledge that you have since fallen under your
bride's spell. I wouldn't want to think that Adrienne was
living with an inconsiderate rake."

"Yes, I've changed my ways." Nathan threw his father
an annoyed glance. "You of course were a model suitor and
husband?"

"No, but I was young and foolish." André wandered over
to inspect the pale golden silk that covered the ballroom's
walls. A motif of palm trees had been painted on it, so that
the trees marched all the way around the room. This was
one of the few homes so decorated, for silk would soon rot
in the humidity of Barbados.

"Ah. Were you not older than I am now when my sister
Mouette was born?"

The elder Raveneau turned back, clearing his throat.
"Possibly."

"And didn't Mouette's birth precede your wedding to our
mother?" Nathan was right behind him, waiting for his reluctant nod. "You were even more debauched than I, Father! I rest my case."

Slowly André began to laugh. "I think that my happy
marriage has blocked out the follies of my youth." His clear
gray eyes held Nathan's then and he spoke with conviction.
"I haven't been one to dispense a lot of advice since you've

reached adulthood. However, now that you are married, I would tell you one thing . . ."

Nathan merely nodded, waiting respectfully.

"If you can maintain this one area of your life—your relationship with Adrienne—all the rest will settle into place. And if your marriage is fulfilling, you'll find that the pleasures of your bachelorhood will pale in comparison." André touched his son's arm for emphasis.

Nathan nodded. "I used to think I could never have a marriage as wonderful as my parents. So did Adrienne. And I begin to see now that I may not have recovered from losing Eloise as easily as I thought." Smiling, Nathan began to search the ballroom for his wife. "All things come in time, though. Adrienne and I formed this alliance for other reasons, expecting nothing, and I believe we are falling in love."

"Your mother is going to be ecstatic, you know."

"Yes. Oh, Father, there is another matter I must discuss with you . . . about the *Golden Eagle*. Can you visit us at home?" Nathan spoke absently, looking for Adrienne, and then he frowned. "I should have known better than to leave her—"

"What's wrong? Isn't she there?"

"Oh, yes," Nathan replied grimly, "and she is talking to Eloise!"

"Eloise Sinclair—Crowe?" André stared. "But I didn't know they were acquainted—"

"They were not, until I turned my back for a few minutes!" He started off through the crowd, and his father decided to remain behind. By the time Nathan reached his wife, Zachary Minter had joined the two women.

"Oh, Nathan!" Eloise cried, and her flush deepened. "I have met your charming bride."

"So I see." He was scowling.

"We didn't know," Adrienne said. "I mean, we began to talk, and we seemed to be getting along quite well, and then Zachary appeared—"

Eloise turned nervously to Minter. "I haven't said how nice it is to see you again, Zachary. It's been a long time."

He was bright red. "Yes, Miss Sinclair—I mean, Mrs. Crowe."

Before Nathan could interject, Eloise fixed him with her beautiful, brimming eyes. "I didn't know you were married." She tried to smile. "How fortunate you are to have found true love."

"Yes," he agreed without a hint of emotion. It was disconcerting to feel his heart sting in her presence. "Look, I don't think that your husband would want you to be chatting with us, so we'll bid you good evening."

"Of course," she whispered.

Adrienne put a hand on the other woman's gloved forearm. "Why can't we be friends? Aren't women supposed to be above the petty differences of their husbands?"

Eloise looked sadder than ever. "I just don't think, in this case—"

"No, I won't accept that. We shall have tea together. I will write to you." Adrienne paused, eyes flashing. "I am very fond of Lady Thomasina, your houseguest. I should like to see her as well."

"She's here tonight . . . somewhere." Smiling vacantly, Eloise looked around. "Such a crush, isn't it? Yet so lovely. It was a pleasure meeting you, Mrs. Raveneau. Tea would be lovely, but my husband is temperamental about guests. Good evening."

Nathan was pale beneath his tan as he watched Eloise go, his emotions in conflict. There wasn't an opportunity for him to speak with Adrienne, because dinner was served, and everyone began to move toward the dining room. They were separated then and Nathan sat across a huge table from her, watching as his bride chatted animatedly with two rum-soaked planters, her beauty aglow in the dancing light of hundreds of candles. The food was rich, but there was too much of it. The guests feasted on suckling pig, sugar-fed mutton, three kinds of fowl, and an abundance of shellfish. It was impossible to choose among the countless dishes, so Nathan contented himself with a slice of pork, yams, breadfruit with bay sauce, corn pudding, and warm bread with guava jelly. All of this was washed down with powerful madeira.

During the long meal, Nathan was drawn into a spirited debate over slavery, and he found himself arguing for abolition. "The slaves want it; they made that clear during the rebellion of 1816," he said. "We all know what is right. There's no point in making excuses any longer."

Lord McGrath turned red and shouted, "My slaves didn't join in that revolt, and they wouldn't know what to do if they were free! They couldn't fend for themselves. They depend on me!"

"You are fooling yourself, my lord," Nathan replied. "We tell ourselves such things so that we can look ourselves in the mirror each morning—and step inside church on Sunday. But we all know in our hearts that they are people just like we are. If we want them to do our work, we should give them a choice, and if they agree, we should pay them."

Another planter chimed in, "We all know that the sugar industry's in decline on Barbados! The land is wearing out, and there's too much competition from other islands. If we free the slaves, or have to pay them wages, we'll lose our plantations!"

"I didn't say it would be easy. But it is the right course," Nathan replied.

Halfway down the table, Major Carrington rose, goblet in hand. "I perceive that an argument has broken out, and it is up to me to calm tempers." He smiled genially. "After all, I am your host, and I would see my guests laughing. We are here to celebrate the Crop-over, after all. Let us leave our cares outside these walls, shall we?"

"Here, here!" cried Xavier Crowe from the other end of the table.

Carrington looked a bit discomfited. Nathan guessed that the notorious Crowe had been invited only because of the other members of his household. Honoria Carrington, in particular, was noted for her kind heart and desire to make all newcomers to Barbados feel welcome.

"You have reminded me, Crowe," Major Carrington boomed, "that I must propose a toast to Lady Thomasina Harms and her son, Lord Huntsford Harms. They have come to Barbados from Hampshire, England."

Glasses were lifted all along the table, reflecting the candlelight, and good wishes were murmured by the countless guests. Far away from Nathan, Lady Thomasina managed to stand, supported by her fair-haired son. She wore a jewel-encrusted toque, too much rouge, and a stifling old gown, while Huntsford sported blue gloves. They smiled and nodded, and were toasted again.

Nathan leaned back in his chair, unwilling to seek eye contact with the Harmses just yet. Across from him, his wife looked as if it were just now sinking in that they really were all on the same island.

Lord Carrington raised his glass again and introduced the new Mrs. Nathan Raveneau and her father-in-law to his guests. More toasts followed.

As Nathan watched, smiling, he became aware that someone was looking at him. His hooded eyes touched the guests one by one until he reached Eloise, and their gazes met. It was disturbing, seeing her here tonight, and it came to him how little contact they'd had since her marriage.

It still hurt like the devil to look back on those weeks during 1814, when he'd fallen in love with the shy, elegant beauty and had striven to win her heart. It had been the first time that a woman hadn't wanted him more than he'd wanted her. He'd loved the thrill of the chase, and each word of hope, each kiss, each gaze from her luminous dark eyes had driven him mad with joy. Sweet and uncertain, Eloise had brought out all his protective instincts, and so when Xavier Crowe appeared on the scene and began to court her aggressively, Nathan had been furious.

How could she have wanted a brute like Crowe? Nathan still didn't know the answer. Even though his pride was battered by her farewell note and subsequent departure with Crowe, he had cared enough to worry that Eloise might not have gone of her own free will. Had he been foolish to go after her and offer rescue?

Now, as their eyes met and the memories flooded back, Nathan's pain rose to the surface. Her rejection on the deck of Crowe's ship, when he'd offered to fight for her if necessary, had gone to the core of his spirit. If a kind, delicate girl like Eloise Sinclair could be so false, what point was there in loving at all?

How much was she tangled up in his quest to bring Xavier Crowe to justice? Perhaps it was possible that a part of Nathan had hoped he might win Eloise in the end, after her husband was exposed as a criminal. Thank God for Adrienne. He knew now that he had needed a different sort of woman all along.

Clearly, Eloise Sinclair Crowe wasn't happy, but Nathan didn't take satisfaction in that knowledge. What should be done about her now? Should he encourage Adrienne to turn her back on Eloise, the way Eloise had turned her back on him?

The toasts were finished and, to his right, Honoria Carrington was eating a sugar cake. "Would you care to dance with your hostess?" she asked, eyes twinkling. "That will signal the others that they may return to the ballroom."

"I would be honored, my lady." He rose and offered her his arm. When they passed his wife, Nathan winked, winning a radiant smile in return.

Adrienne had settled back to wait for him when she noticed Lady Thomasina sitting alone, fanning herself. Within moments she had slipped into the chair next to Lady Thomasina and put a hand on her arm.

"Oh!" her ladyship cried out. "What do you want?"

"Don't you know me? I am Adrienne Beauvisage—Miss Beau!"

"Gadzooks, so you are. . . ." Trembling with excitement, Lady Thomasina leaned forward to caress Adrienne's face, and musty powder from her wig sprinkled both their gowns. "Hunty will be so pleased. He's come to find you, you know. I've missed you, dear girl."

Affection and pity welled up in Adrienne. It seemed to her that Lady Thomasina's powers of concentration were erratic at best. "I have missed you too, my lady. How is your health?"

"Wretched. Some days I don't get out of bed at all. What's the point?" She stared off into the distance again, bleary-eyed. "That beastly scoundrel should not have kidnapped you from Harms Castle."

"Nathan has been very good to me." She broke off when Lady Thomasina responded by sticking out her lip in a pout and turning the other way. "Did you know that we are taking care of Angus?"

This news made her brighten. "Are you, Miss Beau? Is my darling as charming as ever?"

Just then Huntsford Harms loomed over them. "Ah, Adrienne, you cannot imagine how I have dreamed of this moment. Ever since that lout carried you off through the window, I have worried for your safety—"

"I doubt that," she replied crisply.

"I've come a long way to prove it. Won't you dance with me?"

Adrienne agreed, wanting a chance to give Huntsford a piece of her mind without being overheard by Lady Thomasina. She rose and her ladyship beamed as they walked together toward the ballroom. From the shadows, Xavier Crowe stood with his wife, watching intently.

"I must tell you, Huntsford, that I was very surprised to hear that you and your mother had come to Barbados," Adrienne said as they began to waltz, his blue-gloved hand holding hers firmly. "Are you certain that her health can stand all this?"

He cocked his head to one side. "Well, who can say? She is very old, and death is inevitable, is it not? In any case, if you were so concerned for her health, you would have stayed with us rather than going off without a word of good-bye."

"I am not her child; you are."

"She thinks of you as a daughter." His gaze turned adoring. "You know that the greatest restorative for her health would be a union between you and me—"

"Oh, Huntsford, that isn't possible. Haven't you heard? Nathan and I are married." Firmly she added, "We've realized that we were in love all along. I am very happy."

The pace of the waltz picked up. Muscles twitched in Huntsford's boyish face, but he kept smiling, remembering Crowe's insistence that he had more than enough charm to win Adrienne away from Raveneau. "When did this wedding occur?"

"I don't see any point in discussing this with you. Clearly, you don't wish us well. Furthermore, I have a great many questions about the goings-on at Harms Castle. I believe that you were not my friend, as you insisted, but the friend of Walter Frakes-Hogg, who wanted to harm me! And now you are in league with Xavier Crowe, my husband's sworn enemy. How can you expect me to be civil to you?"

"Don't make a scene." He pouted. "I do care about you, I do! I saved your life! I told you how I felt, but—"

"I don't understand this preoccupation you have with me," Adrienne interjected. Suddenly it felt very warm in the ballroom, and they were spinning too fast for comfort. "I suggest that you turn your attention to your mother. She needs you."

Something flashed across his face that gave her goosebumps. Before either of them could speak again, Nathan tapped on Huntsford's shoulder and Adrienne stepped back out of his arms.

"I've come to fetch my wife," he said with a cool smile.

Adrienne was overjoyed to take his arm. Next to the sunburned Englishman, her husband looked more rakishly attractive than ever.

"It seems that you've won after all, Essex," Huntsford muttered as the dancers whirled all around them.

"Were you in a contest? How lonely you must have been. No wonder it didn't work out." Nathan arched a sardonic eyebrow. Before leading his wife away, he glanced back and added, "My name is Raveneau—but of course you knew that. Good night."

The beach lay ahead of them through the palms, iridescent in the moonlight. Water lapped gently at the edges of the sugary sand. The ocean was still, and the air was warm and scented with plants, flowers, and the sea.

"There are moments when I think that Barbados is a fairyland," Adrienne whispered. "I'm so glad that you brought me here tonight." Barefoot, she held her skirts in one hand while her other hand was linked with Nathan's. In the distance, the water twinkled with the reflections of a million stars.

Clad only in his starched shirt, waistcoat, and dark trousers, Nathan smiled back at her. His grip on Adrienne's hand tightened as he pulled her into his arms. "You mentioned that you wanted to come to the beach again and go swimming. Somehow, this seemed just the night."

She relaxed in his embrace, twining her arms around his neck as they kissed. Great waves of bliss washed over her. "Can we have a talk before we . . . swim?"

"Of course." He pushed his trousers up to his knees and they waded along the water's edge. There was something wonderfully decadent about walking through water in evening garb. "What would you like to talk about?"

"Eloise."

Nathan's shadowed face was pensive. He nodded but did not look over at Adrienne immediately. "I suppose I should have guessed that you might want to know more. And I should have told you without waiting for you to ask." He paused, threading his fingers through hers and lifting her hand to his lips. "I think that, until tonight, I was blocking her out of my own thoughts—so I couldn't guess that she might be in yours."

"Explain to me, please? What was between you, and what remains?"

They continued to walk through the ankle-deep water as he talked, following the shoreline. "We met in London, as I think you've heard. I was there for my sister Lindsay's wedding, and a mutual friend introduced us. Romance was in the air." He tipped his head back and gazed up at the sky.

"How did Xavier Crowe come into the picture?"

"He was at Almack's one night while we were waltzing. Eloise was fond of society, and even though I should have realized that we weren't suited in the least, I was bewitched. There was something about her that made me want to take care of her. . . ."

Adrienne sniffed. "I don't think that's a very good basis for a marriage."

"And you're absolutely correct, darling. It would have

been a disaster—though it's hard to imagine Eloise's lot being worse than it is with Crowe." He stood still then and held both her hands. With care, he explained how Eloise had seemed almost frightened of his passion and his unpredictable style of living, and how Zach guessed that Crowe's great wealth and charm may have appeared less risky to Eloise. "He gave her lots of presents and doubtless made lots of promises. When she left with him, I was stunned by the rejection . . . but I couldn't help wondering if he'd coerced her somehow."

"You tried to rescue her?" There was a lump in Adrienne's throat as she imagined the scenario and how deeply he'd cared.

"Yes." His tone was flippant. "I gave chase. I was ready to do battle at sea if necessary, but Crowe invited me on board to see Eloise for myself. I still couldn't believe it. I challenged him to a duel, but she forbade it—and sent me away."

Her heart ached for him. "Have you loved her all these years?"

"Well, I realize now that I'm only just learning what love should be." A self-deprecating smile touched his mouth. "And I realize now that Eloise has been with me more than I thought. It's been hard, living on the island with them, and so I've avoided the entire situation by dashing off to sea so often."

"Do you think that Eloise is part of the reason you hate Crowe so much?"

He bit his lip, and they began to walk again, slowly. "Who knows? Perhaps. But I hated him before that. I know I am right about the ships he's lured onto the rocks and the men who have died as a result." For a moment Nathan was silent, and there was only the sound of the water. "I want you to know, though, that tonight I've realized how much I've changed, knowing you. Your love has healed my old wounds . . . and helped me to understand myself."

Adrienne was tingling from head to toe. He was saying the word *love*! Of course, Nathan hadn't actually admitted that he loved her, but she could feel the last of his resistance melting away. "You've helped me to understand myself as well," she said. "And I think I've grown up."

"We're rather alike, I've decided. You and I both have tended to rebel against any sort of constraint."

"Perhaps being alike helps us to understand one another." Adrienne paused, gathering courage. "There's something I've been wanting to ask you. The clothes I wore on board the *Golden Eagle* . . ."

"Yes?" Nathan couldn't resist.

"Did they belong to Eloise?"

Her small voice melted his heart. "Is that what you thought? My dear wife, Eloise never went to sea with me. I never made love to her; I held her above that. I won't say that I never had another woman in that cabin, but the truth is that I went to sea to *escape* romantic entanglements." He paused. "Those clothes belonged to my lovely sister Lindsay. She left them by mistake the last time I took her from England to Connecticut to visit our family."

Adrienne found this highly amusing. "Do you have any idea how much I tortured myself with jealousy?"

"I might." He joined in her laughter and then fell silent. The sight of Adrienne, standing in the moonlit ocean while clad in pearl-embroidered silk, was awe-inspiring. He wondered what she would look like wearing only the damask roses in her hair. . . .

"I am ready to swim," he announced.

"I would love that. Are you certain we're alone?"

"Yes, but to set your mind at ease, I know a completely secluded cove on the other side of those trees. Come with me, my little sea nymph."

Her heart was pounding as they walked around a gentle point of land and found themselves in a cove thickly lined with slender palm trees. It appeared to be their own private beach.

Nathan stripped off his clothing while Adrienne gazed dreamily at the water. "The idea of actually swimming seems—" Her voice broke off when she looked back and saw that her husband was completely and splendidly naked. His body was more gorgeously lean-muscled than ever in this setting.

"You were saying?" His wicked grin flashed in the shadows.

"I—I've forgotten." Her face was very warm. "I think I was going to say that the notion of swimming seems so natural and wonderful, yet—well, naughty."

"That's perfectly fine. You're a married woman, in the company of your husband."

"What wonderful words. I think that marriage is much more romantic than I ever dreamed." Nathan had come around behind her to unfasten her gown, and the touch of his fingers on her back made her melt. "Wait! Hold up your shirt in front of me while I undress."

Remembering the wild tigress who had shared his bed this past week, Nathan decided that he would never completely understand Adrienne. Somehow, this added to her allure. Shaking his head, smiling, he walked naked through the sand to get his shirt, then stood before her, holding it open with both hands to shield her. When her silk gown, stockings, and undergarments had dropped at her feet, she peeked at him playfully over the top of the makeshift curtain.

"Close your eyes."

He heaved a long-suffering sigh but obeyed.

"You can open your eyes!" Her voice came to him from a distance, and Nathan looked to see that Adrienne was in the water, waving to him. The shirt fell from his hands, and he plunged into the sea.

Starlit, her face radiant and her skin wet and gleaming, she had never looked happier or more beautiful. When Nathan reached her side, she put her hands on his shoulders and murmured, "Oh, the water feels better than I ever imagined. It's warm!"

"I know. This is one of the reasons I love Barbados so much. It's as close to heaven as one gets on earth. . . ." He paused and laid a hand on her cheek. "At least I thought so until our wedding night."

It was almost more pleasure than he could bear when Adrienne moved forward, into his waiting arms, and linked her arms around his neck. They bobbed gently in the calm sea, buoyed by the saltwater and caressed by the soft night air. He held her close, kissing her tangy lips. There was no need to hurry, or even to talk.

After a bit, Adrienne slipped away and swam in front of their cove. She unpinned her hair and dove down, then floated on her back and looked at the star-strewn summer sky while the roses from her hair drifted to and fro on the current. The sensation of the warm water moving over her bare flesh was deliciously liberating and erotic.

Nathan swam too, but his eyes never left his mermaid-wife. At last, when he saw her lying on her back, watching him, he glided over and slipped his arms around her from below. Bending near, he gently kissed her breast, and when he reached the nipple, it was taut, tasting of salt. His hands slid around her narrow waist, caressing, then over her legs. Parting her thighs to his exploring fingers, she moaned at the first touch. Minutes passed as she lay under his skilled hands and lips, allowing herself the extreme pleasure of heightening desire.

When he bent his head again, lower, and touched his tongue to her wet, delicate curls and then to her swollen womanhood, Adrienne cried out, pushed abruptly over the precipice. Every nerve in her body seemed to be between her legs, contracting and releasing in intense waves of pleasure.

At last she could bear no more. Adrienne turned and came into her husband's powerful embrace, and they kissed with new abandon.

"I want you," Nathan breathed, uncertain if he'd even spoken aloud. Adrienne's hands were roving over his chest, and he realized that he'd been aroused a very long time, perhaps even before they'd reached the cove.

"Oh, Nathan, I want you too." She swallowed tears, still afraid to let him see how desperately she cared. Every time they came together, Adrienne tried to memorize the savage beauty of his face, yet the next time he was always more breathtaking. Now, as the midnight-blue water glimmered around them, she wrapped her legs around his waist. They kissed and touched for long minutes, as if starved for the taste of one another, and she let herself brush against his pulsing member. Nathan held her hips and, panting, they pushed until their bodies were united.

Adrienne sank her fingers into his wet hair. It seemed that he was touching her very heart. "Nathan!"

Their eyes met, souls bared, and there were no words. The fire they created together was greater than anything either of them was capable of alone, and it burned brighter and brighter as she met his thrusts, her head thrown back so that her streaming hair poured over the water.

When at last Nathan found his own scalding release, he heard himself saying "I love you."

Her breasts pressed to his chest and her cheek against his temple, Adrienne began to cry. "You'll never give me a finer gift than that. Oh, Nathan, I love you too."

Chapter Twenty-three

GOLDEN LIGHT POURED THROUGH THE JALOUSIE SHUT-
ters and across the mahogany four-poster bed. Nathan
Raveneau lay amid rumpled sheets, watching his wife
sleep, while a pair of Barbary doves cooed from the sandbox tree behind the house.

"The rain must have stopped for your birthday," he whispered when he saw her eyelids flutter.

"Mmm. I rather like the rainy season. You are in the
house more." Sensing that he was about to get out of bed,
Adrienne quickly snuggled back against him, fitting her
bottom to his hips and caressing his sun-darkened arm
when he embraced her. "Don't get up yet."

"I'm already late, love. I only stayed this long because I
wanted to kiss you and tell you how glad I am that you are
twenty-one at last. I don't have to worry that your father
will change his mind." The heat was building in his groin,
and he tried to will his body to behave. By the smile on
Adrienne's face, he knew that she could feel the first stir-
rings against her backside. "Have you forgotten that we
have a visitor coming for luncheon today?"

"Oh, yes—André!" Her eyes lit up. "It will be wonderful
to see him. Darling, did I tell you that Orchid is making
callaloo? I love it, and we're going to serve it to your father
for lunch. Orchid says that it's one of the dishes her people
brought from Africa."

He kissed her glossy hair. "You seem to be quite at
home."

"I am." Her smile widened. "Every morning, when I awaken, I feel happier. I look at the yellow walls in this room and they are my world. Even the rain is fresh and cheerful to me. I smell the air and listen to the guinea fowl in the garden and it's as if I have always lived in this house." Turning in his arms, she burrowed into Nathan's wide, wonderful chest. "And when I find you in my bed, it's as if we have always been married."

"Excuse me, but *you* are in *my* bed!"

"A slip of the tongue. I meant to say *our* bed."

"Naughty chit, I must leave you. There are arrangements to make for your birthday—"

"Wait—I've been meaning to tell you that I already know what I want. I want you to help me rescue Lady Thomasina from Crowe's Nest, and perhaps Eloise as well!"

André Raveneau gazed around Tempest Hall's interior and smiled. At last, his son's house was a home. Orchid may have done her best to take care of him in the past, but only a wife could fill a room with so much spirited charm.

Everywhere he looked there were bright exotic flowers, in Chinese vases and glass flasks and crystal bowls of all sizes, and their soft fragrances filled the air. The walls had fresh paint, the furniture had been polished, and the wood floors wore a burnished glow. Every bit of brass had been cleaned, and even the windows had been washed.

"The house looks splendid," he said when his son came into the room.

"Oh—yes." Smiling, Nathan nodded. "That's Adrienne's doing, of course."

"So I surmised. And it goes beyond mere appearances; there is a different feeling in the air."

"Yes. I think it may be joy."

As Retta came in with two planter's punches on a tray, André sniffed the air appreciatively. "What is that delicious smell?"

"Callaloo, sir," she replied.

"What?"

"It's a kind of stew," Nathan explained. "I think it is made of okra, crab, coconut—"

"An' pork fat," Retta interjected.

"Adrienne loves it, and I think she's in there helping with the preparations now." Nathan led his father to the settee of Barbadian mahogany. "Before we eat, I would have a word with you in private."

"Without your wife?"

"For the moment. You see, Father, I would like you to change your plans about taking the *Golden Eagle* on a trading voyage. We may tell people that you have sailed for Europe, but I have something else in mind." He paused and they both drank from their glasses. "I believe I've thought of a way to catch Xavier Crowe in the act."

The white scar along André's jaw stood out for an instant. "You have captured my interest."

"In the past, he's known in advance when ships were approaching and he could lay his plans and make certain that he was visibly present elsewhere. That has always been the speech made by his defenders: 'Xavier Crowe was not even near the eastern side of the island when the ship in question was lost!' However, if we use the *Golden Eagle* as bait, and send word to Crowe's Nest very suddenly that a ship is approaching, he'll have to be involved."

"I think it's a brilliant plan." The elder Raveneau's gray eyes were agleam. "If we prepare the entire crew for the confrontation, he won't have a chance. His success is based on taking ships by surprise!"

"Of course, I'll have to come along—and Zach. You'll need as many men as possible, and it would kill me to miss it."

"I understand completely," his father replied, nodding.

Just then Adrienne came out of the dining room. "Well, I don't understand! Nathan, how can you conceive of such a dangerous plan when you have been married only a short time? I could be a widow while I'm still a bride!"

The two men exchanged glances. "Darling," Nathan said, going to her and clasping her hands, "nothing is going to happen to me. Just the opposite, I can assure you."

Adrienne could see the unswervable determination in his

eyes and knew that all her arguments would be wasted. Sighing, she leaned into his chest, then took a different tack. "Well, if you are going to do something outrageous and dangerous, then you will have to let me rescue Lady Thomasina."

"What's this all about?" her father-in-law asked. His eyes swept appreciatively over her buttermilk-colored round gown and the wild orchids in her hair. "You look particularly fetching today, my dear. Can you tell me when we eat? I am ravenous."

Hortie appeared then to oversee the service of luncheon. After the trio had taken their seats in the dining room, Retta brought each of them a pineapple half along with a tray of freshly baked bread. There was jam made of native cherries, and sweet butter.

"Now then, lovely daughter," André said, "tell me what you're up to."

"I'm terribly worried about Lady Thomasina. Although she was always a bit eccentric—"

"She's barking mad!" Nathan put in. "You saw her, Father!"

Adrienne gave him a quelling stare. "As I was saying, her ladyship is odd, but at the Carringtons' ball I became concerned that she might be drugged. She didn't recognize me, and her eyes were so strange-looking! Furthermore, Huntsford behaved very badly when I mentioned his mother's health. Something in his manner gave me chills!"

"I hate to admit it, but you may have a point," her husband said. "I've feared from the moment I heard that she and Hunty had come to Barbados that Crowe might try to get at her money. It would be like him to bend Hunty to his will and try to get rid of Lady Thomasina so that Hunty could inherit. Drugging her ladyship would be a logical first step." The callaloo was served then and Nathan inhaled its fragrance appreciatively. "Have I told you about Crowe's brother? He and his brother, Francis, jointly owned the land where Xavier's mansion now stands. Francis and his wife, Jane, drowned together while swimming off Cobbler's Reef. Xavier was left to raise their five-year-old son, Martin, who was Francis's sole heir."

"Do you mean that a little boy owns half of Crowe's Nest?" André asked in amazement.

"Yes. And many believe that if Eloise hadn't appeared on the scene to take Martin under her wing, he might be dead now as well!"

"That's ghastly!" Adrienne cried. "No child should be raised in such a home!"

"Well, you can't just burst in and start rescuing everyone, dear chit. For one thing, they may like their lives there. It's entirely possible that Lady Thomasina is just teetering a bit farther over the edge than she did before. She is incredibly old, after all."

André had finished his bowl of callaloo and Hortie signaled Retta to serve more. Adrienne, meanwhile, was not in a mood to be placated by her husband. "Why is it that your suspicions deserve to be acted upon but mine do not? Your plan is *much* more dangerous!'

"Let's discuss it later, shall we?"

"I shall follow through this week with my promise to invite Eloise Crowe to lunch. Perhaps I can learn more from her."

The elder Raveneau spoke then. "Adrienne, I have been wanting to ask you if Nathan told you how he got his name."

Remembering her duty to be a charming hostess, she smiled. "No. No, in fact, there are still a lot of stories I haven't heard. I begin to think I'll only hear them from his family." She leaned forward, dimples winking. "How *did* Nathan get his name?"

"Devon, my wife, was raised in New London, Connecticut. She went to the little village school, and a fellow named Nathan Hale was the schoolmaster." He held up his hand before she could speak. "Devon always loved books, and so she became very attached to Master Hale and was sad when he went off to fight in the War for Independence—"

"Where were you then, André? In France?"

"No, in New London, actually. I was the captain of a privateer, helping America, and I met Devon in 1775, when she was only twelve—and I was rather older, and still very

French." He laughed at the memory. "It wasn't until 1781, when the British attacked New London, that we were thrown together for good. In the meantime, Nathan Hale had been captured while spying on the enemy."

"'He was hanged, wasn't he?'" Adrienne said. "I may have been raised in France, but my parents were American, and I learned all the stories of the war." She turned to look at Nathan, awestruck. "You should have told me that you were named for Nathan Hale! It's terribly sad and romantic to think of him being your mother's schoolmaster."

"I didn't know I had to divulge every detail of my life before your twenty-first birthday! I can assure you that there are still plenty of adventures left, and I'll relate them one at a time for the rest of our lives."

Over coconut pudding, they talked about the next crop of sugarcane. Nathan said that he and Zach had decided to wait before planting any more, to give the ground a rest. He added, "I can see now that Owen Horner's methods served only the present, not the future."

"And I don't doubt that the field slaves need a rest as well!" Adrienne straightened her shoulders. "It makes me ill to say that word—'slaves'—and realize that we believe we can own human beings!"

"Adrienne—"

"Don't furrow your brow at me! All right, I will give you credit for at least *saying* the right things at the ball. . . ."

"I intend to follow my words with deeds, but there are plans that must be laid first."

André finished his drink and observed, "You two will never be bored! I don't understand where you get the energy, though. This island and the rum make me feel like lying back in a planter's chair and dozing all afternoon."

"You are welcome to borrow ours!" Adrienne said. "I hope our squabbling hasn't spoiled your afternoon. I know that I have a lot to learn about being a proper planter's wife . . . and I am not certain I'll ever master the role."

"Nonsense. You are utterly delightful just as you are," André replied.

"Quite true," Nathan agreed. "Barbados has long been in need of a hellion hostess."

They all began to laugh, then André took a velvet jewelry case from his coat pocket. "I happen to have a gift for my new daughter's birthday. It is also a wedding present."

"Where's *my* wedding present?" Nathan complained good-naturedly.

"Hush," Adrienne said, and accepted the box with a reverent expression. Slowly lifting the lid, she glimpsed a sparkling collarette of sapphires and tiny diamonds. Tears sprang to her eyes. "Oh, André, it is too beautiful! I—"

"I gave it to Devon before our wedding, and she has always wanted Nathan's bride to have it. When she knew that I was coming here, she packed it with my things—hoping against hope that you might have come into his life."

Dabbing her eyes with a fragile lawn handkerchief, Adrienne could scarcely speak. "I am honored. This will be precious to me for the rest of my life." She rose to embrace her father-in-law, and he put the choker around her neck and closed the clasp. "It's the most beautiful piece of jewelry I've ever seen!"

"It suits you, my dear."

As Nathan watched them, his throat closed with emotion. He'd never dreamed how meaningful it could be to begin a real family of his own and to feel the ties to his parents and siblings strengthen. Adrienne really did seem to be the mate God had created for him, and he silently gave thanks once more that they had found one another.

"I have a gift for you also," he said softly. "Come into my—I mean *our* library."

The trio walked together, Adrienne fingering her choker and looking in passing mirrors. At the library door, she told André the story of Nathan's early efforts to keep her out of his masculine sanctuary.

Enjoying herself, she added, "He was selfish and arrogant—"

"Hardly surprising." André laughed. "Devon would tell you that it runs in the family."

"Not anymore," Nathan vowed as he slipped an arm around her waist. "I have changed."

When the door swung open, Adrienne beheld a completely new piece of furniture that had been placed in front of the garden window, opposite Nathan's desk. It was a mahogany chaise with a double shell-shaped base that curved up at either end. Upholstered in blue silk shadow-striped with gold, it was both lovely and inviting.

"Oh, Nathan, it's beautiful!" She hurried over, plucked a book from a shelf, and practiced reclining on her new chaise.

"I couldn't decide whether you'd rather have it here or upstairs in our bedroom. But this seemed a more symbolic location, and the ocean is visible from the window." He grinned. "I liked the shell motif and the idea of you lying between the two halves."

"Why," André complained, "do I get the idea that there is some hidden meaning in all this?"

Adrienne's color heightened and her green eyes sparkled. "You two come over here and sit with me." When they had complied, she put an arm around the backs of father and son and beamed at each of them in turn. "I adore my gifts, and I thank you, but of course I didn't need presents. I am already enormously blessed, to have so wonderful a husband and father-in-law. Today my very life is a priceless gift."

Raising a finger, André said, "I predict that the next time I visit here, you will give *me* a gift—the announcement that you and Nathan will be presenting Devon and me with a grandchild!"

Nathan laughed, and Adrienne joined in, hiding her face in his shoulder so that he wouldn't notice her rapidly deepening blush.

Eloise Crowe watched her husband's nephew from the entrance to the dining room. Martin didn't see her, as he was sitting alone at a Sheraton rent table, engaged in a game of chess that required him to play both white and black.

It was a shame, she thought, that virtually no one was able to enjoy the trappings of this magnificent house. The ornamented plaster ceilings, the intricately carved staircase and the mahogany columns that divided rooms, the dining table for twenty-four with brass lion-claw feet, and the priceless portraits; all were rarely seen by anyone but the lonely band of misfits who inhabited Crowe's Nest.

"Martin," she called, "it's quite pleasant today. Wouldn't you like to go outdoors?"

He glanced up. Through two sets of double doors, he could see the lawn that glided past gardens and fountains down to the beach where Crowe had built a turtle crawl. There, beyond the coconut palms, swept the stunning ocean with its froth of white surf. Martin stared, then frowned. "No. I don't think Uncle wants me to go outside. He said that something might happen to me, just like my parents."

"I don't think he could have meant for you to stay indoors all the time!"

"I like this, Auntie. I am enjoying myself."

It broke her heart to see a child behaving as if he were a stuffy old man. However, everyone seemed to bend to the force of Xavier's will, and she was no exception. For four years, she had drunk his laudanum-laced tea that helped ease the pain in her heart. This week Eloise had summoned new strength and had begun weaning herself off the stuff.

Slipping her hand into a pocket hidden in her gown, she fingered the invitation to tea from Adrienne Raveneau, that had arrived three days ago, hand-delivered by a charming freed slave named Philip Smythe. At the time, she had been relieved that Xavier was away from Crowe's Nest. If he knew that she and Nathan's wife were in contact, there was no telling what might happen.

And of course, tea was impossible.

"Ah, there you are, Mrs. Crowe. You are ravishing as always."

Eloise turned at the sound of her husband's voice, leaving Adrienne's note in its hiding place. Xavier's constant charm had an edge that made her feel as if he were taunting her. Before she could reply, he had clasped her arm and guided her onto the wide stone verandah that spanned the front of the house.

"Did you do as I asked and have Clarice get a turtle and make soup?" he asked.

"Yes." She felt sorry for the turtles. "Where is Lord Harms today?"

Sipping rum, Xavier showed his teeth in a feral smile. "Why do you ask? Do you find his blue gloves unaccountably appealing? No, never mind, your replies are always predictable. Harms is taking a stroll up the coastline."

"A stroll?"

"I've sent him to hunt treasure." Once again he grinned. "I thought that he needed a project to occupy his mind! That's the trouble with those London beaus, don't you think? They need projects."

"I am worried about Lady Thomasina, Xavier. She seems to be failing more each day."

"By jove, I do hope so!" His eyes glittered. "The old cow ain't any good to us, is she? And I hear that she's rich. If she dies, Harms won't have to hunt treasure any more!"

Watching her husband laugh, Eloise couldn't decide if he were drunk or simply more evil than she'd imagined. When Crowe spotted his favorite slave, Abraham, walking nearby with Owen Horner, he turned and walked away from Eloise without a word of parting.

Curious, she wandered to the other end of the verandah and paused behind a thick bougainvillea vine. As long as they didn't keep their voices too low, she would be able to overhear.

"Well, did you uncover more information? Is it really true about the Dutch ship?" Crowe demanded.

"I hear it, Massa Crowe," Abraham said. "A ship from America just come in Careenage, and we hear them on the docks say a Dutch packet close behind."

Owen Horner was nodding his sunburned head. "Yes, it's true. I didn't just hear the rumor in the pub, but I paid a young fellow named Crenshaw for information, on the docks. He said that there was a splendid Dutch packet, weighted down with fine goods, and his ship had passed it perhaps two days ago. Crenshaw said his captain was informed that the packet would be sailing around the south coast into Carlisle Bay, and they hoped they wouldn't get lost since this was their first time to Barbados. When I wondered aloud how soon Crenshaw thought the packet might come into port, he estimated tomorrow morning."

"Which means they would sail down the eastern coast during the night. It's rather too good to believe, hmm?" The sound of Crowe's heavy breathing carried to the verandah where Eloise listened. "How could we not have heard before?"

"Perhaps this is an unscheduled stop, off their planned course. They may have gotten greedy and decided to buy up more goods."

"Oh, Christ! If they have a hold filled with not only goods but gold as well, it would be more than I could resist!"

"Massa, you like to plan so you far from islan' when we strike! This is danger!" Abraham shook his head doubtfully.

"Nonsense. No one except the American ship even knows that the packet is coming this way, and there are many reasons why it might not reach Carlisle Bay. You've already heard that the Dutch captain is unsure of his way, so trouble could befall them, or they could change course again!"

"I for one would enjoy the adventure!" Owen Horner exclaimed. "I've been waiting for a night like this ever since our association began, sir!"

"What you going to do with that other one?" Abraham asked.

"You mean Lord Harms?" Crowe laughed and drank down the rest of his rum. "Oh, I've found a diversion for him. I have him looking for the treasure marked on the Stede Bonnet map."

"We already dug for that!" the slave cried.

"A pirate treasure?" Owen Horner's voice rose at the thought.

"Don't fly off into the boughs, old man," Crowe cautioned. "You'll have your real treasure tonight, if all goes well. Meanwhile, I've sent Harms to Cave Bay to dig for a treasure that doesn't exist. I found the map a few years back and, as Abraham has said, I gave it a try and had the slaves do some digging. Didn't really expect to find anything, after a century, and sure enough, it turned out to be the grave of three of Bonnet's pirates!"

Abraham shuddered at the memory. "Bad, real bad!"

"What makes you think he'll stay there and dig into the night?" Horner asked.

"I told him I had heard that the land, which used to belong to a Frenchman, has been purchased by someone on Barbados. That part is true, but I have no idea who the fellow is. He may not set foot on his property. However, I lied to Harms and said that the new owner is going to take possession tomorrow morning, so he has only this one night to find Bonnet's plunder!" This speech was followed by caustic laughter, and Eloise felt ill.

"Hard to imagine that peacock of a lad digging by the light of the moon!" Horner rejoined, and all three men laughed together. "If he finds one of those skeletons, he'll jump right out of his soft, pale skin!"

Crowe put one arm around his overseer and the other around his favorite slave. "Abraham, you'll have to assemble the crew and prepare them for this night's work. I'm counting on both of you to make our adventure a success! I must say, I'm glad to be at home for once. I find that I am ready to join in the fun myself!"

Chapter Twenty-four

By the light of a guttering candle, Adrienne dressed in one of Retta's old gowns and fastened a green fichu around her shoulders. After covering her hair with a coral-and-white-striped headtie, she surveyed the results in the pier glass. She could see Angus in the reflection, sitting beside Hortie on the bed. The terrier's head was cocked to one side as he watched intently.

"What do you think?" she asked. "Will I blend in?"

"Are you expecting to be mistaken for a white slave?" Hortie thinned her lips. "Captain Raveneau would be furious if he knew what you were doing. I don't feel right at all about involving myself in such a scheme."

"I told him quite plainly that I wanted to rescue Lady Thomasina, and I asked for his help. However, we couldn't find time to make plans before he had to go off with his father and Minter." Adrienne turned back to her housekeeper and fixed her with an imploring gaze. "What about your loyalty to Lady Thomasina?"

Suddenly Angus began to howl mournfully. Hortie cried, "Hush up, you infernal beast!" She shook her head. "I vow that animal understands English. He's been in mourning for her ladyship ever since we left her, and any time she's mentioned, he begins to make that hideous noise! Every piece of clothing I have that she might've touched, he finds and hides in his bed."

"But that's very sad! Don't you see, then, we must go to

her aid—and bring her back here to be reunited with Angus!"

The terrier rushed to lay his head on Adrienne's hand while looking up imploringly. "Ahh-ooooooo!" he cried. "Wooo-wooooo . . ."

Hortie rolled her eyes. "Do I have any choice?"

"Oh, good! I'm so pleased! You won't be sorry, and I promise you a rare adventure!"

"I can see why you and Captain Raveneau are married," she grumbled. "You're both fire-eaters. I only hope you don't meet untimely deaths because you've taken one risk too many."

"How kind you are to say that." Still smiling, Adrienne clenched her teeth. "I'm quite certain we'll both live long and happy lives. In the meantime, let us be on our way. It's a rather long journey to the southeastern side of the island, and Philip is waiting. I've had him bring the carriage around, since Lady Thomasina will be returning with us and we'll need plenty of room."

"I just hope I can remember my way around that great maze of a house. There were times I couldn't remember which room was her ladyship's when I was there, in broad daylight! I don't feel right about this, ma'am. . . ."

"Everything will be fine."

The two women left the bedchamber, discussing their plan, and Angus hopped from the bed and scurried after them down the stairs. Philip was waiting with a closed carriage behind the house. The great sandbox tree shielded him from the evening's intermittent showers, and when Adrienne and Hortie appeared at the back door, he rushed to meet them.

"Dere you are, Mistress." He looked shocked by the sight of her in Retta's clothing.

"Philip, are you certain you can leave Orchid tonight? Is she resting?" Adrienne's brow was etched with concern for his brave wife. Lately, although Orchid had continued to work in the house and pass on as many of her secrets and skills as possible, it was clear to those who knew her best that her health was worsening by the day.

"She say dat I mus' see 'bout you, Mistress. Dat what Captain want."

"It's raining!" Hortie cried as she stepped into the darkness.

"No more dan mist, Miss Hortie," Philip replied.

"Are these primitive roads safe for travel? Perhaps we ought to postpone this mad undertaking—"

"No" came Adrienne's firm reply. "If Nathan's plans come to fruition tonight, there's no telling what will happen next at Crowe's Nest. And if something goes awry and Xavier Crowe escapes, Lady Thomasina's lot could be worse than ever. We cannot wait."

Angus began to howl again, higher and louder than ever, and dashed through the open door. Before anyone could catch him, he had jumped into the carriage and was sitting on one of the upholstered seats.

"Wait, Philip—let him stay. Hortie tells me that Angus can track Lady Thomasina's scent, so we may need his help at Crowe's Nest!" She looked at her housekeeper, grinning. "I knew I would think of something!" And with that, they joined the terrier in the carriage. Philip climbed up to the driver's perch, flicked the horses' reins, and they set out for Crowe's Nest.

The journey to the easternmost parish of St. Philip was tedious by carriage. Adrienne curled up to one side and dozed, dreaming of pirates and shipwrecks and a house with corridors that were more confusing than the maze at Harms Castle. It was the sound of Angus snoring that brought her awake at last. The carriage was jouncing over a bumpy road and Adrienne looked out to see that they were skirting cliffs that dropped to an angry sea. The rain had stopped. The air was fresh, and the light from the full moon was broken only by dark clouds that hurtled across its face.

She shivered with excitement.

Hortie cowered in the other corner of the carriage. "I wish I'd never left Hampshire." She paused for a moment, then added sulkily, "I can't even find a man here."

"Oh, now, Hortie, it isn't as bad as all that. Wouldn't you

rather be working for Nathan and me than be back at that
dreary Harms Castle?"

Just then Philip tapped on the box to let them know their
destination was in sight. Angus began to howl again, and
Adrienne wrapped a hand around his muzzle.

"You must be quiet, darling cur, or we'll never be able
to find Lady Thomasina." When she took her hand away,
he stared at her in attentive silence. Adrienne decided it
couldn't hurt to test Hortie's theory that Angus understood
English. "You do want to find Lady Thomasina, don't
you?"

The terrier whimpered pitifully.

"Then I shall let you help us—but you must be very
quiet, Angus. Do you understand? Good. When we go into the house, you will lead us to Lady Thomasina. It's an
enormous house, I think, so you must be careful. And I
may pick you up if we need to hide! Some people there
would harm us, so we can't make a sound, and we have to
be prepared to escape at a moment's notice!"

Angus rested his chin on her lap and seemed to nod. He
made a small wheezy sound rather like "Uhh-huhh."

She nearly told Hortie how foolish she felt, but now
there was a chance of hurting Angus's feelings, so she
merely smiled and petted his head.

Tall casuarina trees lined the approach to Crowe's Nest,
their feathery, silver-green tops silhouetted against the
moonlit sky. When the wind blew through them, the leaves
made a whistling sound so eerie that Hortie hugged herself
in the sultry air.

Philip slowed the horses to a walk when they drew near,
and it was agreed that he should stay back in the trees until
it was time for him to bring the carriage closer for Lady
Thomasina. One of the greatest dangers they faced
stemmed from the old woman's age and weight. Clear-
headed, she could scarcely get out of a chair unaided, so
they could hardly expect her to run across the wide drive
and through the palm trees during their escape. The probability that Lady Thomasina was drugged merely multiplied
the risks they faced.

Adrienne's palms were clammy, but she decided that

there was no room in her mind for fear tonight. If she let fear in, there was no point in going on, since danger lurked at every turn.

Since her tearful farewell to Nathan early that morning, it had occurred to her that she might be undertaking this rescue mission in part to distract herself from the dangers *he* faced tonight. It was not in Adrienne's nature to wait dutifully at home, worrying and wringing her hands.

When they had come to a stop, Philip opened the carriage door. Adrienne was holding Angus in her arms, and Hortie followed her out into the breezy night.

"I watch for a sign to come wit' carriage," Philip whispered. "I wait 'nuff time, den I go in an' save you."

"You are very dear," Adrienne said with feeling, and shocked him by kissing his cheek. "We are so fortunate to have you and Orchid at Tempest Hall, Philip."

"We de fortunate one, Mistress," he replied gravely.

Hortie led the way through a grove of palm trees, and soon the square white mansion with its castellated roof came into view. Nearly every window was dark; Adrienne realized that she didn't know the time. It could be midnight, or later! From a distance came the sound of the waves breaking on the beach.

"Look," Hortie breathed. She was just far enough ahead to have a view down the moonlit lawn toward the shoreline.

Adrienne looked, and her jaw dropped. Barely visible were dozens of dark figures wearing the short white pants favored by male slaves. They were partially illuminated by the lanterns that they were hanging on the palm trees and even from the horns of cattle. Terror spread through her body as she realized that the party of wreckers was lying in wait for the *Golden Eagle*.

"Come!" Hortie pulled on her mistress's arm and led her up some verandah steps and into the rear door used by servants. The house was very quiet and very grand. Adrienne could smell furniture polish and see the outlines of great, gilt-framed portraits hanging on the walls.

Turning down a narrow corridor, Hortie signaled Adrienne to set Angus down at the foot of the back stairway. When the terrier was free, they waited nervously for him to lead them up to Lady Thomasina. However, Angus turned away from the stairs and started quickly and quietly to re-trace their route until he had reached the reception rooms again.

The magnificent tall-case clock at the base of the hand-carved mahogany staircase struck one, startling Adrienne so that she covered her mouth to keep from gasping aloud. When Angus trotted up the stairs, the women had no choice but to follow. Adrienne felt weak with fear, and when she reached for Hortie's hand, she found that the housekeeper was shaking.

It was madness for them to just march up Crowe's Nest's grand staircase in full view! Why couldn't Angus have gone the way they'd originally pointed him?

Upon reaching the top step, he turned right and began sniffing at the doors, one by one. Adrienne and Hortie hung back, waiting for him to make a decision. Then, unexpect-edly, Angus lifted his leg, relieved himself on a door frame, and strutted back in their direction. Adrienne turned to her companion with a look of horrified disbelief, and Hortie, nearly smiling, leaned up to her ear and whispered, "Lord Harms's room."

Angus had stopped by then, in front of a room on the other side of the staircase. His tail was wagging madly but he didn't make a sound. Hortie nodded confirmation, and Adrienne gently tried the door. Her heart beat so hard she thought it must burst. Slowly the door eased open and she could see a rather plain room with a high four-poster bed. Lying in the middle of it was Lady Thomasina, and Adrienne's first thought was that the bed's height would not allow her to get up or down without assistance. The bed was a prison in itself!

Angus scampered across the floor, nails clicking, leaped lightly onto the feather tick, and began to lick Lady Thomasina's face.

"My little darling!" she murmured hoarsely. "You have come back to Mummy."

The terrier snuggled onto the pillow beside her while the women hurried to her bedside. "My lady, it is Adrienne and

Hortie." Her voice was clear and soft. "We brought Angus—and we are going to take you away from this place."

"They are poisoning me," Lady Thomasina gasped. "The middle of the night is the only time my mind clears."

Although shocked by her puffy eyes and bedraggled appearance, Adrienne was heartened to realize that Lady Thomasina had her wits about her—and perhaps a bit more physical strength than at any other time of the day. Hortie took her ladyship's swollen hand and began to weep.

"We haven't a moment to lose," Adrienne said crisply. "We must get you out of bed, my lady, and then out of this house."

"But Hunty . . . !"

"He's not here. Don't worry," she lied, "we'll send for him when you are safe at home with Nathan and me."

While Hortie was helping the old woman to sit up, Adrienne hurried over to the windows that faced the ocean, compelled to look. Pushing back the drapes, she saw that the coconut palms ringing Long Bay were hung with more bright lanterns. Adrienne shifted her focus to the sea. When she saw the sails of an approaching ship in the distance, waves of panic took her breath away.

"Nathan!" Her voice was scarcely audible, yet seemed to be a scream inside her. It was Angus, tugging at her skirt, that brought her back to the moment.

"Ma'am—" Hortie called. "We need your help."

"Of course." She rushed back to the bed and together she and Hortie got Lady Thomasina on her feet and helped her into a loose robe. "My lady, we must be very quiet, or we shall be discovered. Do you understand?"

"Yes!" she cried tearfully, then peered at Adrienne's costume. "Why are you wearing your hair in a kerchief? And that dress! Are you a slave here too?"

Adrienne nearly laughed, and was grateful for it. "I am in disguise, my lady." They started slowly toward the door.

"Hmm." Lady Thomasina sniffed. "Rather ridiculous, since you're clearly not colored."

"Perhaps, but I was just trying not to be noticed."

They had come to the door, and Adrienne peeked into the long corridor. It was thick with shadows, but there was no sign of anyone moving, so she nodded, and they shuffled forward. Lady Thomasina was a tremendous burden, for she leaned heavily on both women, breathing loudly and moaning from time to time.

Angus lightly trotted ahead, sniffing the air, and ducked into the room he'd marked earlier with his scent. Just as the others reached the top of the stairs, he reemerged, one of Huntsford Harms's new blue gloves dangling from his mouth.

Suddenly he stopped, teeth bared. "Grrrrrrr!"

At the other end of the corridor, a door flew open and a boy's voice shouted, "Auntie, look! I was right! I can see the intruders, and they have a wild animal who is growling at me!"

They were teetering on the top step, and a speedy escape was impossible. To ward off a possible assault, Adrienne called back through the darkness, "We aren't intruders. I am Adrienne Raveneau. We have come to take Lady Thomasina with her consent. And the animal is her little terrier, Angus."

A light shone in the doorway. The oil lamp haloed the face of Eloise Crowe and, lower, a young boy with dark curly hair. She took the boy's hand and they walked down the corridor, stopping a few feet away from Lady Thomasina and her rescuers.

"You see, Martin, there's no cause for alarm," Eloise said gently.

Adrienne picked up the growling Angus and petted him. It was hard for her to look into Eloise's haunted eyes. "Will you let us go, please?"

"Only if you take us with you." Her tone grew firmer as she spoke. "I don't want to stay here with Xavier any longer, and I want Martin to have a fit life for a boy his age."

"Auntie! I don't—" Then, abruptly, he fell silent, staring at the carpet. "I shouldn't betray Uncle."

"It's your welfare that concerns me, my dear," Eloise replied. "Your uncle is used to taking care of himself . . . and I don't believe he has earned our loyalty. He'd never let us go—"

"We should be delighted to assist you," Adrienne said.

"Good show!" Martin exclaimed. "A moonlit escape!"

"How kind you are, Mrs. Raveneau. We are deeply in your debt." Eloise smiled into Adrienne's eyes before urging "Let us make haste before my husband returns and discovers us!"

Lady Thomasina gave her a faint smile of approval. "Brave girl. I like you."

The younger woman was unable to speak. In the shadows, her luminous eyes swam with tears of guilt for her part in Lady Thomasina's suffering. Could anyone ever forgive her?

As they helped Lady Thomasina down the stairs, Martin and Angus ran ahead to scout their path and to signal Philip to bring the carriage around. All went smoothly until they looked through the double doors downstairs and saw a familiar figure pacing on the front verandah and smoking a cheroot.

Martin waited for Adrienne. He was tellingly pale as he whispered, "Uncle is watching the ship that's sailing toward the reef. Perhaps he won't notice us—"

Adrienne glanced down at the boy, surprised by his knowledge of Crowe's clandestine activities. She led them on then, entering the rear corridor. Escape was in sight when the verandah door clattered behind them and Xavier Crowe's voice broke the silence.

"Eloise! Is that you?" His cheroot smoke wafted into the stairhall. "I can smell your perfume!" He paused, then took a step forward on the marble floor, calling slyly "Don't make me hunt you, my beauty!"

All six of them, including Angus, froze in sheer terror. Martin grasped Eloise's arm, but she freed herself. "I'll join you outside," she commanded softly. "Go!"

Adrienne realized that, with Lady Thomasina in tow, they had no choice. They exited through the rear door, while Eloise retraced her steps, and the sound of her voice as she spoke to Crowe had a nightmarish quality as it followed them into the night. Martin did his duty and ran to signal Philip. Even as the carriage rolled toward them, Adrienne knew she couldn't leave Eloise behind so quickly.

Hortie and Martin were pulling and pushing Lady Thomasina into the carriage, and Adrienne caught Philip's arm. "Take them back into the sheltered area and wait— only a minute or two. I must see about Mrs. Crowe—"

"Go den, Mistress."

Looking into Philip's wise eyes, she knew that he would use his best judgment. With that, Adrienne lifted her skirts and hurried back inside. Raised voices immediately reached her ears.

"If you're looking for Raveneau, Madame," Crowe was saying, "I can assure you he won't be riding to your rescue tonight or any night. He lusts for his bride, not you."

"I told you, the moonlight woke me. I just wanted some air."

"Must I lock you in? Would you like to join her ladyship?" Biting laughter followed this suggestion. "Thank God for laudanum. It's the only way to keep my women docile!" There was a pause, then, "You didn't forget to give Lady Thomasina her special tea, did you? You know what will happen to Martin if you dare to defy me!"

"I know better than to defy you," Eloise said in a voice thick with tears. "I'll do anything you say if you just let me keep my mind clear. All these years, I haven't known which was worse—starving myself to be free of the laudanum, or eating your food and remaining a prisoner of that poison!" She began to sob. "Do you have any idea how much I despise myself for inflicting the same torture on Lady Thomasina?"

"Of course. Why do you think I chose you to take her the tea each day?"

"No, you tell me—why?" Eloise's voice teetered on the verge of hysterics.

"Because it amuses me. Amusement is my *raison d'être*." Crowe's tone was bored. "You, however, do not amuse me, and you are keeping me from this night's real entertainment. Go back upstairs and stay there."

From her hiding place, Adrienne recognized the threat in his voice. Sickened by the revelations in their conversation, she was determined not to leave without the tragic Eloise. She tiptoed lightly up the stairway and called down in a high voice, "Mistress, de ladyship callin' you! Come quick!"

Crowe barked, "Who's that?"

"Oh—" Eloise stopped, then exclaimed, "It's the new maid, Addie. She's been helping me with Lady Thomasina!" She started toward the stairway. "No, no, I'll go up—Xavier, don't trouble yourself." And still he was behind her.

Adrienne stepped back into the shadows so that only her headtie and fichu were identifiable. "Hurry, Mistress!"

As Eloise ascended, Xavier Crowe peered upward, puffing on his cheroot. "Addie, hmm? Are you one of our lovely quadroons?" And then a gust of wind rattled the verandah doors, reminding him of the adventure unfolding on the beach. "I'll be back . . . later," he promised, and turned on his heel.

The two women clung together on the top step, weak-kneed, each taking strength from the other. When the door had banged shut behind Crowe, Adrienne whispered, "Now. We'll have to run."

Hearts pounding, they went racing down the stairs. Eloise nearly tripped at the bottom, but Adrienne pulled her along, and then they were out the rear door, skirts lifted, running barefoot over the gravel toward the carriage hidden among the palm trees. Philip was waiting with the door open, and when they were inside, he climbed onto his perch and flicked the reins.

Exhausted, Adrienne fell back against her seat and pulled the headtie from her damp hair. "Thank God that is over. Now—"

"Now," Eloise interjected, "we must travel a few miles north to find Huntsford. He is searching the cove at Cave Bay for a treasure that doesn't exist. I heard Xavier talking about it today, and laughing. Not only is it appalling that Huntsford has spent hours digging, but I shudder to think what fate awaits him if he returns to Crowe's Nest after all of us are gone!"

"No!" Hortie protested. "No more adventuring!"

"I am inclined to agree," Adrienne said. "We are utterly fatigued, and I—"

"I want my son," Lady Thomasina said suddenly. Moments before she had appeared to be dozing, but now her eyes were open and her chin jutted out. "If you won't save my Hunty, you needn't bother with me!"

Angus took up howling again, and Adrienne threw up her hands. "All right! As soon as we've gained the open road, I'll instruct Philip to turn toward Cave Bay. I just hope that we all live to tell this tale!"

The wind was warm against Nathan's face as he leaned over the rail and studied the moonlit water. "I think I see Cobbler's Reef," he told Crenshaw. "Call my father."

Instantly André appeared. Zachary Minter was right behind him. "If you're certain, we must drop anchor—"

"You can't risk actually hitting the reef with this ship," Zach cried. "There's no time to lose!"

Nathan straightened and fixed both of them with steel-blue eyes. "We also can't risk backing off too soon and giving ourselves away. Xavier Crowe is profoundly shrewd. He'll smell it if we don't seem to be the genuine article."

"Why the devil would he suspect anyone of going to so much trouble to trap *him*?" Zach asked. "I mean, it's hardly a lark. We could die!"

"That's precisely why we mustn't assume that he won't be suspicious," Nathan insisted. "Crowe takes nothing for granted, and neither can we."

The ocean was choppy, each swell tipped with white froth, and far ahead in the distant dark, countless lights winked. It was a magnificent night for adventure. There was salt spray and the threat of storms and the eeriest sort of moonlight, and beyond the reef there were land pirates who would come on board their wrecked ship with the intention of killing every one of them before plundering the hold.

It was the killing part that had caused Nathan to think twice before setting out tonight. He'd grown wise enough to know that adventure wasn't reason enough to risk anyone's life. There had to be more, and he realized that other innocent souls would die in the months and years to come if he did not try to stop Xavier Crowe.

He clearly understood now how the ships had been wrecked in the past. From far off the coast of Barbados, the sight of so many bobbing lights seemed to signal the riding lights of ships in a harbor. What else could it be? If it was a house, the lights wouldn't move like these. It wasn't until one was upon the reef and it was too late that a clearer view of the swaying palm trees and the lanterns emerged. Those unsuspecting ships that were approaching Barbados for the first time would sail into the trap, and it would snap closed before they could realize what fate had befallen them.

"The men are ready," Zach said. "They are overjoyed to be able to serve you again, sir."

"My father has had more experience with sea battles than I, so we're fortunate to have him." Nathan put a hand on André's shoulder and they shared a moment of rare unfettered love. "Thank you."

André nodded. "We shall prevail, son."

"I know." For an instant, Adrienne's face appeared to him, intensely beloved. "The truly meaningful years of my life have just begun, and I intend to make my wife a happy woman."

Nathan signaled Zach then, and the order was given to drop anchor. The expert anchor-men on the forecastle had been instructed clearly, and they took care to scrape the cables against the ship's hull methodically. It was Nathan's hope that this grinding noise would simulate the sound of the *Golden Eagle* hitting the reef. And he wanted Crowe to think that the ship wasn't certain *what* had caused the collision. If they acted as if they feared attack, and appeared to take an immediate aggressive posture toward Crowe's henchmen, it might be enough to draw out the master pirate himself.

On cue, André shouted loudly enough to be heard on shore: "All hands on deck! We've been hit!"

There was always the remote chance that Xavier Crowe was watching through a telescope, and as they drew closer to the lights he might recognize his old enemy. For safety's sake, Nathan slipped on the spectacles that he'd worn at Harms Castle and covered his hair with one of Crenshaw's striped caps. In spite of the hazards at hand, many of the men couldn't help grinning when they spotted their captain.

"I see movement on the beach," André said as he looked through his spyglass.

Zach reappeared, pale and tense. "I've repeated your orders to the crew that we're to spare lives, if possible, and take prisoners. Those men on the beach are Crowe's slaves, after all, not criminals."

The moon was hidden behind banks of clouds, which doubtless pleased Xavier Crowe even more than Nathan. Men from the beach were coming out into the lagoon beyond the reef, some in small boats, some swimming, but all appeared to be armed.

"Battle stations!" André shouted, then blew a whistle. "Lower the boarding nets and take up your swords!"

The scene of chaos was exciting. The crew of the *Golden Eagle* came pouring onto the decks, and they numbered many more than those who had been hoping to take them by surprise. Nathan could see the lethal pikes, cutlasses, and other weapons that rattled around in the approaching boats.

On the *Golden Eagle*, boarding nets were unfurled to keep the enemy from climbing over the rails. Seamen on platforms high in the topmasts began to lob grenades into the surf, purposely missing their targets. Crowe's slaves began to look uncertain.

"We've got them," Nathan muttered to his father, "but I'm not certain what to do with them. Where is that coward Crowe?"

Just then Owen Horner showed himself in the bow of the nearest boat. He stood up partway, hanging on for balance, and took off his crumpled hat. "Hey, Captain!"

André Raveneau moved forward but did not speak.

"We're coming to save you! Put away your weapons!"

"We have too much gold and silver on board to take chances," André replied. "You shot at us, and I don't trust you."

"That wasn't a cannon shot, it was your ship hitting Cobbler's Reef!"

On the beach, Xavier Crowe stood in the sheltering palm

trees and considered his predicament. Horner was an oaf. It seemed that only he could calm this captain and crew sufficiently. Even if it meant inviting them all into Crowe's Nest for soup and rum, then locking them in the storage cellars, he would have his way.

When Abraham saw his master waving from the beach, he went back with his skiff to fetch him, and they rowed through the waves to the ship. Crowe held a lantern and wore a worried look.

"Foolish captain thinks the reef is cannon ball," Abraham muttered, shaking his head.

"I shall tell him otherwise."

The boats holding Horner and the rest of the slaves made room for Abraham to pass with their master. The packet's sleek bow rose before him as they came near, and a man who appeared to be the captain called down from the darkness.

"Call off your sharks or we'll attack."

Crowe laughed as if that were a marvelous joke. "My good friend, you are new to our waters, and you do not know Bajan ways." He nearly introduced himself but was worried that rumor of his past crimes might have reached America. "I am a respected planter on this island and these men you would kill are my simple slaves. Quite harmless, I assure you. You see, you have happened onto our reef by mistake, and I sent them out to offer assistance. I fear that you will have to disembark before you sink."

"What about those lanterns hanging on the trees? We thought we had reached Carlisle Bay!"

"Ha-ha-ha! Ah, my friend, we never dreamed such a mistake could occur. You see, my slaves are sweet, but quite primitive, and they amuse themselves with African rituals these summer nights. The lanterns were their doing."

The captains seemed to be considering this. "I shall allow you, and you alone, to come on board, sir. I would look into your eyes before I decide what to do."

"Well, certainly!" Chuckling indulgently, Crowe grasped the rope ladder that someone lowered from the deck above. As he climbed, Crowe added, "You must see, however, that you really have no choice but to put your trust in me and my men. Your ship will be taking water, and it is only a matter of time—"

Nathan Raveneau was standing at the rail when Xavier Crowe, sweaty and salty-haired, clambered over the top. Nathan drew off his cap and spectacles while Crowe brushed mud from his shirt.

"I fear," Nathan said, "that you won't be able to convince me."

Crowe let out a yell. "Where the devil did you come from? That wasn't you speaking—"

"No, it was my esteemed father." When he gestured, André Raveneau came forward, tanned and silver-haired and a commanding presence at more than seventy years of age.

"Crowe," he murmured, and sketched a mock bow.

Nathan lit a cheroot and narrowed his eyes at his nemesis. " 'Twould seem that you have been ensnared in your own evil trap. Shall we do unto you as you were prepared to do unto us?"

"Christ, no!" Sweat ran into Crowe's eyes. "I'm warning you, Raveneau! If you lay a hand on me, my men will hunt you to the ends of the earth—"

"Spare me." Nathan held up a hand. "It's far too late for such dull speeches." Then, briefly, their eyes met and it came to Nathan that Xavier Crowe was terrified because he was imagining what he would do if the situation were reversed. "You think I'm going to bury you in the sand, up to your neck at low tide, don't you? It's a tempting thought."

Crowe went dead white. "Please. Please, no. You can have everything. Even Eloise—"

"You are a revolting excuse for a human being. Don't say another word, I beg you." A muscle twitched in Nathan's jaw, and he exchanged glances with his father. "You deserve that pirate's punishment, but that sort of thing is not in my nature, I fear. Nor is it my place to decide your fate. We'll take you to Bridgetown and deliver you to the authorities. . . ."

Crenshaw and several other seamen were standing by. They shackled Crowe and led him away to the hold at gunpoint, and Nathan felt as if a tremendous weight had been lifted.

"Well done," André said. "This is one of the proudest nights of my life."

"Because you see that I've turned out so much like you?" They laughed together, then embraced, and Nathan's eyes stung. "Not so long ago I would have said we were different men and I didn't need your approval, but now I can admit that it means a great deal. Thank you, Father. I would say that this night's work was a joint endeavor, and that you and Zach and all the crew deserve a great deal of the credit."

"Thank God it all worked out," Minter said weakly. "I had my doubts. . . ."

Nathan went to the rail then and shouted down to the boats filled with slaves. "I am Nathan Raveneau, and this was no shipwreck. We came around the island to trap Xavier Crowe, and he is below, in irons, at this very moment—"

Strenuous cheering broke out and filled the warm, misty air. The slaves who had obeyed their master rather than face his wrath were able at last to express their true feelings. When the noise subsided a bit, Nathan looked for Owen Horner.

"Horner, I must ask you to come up and join your employer in the hold. I suspect that we can find crimes to charge you with as well!"

The overseer tried to dive into the ocean, but the other men in his boat caught him and held a knife to his throat. Abraham promised to escort Horner on board the *Golden Eagle*.

Before all the boats filled with slaves could return to the beach, Nathan had one more announcement to make to Zach and his father. "I am counting on you, and the crew, to alert the magistrate and see to it that Crowe and Horner are jailed."

"Where will *you* be?" cried Zach.

"I am going home from here. I know that Adrienne is worried to death about me, and it's the first time in my adult life that anyone has ever cared so deeply about my well-being. I want to see her face before dawn breaks." A wry smile curved his mouth. "You see, I *am* changing. Do you suppose I might borrow one of Crowe's horses?"

André laughed, but another thought had struck him. "Adrienne will be happy to hear the news about Xavier Crowe for more reasons than one. Now, with his arrest, she won't have to worry any more about the safety of Lady Thomasina and Crowe's wife!"

Chapter Twenty-five

WHEN NATHAN DISCOVERED THAT THE OCCUPANTS OF Crowe's Nest were missing, he went back down to the beach to look for Abraham. In the distance, he could see that the *Golden Eagle* was in full sail once again, tacking southwest for Bridgetown.

The slaves were crowded together on the beach, talking all at once, and Nathan realized that he couldn't just leave them in this state of uncertainty. Clearly, Abraham was the authority figure among them, so Nathan walked through the gleaming coral sand to meet him.

"I must have honest answers, Abraham," he said. "You were Xavier Crowe's assistant. How do you feel about his downfall?"

The tall, handsome man was somber. "Good. I feel good. I seen too much ugliness and deceit these past two years, and I had no choice but to go along. Now I can do right again."

"Where do you come from? Your voice sounds—"

"American," he confirmed. "Master Crowe bought me from a planter in Carolina. Lots of Barbadians live there." He shook his head. "I never had respect for Master Crowe, and I hate the things he makes me do, but he didn't beat me, and he let me have my wife. He just treat us all like pets, not people."

"Abraham, would you like to come and work for me? I'll give you your freedom, but I can't pay much—not yet. I'll hire as many of Crowe's slaves as I can. Perhaps with more field hands, I can find a way to free all of you, and my slaves as well."

"I'd be honored and blessed to labor in your fields as a free man, sir! I come with you now. I tell them what you said, and come back tomorrow to talk more."

"Yes. Dear God, I am exhausted. I have to ride home yet tonight, so perhaps you will watch me to see that I don't fall off the horse!" Nathan paused. "I also came back to find you because none of Crowe's family or guests are in the house. I have to tell Mrs. Crowe the news about her husband. Do you know where they might be?"

Abraham looked down at his bare feet. "I know where the young Englishman is. Massa want him out of the way tonight, so he had him dig for treasure—"

"Never mind. I know exactly where he is—and perhaps Harms can tell me the whereabout of the others. I can't go home if there is any chance that they are in danger."

With Abraham's calm assistance, Nathan soon found himself riding a magnificent gray gelding up the road that skirted the dramatic limestone cliffs. The two men were separated while Abraham hurried back to his hut to explain to his wife where he was going, but, after taking Owen Horner's horse, he caught up with his new employer just north of Crowe's Nest.

They were galloping along side by side, in silence, when they came over the brow of a hill and sighted a carriage in the distance.

"Devil take it, I think that is *my* carriage!" Nathan cried, outraged, as he squinted through the moonlight. "How can it be?"

"A thief?" Abraham speculated. "You have a pistol, sir?"

"Yes, but I don't think it's a thief."

"Who else, in the dead middle of the night?"

"I think—" Nathan winced. "I believe it's my blasted wife, on a mission of her own."

Abraham lifted his brows, curious and slightly amused. "Doing what, sir?"

"Rescuing the occupants of Crowe's Nest, I surmise. She—ah—has mentioned such a plan. . . ."

Unable to think of a polite reply, Abraham said nothing.

As they drew alongside the carriage, Nathan shouted at Philip to halt. As soon as the old man saw his pursuer, he obeyed, cringing a little as he watched Nathan jump to the ground and reach for the carriage door handle. "She mean good, Captain."

"The bloody chit will turn my hair white before the New Year," Nathan raged, and yanked open the door. The sight that met his stormy gaze was beyond belief. Lady Thomasina looked more outlandish than ever, if possible, with her hair wild and her clothes unfastened. Eloise and Martin cowered in the seat opposite, wide-eyed and pale, and Angus leaped toward the door and began growling ferociously while Hortie tried to quiet him. The terrier had a blue glove in his jaws! Finally, Raveneau saw Adrienne, her slight form tucked into a darkened corner. She wore the colorful garb of a slave woman, including a coral-striped headtie, and she was rubbing her eyes as if he'd roused her from a deep sleep.

"I beg your pardon, Madame, if I have disturbed you," Nathan ground out. "I would have a word with you."

"Don't hurt her!" Eloise begged.

He threw a sharp glance her way. "Pray do not judge me against the standards of your husband."

Adrienne's chin trembled as she struggled out of the crowded carriage. Standing in front of Nathan, she looked pitiful. "I have been so very worried about you!"

"That's a very interesting disguise you've chosen." He shook his head. Then, relenting, Nathan opened his arms and she threw herself into them. "If I had known what you were planning for tonight, I would have chained you to the bed. Naked."

"A game?" she dared tease. "I might like that if you were there." Her arms were fastened tightly round his neck. "Oh, Nathan, I love you more than I thought possible! Please, from now on, promise me that you will try to stay out of harm's way!"

"I was trying to go home to you, to put your worries to rest, when I discovered that the occupants of Crowe's Nest were *missing*! I am furious with you for rushing into such danger without even telling me!" He buried his face in her neck, drinking in the dear scent of her skin. "If Crowe had caught you, all of you might be dead!"

"I was too crafty for him. Have you no faith in me at all? Besides, I tried to tell you, and I tried to enlist your aid, but you had more important business." Her story tumbled out then, in a shortened form, and she listened to the outcome of his trap for Xavier Crowe.

"I'll tell you everything when we are at home, but for now I must know why Eloise and Martin are with you, and why you are on this coast road."

"Eloise insisted that we find Huntsford. She said that he has been digging for treasure all night and that she heard Crowe saying that he won't find anything." Lowering her voice, Adrienne added, "Oh, Nathan I've discovered so much tonight about Eloise and Xavier Crowe—and that entire coil. He is evil! Why, he—"

"We haven't time for this now," Raveneau said fondly.

"Well, as for Huntsford," she hurried on, "I think that Eloise decided that he was also manipulated by Crowe, and she feels sorry. I believe she wants to take Martin back to England, where no one will know about Xavier Crowe and they can have a decent life. Perhaps Huntsford can escort them, with Lady Thomasina, on the return voyage."

"I perceive that you are trying to take charge of this matter, my dear, but it won't be decided by the side of the road. I haven't decided what to do with Harms yet. I remain convinced that he plotted to murder Walter Frakes-Hogg—"

"Let's go and talk to him. I agree that Huntsford is weak and flawed, but perhaps he's worth saving."

"You aren't going anywhere except back to Tempest Hall!"

"Yes I am. I am going with you and—"

"Abraham. I've taken the liberty of freeing Crowe's slaves, whether it was legal or not, and I have offered them work at Tempest Hall."

She beamed at him. "I am proud to be your wife, sir." And then, Adrienne's tired lips found his and she kissed him with every ounce of love in her heart. "I believe I would have died of worry tonight if I hadn't been occupied with my own adventure."

"All right, I surrender," he moaned. "Philip will drive the others back to Tempest Hall, and you may come with us."

Guided by moonlight, the trio rode farther along the cliffs overlooking the treacherous Atlantic Ocean. Sitting in front of Nathan on the gelding, Adrienne was flushed with excitement and thrilled to be in the circle of her husband's embrace.

When they turned off the overgrown road and came around a stand of fiddlewood trees, Victoria Villa loomed abruptly before them. The crumbling, hollowed-out plantation house was like a specter against the night sky, and for an instant Adrienne imagined the distant strains of a waltz and the murmuring voices of guests. The moon, glowing fitfully behind restless violet clouds, illumined huge cave bats fluttering in and out of the verandah's arches. As the ocean pounded the cliffs below, Adrienne sighed.

Nathan laid a finger over his wife's mouth. "Shh." He then raised a hand to signal Abraham that they were near the beach where he guessed they would find Huntsford Harms. After tethering the horses to the cannonball trees, Nathan took Abraham off to one side and conferred with him at length. When they parted, the black man went off toward the south end of Cave Bay.

"What was that all about?" Adrienne queried softly. She was bursting with curiosity.

"I can't go into it now. I would only suggest that you forget anyone came with us tonight. Pretend we are alone, except for Hunty."

She tugged at his sleeve as they walked. "Isn't this a violation of your marriage vows? Didn't you promise to tell me the truth at all times?"

Nathan arched a brow at her. "The only marriage vow that matters right now is your promise to *obey* your husband. All else can wait until—"

His hushed voice broke off. They had reached the edge of the vertical cliffs that plunged down to the beach, and

Nathan drew Adrienne down beside him so they were concealed by oleander shrubs. When a bat flew low over their heads and swept out over the water, they watched as it skewered a fish with its clawlike toes.

Seeing his wife's look of horror, Nathan whispered, "Are you still glad you came?"

She squared her shoulders, nodded, and stared down at the wide crescent of white sand shadowed by coconut palms. A movement caught her eye. Was it a man? Then, as clouds blew past the moon, a beam of light shone on pale hair and shoulders that she recognized as those of Huntsford Harms. He was digging into the sand with a shovel.

Nathan found her hand and squeezed it. Slowly they moved around the cliff to the place where steps had been carved into the rock. Adrienne knew a sudden tide of fear. The cliff went straight down, and the indentations were hard to see in the darkness. But Nathan bent down, boldly kissed her, and murmured, "I'll keep you safe."

He went first and she came right after, so that his arms shielded her lower body. Nathan helped her feet find the steps. Once or twice she slipped, but he was quick to catch her, and before long the sand was within jumping distance.

On the beach, they crept around palm trunks and through sea grape leaves, thankful that Huntsford was making enough noise with his shovel to drown out their progress. Drawing closer, Adrienne saw that all around Huntsford the sand was pocked with dark holes, many of them were half full of water. It was an eerie sight, rather like Adrienne's imagined vision of the moon. When she focused on Huntsford, it was a further shock to see that he was standing in one of the holes, water splashing as he flailed away with a shovel. His face was dripping perspiration, his clothes were torn and soiled, and he wore the expression of a madman.

"This is the spot," he muttered to himself with feverish intensity. "It must be! Yes, yes, keep going, that's it—"

Nathan and his wife exchanged glances in the shadows. There was the sound of metal clanging against a hard object. Huntsford Harms began to sob and laugh at the same

time, his face contorted with joy. Bending over, he pushed
his hands down into the watery mess to find his treasure
and moments later brought an object out that was far too
small to be a pirate's chest.

Adrienne nearly gasped aloud as Harms lifted the pale,
curved thing higher, squinting at it in the moonlight. Pure
horror spread over his face.

It was a skull—apparently that of a human!

Reaching down again, as if in disbelief, he yanked again
and this time came up with a leg bone. Back in her hiding
place, Adrienne had to cover her own mouth to contain her
shock. What could be more ghastly than to dig for treasure
and find a skeleton instead?

Just as Huntsford began to scramble out of the watery
grave, a deep, chilling voice called from above. "You
betraaayed me, Harms! I trusted yooou, and you killled
me!"

Adrienne's heart threatened to come out of her chest, but
Nathan quietly pointed upward and she spied Abraham,
wrapped in shadows and clinging to the top of one of the
coconut trees. Huntsford Harms, meanwhile, was staring
straight at the heavens. At that moment in his life, he was
ripe for all manner of guilt and ghostly suggestions.

"Walter?" he quavered, then pressed a hand to his mouth,
trembling. "Is that you?"

"Admit the truuuth! You'll feel—" Abraham paused for
effect and spat out the last word: *"better!"*

Huntsford Harms looked as if he feared that the ghost of
Walter Frakes-Hogg might thrust him into the hole filled
with water and human bones. His confession tumbled out.
"I'm sorry! So sorry! Even though we were in league, I
couldn't let you have your way with her! And I admit it, I
wanted Adrienne for myself, and I hoped that if I killed her
tormentor, she might be grateful—"

Holding Adrienne's hand, Nathan stepped out of the
palm trees and into the moonlight. "You needn't go on.
That's all we had to hear." He nodded slowly, and
Huntsford, meanwhile, looked more confused and terrified
than ever. Moments later Abraham had descended to join
them, and Nathan gestured toward the former slave with an

ironic smile. "Sorry to disappoint you, my lord, but Frakes-Hogg's ghost was really Abraham speaking to you from the top of a palm tree."

In spite of himself, Huntsford was relieved to see other people and to know that he might escape the haunted beach after all. "By Jupiter, do you have any notion what's buried down there? Bodies! Pirate skeletons! A fellow would admit to anything when it seems that a lot of cutthroat buccaneers are about to rise up out of the sand and—"

"Too late, Harms," Nathan replied calmly. "You've told the truth, and it is just as I suspected from the start. Not that I'm sorry that Frakes-Hogg is dead, but I did hate to have you strutting about playing the hero. In truth, you first conspired with him against Adrienne, then you turned traitor against him and lay in wait to murder him that night in her bedchamber."

Huntsford came stumbling toward them, a broken man. "Yes, yes, but I did care for her, and he was a hideous beast! He wanted me to let him into her room so that he could force himself on her!"

"Don't worry," Nathan murmured, waving a hand in the air, "I won't have you sent to the gallows for it. Just tell me the truth about what's been going on at Crowe's Nest. You've let him drug Lady Thomasina, haven't you?"

"Oh ... I suppose he has been, but I've tried not to know. I've been more worried about this blasted treasure! It was buried by Stede Bonnet, and Crowe promised me part of the booty. He said we'd have wealth beyond imagining!"

"I hate to dash your dreams, but he only kept you occupied down here so that he might undertake another wrecking party without involving you. Crowe was doubtless afraid that you might betray him at some future date, if you witnessed the full extent of his crimes."

"How do you know all this? And how did you find me tonight?" Suddenly the last bits of life seemed to drain from Harms's body and he slouched against the trunk of a palm tree. His face was blue-white in the moonlight.

"I own this land, old fellow," Nathan replied coolly. "I was here, just yards away, the day you and Crowe stood on the beach and discussed Stede Bonnet's supposed treasure map for the first time." Then he went on to describe the adventures of that very night, ending with Crowe's capture and the removal of Lady Thomasina, Eloise, and Martin from Crowe's Nest. "The women seemed to think that you ought to be taken to safety as well. I've freed the slaves there, and given their mood, I don't know if they'll welcome you back tonight—"

Abraham, standing off to one side, shook his head doubtfully.

"Please!" Huntsford cried. "Let me come with you!"

Nathan reflected that it almost wasn't any fun to have a victory like this over the once-pompous Lord Harms. He was groveling a bit too much. "Only to please your mother, and because you may need to escort her back to England. Her health may be ruined for good, no thanks to you." He paused, his expression harsh. "If it wouldn't make her worse to know the truth about her own son, I'd force you to own up to your unpardonable behavior."

Harms nearly went down on his knees to beg forgiveness, but something in Raveneau's eyes told him that would do more harm than good. Even Adrienne's eyes were unsympathetic. "I'll prove to you that I've changed," he pledged in quieter tones.

"Let's be on our way to Tempest Hall," Nathan said.

"I have my own horse," he called over the roar of the surf. "I've hidden him."

Adrienne walked with her husband back up the hillside, bone tired but loving the feeling of his strong arm around her waist. "Yes," she whispered. "Let's go home."

It was the middle of the night when Nathan saw Tempest Hall again, and he thought that her three Jacobean gables had never looked grander. Hurricane lamps burned in the windows, welcoming them home, and the servants were waiting in the doorway.

Hortie took one look at the filthy, battle-weary Lord Harms and announced that she would show him his room. Abraham went off with Philip, and Adrienne walked with Nathan to the bottom of the staircase.

" 'Twould seem that our other guests are fast asleep," she murmured. "No more crises tonight."

Before he could reply, the library door swung open and they saw Eloise standing in a beam of lamplight. Still clad in the frilled muslin gown she'd worn throughout the night's adventure, she had washed her face and repinned her hair. "I hope you don't mind," Eloise whispered. "I could never sleep without speaking to you. Both of you. I need to explain—"

Adrienne saw that she was looking only at Nathan. "Eloise, I overheard some of your conversation tonight with Crowe, so I may already know what you are going to tell us." She paused and made a decision. "I think that you really need to speak to Nathan, don't you? You two have old business that needs settling."

Too tired to argue with her, Nathan capitulated. "You win. I'll join you upstairs shortly—" That quickly, Adrienne scampered up the staircase and disappeared from sight. Looking back at Eloise, he said, "I'm going to have a brandy, and I imagine you could use one too."

Eloise sat on the edge of Adrienne's new mahogany chaise, sipping her brandy, and Nathan decided that it was odd to see his old love in this setting. How many times had he dreamed that she would come to live with him at Tempest Hall?

Eloise found her voice. "It's ironic, isn't it, that now that I've gotten away from Xavier, you have a wife?" Another sip of brandy, then, "But I do like Adrienne. Very much."

"Everyone does." He smiled. "She's irresistible, I think. She's also headstrong, and has made mistakes, so she understands whatever it is that you've been struggling with. Eloise, won't you tell me?"

It was bittersweet to be so close to him, to be in his library, surrounded by his things. It could have been her home, once. "I didn't want to stay with Xavier, you know," she said suddenly. "I prayed that day, when you boarded his ship, that you would understand somehow and take me with you."

"You told me in London that you wanted him, and then you told me again at sea," Nathan said. It was odd to real-

ize that all his conflicts over Eloise had vanished. Now all
he could think was that if Adrienne had been carried off by
Xavier Crowe, she would have found a way, somehow, to
let him know she needed rescuing. "I am sorry if you've
been unhappy—"

Tears filled her great dark eyes. "He fed me laudanum,
and he made so many cunning threats . . . for years . . ."

"Oh, God, Eloise—if only you'd found a way to let me
know!"

"I was afraid he'd kill us both, afraid that you didn't
want me any more." She dabbed at her eyes with a handkerchief, sick with regret. Nathan had never been more
dashingly handsome, and now he had grown a strong and
tender heart. "But that's past now. You have a wife whom
you love, and perhaps we both owe our blessings to her. I
wouldn't be here tonight if not for Adrienne. I just wanted
to explain—why—so that you would never think that I rejected you."

Nathan started to rise. He was dead tired. "I understand."

"There's something else." The words spilled out. "I'm
the one who drugged Lady Thomasina. He made me take
her the tea every day! I've been torn apart with guilt, and
I don't suppose there is any excuse—except to say that
Xavier is an evil man, and he has a way of using threats
and twisting words—"

"I understand. Eloise, you helped her to escape, so I
think that evens the score." Patting her hand, he added,
"We'll see to it that you go home to England for a long
rest, with lots of fresh air and good food and love from
your family. All right?"

She walked with him to the staircase and blurted,
"Xavier killed Martin's parents, you know. And he would
have killed Martin as well one day. He had no scruples at
all."

"I'll tell the magistrate tomorrow." Nathan brushed the
back of his strong, dark hand over her cheek, and for an instant their eyes met, memories mingling. "For now, you
should go upstairs and get some sleep. That's exactly what
I intend to do as soon as I've spoken to Hortie."

Eloise nodded and obeyed, drained now that she'd unbur-

dened herself. Nathan went off to confer with Hortie about
plans for the next day and then decided to peek in on Orchid, who seemed to be waiting for him. Philip had already
told her as much as he could, but it was Nathan's habit to
share not only the details of his life with Orchid, but his
feelings as well.

"I do feel better," she said to him, smiling as she lay
against plump white pillows. "I worries 'bout dat Crowe
fellow. Evil. Sometime evil do win jus' because it stoop
lower."

"No need to worry anymore, darling Orchid. Crowe and
Horner are jailed, and Eloise, Martin, and the Harmses are
returning to England as soon as passage can be arranged."

"It's good 'bout dose slaves from Crowe's Nest too.
You're a fine man." She paused. "You goin' to free de
folks here?"

He nodded. "You have Adrienne to thank for opening
my eyes to the truth in that regard. It was easier for me to
make excuses, but she wouldn't let me."

She opened one twinkling eye. "Mistress tell you she
news yet?"

"News?" His brow furrowed. "You mean her escapade
with Philip to rescue the people at Crowe's Nest?"

"No ..." Orchid patted his hand. "Go an' ask."

Nathan leaned down to kiss her cheek and saw that she
was already asleep, breathing with difficulty. Philip was in
the doorway, his tired eyes filled with tears.

"It won' be long now," he murmured. "She need to see
how it all do turn out."

Slowly Nathan went in to the back of the house and
looked around at the still rooms. The soft bluish-rose light
of early dawn filtered through the shutters and the air
caught the evanescent perfume of the ylang-ylang trees.
Angus was curled in a planter's chair, eyeing Nathan chal-
lengingly as he held fast to his blue glove, and Nathan gave
the terrier a wry smile.

The interlude with Eloise had left him numb, but now a
mixture of feelings crept over Nathan as he mounted the
Chinese Chippendale staircase. His eyes stung at the
thought of losing Orchid, yet there was a sense of peace in

knowing that he and Adrienne had laid a strong foundation, with Orchid's help, for the future. They were a family now, and the love he felt for his wife was a blessing he'd never expected, and thus treasured all the more.

They'd come a long way from the fanmaker's shop in Oxford Street and the library ladder at Harms Castle. Despite their own efforts to break each new bond that formed, here they were, showered in blessings. Nathan simply could not imagine his life without Adrienne.

Lady Thomasina's snores rumbled from inside her bedchamber, and the door to Martin's room had come open a bit. Pausing there to fix the latch, Nathan peeked at the boy and sighed. It was chilling to know that Xavier Crowe had killed Martin's parents so that he might have his brother's portion of the estate. How long would it have been before Martin met an accidental death?

Entering his own chamber, Nathan expected Adrienne to be in bed, sleeping soundly. Instead, he found that the jalousie shutters were open to admit the dawn light, and she was sitting at his desk, wearing a nightgown and studying a piece of paper.

"What the devil are you doing, my beautiful bride?" he chided. After pulling off his own clothing as he crossed the room, he poured water into a basin and began to wash. "I expected you to be unconscious, snoring louder than Lady Thomasina!"

She glanced up distractedly. "It is fun to have her with us again, isn't it?"

"Perhaps, in a rather warped sense of the word, but that doesn't mean I would like them to stay on Barbados."

"How was your interview with Eloise? You needn't tell me—"

"Are you trying to offer me some privacy?" Nathan laughed. "That's very amusing, my love. As for Eloise, as much as I hate scenes like that, I suppose it was beneficial to put the past to rest. So much had to do with my pride. I realized more clearly than ever that we were never suited, and I was only infatuated with her beauty and the notion of protecting her." He shook his head. "I am appalled by all that she endured at the hands of Xavier Crowe ... but I also realized that it wasn't my fault—"

"You are saving her life right this moment, Nathan."

"More you than I. But we'll send her back to her family in England, and she can mend slowly from all that she's endured these past years."

"To think that Crowe was feeding laudanum to his own wife!" Adrienne was examining the paper again.

Toweling his damp hair and face, Nathan went to look over her shoulder. "Adrienne! How did you get hold of that ridiculous treasure map?"

"You so effectively convinced Huntsford that it's a fraud that he wanted to pitch it in the trash. I rescued it and find it fascinating!" She gave him a winning smile. "What if—"

"My dear, I can assure you that if there were *ever* a treasure buried there, it was recovered long ago. I rather suspect that Crowe drew the damned thing himself, but even if it is authentic, it's a century old and other people have had their hands on it before Crowe." He shook his head. "Forget about that and come to bed with your husband. I'll give you a treasure that's *real*." He flashed a roguish grin that made her giggle.

Adrienne rolled up the map again, sighing. When she stood up, her hair fell over her back. "Well, I shan't destroy it. I'll hide it, and perhaps our descendants will find it and have a more adventuresome spirit than you."

He lifted her into his arms. "Madame, I take issue with that statement. Living with you requires an exceedingly adventuresome spirit. I haven't any left over for nonsense like treasure hunts."

Both of them collapsed on the big bed and made contented noises. "It's shocking how tired I really am," Adrienne admitted.

"We're past tired."

"Delirious?"

Their laughter mingled with the songs of the waking birds and the first faint voices from the slave huts. Nathan rose up on one elbow and looked down at her, captivated by her sparkling green eyes. "Promise me that you'll never secretly embark on another dangerous escapade like to-night's, all right? If anything were to happen to you . . ."

She put a finger over his mouth and drank in the sight of his beloved face. "I promise to be very careful from now on. I have to look out for the welfare of our child."

"Our—what?" His eyes were shocked, then stormy, then tender. "You are an incorrigible chit! So this is the news Orchid mentioned. Why didn't you tell me?"

"I had to see to Lady Thomasina, Eloise, and Martin first, and I feared that you would truly lock me up if you knew—"

"As well I should have done!"

"But I *was* very careful, Nathan. It only seemed like a dangerous undertaking to you because you didn't know about it! I wouldn't have taken chances with our baby's well-being."

"A . . . baby." He fell back on the feather bed and stared up at the mosquito netting. "Our baby. It's incredible. Like a . . ."

"Miracle," Adrienne supplied happily, and snuggled against his brown chest. "The baby will come in the spring, and I thought we might invite our families to visit for the christening. Wouldn't that be lovely?"

Suddenly he said, "Let's get married again when they are here. Properly. I was a scoundrel at our first wedding ceremony."

"If you want to, we will, but you know it's not the wedding that matters but the marriage itself."

Nathan rolled her onto her back, pressed himself between her thighs, and captured her mouth in a long, ardent kiss. "I am doing my best, you know. It is very *rewarding* work." His tone was laced with laughter.

Wrapping her arms around his broad shoulders, Adrienne felt herself lifted on a tide of bliss that was every bit as real as the ocean waves. Nathan was kissing her throat, her collarbone, then opening her gown to find a swollen breast. "I love you so desperately." Her fingers traced the curve of his cheekbone.

He had drawn back to look at her breast. "I've been dense not to notice the changes, haven't I?"

"Not dense." She smiled. "Merely male."

His eyes burned with fatigue and emotion and, closing them, he imagined the child who was growing out of their love. "When do you think it happened?"

"Looking back . . . I suppose it must have been that first time, in your cabin on the *Golden Eagle*. Love knew better than we ourselves what was best for us."

Holding her near, Nathan gently lay his stubbled cheek against her pale breasts while a tear slipped from his eye. "We're going to have a wonderful life together, aren't we?"

"Mmm-hmm. And when we free our slaves, the mood of the plantation will change."

"Something to do with a clear conscience?" He kissed her throat, aching with the love only she could inspire. "Tempest Hall will be a place we can all be proud of—a place where we can raise our children amid—"

"Riches of the heart." Adrienne stroked his crisp hair as the tide came again, lifting them together. She savored the miracle, then murmured, "Are you asleep?"

"Not quite."

"Take me to the beach."

"You're mad. I can barely talk, let alone ride a horse."

"Of course you can! I want to go back to the beach where I first swam in the waves, and we can make love there, seal our future—"

"In broad daylight?" He laughed dismissively. "Besides, we need to sleep."

"Has marriage tamed you completely?" Her eyes roamed over him. "A little madness can be delicious."

The guinea fowl were scratching in the garden below, sending up their incessant creaking call, and a rosy-gold light filled the bedroom. A soft island breeze wafted in, carrying with it the distant sound of the Atlantic rollers breaking on the beach.

Nathan looked into Adrienne's sultry eyes and felt the answering heat in his own loins. "Are you accusing me, your husband, of going soft?" He arched a dark brow.

"I know better than to make such a foolish charge." She grinned.

"Might I remind you that I have done battle at sea to-night?"

"My hero!" Adrienne climbed onto his lap, and they exchanged a long, smoldering kiss. "You can tell me all about your shipwreck on the way to our beach. Then you can lie back on the sand and let the water come over you, and I'll straddle your hips ... if you take my meaning ..."

"I *am* persuaded that we can sleep another day."

With that, they scrambled off the bed, grabbing up clothes and laughing, heading off to enjoy another Barbados sunrise.

Author's Note

Like most of my books, *Barbados* has evolved over a period of years, beginning with a brief trip I made to the island in 1987. I learned about Sam Lord, "The Regency Rascal," who *may* have lured ships onto the rocks near his mansion on the island's east coast. Since many doubt that Sam Lord carried out the evil deeds with which he's been credited, I decided to create my own character—Xavier Crowe!—based on Sam Lord's legend. "Crowe's Nest," the home of my character, Xavier Crowe, is nearly identical to Sam Lord's Castle, which has been restored and is now the centerpiece for a Marriott resort.

My husband, Jim Hunt, and I have come to love Barbados while doing research for this book and its companion, *Tempest*. We've found a home away from home at the hundred-year-old Ocean View Hotel, where owner John Chandler and the rest of the Ocean View family have happily made us welcome. John, his staff, and his friends have spent hours answering my questions and telling incredible stories. We've tasted all the great Bajan dishes, home cooked at the Ocean View, and learned about the flora and fauna from John, who fills the hotel with his own floral arrangements, gathered from all over the island. On our last trip, John took us for a customized all-day tour—and, among other hidden treasures, introduced us to Cave Bay (the sight of "Victoria Villa"). Incredible! You can't even imagine the color of the water, and there really is a ruined plantation house there (circa 1910, John reckons). Its real name is Harrismith.

If you have a chance to travel to Barbados, you may hear

people of all colors speaking Bajan, a rich, hybrid language that intermingles African and European speech. You'll also be able to visit many of the locations from *Barbados*, and you can tour St. Nicholas Abbey, my inspiration for Nathan's home, Tempest Hall. St. Nicholas Abbey is a wonderfully maintained seventeenth-century Jacobean-style plantation, where the four fireplaces have never been used, the sandbox tree still towers in back, and the guinea fowl scurry about.

Most of all, if you go to Barbados, you might sample the flying fish and callaloo, smell the fragrant plumeria, see the wild green monkeys playing, and swim in the ocean at sunrise, imagining all the while what the island was like for Adrienne and Nathan. . . .

Jim shared the pleasures of Barbados with me, and acted as co-researcher. Thanks, honey, for always driving a few miles more on the left and touring one more house with me. You're the best! Love to my mom and daughter, Jenna, who complete our wacky, wonderful family.

Biggest thanks to you, my readers. I hope you'll all read *Tempest* next year! It's set partly in Newport, Rhode Island, but mostly on Barbados, in 1903. The hero is Nathan and Adrienne's grandson, Adam Raveneau, who's gambled away most of the family fortune and needs funds to restore the crumbling Tempest Hall. Cathy, the heroine, is a Newport heiress who must be rescued from an arranged marriage to a boring duke. They need each other, but is it love? Come back to Barbados with me and find out.

Until then, I treasure your letters. Tell me everything, including what *you'd* like to read next!

Cynthia Wright Hunt
P.O. Box 2053
Sioux City, Iowa 51104

P.S. In case you are wondering, André and Devon Raveneau's story was told in *Silver Storm* (1979), and Nicholai and Lisette Beauvisage starred in *Spring Fires* (1983). Lindsay Raveneau was the heroine of *Surrender the Stars* (1987).

CYNTHIA WRIGHT

Published by Ballantine Books.
Available in your local bookstore.